SEARCHERS TESTIMONIALS

Searchers: The Irish Clans Book One

Archer has created colorful, sympathetic characters, all striving for better lives. He packs this dense volume with pungent details, giving the reader necessary context . . . he leaves the characters adrift at the book's end (literally, in two cases), with the reader wanting more. But throughout, the author takes what could have been dry genealogical research and skillfully converts it into a layered historical drama. An engrossing beginning of what promises to be an involving generational saga about Irish immigrants. Kirkus Reviews

Amazon 5-Star Reviews ★ ★ ★ ★ ★
Searchers **Amazon Review: Irish Lore/History Brought to Life**

Having family from Scotland, I am very familiar with the clans/history/politics/struggles of the Irish people. Mr. Archer has taken not only your heart by the hand, but also his love of history and guided you through the lives and loves of his characters. I anxiously await the ongoing chapters of his trilogies. Pull up a wee dram of Irish whiskey and lose yourself!

Searchers **Amazon Review: A Great Read**

I read this book on my trip to Ireland. The fact that it is fiction, based in fact, and that many of the characters were actual historical figures made the story most compelling. I recommend this book very highly and am eagerly awaiting the next books in the series. If you have any interest in Irish history or just enjoy fast paced historical fiction, then this is a must read.

Searchers **Amazon Review: A Lively and Interesting Story**

A lively and interesting story set in early 20th Century America and Ireland. Stephen weaves an intriguing tale of fact and fiction set against the struggle for Irish independence, so relevant as this year celebrates the 100th anniversary of the Easter Rising. The young characters in the story begin to find a link between themselves and two of the ancient, noble clans of Ireland. The discovery of a secret pact between these two clans and the possibility of finding the whereabouts of hidden treasure all adds to the making of a first class mystery. A very enjoyable read. I look forward to Book 2 `Rising` with eager anticipation.

The Irish Clans

This is an epic story immersed in the tumultuous Irish revolutionary period of 1915 through 1923, while the world is embroiled in the Great War and its aftermath. The once mighty McCarthy and O'Donnell Clans, overthrown in ancient times, are not extinct. They are linked on two continents by a medieval pact entwining military history and religious mythology. Divine intervention plays a pivotal role in unearthing the secrets of the Clans' treasure and heroic exploits. The patriotism and passion of Celtic heritage lies at the heart of this intriguing story.

A tragedy at sea sets in motion the search for life's true treasures, both in 1915 Ireland, when the funeral of Fenian Rossa fans the flames of revolution, and in America, where the clans begin a journey toward their destiny in **Searchers**, the first book of the series.
Published March 2016

The mysteries of an ancient Clans Pact deepen beneath the horrors of WWI as Irish Rebels march toward revolution in **Entente**, the second book in the series.
Published May 2017

Irish Republican martyrs rise against overpowering British forces to spark the revolution in the 1916 Easter Rising, while the Clans search for unity and treasure to honor the Clans Pact of their ancestors in **Rising** the third book in the series.
Published January 2019

In the aftermath of the Easter Rising, the Clans seek the McCarthy treasure as Collin searches for his missing sister in **McCarthy Gold**, the fourth book in the series
Published January 2020

While fighting for Irish freedom, the McCarthys suffer brutal consequences of the merciless British oppression in the early years of the War of Independence in *Revolution*, the fifth book in the series
Published March 2022

The mysteries of the O'Donnell Clan are explored in *Fortunes*, the sixth book in the series, set in the last year of the Irish Revolution's War of Independence upheaval, leading to the Anglo-Irish Treaty of 1921.
Published September 2023

Future Books in the Series

The Clans, fractured at the start of the Irish Civil War in 1922, follow the ancient clues in an attempt to recover the O'Donnell Treasure they have lost, in *Asunder*, the seventh book in the series.

The Clans, while supporting the Irish Civil War in 1922-1923, seek to unravel and unearth an ancient religious mystery that has confounded civilization for centuries in *Revelation*, the eighth and final book in the series.

Entente

The Irish Clans

Book Two in the Series

Stephen Finlay Archer

Manzanita Writers Press
Angels Camp, California

Entente: The Irish Clans
Book Two in the Series

Copyright © 2017 by Stephen Finlay Archer

ISBN: 978-0-9908019-5-5
Library of Congress Control Number: 2017940284

Publisher: Manzanita Writers Press
manzapress.com
manzanitawp@gmail.com
PO Box 215, San Andreas, CA 95249

Cover Design: Lilia Lalova
Book Layout Design: Joyce Dedini-Runnells
Cover photo credits:
  Front cover: The Belgium Front, WWI, 1915, painting by William Barnes Wollen, titled *Canadians at Ypres*, courtesy of the Princess Patricia's Canadian Light Infantry Museum, Calgary, Alberta, Canada (cropped)
  Back Cover: British WWI Poster, *Support for Belgian Red Cross*, painting by Charles Buchel, 1915, Library of Congress LC-USZC4-11243, and *Portrait of Sir Roger Casement*, Painting by Norman Teeling, Artist
Searchers: Book One - Front cover:
  The Sinking of the Lusitania, Painting Courtesy of the Everett Collection
Rising: Book Three - Front cover:
  Montage of the Irish Easter Rising 1916, Painting by Norman Teeling
McCarthy Gold: Book Four - Front cover:
  The Money Diggers, Painting by John Quidor, Courtesy of the Brooklyn Museum
Revolution: Book Five - Front cover:
  Roadside Ambush, Painting by Martin McGrinder
Fortunes Book Six - Front cover:
  Front cover: *Customs House in Flames*, Painting by Norman Teeling
Asunder: Book Seven - Front cover:
  Montage of the Irish Civil War, Painting by Norman Teeling
Revelation: Book Eight - Front cover:
  Iona Abbey, Painting by Reverend John Butterfield
Author photo: Kathy Archer

This is a work of fiction. Any resemblance of my fictional characters to real persons, living or dead, is purely coincidental. The depiction of historical persons in these novels is not coincidental, and to the best of my knowledge, is accurate to events and their character in life. Some historical aspects may be augmented or adjusted for dramatic purposes.

IN FLANDERS FIELDS

by John McCrae, May 1915

In Flanders fields the poppies blow
Between the crosses, row on row,
That mark our place; and in the sky
The larks, still bravely singing, fly
Scarce heard amid the guns below.

We are the Dead. Short days ago
We lived, felt dawn, saw sunset glow,
Loved and were loved, and now we lie
In Flanders fields.

Take up our quarrel with the foe:
To you from failing hands we throw
The torch; be yours to hold it high.
If ye break faith with us who die
We shall not sleep, though poppies grow
In Flanders fields.

DEDICATION

To the brave men and women who fought in WWI

THE WESTERN FRONT, WWI

by Stephen Finlay Archer

Brave millions dead, we mourn them still,
Ghastly trenches, entomb, enslave,
Generation gone, foul muddy grave.
Machine gun mowing,
Poison gas blowing,
Evil flame throwing,
Phosphorus glowing,
Oozing muck flowing,
Officers crowing,
Such hatred sowing.
But overall,
Governments knowing,
Arms merchants growing.
Brave millions dead, we mourn them still.

CONTENTS

Contents

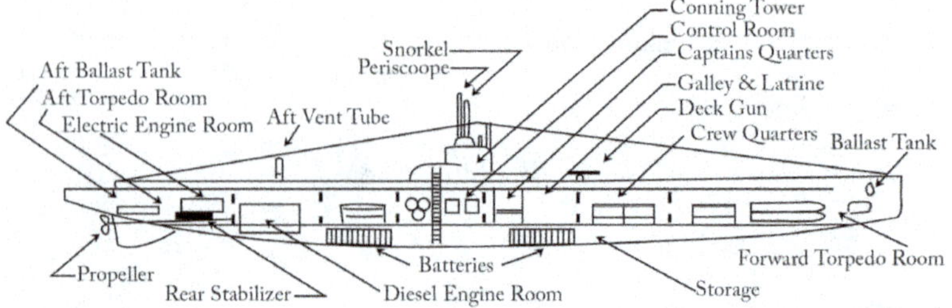

WWI Unterseeboat (U-19)

U-19 and *U-20*
(Second and Third from the Right) in Kiel Harbor, 1914

Chapter One
Captured

October 19, 1915
Five Months and Twelve Days After the
***Lusitania* Was Torpedoed**
Site of the Sinking, Eight Miles off
Old Head Kinsale, Ireland

The thought of being pushed toward the German dinghy brought Morgan back. "Tadgh!" she screamed, remembering that her partner had flung her overboard from their disintegrating fishing hooker moments before. How long had he been trapped under *The Republican?* Morgan heard the German seamen shouting, and one held her fast in the small boat foundering in the choppy ocean swells. She remembered one of the Germans diving off the craft just as she hit the water. *He must have been the one to pull me out.*

Her mind vacillated between two terrible realities. Tadgh, her normally strong and in-command Irish rebel lover, trapped under their overturned Galway hooker—what was left of it after the freighter had exploded. He never should have tried to save the crewmen after the boat was torpedoed by this German U-boat. And here she was, right on top of the site where the *Lusitania, with her on it,* had been sunk just five months earlier by a German submarine.

The veil of her amnesia parted for a moment. The explosion of the freighter brought on another memory of a distant ship, another disaster surfacing. She remembered the lighthouse off in the distance to the north. She remembered the devastation on the deck of the ocean liner as port lifeboats crashed onto the deck, spilling and killing their inhabitants. The fire engulfed the decking where the funnel had collapsed. She felt the ship shudder beneath her and sensed the tearing of the ship's bowels as bulkhead after bulkhead gave way. And she could vividly remember anguish that her man—*what was his name?*—was overdue with the babies from below decks in the nursery. *My babies?* Her spine shook with the fear of it all. *Why can't I remember their names?* A crewman insisted she jump into the last lifeboat dangling over the side. Then the plunge into the icy sea. *God preserve me.*

Morgan startled back to the present peril. The men pointed behind her, shouting. She spun to see a German dive overboard. Her heart leapt. Tadgh's head surfaced in the ten feet between the dinghy and the sinking hull of the hooker, just outside a pool of burning wreckage. His head lolled violently side-to-side, eyes in a vacant stare. A gash bloodied his forehead, a deep one by the look of it.

Morgan squirmed to break free of her captor. "I've got to save him!" But the seaman held fast, and her legs buckled.

The swimming German reached Tadgh and dragged him back away from the burning wreckage and towards the dinghy. Germans hoisted Tadgh out of the water and onto the bottom of the boat. Blood flowed freely from his left calf where a wooden stake protruded, and the gash on his head bubbled.

Morgan's hands went to work. *Stop the bleeding on the leg first, then the head.* Someone threw her a rag. She ripped it in two strips, tying one on the leg and pressing the other to the forehead. No pulse at the neck. Tadgh wasn't breathing. Morgan checked his airways for obstructions. None. She pumped his chest with her palms, stopping every few seconds to blow air into his lungs.

Tadgh didn't respond to her efforts. What if he didn't make it? What would her fate be? He had pushed her into the icy sea to save her, while he had remained trapped on *The Republican*, thinking he would die there. This time, it was her turn. He had saved her from the *Lusitania* wreckage, nursed her back to health. She vowed she would repay him. She got no help from the Germans who were still focused on the roiling sea, shouting at their struggling comrades. The dinghy lurched as the crew pulled two of their own out of the water, dragging them to one side near Tadgh. The one who had saved Tadgh was spent, and the other was badly burned. *God save us all.*

Suddenly Tadgh belched just as Morgan blew once more into his lungs. Vile liquid flowed into Morgan's mouth. She spat it out. Her arms ached, and one of the Germans took over as she lagged. "Keep pumping," she shouted. Water streamed out of Tadgh's mouth, and he coughed. Morgan found a pulse in his neck, weak but stable. *Thank God!*

She turned her attention to the leg. Blood pooled in the bottom of the dinghy. Plenty of it. The rag hadn't held. Morgan pulled out her utility knife and cut away Tadgh's ripped trouser leg applying it as a tourniquet above the knee. That stopped the bleeding. She winced at the piece of wood lodged in place but knew better than to try to remove it. Then she checked his head injury. *Superficial. Doesn't look like the cranium is cracked.* She checked his pulse again. Still stable. But he had slipped back, unconscious.

Frightening memories returned. Tadgh had almost died three months earlier when *The Republican* was attacked during the arms transfer. The agony of it flooded over her. She didn't lose him then, and she wasn't going to lose him now. She was alone then, but she had help now. But these were Germans. Were they the ones who had sunk the *Lusitania* and killed all those innocent people? How could Tadgh have said that they were allies? It didn't make sense to her, but here they were attempting to save them.

The dinghy banged up against the hull of the submarine. The sinister black killing machine wallowed in the chop, a giant sea snake looking for its prey. Seamen from the U-boat jumped down into the dinghy with two stretchers and lifted Tadgh and the injured German onto them. They were strapped down tight, chest and legs. "Take it easy with him," Morgan cried, but they paid her no mind. One of the seamen injected the wounded German with a needle, and soon the man stopped crying out. Another German pointed at the horizon, shouting. Morgan could see what looked like a warship headed their way out of the northeast, from Queenstown, their destination before this nightmare descended.

"*Schnell, schnell,*" the German screamed, and another seaman grabbed Morgan and pushed her toward a tiny hatch revealing the inner belly of the snake. She protested but was in no condition to argue. The stretchers were lowered first, and everyone had to wait his turn to descend. A claustrophobic feeling gripped her as she waited. Then it came to her. She had seen this before. The throng of passengers clawing their way up from the bowels of the *Lusitania* towards the light of the open deck above. She had almost died right there on the stairs. And the babies? What happened to them? *Her babies?* She couldn't shake the foreboding feeling, the dark dread of death.

When it came to her turn to descend, she balked. The rasping siren was sounding and Germans pushed behind her. Just like inside the *Lusitania,* people pushing, but this time she forced herself onto the ladder, dropping down into the darkness of the ship below the surface of the sea instead of escaping it. She stumbled and fell the remaining short rungs of the ladder, landing on the bodies below her.

The smell was overpowering—sweaty men and the stench of urine gagged her. An oily choking mist made her cough. She could barely see in the dim lights illuminating the cramped stomach of the snake. She knelt at the foot of the ladder, now encompassed by a small room with so much equipment within its walls that the men stood shoulder to shoulder. It was a control room filled with pipes, wheels, and gauges.

She felt the same panic as when she had awakened with amnesia that first time in Tadgh's bed. He had saved her from the sea in what seemed like ages ago. The feeling of being totally out of control, defenseless. Several seamen worked to close the hatch above her, spinning wheels, calling out gauge readings and pulling levers. Suddenly she felt a sinking sensation as the beast with the warm, wet vibrating floor nosed down. But no loud engine noise intruded. Just the soft drumming of a motor somewhere as she imagined propellers spinning, machinery working to move through the heavy darkness beyond the walls.

God, let me out. She pulled herself up to climb the ladder, but then a thought stopped her. She faced the men and shouted, "Where is he? I demand to see him."

"*Kommen Sie mit, Fräulein,*" an officer addressed her gruffly, grabbing her arm and pulling her off the ladder toward a bulkhead on the forward end of the control room. Was that cologne she smelled on the man? How strange. He yelled something to his crew as he dragged her forward.

Morgan smashed her elbow when the officer tried to pull her through the opening of a circular hatch. Her arm went numb and it hurt like hell, but it didn't bleed. This wasn't one damn bit funny.

"*Jetzt, bitte.*" The officer yanked her forward past more electrical gear tended by seamen wearing headsets, and past sleeping bunks and a makeshift kitchen, until they were opposite two portside bunks one above the other. *How can men live like this, like rats in a hole?*

"Tadgh," Morgan cried, seeing her lover face up, strapped into the upper bunk with a rubber sheet covering him. Moisture condensed on the ceiling and walls, yet the floor was hot. Stinking water dripped down onto him. At least his wound was covered. *This really is hell.*

Tadgh's face glowed white and his cheeks felt clammy, his pulse steady but still weak.

"Do you have a doctor on board?" Morgan asked the officer.

"*Nein.*"

"You speak English."

"*Jawohl, Fräulein.* You are English?"

Morgan had no idea what her nationality was. Maybe American since she had been on the *Lusitania,* which had come from New York. But certainly not German. She thought it wise to reply, "Irish, Captain."

"I am not the captain. Our *Kapitanleutnant* is on the bunk," he pointed to the wall. "He saved your life and that of your companion. I am the Watch Officer, Fritz Schmidt. What is your name?"

"Morgan."

"Morgan what?"

"Just Morgan." She eyed her captor carefully, sizing up his sinewy, five-foot-three frame. What he lacked in height, he made up with a fierce handlebar moustache that all but covered his mouth. A rugged beard from weeks at sea masked what may have been a square-cut chin. She noticed that most of the sailors were small in stature, perhaps a prerequisite for sardine duty. "What are you going to do with us?" Morgan asked, her senses clearing.

"This I cannot say. I must return to my men now."

"I am a nurse. This man needs care." She pointed to Tadgh. "Do you have medicine?" She lifted the sheet from Tadgh's leg to examine it, but before she could uncover the wound, the officer spoke, "I have a kit in the galley, and we are trained to use it."

"Get it, please."

"You will look after the captain first," he commanded.

Morgan glanced to where the officer lay face down on the lower bunk. He seemed to have passed out. The back of his head and neck, his shoulders, and what was exposed of the top of his back were badly burned. At least second degree, if not worse, Morgan thought. She shook her head.

"He ran out of air saving your man and had to surface through the fire."

Morgan noticed that the standing officer had minor burns on the back of his hands. "You mean that you had to pull him out," Morgan said. She took the palm of his hand and turned it over gently.

He pulled his hand away. "It is nothing, Fräulein." He coughed. "But you will address me as *Sir.*"

"Bring me your kit and I will see what I can do, sir. Can you boil water down here? Do you have any clean cloths? How about alcohol?"

"We have a small electric burner, when it works. We ration water, and there are a few supplies."

"Well, I need your ration hot. The kit and alcohol. Bring it, now, *schnell.*" That's the word he had used to get them all back in the U-boat.

"I will send the help. Tend to my Kapitan first, as you are told." The man turned on his heel and headed for the control room.

Morgan ignored the order and lifted Tadgh's sheet. At least they had put a sheet under him as well. Morgan was relieved that the amount of blood pooled under his calf was not as much as she had expected. The tourniquet had survived the descent into the U-boat. On the other hand, she had no knowledge of how much blood Tadgh had lost in the ocean before he was brought into the dinghy. The skewer, a piece of wood about three quarters of an inch in diameter, protruded sideways from his calf about six inches from the ripped skin, the ragged flesh surrounding it like raw meat. She had thought better of trying to remove the obstruction until she knew what first aid materials were available. She would definitely need to stitch him up as soon as the wood was removed. No telling whether it would come out cleanly. Morgan noticed that several of Tadgh's fingernails were ripped and bloodied, most likely from clawing at the decking to free himself in the sinking debris.

The drumming of the engines suddenly stopped. The U-boat tipped, and she stumbled in the dive. A minute later, the submarine leveled again, and she imagined it hovering in the blackness of the sea. Above the creaking of the vessel's joints, Morgan thought she could hear another churning noise above. She looked aft through the bulkhead opening toward the control room. The men there stood motionless, as if anticipating something.

A sudden noise boomed like an explosion. Maybe something rammed them. The vessel shook and lurched. Morgan lost her footing and crashed into the corner of the bunk, collapsing on the flooring, ears deafened by a high-pitched screeching sound. A seaman rushed through the bulkhead opening and lifted Morgan up, warning her, "Be quiet. Depth charge. Deadly new invention of the English," he muttered.

No telling what would happen to them all now. She awaited the next jolt, imagined the ship splitting apart. At least this time she and Tadgh would be together. She moved closer to him and touched his arm, still warm.

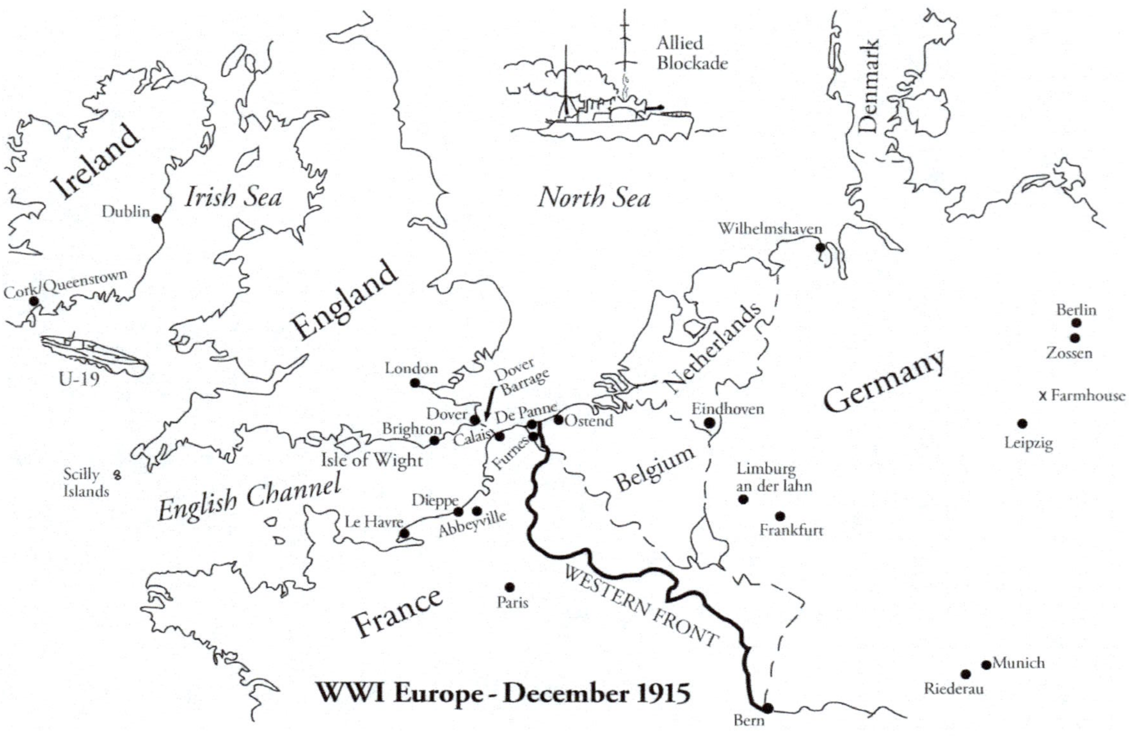

Ireland
Dublin
Irish Sea
Cork/Queenstown
U-19
Scilly Islands
England
London
Brighton
Isle of Wight
Dover
Dover Barrage
De Panne
Calais
Furnes
Ostend
English Channel
Dieppe
Le Havre
Abbeyville
France
Paris
WESTERN FRONT
WWI Europe - December 1915
Bern
Allied Blockade
North Sea
Wilhelmshaven
Denmark
Netherlands
Eindhoven
Belgium
Limburg an der lahn
Frankfurt
Germany
Berlin
Zossen
x Farmhouse
Leipzig
Munich
Riederau

Chapter Two
Command Decision

October 19, 1915
One Hundred Feet Down and Two Hundred Feet
Above the *Lusitania*

A crashing sound from above startled her. The vessel shook violently, pipes rattled, and salt water spewed out of a joint above Morgan's head. The seaman held her fast, then guided her to hold on to the bunk. "Pressure wave," he said. Tadgh's leg had rolled precariously out over the edge. Morgan moved it back and noticed blood seeping from the wound. The tourniquet had loosened. She quickly cinched it up.

The seaman brusquely pushed her out of his way. Then, using a wrench on the leaking joint, he soon reduced the flow to a trickle. The tool had made scraping noises, and Morgan could see the same officer shaking his fist at the seaman from aft in the control room. The crew waited for the next attack. It never came. Morgan grabbed the seaman's shoulder. "Can we get the medicine kit and hot water now, so I can fix these men?" She motioned to the injured in a gesture to indicate sewing and stitching. The man disappeared through the bulkhead opening. She could see him consult with an officer who shouted some orders, pointing back towards the small galley.

Morgan examined Tadgh while she waited. At least he didn't seem to have any broken bones. She heard him groan when she moved his leg back. A good sign. "*Mavorneen*, it will be all right, my love." She stroked his cheek. First, she would attend to him, and then she would convince the Germans to put both of them ashore near Baltimore. They were prisoners trapped in the belly of a snake, but she would try anyway to get them out of there.

The seaman returned with a badly banged-up tin box. Morgan saw that it had a worn red cross on the outside. At least they acknowledged that universal symbol. On opening the box, she saw it contained liquid-filled bottles labeled *antiseptikum*, a jar of ointment, gauze, tape, a sewing kit, and stout surgical thread. But a box of needles and vials labeled *das*

9

morphium piqued her curiosity the most. That must have been what they gave the captain. Morgan opened one of the bottles and sniffed. Pungent, it smelled like Dakin solution, a diluted mixture of boric acid and sodium hypochlorite, used as a wound antiseptic. How she knew that, she wasn't sure. She was getting used to remembering some nursing skills, although her amnesia still persisted. Morgan thought that she could work with these supplies.

She had to stabilize Tadgh before the officer came back. She needed to extract the wooden piece first. The seaman returned with a bowl of hot water and a bar of foul-smelling soap, but no alcohol. Must be drinking water in the bowl. It looked clean. All the cloths the man brought were soiled. "This won't do," she told him. "Find me something clean." Morgan removed her tunic. It would have to do. She poured some water on her dirty hands and lathered the soap. It left behind a scummy film. She dabbed some of the Dakin solution, or whatever it was, on her fingers for good measure. The seaman returned with a work shirt. It wasn't clean, but it would do. Again the perfume smell. Instinctively, she reached for his hand to thank him and smiled. Maybe this wasn't a hellhole after all. He pulled back, and his face reddened.

Morgan tore her shirt in strips. "Hold his leg still," she told the man. He pointed at the captain, but Morgan insisted he follow her directions, even if he might not understand. He complied and held down Tadgh's leg. Then, with a slow but forceful tug on the wood, she pulled it from the wound. Blood gushed out, but she was ready for it. Pouring the disinfectant on a strip, she pressed the strip to the wound, applying pressure to slow the bleeding. She realized that there were probably splinters still in the wound, judging by the rough edges of the wood, but she dared not lift the sodden cloth for fear of risking more blood loss. Tadgh involuntarily flinched. The seaman held the leg fast.

Morgan's arm shook with the effort, but after several minutes, it seemed safe to check the wound. The poor lighting made it difficult for her to work efficiently, but it couldn't be helped. The flow had slowed considerably, and she could see two large splinters embedded deep in the wound. Using her thumb and middle finger, she gently pulled out one of the splinters, and it came out cleanly, but the second one seemed to be deeper and would be more difficult to extract.

She noticed that the seaman watched her carefully. He produced a knife from his scabbard and held it out. It looked dirty. Morgan took some gauze, and dipping it in the antiseptic solution, she wiped the blade then probed with it to catch an edge of the splinter that had popped up closer to the surface of the wound. Then the blade tip snagged on the soft tissue. Blood spurted afresh, nearly hiding the splinter. Her fingers touched the tip of the splinter, and she pulled it out, immediately applying the compress again. She was fairly certain that most of the damaging wood was removed. At least as far as she could tell.

Fortunately, the bleeding had slowed enough for her to continue. Morgan carefully prepared another strip laced with disinfectant. Tadgh moved fitfully but did not wake. She threaded the needle and looped a knot at the end. Then she commanded the seaman, "Keep holding him still," and he tightened his grip. She sewed the ragged edges of the wound together as best she could, and a vague memory that she had done this before came to her. She dressed the wound and prayed that her work would hold. Morgan noticed evidence of increased bruising down to Tadgh's ankle. That was to be expected, not dangerous, but then she wondered how she knew that. These Germans at least had the basics for treating injuries, but if the depth charges had found their mark, the supplies would be useless.

Morgan removed the tourniquet and noticed that the gauze didn't immediately turn red. Her stitches must be holding. After checking Tadgh's forehead wound, Morgan decided it was superficial. While applying antiseptic and bandaging his head, she detected an elevated temperature. She would have to monitor closely for infection. Then she ministered to the raw fingers on his right hand, binding them tightly with the gauze. She checked his pulse again. Still weak. She had done the best that she knew and had to hope that it was enough.

Her guard looked on approvingly, then covered Tadgh's legs with the rubber sheet and strapped him down once more. He pointed over to his captain, indicating that Morgan was to tend to him right away.

Morgan checked the captain's pulse. Regular. But the burns were extensive. She wondered why a German officer would risk his own life to save someone whom he didn't even know. Look at all the men on board the freighter that they didn't try to save. They had probably already been blown up, she supposed. He must have seen the English warship bearing down on them. That made her wonder whether they tried to save anybody on the *Lusitania*. She felt the electric engines whir into life again, and the deck vibrated beneath them.

Watch Officer Schmidt jumped through the bulkhead opening and strode with purpose into the temporary sick bay. In perfect English, he asked, "How is Kapitanleutnant Weisbach?"

Morgan addressed his concern. "The good news is that the burns are second and not third degree, sir. No black skin, which means that the subsurface fat layers have not likely been affected. I am worried about the large area of his burns, however. He could lose body heat and blood flow." *Where did that knowledge come from?*

"Well, fix him, then. We need him back in command. You will help him."

"This man is not going anywhere for quite a long time. Especially back in command. I am concerned about his very life, sir." She dipped another strip in the pail of now-cooled water and pressed it to the back of the captain's neck. Raw red blisters had formed, but they were small and could be left alone. That would be preferable.

"How long will this take?"

"You will have to see how he responds. At least three weeks."

The officer scowled. "*Drei wochen? Inakzeptabel.*"

"Your captain will be in great pain and should not be moved," Morgan said, ignoring the officer, remoistening the cloth and dabbing the top of his back. She examined the top part of his burned-away tunic. "We'll need to cut the cloth out of the blisters. With something better than a knife. Find scissors."

The seaman disappeared into the galley and reappeared with a pair that she doused in disinfectant. Morgan set to work cutting the cloth below the burn area, leaving only a narrow strip still attached.

"Right, you can remove his shirt later without disturbing the wounds." She turned to the red-faced officer and asked, "Are you the second officer?"

"*Jawohl.*"

"Not anymore. You are the captain, now."

The officer scowled. "Don't you give me orders."

Morgan lifted her chin and continued defiantly, "I'm going to attend to your captain here until Tadgh awakes. Then after I have done my part to save him, you are going to put us ashore in that dinghy you have strapped and netted to your submarine."

"I will do no such thing. You are my prisoners. When the captain awakens, he will decide what is to happen. Not you."

Gently touching the injured officer's head, she said, "Your captain may die tonight. He's burning up with fever. If he lives, he will be in no condition to decide anything. He will need to be on morphine for the pain until his wounds heal."

Morgan cringed at the thought of being trapped inside this foul snake with these men for even another few hours. But she couldn't leave Tadgh, even for a moment. She touched his brow, as hot as the captain's below him. A sudden wave of nausea rolled through her. *I can't show any weakness. I have to be strong.*

"You must tend to the captain, Fräulein. I will be back." Fritz turned on his heel and disappeared into the control room. She could hear him in agitated conversation with his crew.

Morgan applied cool water to the captain's neck, shoulders, and upper back in a dabbing motion until the whole area was moistened. The burn area had swollen with splotchy red and white skin. Oddly, even through the dabbing cloth, the area seemed cool, not hot as expected. That's when she noticed that his teeth chattered uncontrollably, but his breathing seemed regular.

"We've got to get him out of his wet uniform," Morgan commanded the seaman. "But don't touch his burns. And bring blankets." She wondered how large a dose of morphine had been given him. Working as quickly as she could, Morgan dabbed disinfectant on the burn areas and covered them loosely with gauze strips from the medical kit.

The seaman assigned to her disappeared aft and brought back a fresh set of clothes and a thin wool blanket. Another seaman accompanied him, and they carefully lifted and re-dressed their captain, while she averted her eyes. Gently returning him to his face down position, they covered him and tucked him in securely. The seaman brought another blanket at her request, and she laid it gently over her patient's head, shoulders, and upper back. In a few minutes, the chattering stopped. The U-boat lurched forward and she instinctively held onto the captain's bunk, keeping him in place. Fortunately, the injured were lashed down, even though the cinch on the captain's upper torso had been removed. The seaman told her they had surfaced. She imagined that she could smell the sea air. Had they come into port? What a relief. *Maybe they are going to take us ashore,* Morgan prayed.

The officer came forward to the sick bay. "Well? His status?"

"Stable, with his burns cleaned as best I could."

"When can he resume his duties?"

Why wasn't he listening? "Three weeks at the earliest. The next few days—"

"Not acceptable. We need the captain now. We are heading home through the English Channel, and it is dangerous."

"Put us ashore first, sir."

"No. You must continue to tend to my captain."

Morgan held her tongue and wished she hadn't painted such a dismal picture of the captain's condition. The nausea returned, and she had to get out. She pushed past him, and before he could stop her, she dashed through the bulkhead and up the ladder for the open hatch. She could feel someone trying to hold her back at the ankles as she struggled to escape. She kicked them away and pushed her head through the opening.

Morgan gulped in fresh air and rested her elbows against cold steel, propping herself up. She turned her face to the stars winking in the cool night sky, high above the calm sea. Off to the northwest she could make out dim lights on the horizon. Queenstown Harbor, she guessed, her intended destination when they set out that day. Oh, to be in Ireland again, where they had been safe in Tadgh's home early that morning, having a simple breakfast. If only she hadn't suggested that they take a sail in the hooker with the hope of convincing Tadgh to visit the Cunard offices searching for her identity. How selfish she had been.

Below her, someone bellowed and Morgan felt a pull on her legs. "Oh, God preserve us," she cried out. Backing down, too tired to fight them anymore, she sank into the belly of the snake.

Chapter Three
Awake

October 20, 1915
South of the Scilly Isles,
Entering the English Channel

*I*n Tadgh's nightmare, he was pinned down on a slab in a lumber mill, a whirring sound in his ears. He couldn't move, and his leg hurt like hell. In his foggy mind he saw the whirling saw blade cut his left leg to shreds. He cried out in agony.

That cry wakened Morgan who had finally managed to fall asleep in the captain's quarters between the galley and the control room. The same instinct a mother has to pick out her baby's cry from confusing background noises roused her from her own nightmare. She bolted upright hitting her head on the overhead piping. She scrambled into her clothes as quickly as she could within the cramped space, then rushed forward to Tadgh's bed and checked his pulse and brow. Morgan reflected on the fact that Officer Fritz had given her the only bunk onboard with a modicum of privacy. At least the curtain closed it off from the rest of the U-boat. Perhaps he had seen how she had carefully tended to his captain—*they said the captain's name was Weisbach, didn't they*—and Fritz may have softened his view of her. Maybe he had noticed some of his men staring at her.

She used the last of her cloth strips, dipped in the cool water pail, to cool Tadgh's face and neck, carefully avoiding the gauze on his forehead. "Tadgh, it's me, Morgan." He was unresponsive, although she could see his biceps strain against the cinch that tied him to the bunk. "You've been hurt and we are on a submarine." Morgan gently opened his right eyelid with her thumb. The normally calm amber eye that she loved so much shifted left and right. He seemed to be in severe distress. Sweat dripped from his face, and she could see his neck muscles straining as he tried to raise his head.

"It's all right, my love," Morgan whispered, wiping his brow again with the cool cloth. She wondered if this was how he had tended to her when she was so ill after the *Lusitania* sank, those days spent in the bedroom of his home at Creagh, in that very same bedroom where they had so magically made love. Their home. Or, at least it had been as late as yesterday morning. They had survived the attack by the RIC goons at the Beamish & Crawford Brewery loading yard in Cork and subsequent chase from that villain Boyle in Dublin, so she wasn't going to let this encounter with a German U-boat be the end of them. "Damned if I will let them get to us, Tadgh."

"What's that you say, Fräulein?" Now Captain Fritz hailed her as he strode forward from the control room. "*Haben Sie gut geschlafen?*" He smiled at her as she tried to understand him. "Slept good?" he pressed.

Morgan shrugged her shoulders. She thought it best to humor him. "Yes, *danke,* is that right?"

"*Jawohl, danke.* How is your patient?"

"He cried out in his sleep. I am checking on him now." She moved close to Tadgh's leg.

"*Nein. Erst der Kapitanleutnant.*" He gripped the back of her neck and forced her to look at the burned officer. "The captain comes first. How many times do I have to tell you this?"

Morgan complied and put her hand to Weisbach's brow. Cooler. "How much morphine did you give him?"

The officer did not answer her question. "He should wake up *an diesen morgen,*" Fritz responded, then in English, "Sometime this morning."

"What time is it now?"

"It is already six. What condition is he in?"

Morgan gently lifted the blanket and carefully peeled back the cloth covering Captain Weisbach's neck. It adhered in a couple of places due to the pressure of the cover, but when the material was removed, she saw that the blisters were intact except where the cloth had stuck. The small areas that had been affected ran with a clear liquid, so she dabbed at them carefully with the Dakin solution and replaced the gauze. After carefully tending to the man's wounds, she announced, "I don't see any signs of serious infection." She certainly didn't want to paint an overly negative picture, yet she knew that the healing process would not be easy.

Fritz seemed unconvinced. "It doesn't look good to me."

"He survived the night, didn't he?" Morgan turned away from the injured captain and resumed her inspection of Tadgh's leg. She fretted about the lack of cleanliness in her operation the night before. She had sewn up the wound potentially trapping the infection inside, but at least there wasn't a lead bullet or shrapnel to worry about. That monster, gangrene, still lurked in her mind. "What will you do with us?"

"Never mind. You appear to be more skilled in the medical way than any of us on board, so you will nurse my captain until we reach our port of Wilhelmshaven. For your sake he had *besser nicht sterben.*"

"*Sterben?*"

"He must not die, Fräulein Morgan."

Morgan, appalled at the threat, dared not display her feelings. She turned her attention to Tadgh and loosened the upper leg cinch to peel back the blanket covering his left calf. She asked the officer, "Where are we?"

"We are just entering the English Channel south of Cornwall. Sunrise will be in another hour, and we will have to submerge to avoid the English ships and airships."

Morgan scrunched up her nose. "What's that horrible stench?"

"It's normal that the air is foul down here," Fritz explained, "but it gets much worse after we have been under water for several hours. Your eyes will sting from the chlorine. Although it is dangerous to do so, we must surface occasionally to charge batteries and vent the hydrogen gas that builds up when we use them underwater. If water gets to the many batteries under this floor, the chlorine gas can become deadly." He cleared his throat.

Morgan realized that this really was hell on earth, or rather under it, but still not anywhere near the agony of being in the sinking *Lusitania*. At least these men had a chance for survival in this miscrable war. But then, she imagined what chlorine gas may do to them all. "How long do we have to be down here?"

"Four days to port if we are not attacked. We travel 65 miles under water in the daylight hours at this time of year before we have to surface. Our speed is only six knots, I'm afraid." He frowned. "We travel on the surface much faster under the cover of night, though, but only for ten hours or 180 miles ." Fritz looked up at the ceiling, calculating in his head, perhaps.

Why was he telling her all this? To frighten her? If so, it was working. "Four days? My God, I don't think these two men will last that long without proper medical care."

"If they don't, then you won't," Fritz muttered, grabbing her wrist. "You are the best that we've got right now. We make do down here to survive. Now tend to my captain, without another word." He shoved her down, and she nearly crashed into the prone officer.

She pressed him again, more adamant this time, "Let me repeat my question from last night. What will you do with us?" Morgan looked up at him. She was not going to give up without a fight.

"When my captain is awake and well, he will make that decision. At any rate, you will be visiting Deutschland as our *guests*."

Morgan fought to keep her face calm as her brain reeled with the realization that there seemed to be no way out of their captivity in this underwater tomb.

♣ ♣ ♣ ♣

Tadgh's leg throbbed, the pain excruciating. His forehead hurt like hell. The last thing he remembered was his beloved boat *The Republican* breaking up in the water. In the dim light, he could see the interior of what appeared to be a U-boat. He could hear the whir of motors. Then he thought of Morgan and cried out for her.

Morgan was eating a meal of what Captain Fritz called "diesel food" in the tiny galley when she heard Tadgh's raspy voice call out her name. She jumped up, knocking over the makeshift table and spilling her precious ration of water. "Tadgh, I'm coming!"

God be thanked. She survived. Tadgh turned his head and saw her rushing towards him, a vision of loveliness.

She leaned over his bunk, took his hand, and raised it to her lips, wishing she could kiss his mouth instead. That would have to wait until his recovery.

"Are you all right, *aroon?*" Tadgh whispered.

"Yes, yes. I'm fine." She soothed his head with the cool water cloth. "You have a bad leg wound, but I cleaned and sewed it up. You will be better soon, I hope."

"How, in the name of God, did we get into this predicament?"

"The U-boat captain saved us both, first me from the water, and then he pulled you away from the wreckage of *The Republican*."

"Where is the man? I want to thank him, sure I do."

"He's on the bunk below you, badly burned from the flaming wreckage. He hasn't regained consciousness."

"Burned?"

"He surfaced into a patch of burning debris after he freed you and pushed you up and out of harm's way. I saw him do it," she paused, "a brave man, indeed."

"Where are we headed, Morgan?"

"To Germany, *mavorneen*. Apparently we are their prisoners. I tried to get them to put us ashore, but they are heading home instead to get their captain medical attention. We're in the English Channel, I think. We almost got blown up by the depth charges from an English warship going after the U-boat when they were saving us."

"I guess I missed all the fun." He winked at her.

"This place is filthy, not the fun I had in mind."

"So you like *The Republican* better than this submarine, then."

"This water snake terrifies me, Tadgh."

"I have no doubt, lass, after what you must have endured on the *Lusitania*." He tried to shift on the bunk and realized he must be tied down.

"I remembered some of it, Tadgh! The ship."

Tadgh recalled how Morgan had appeared disoriented just after the freighter blew up, calling for her loved one and her babies. Could that man, presumably her husband, have survived? Was he the one who put the ad in the *Southern Star* newspaper, identifying her as his missing Claire and asking anyone who knew her to contact Jack Jordan at Cunard in Queenstown? The pieces of the puzzle now seemed to make sense. Morgan was most likely a married woman, then, with babies that may have been rescued from the *Lusitania,* and a husband who must be looking for her. And Jack Jordan, the boson's mate on the *Lusitania,* was the key to it all. It pained him to realize that these devastating facts formed a truth he did not want to share with her. His head ached with the weight.

"I remembered. We were just at the spot where the *Lusitania* sank. I recalled seeing the lighthouse in the distance. Then the freighter exploded. It was just like the first disaster, like being back on the deck of the *Lusitania.*"

"With your husband and your babies?"

"I don't know anything about them. That part is still fuzzy. There was a lover, I think. And he had babies. I had one, too. Oh, Tadgh. The panic and misery of all those people struggling to get up on deck and then crashing in the lifeboats." She shook her head. "It's a vision that's trying to form."

"What else do you remember, aroon?"

"I remember that a kind man helped me to the last lifeboat, and then it plunged into the sea with my holding onto the back for dear life. Just like when you threw me off *The Republican.*" She looked into his eyes. "Why did you do that, Tadgh?"

"You would have died with the boat capsizing, don't ya know. What else do you remember?"

"Nothing, damn it. Everything else before that is a blank."

"Your real name? Do you remember it yet?"

"No idea. It's Morgan now, that's all I know."

Then he remembered something. "Do you have my locket, lass? I tucked it inside your shirt."

"I took my tunic off right here by your bunk to use it for bandages. It has to be here somewhere. Maybe it fell between the slats of the grating." Morgan searched the floor by the bottom of the bunk. "Oh no! I've lost it, love. I didn't know it was there. I was so preoccupied." She wanted to cry. That locket was important to him.

"You'll find it. And if not . . ." He shrugged his shoulders and changed the subject. "I noticed that you're wearing a German officer's shirt, lass. Blending in with the natives, are we?" He wondered how much the men had seen when she took her shirt off.

"The sailor was very kind."

"Did you say something about the English Channel?"

"Yes. Fritz talked about taking the fastest route home."

"So you're already on a first name basis with these men, with this . . . Fritz."

"He's the acting captain now. He's all right." She saw Tadgh shake his head. "He seems to think I'm some sort of miracle healer and needs me to tend to the captain."

"I need you to tend to *me*." Tadgh wondered what all had happened while he was unconscious. Morgan had become much too friendly with these men.

"That I have been, my love. And that I will. You have no idea what it has been like here while you were asleep. Now, what were you saying?"

"The English Channel is a much faster route than going north around Scotland, but it is highly risky, I've heard."

"Risky? This whole contraption is more than risky. It's a death trap. I keep getting this feeling of impending doom."

"I'm sure it seems that way, especially after your ordeal on the *Lusitania*. We will make it out all right, aroon." He was seriously wounded and strapped down, but he believed in Morgan and their love, and that they would be fine. They had survived thus far, and they would endure whatever the future brought them. "Can you bring this Captain Fritz to me *?*"

"I'll get him." She kissed Tadgh's hand again. She heard the wounded German officer moan below. Morgan looked down at the man's face and saw that he was definitely waking up. "Lie still, Captain Weisbach. I will be right back with your officer."

"Weisbach?" Tadgh remembered the name from his first German encounter just after the

U-boat sank the *Lusitania*. Was this the same Kapitanleutnant Weisbach? Wasn't he the second in command, then?

"Yes, that's his name. I'll be right back, my love."

Tadgh heard the captain cry out below him, "*Gott im Himmel!*" and he called out to the man, "Don't move, sir. You've been burned."

"Who are you, talking to me in English on my own ship?" the man growled.

"I am the Irishman you saved along with my partner Morgan, who was on the *Lusitania,* I believe, another ship that you may recall. We are in your debt, sir, once again."

"I fired the torpedo that sank the *Lusitania,* you know," he groaned.

"Well, you saved one of the passengers then, and now you've saved her once again—that is twice now."

"I saved someone?" He took a breath. "*Gott sei dank. Zweimal die selbe,*" he whispered.

"You saved my companion Morgan once before, remember? You directed me to look for survivors when we met at sea that day of the sinking. Morgan said it was you who pulled her out of the sea yesterday, so that makes two saves for you. She's the one who dressed your burns."

Officer Fritz strode down the companionway with Morgan in tow. "*Herr Kapitan,* you're awake!"

"Ja, Fritz. I'm back in the world. What is our status?"

"We are in the channel, now."

"And what about my condition?"

"Your shoulders and upper back up to your head are badly burned. You may have noticed that you cannot roll over. We are heading home via the English Channel to get you proper treatment."

"It seems that our young lady, here, is taking good care of me. What about the nets and the Dover patrol?"

"*Ja, mein Kapitan,* I couldn't take a chance with your life by going around Scotland."

Morgan stepped in and touched Weisbach's forehead. "You are very sick, sir. High fever. Your body is likely in shock because of the burns. We don't have the needed medicines on board that can help you. The burns are serious, and you must rest."

"We are taking you to the hospital in Wilhelmsholm, the one specializing in burns from the Western Front." Fritz spoke with authority. "They know how to treat burns from these new flame throwers the English invented."

"Can you move me to the control room?"

"I don't advise it, Captain," Morgan told him, lifting the blanket and then checking under the gauze covering his neck. She didn't like the white liquid oozing from the broken blisters. "I need to examine all your burns. Lie still." She carefully removed the gauze strips, studying the condition intently. "I'm going to use the Dakin solution again."

"Dakin? That is only used for minor cuts ."

"Well sir, that's all the disinfectant you've got available on board." She raised the bottle so he could see it. "Do you want more morphine? This is going to sting."

"No. It can't be any more painful than it is right now. When I move a little, it feels as if the skin is splitting open."

"It is not ripping open yet, so don't move. That's why I need you to stay still and rest. This will bite a little." Morgan dabbed the Dakin on the worst of the open sores where the gauze had stuck. Weisbach's limbs jumped, but he didn't let out a sound. "You were very brave in risking your life to save us, sir. We are in your debt."

"I was the one who caused the freighter to sink in the first place, you know. I pushed the button that sank the *Lusitania*, apparently with you on it. You should hate me." His voice sounded weary. "It's my job, and I have my orders."

When she had finished dabbing, she carefully laid a new set of gauze strips over the burns. There was no tape to secure them. She didn't like the condition of the infected skin.

Fritz returned with a needle. Before Weisbach could resist, more morphine coursed into his system as Morgan watched the syringe level drop. "Damn you, Fritz . . ." he moaned. She was glad the captain fell into darkness again. Easier for him that way.

Morgan turned her attention back to Tadgh. She did not like the look of his festering leg under the bandage. There appeared to be the start of an infection along the line of stitches. "How does it feel?"

"Like it's on fire. There's no burn, is there?"

"No. I'm going to dab it with Dakin now." The disinfectant foamed on the surface as it sank into the ragged suture line.

The wound now hidden under the bubbling Dakin reminded him of something else that was tucked away beneath the surface—the truth. Tadgh wanted to talk to her about what he had read in the newspaper article he had kept hidden from her. Maybe she would remember her name in the process. Especially after her memory jog. But it wasn't the time nor place. "We will get out of this together, my love. I promise you," he repeated to her as if it was a prayer.

"You will be prisoners of my country—that is, if we all make it through the gauntlet," Fritz stated, removing his cap and rubbing his wrinkled forehead.

"What do you mean *prisoners*?" Tadgh asked. "Aren't we Irish your friends?"

"That depends on the situation. In Germany, no." Fritz frowned and changed the subject. "We normally don't go through the English Channel. Our admiral has banned it unless absolutely necessary. The English have light steel indicator nets with mines at various heights from Dover to Calais that ensnarl our U-boats, giving the enemy warships of the Dover Patrol time to depth charge our trapped submarines."

"Like shooting fish in a barrel," Morgan said, as she covered Tadgh's leg with the gauze and then the blanket.

"I'm afraid so. But we have maps, and at night we can usually avoid the higher nets. It is difficult to get precise bearings in the dark."

"What kinds of ships do they have in the Dover Patrol?" Tadgh asked, squirming a little from the residual sting of the disinfectant. He wondered why Fritz was so open with him, giving him information that would be reserved for his own crew.

"Anything from tribal-class destroyers to armed yachts and trawlers, most of them equipped with powerful searchlights. There are also seaplanes and observation blimps during the day."

"How many U-boats have been sunk there?" Tadgh pressed, hoping to get as much information as possible.

"Before they stopped us from running the gauntlet, five in the English Channel with two tangled in the nets."

"I think it wise to take the swiftest route," Morgan said, checking Weisbach's temperature once again. "If you want to save him," her voice wavered.

"When will we be at the nets?" Tadgh asked.

"Overnight we will be on the surface off the coast, opposite the Isle of Wight. Tomorrow morning we submerge before dawn south of Brighton. After twilight tomorrow at about 1900 hours, we will have to surface to charge batteries, just ten miles short of the nets and south of Dungeness Lighthouse."

"Then what?" Tadgh's voice wavered. Being tied down and useless like he was, it would be better if he knew what was going to happen and when.

"It takes three hours to charge batteries. Then we can be off to the nets." Fritz calculated in his head. "We should clear the nets just after midnight." He turned to leave and stopped, facing them, his brows knitted. "I've told you this because we are in dangerous waters. No telling if we will all see the light of day. Now I must return to the control room." He pointed toward the captain and said to Morgan, "Let me know if he gets worse."

"I will monitor my patients. You can count on me."

"Fräulein. I am *counting on you* to remember what I said."

"What did you tell her?" Tadgh asked.

"That she had better not let my captain die, for both your sakes." He turned on his heel and disappeared into the control room.

Time passed with agonizing slowness for Morgan. During the night, her patients' fevers rose, and all she could do was mop their brows with cool water. She learned a lot more about this U-boat from her observations. They had crammed fresh food and stores into nooks and crannies of the boat, even packing one of the toilets with food. The thirty-five sailors on board worked and slept in eight-hour shifts, so they needed only enough bunks or hammocks for a third of them. They slept in the torpedo room forward of the temporary sick bay once the two of the four torpedoes had been launched. She had no idea where they would have slept before that. She likened their condition to sardines in a can, stacked, trapped, and wet to the bone.

The sailors, as superstitious as any seamen, made it clear that it was bad luck to have a woman aboard and gave Morgan as wide a berth as possible in the cramped quarters. She hadn't been allowed back into the control room or beyond it. Fritz had told her that the aft end of the U-boat contained the engines and a torpedo room where more sailors slept. Fritz had bragged to her that both fired missiles had found their mark, so it had been a productive mission, a necessary outcome if the submarine command was planning on sinking enough tonnage to upset England's food and munitions supply. That left them more room.

Overnight, Fritz let Morgan go topside with the new watch officer to get some fresh air. What a relief. At least the submarine wasn't sinking under her. The salt air pierced her lungs, and she felt almost human again. She imagined that this was how a miner might feel when he surfaced after digging down in the tunnels all day. Standing on the bridge at 4:30 in the morning, Morgan could see moonlight glistening on the forward deck. The sea was calm with only the occasional wave whipping over the bow and splashing them. It was the first clean water that had touched her face since she was pulled out of the sea. The fresh air and star-jeweled sky above her head starkly contrasted with the tight spaces and dank odors of stale sweat below. The men were only allowed skimpy rations of fresh water, with none allowed for bathing. No wonder they smelled so bad. They tried to mask the odors of sweat with cologne, but it only added to the stench. Fritz had told her the cologne was called No. 4711. When he offered her some to splash on, she was tempted, but refused. Her own smell was overpowering to her, and she longed to bathe, but it was *her* smell, and familiar to her.

Off to the left she saw lights twinkling on the shore. "Those are the towns alongshore of the Isle of Wight. We're right on track," the watch officer announced, pointing to his left. Suddenly he turned toward a crewmate. Morgan spun around to follow his gaze.

"Dive, dive, aircraft overhead," he shouted into the IMC intercom.

Morgan could hear a distant buzzing sound but couldn't see anything. The officer shoved her back down through the hatch opening following the crewman, and he jumped down after her, turning in the conning tower to secure the hatch. The boat was already diving.

In the control room, Fritz questioned the watch officer, and the man replied, "Felixstowe F.2 flying boat, sir."

"Are you sure? At night?"

"There's a full moon and clear skies. The craft is at about 5,000 feet I guess, half a mile out heading north from Cherbourg, I should think, towards Southhampton. I don't think he saw us."

A bomb struck the water at a distance of about 500 feet ahead of the U-boat. They heard the thump, but there was no concussion. "He didn't see us, eh? What's the depth?" Fritz turned to his pilot who was furiously working the levers to the ballast tanks.

"Thirty feet, sir."

"Right full rudder."

From her place near the sick bay, Morgan could feel the sensation of the boat turning as it continued its descent at a tilt. She rushed forward to make sure that both patients were secured in place. She had just stepped through the bulkhead when a loud explosion shook the vessel, seemingly right above them. The concussion knocked her sideways into the latrine.

Sirens blared, then Fritz yelled, and they were quickly silenced.

"Damage control!" Fritz shouted.

Morgan heard several men sound off. No one appeared panicked. The lights flickered and then came back on. Then she heard clanking sounds, like tools pounding against metal. She imagined the worst and checked the floor around her for water gushing in.

By the time Morgan had picked herself up, she noticed a definite pain in her left shin. It wouldn't do for her to get injured now. She felt the U-boat level off and she heard Fritz's order. The engines stopped. Morgan reached for her patients who thankfully were still strapped in.

"What's going on, lass?" Tadgh asked, clutching at Morgan's sleeve.

"I'm not sure. I heard someone say the word *Luft*. I know that means 'air' so maybe it was an aircraft bomb drop ."

"Is it night? I can't tell. How could this ship have been spotted?"

"The boat was running on the surface under a full moon, love." She didn't tell him that she had been out there, enjoying the fresh air and view.

Morgan held Tadgh's hand and wondered when the next bomb might drop. But none did.

Fritz ordered the U-boat to come up to periscope depth. Then from up in the conning tower, someone said, "*Aufstehen periskop*." Soon afterwards, Fritz announced, "The damn flying boat is up there, not 400 yards astern, bobbing on the sea like a giant seagull."

"Will we torpedo it?" someone asked. "They may have dropped a line trying to hear our signal."

"Do they have ship-to-shore communications?" No one knew. It was unlikely.

"Come about to firing depth. Left full rudder. Prepare forward tube."

"Aye, sir."

Fritz ordered, "Rudder amidships. All stop." They waited for the next direction.

"Damn, the plane is taking off," a nearby sailor announced, clutching his headset.

"I can see that," Fritz yelled down from the conning tower. "Secure the torpedo tube."

"Maybe they can't be sure that we are down here," one seaman offered.

"Wishful thinking. They'll be waiting for us at the nets."

No further attack came and Fritz ordered them back on course. An hour later, they surfaced to a tranquil world devoid of aircraft. The moon had set.

Chapter Four
Running the Gauntlet

October 21, 1915
Southeast of Brighton in the English Channel

*T*he mood aboard *U-19* was grim. They had been submerged since 0730, and now, almost twelve hours later after twilight, the air became intolerable. Morgan felt the boat rise and then break the surface with a jarring slap as it leveled out. The hum of the electric motors stopped as the diesel generators kicked in.

Fritz came forward to inform Weisbach that they were ten miles west of the Dover nets. "Fräulein, the captain looks worse."

"Yes, sir, his situation is grave." She knew that Tadgh wasn't faring any better, either. "What is our status, Captain?"

"We will charge our batteries for three hours." He paused, and his voice wavered. "Then we can submerge again and be on our way to the nets."

Morgan heard the hesitation in his voice. The upcoming maneuver at the nets was going to be dangerous.

During the charge, they dove for cover twice. Both times the watch officer signaled that a Felixstowe F.2 came at them from the horizon, lights flashing. There was every indication that their presence in the channel the night before had been reported.

At midnight they were at periscope depth a thousand yards west of the nets. Even at that hour, Fritz could see armed ships of the Dover Patrol plying back and forth between Dover and Calais, searchlights focused on the net. They would have to time things carefully. He was consulting the rough net and minefield chart they'd been given by the admiralty when Morgan popped her head up into the conning tower. "How long until we get through the nets?" Heads turned toward her.

"I told you to stay with your patients. Get back there."

"Not until you answer my question," she demanded.

"I want to wait until the moon sets at 0200 hours," Fritz replied.

"I don't think you should waste precious time, sir. Without the proper equipment and medicines, your captain's condition is now critical."

"It's your job to keep him alive and well, remember."

"In this hellhole with dirty water dripping from the ceiling and no clean bandages?"

"That is not my problem. Get back to sick bay and stop bothering me."

"How long until we reach the port at Wilhelmshaven?"

"About thirty hours after we clear the nets."

"I expect Captain Weisbach will die from infection well before that. His skin is bubbling and blistering."

Fritz jumped down from the conning tower and dragged Morgan with him to sick bay. "Show me," he snapped.

Morgan carefully lifted the dripping rubber blanket and pulled off the neck gauze first. White pus oozed from the sores, and the area had taken on a purple tinge. Weisbach was on his third dose of morphine. "We will run out of the disinfectant well before we reach your port, and you are most likely low on morphine. I'm not sure that any of this is doing any good. Brandy would probably work better."

"That we do not carry for obvious reasons." Fritz put his hand to the captain's forehead. "He's burning up."

Morgan didn't dare mention her real concern. She glanced over at Tadgh. His leg was swollen, and it seemed that the infection was spreading. Tadgh was conscious, having refused morphine, but delirious.

"There is an option." Fritz took another look under the shoulder bandages. "There is a U-boat base at Ostend in Belgium. It is much closer and just behind our lines, but our hospital facilities there are limited."

"Better to treat a live person than a dead one. Can they deal with major burns there?"

"I don't know. I've never been to that medical facility."

"How long until we could get there, sir?"

"About six hours after we clear the nets. That would put us there on the surface, but well after sunrise."

"I would take that risk and make all-speed to arrive there."

"Transport from there to Germany will be difficult."

"If you don't do that, you may be using a hearse for transport."

"Let's get through the nets first, and then I will decide."

"You don't have much time. You must head to the closest port."

Fritz met her eyes with frank approval. It surprised her that he seemed to take her direction positively. She was, after all, a prisoner whom he should not trust.

♣ ♣ ♣ ♣

Fritz returned to the conning tower and consulted the map. Then, in his new role as temporarily appointed Kapitan, he gave the order to proceed immediately, all-ahead slow. Through his periscope, he could see a slow trawler coming out of Dover, its lights shining along the line of the sea above the nets. With the full moon overhead, it may as well have been daylight. His rough map showed a small gap in the wire nets about ten miles off Dover, so he had positioned his U-boat opposite that spot and a quarter mile from the net line. German intelligence reported that these light wire nets, sometimes as much as three hundred feet wide, were anchored at various depths from the seabed, with floats on the surface to hold them upright and to locate them for the British ships. If a submarine became entangled, a marker buoy would pop to the surface to provide a target for bombers and surface ship depth charges. And if that wasn't dangerous enough, the English had placed mines in the sea. His superiors had commanded him not to navigate this treacherous route unless it was absolutely necessary. He had chosen this path on a woman's advice to save his captain, and now, the mission could be jeopardized by the moonlit conditions. For some reason, he trusted the woman.

"We will stay at periscope depth, but be ready to surface or dive on my command," Fritz ordered from the conning tower. He had decided that it was too risky to surface.

"Screws approaching to port," the sound engineer announced. Every crewmember held his breath.

"I see the trawler," Fritz announced, spinning his periscope ninety degrees to port. "Two miles off," he muttered, returning the periscope to its forward-looking position. He couldn't see any signs of nets breaking the surface of the water ahead, luckily for them.

Morgan held fast to Tadgh's hand in the sick bay. He was either asleep or had slipped into unconsciousness. She prayed for salvation. Suddenly she heard a scraping sound along the hull on the port side. Was it a net, or a mine cable?

"All stop," Fritz yelled down. The submarine's forward progress slowed ominously. When the sound had progressed to the aft torpedo room, there was a sudden jerk, and the forward progress of the vessel stopped dead.

Damn. We almost slipped through the net. Well, at least it isn't a mine. It sounded as if the edge of the net had snagged on the rear port stabilizer fin. "Depth?" Fritz barked.

"Thirty feet."

"All back one third," Fritz commanded. The engines spooled up and the boat inched aft. After fifty feet, the boat again jerked to a stop.

"All stop." *Something is trapped in the rear stabilizer.* Fritz tried up and down planes commands and the stabilizer appeared to be stuck in the neutral position.

"Screws are still approaching," the sound engineer announced.

Fritz spun the periscope left and realized that the trawler was now approximately a mile and a half off their port beam, headed directly for them.

"Retract the periscope." Ten seconds later it was done. The conning tower top hatch was five feet under water and about sixty feet forward of the stabilizer. Blowing the ballast to raise the U-boat would expose the bridge in the moonlight, and they would be picked up in no time. If they sat quietly, the trawler running the net line might miss them, but it may slice them in two, instead. Had a marker buoy been deployed?

Fritz couldn't take the chance. The trawler didn't likely have depth charges, but other warships that it could summon did carry the deadly explosives. Even if the trawler missed them, aircraft would pick them out at first light.

"Wire cutters," Fritz yelled down, stripping off his all-weather coat and hat. The engineer rushed up the ladder from the control room, cutters in hand.

Fritz gave instructions to the sailor, "Help me open the hatch, just enough to let me squeeze through."

The engineer shook his head. "Too much water pressure, sir."

"Nonsense. I can do it. It's only five feet, man. I will knock when I return. You push and I will pull to get back in."

The engineer still shook his head. Fritz estimated the time it would take if he could snip the netting in a few seconds—*three minutes.* That was not an impossible feat. He had no choice. It was the only solution.

Fritz took deep breaths for a minute. There was no time to lose. He motioned to the engineer to close the hatch after him. As they cracked the hatch, water leaked around the seal and spilled down the stairs. The men below watched wide-eyed as Fritz and the engineer put their backs into hinging the hatch upward. Water surged through the opening, and Fritz pushed off from an upper rung of the ladder against the flow to squeeze out of the forty-five-degree opening into the black water. With a groan, the engineer released the hatch and it slammed shut. A moment later, he spun the wheel and crossed himself in prayer.

Fritz became disoriented. He had shot out forward onto the bridge and hit his head on the periscope mast. The water felt damn cold, maybe fifty degrees. Finding the railing, he turned and pulled down the fifteen feet onto the deck and started swimming aft. He could hear the trawler's engines drum through the water. There were few or no handholds to help propel him towards his target. One arm of the cutter had jammed inside his belt and down his right leg, restricting his kicking motions.

How long had it been? A minute, at least. There, right ahead of him and out of the dark, loomed the aft vent tube. The front edge of the stabilizer would be about fifteen feet farther aft, and down about five feet down over the port side.

The moonlit sea surface twenty feet above him radiated a dim eerie gloom down to deck level. Below that, pitch darkness. The cold English Channel seeped through his uniform, weighing him down. Swimming aft, he reached the edge of a steel net that stretched downwards along the U-boat's hull into the cold void. Its top, about five feet above the deck, stretched perpendicular to the hull, then disappeared into the blackness.

Fritz pulled the cutters from his trousers and kicked off from the deck, pulling himself down the wire edge until he reached the stabilizer. Feeling around with his free hand, he determined that the wire edge was lodged between the stabilizer and the hull. He yanked it with his free hand, but it wouldn't budge. He felt light-headed and almost dropped the cutters. *Damn. At least if I can free it, the boat can get away. Stop thinking. Act now. Should I surface for air?*

Fritz could hear the screws of the trawler closing on his trapped U-boat. There was no time for that.

Fritz grasped the quarter-inch-thick wire. Planting his feet through the netting below the stabilizer, he gripped the wire in the jaws of the cutter and squeezed. He had not completely cut through the thick wire, so he carefully aligned the jaws, squeezed again, and the wire snapped.

He wasn't prepared for what happened next. The U-boat was no longer held fast by the taut wire. Now freed, it sagged downwards snagging Fritz's legs in the wire net below.

Inside the conning tower, the engineer sensed the motion. Grabbing one of the levers, he made an adjustment that slightly lifted the stern of the boat, an action that saved Fritz's life.

Refusing to panic when he found that the wire was still firmly lodged,

Fritz went down another five feet to free it below the stabilizer. Twenty seconds and two squeezes later, another section of wire snapped. The sub bobbed up leaving Fritz entangled in the net below the boat. He kicked fiercely and broke free. That used up what air remained in his lungs.

The sound of the trawler's screws pounded in his head. No time to swim up for air and then forward. His shipmates would wait for him until it was too late. The trawler must be upon them. He saw a dim glow from their forward searchlights that were sweeping the sea surface above and behind him. He had to try to get back to the hatch. Fritz dropped the cutters and guided himself to where he thought the bridge would be. He was getting dizzy. Out into the blackness. The helplessness that accompanied the certainty of having to gasp for air when there was just water to take in numbed his thinking. *At least the boat is free.*

The vision of his wife and two children filled his mind. He had never really expected to survive the war in these tin cans. The odds were against that. Especially now that the enemy had the bombs to kill them. *At least I have saved my men, or have I?* "All-ahead full," he willed his crew to action, in vain.

Ten seconds later, his head hit the ladder leading to the conning tower. *Up,* he willed himself. There, miraculously, he touched the closed hatch. He felt for the handle and weakly tapped against the hatch cover. He had no strength to pull. Time had run out.

When the engineer heard the tap, Fritz had already been out there three and a half minutes. Nevertheless, the engineer spun the wheel open and heaved with his back. Seawater flooded into the U-boat, and with it, the body of his new captain. The hatch slammed closed and another seaman from the conning tower spun the wheel shut.

"Fritz is not breathing," the conning tower crewman yelled, cradling his new captain in his arms and breathing life back into him.

"Dive, dive. All-ahead full," the engineer shouted, and the seaman worked the levers. The submarine lurched forward and then dove.

"The trawler's right on top of us," the sound engineer yelled.

The hull of the trawler snapped the exposed portion of the periscope and snorkel, missing the top of the conning tower by three feet. When its screws went by, the cavitations threw the submarine out of control. The crewman held Fritz secure in the conning tower just in time and prevented his fall down into the control room. Morgan held onto Tadgh's bunk and body as the U-boat rocked back and forth.

At that instant, the trawler's propellers became entangled in the wire net. The sound engineer heard the screeching of the wire netting spooling up, most likely seizing both propeller shafts. They all heard it. The trawler had to be snagged. The captain of the boat started blowing the air horns, scanning the sea surface with a search light for any sign of the submarine. Ships on the Dover shore ten miles away blared horns in reply.

Fritz sputtered awake. *"Mein Gott, ich bin lebendig!"*

"That you are, sir. Still alive, after almost four minutes out there under the water. You saved us." The engineer slapped him on the back, and the men below cheered him, even as they fought to get the U-boat stabilized.

"The trawler's engines have been cycling, but they are now stopped," the sound engineer announced.

The helmsman reported in. "The rear port stabilizer is still stuck, but I can work around it."

It took Fritz several minutes to catch his breath and resume command. That harrowing experience had convinced him. "We are going to Ostend. All ahead full, level at fifty feet. We'll be there by morning, God willing." But he was thinking, *I need to be with my wife and children. The admiralty can go fly a kite.*

Morgan heard Fritz's command all the way forward in sickbay. "Thank you, God," she prayed as Tadgh came to.

"What's the news, aroon," he croaked. Then, pale as death, he slipped back unconscious.

Morgan dropped to her knees. "Oh, God, speed us to Ostend."

Chapter Five
Separation

October 22, 1915
Ostend Harbor, Belgium

organ fumed. They had been tied up side by side to other U-boats in the pens for half an hour, and still no one had come to unload her patients. She had also been put under armed guard, the crewman who had given her his shirt the first day in the submarine. Apparently, the rest of the men had gone ashore. The boat was quiet.

When Fritz returned from reporting to his superiors, he explained to her that the delay was due to their not returning to homeport. Fritz told her he had complained that both men aboard his boat were in critical condition, only to be assured that the ambulance drivers were doing all that was possible. He was told that they were only ten miles east of the Front, and the Battle of Loos was raging a mere forty miles southwest. Hundreds of seriously wounded countrymen had been pouring daily into the field hospital, the La Plage Hotel, vacated by the retreated Belgians. They told him the beds were overflowing with scant medical staff available.

"So you're going to let your captain die?" Morgan demanded an answer.

"Of course not. The ambulances should be here in a few minutes. You will remain at my side. Do you understand? You and your man Tadgh are my prisoners, remember."

"I gathered that. Anything to get out of this hellhole."

"You don't like my U-boat? My cozy home under the sea?"

Morgan could see him trying not to smile. "I must admit, the place grows on you." She couldn't believe that she had just said that.

"Like the white fuzz we call rabbits on our potatoes?" Now he was chuckling.

Only two days before she had been revolted and frightened almost out of her wits to be trapped in the vile vessel. But now, Morgan had respect for this crew's courage and fortitude. Yes, they had all been sardines sealed in a can, but she felt a kind of camaraderie with these men. Had they not saved

Tadgh's life, at least so far, not to mention her own? Fritz himself had shown great bravery and selflessness in the face of an impossible task.

She couldn't help herself. She gave Fritz a big bear hug. "You are a fine captain. Thank you for saving us all."

The officer, startled by Morgan's action, stepped back as if he were on a parade ground. "Fräulein, you did your best, and my captain is still alive."

"Barely, sir."

Morgan heard men scrambling down the ladder into the control room.

"*Hier*," Fritz yelled, and orderlies with stretchers appeared in the bulkhead opening.

It took fifteen minutes to get Captain Weisbach and Tadgh strapped onto gurneys and then lifted up and out of *U-19*. The captain was still out like a light. Tadgh had cried out in pain when the orderlies stumbled on the ladder, nearly dropping him.

Fritz led the way after the gurneys, with Morgan and an armed seaman being the last people to leave the U-boat. From the ladder perch, looking back down into the control room, she stopped to have one last look around. "Good girl," she said, patting the wall of the conning tower above her. "You got us home."

Then it hit her. She was a long, long way from home and had no idea what would become of her and Tadgh, if he survived.

Morgan went in the ambulance with Tadgh and her guard to the German hospital. Fritz followed in the second vehicle with Captain Weisbach in the back. During the short ride from the harbor, Morgan focused on Tadgh's condition. His swollen leg and high fever frightened her. Once or twice, he briefly woke up when the ambulance lurched around a corner, but then he lapsed back into sleep. The prior evening, despite his protest, she had given him a small morphine shot.

The ambulance screeched to a halt and the orderlies quickly removed Tadgh's gurney. Even in the morning mist, Morgan could see that the Hotel La Plage on the oceanfront Albert I Promenade, was a grand old lady, a tabernacle of costly splendor. Morgan smelled the salt air blowing off the North Sea and heard the rollers sweeping onto the adjacent beach. It must have been a wonderful seaside town before the war .

Fritz jumped out of the other ambulance, urging the orderlies to get Weisbach into the hospital. They hurried up the front steps and into an entrance hall with a splendid mosaic dome roof. A nurse directed them to the hotel's grand dining room, which had now been set up as a ward for the wounded. The chandeliers suspended from the ceiling and ornate wall mirrors stood in stark contrast to the battered humanity on the myriad of mattresses before them. Amputees and shell-shocked men in various stages of dying crowded the floors. Chaos reigned, with the few nurses and doctors overwhelmed with the injured. Morgan could see through a partially open revolving door that they were using part of the kitchen as an operating room, where a doctor was sawing through a leg.

"God help Tadgh." Morgan prayed that her lover wouldn't be the next casualty on that chopping block. She corraled one nurse to help get Tadgh settled, but the woman didn't speak English. Finally, Fritz came over and got that sorted out. Twenty minutes later the doctor who had been amputating in the kitchen came to assess Tadgh's condition. He spoke perfect English.

"Fräulein, are you this man's wife?"

"I am his partner and nurse."

"A nurse, you say. As you can see, we need help."

"I will gladly help you if you can save my Tadgh."

"She will help you anyway." Fritz spoke up, putting his hand on the butt of the Luger in his holster.

Morgan knew Fritz did that for show, and of course, she understood the game. *Don't make waves.*

The doctor carefully removed the gauze on Tadgh's leg. "Any foreign objects in this wound? Any metal?"

"No, just splinters of wood that I removed in three pieces, and I believe I got it all."

"You did a fine job of suturing, under the circumstances. He is sedated?"

"Twenty cc's of morphine seven hours ago."

"I don't see gangrene at the surface of the wound yet. But it is septic. No telling what is inside, given the swelling. You did a fine job, young lady. Your name?"

"Morgan."

"That's a good German name. It means *morning*," his face creased into a grin. "It will be a new morning outside, a new day of the war," he said, and then his smile faded. "I will do what I can for him."

Morgan sensed his kindly nature. "I did what I could with my limited abilities. Is there any hope for him?"

"There is a new medicine that the English bacteriologist Twort just discovered. Even though it hasn't been fully tested, they are starting to use it in their field hospitals. We captured some of this medicine and one of their scientists when we lay siege to Ypres a few months ago. So now we are making it ourselves. It's called bacteriophages, and it can sometimes offset wound infections."

"How is it administered?"

"It is introduced to the wound in many ways—topical, ingested, or injected. We are also using it to treat cholera epidemics in the trenches."

"Please give it to him, Doctor."

"Doctor Heinrich to you, young lady. I take it that the lad means more to you than just being a partner then, yes?"

"He means everything to me, my world. What about his leg? Will he be able to . . . ?"

The doctor laughed. "He'll be a full man, if that's what you mean."

Morgan could feel her cheeks flush. "I meant walk."

"Well, then, we'll just have to take extra special care of him, won't we. I'll try to save that leg for you. Did you also treat Captain Weisbach?"

"I did."

We'll be giving him the phages also. There's a serious infection, but I think we can get it under control. You clearly saved the man's life by keeping the burns clean. Now can you give me a hand in the operating room? Are you capable? We have three more amputations to perform before noon."

Morgan took a deep breath. "Yes, I am able and willing." This would be the only way she could stay close to Tadgh, she thought.

Doctor Heinrich arranged for Morgan to be billeted with the nurses, and Fritz posted a guard when she was away from the hospital ward. Three days later she finally got to see the beach outside the hotel in the sunshine. It didn't seem like the middle of a war zone out there. But indoors, the wounded kept arriving day after day and night after night. None of the medical personnel got any rest.

At first, the sight of limbs being amputated bothered Morgan to the point of nausea, the smell of rot and decay in the wounds revolting to her. By the third day, the process became routine, and she realized that they were saving lives, German lives. Those who would learn to hobble or work with one arm, or those who would learn to live sightless. What was it proving, all this killing and maiming? Morgan had learned that the front lines on either side had not moved much, one way or another in over a year. Now the men were arriving with chemical poisoning from lethal gas attacks at the Front.

Tadgh was awake and taking sustenance but was still bedridden, not ready to walk yet. Morgan made sure that he was cared for. It appeared that the utilization of phages was working. His leg was tender, he told her, but not as swollen. Morgan tended to him whenever she was not at her other duties. They didn't talk further about her past. There would be time enough when they were free. But Tadgh brought her up to speed about what was going on politically.

"Morgan, when we were in Dublin at the An Stad hotel, Tom Clarke told me that one of our main Irish Republican Brotherhood leaders, Joseph Plunkett, came to Germany a couple of months earlier to gain support from their military. He accompanied one of our own, a Sir Roger Casement[1] who has been in Germany since October of last year with that goal. Apparently Sir Roger and John Devoy of the Clan na Gael in America convinced the Germans to provide arms and to allow him to recruit an Irish Brigade from the Irish prisoners being held in captivity in Germany ."

"Irish prisoners? Why were they fighting with the English against the Germans?" Morgan was confused.

"Not all Irishmen hate the English as we do. The treacherous British pretended to offer us Home Rule if we would help them defeat the Germans. Our gullible politician, Mister Redmond, fell for their lies and convinced the vast majority of our Irish Volunteers to side with the English in this war."

"How do you know that they are lying?"

"They have encouraged the Protestant Ulster northerners to arm themselves and fight against Home Rule while they clamp down on us southerners to prohibit guns of any kind, the bastards."

"Southerners?"

"Catholics, Republicans, us."

"I see. But we aren't in Germany."

"Yes, aroon, but Belgium was invaded and is now occupied and controlled by Germany[2]. Somehow, we need to get in touch with Mr. Casement. Maybe he can help us."

"How?"

"I have no idea, especially since I am a wounded captive."

"I, too, am a captive, Tadgh. They have me under armed guard."

"We're a fine pair then, lass. At least we're together."

"I'll make sure it stays that way." Morgan had no idea how she could make that happen, but at least Doctor Heinrich and Fritz seemed pleased with her work. "I'm going to check in with the captain."

"Is he better? I want to thank him personally for saving our lives."

"He is responding well to the same medicine that you have been getting. They also have a topical ointment that is healing the sores on his back and neck. He will survive to fight again."

"Did he say why he risked his life for us?"

"No, but he said that he was the one who pushed the button to fire the torpedo at the *Lusitania*. That must be a terrible burden to carry."

"You forgive him then, aroon?"

"How can I not when he saved your life, my love."

"Just doing his job, don't ya know. Pushing that button, I mean."

"The job of killing more than a thousand defenseless human beings?"

"He was not the captain then. He was following orders. Military men have to do that, you know."

"But what about moral obligations?"

"You'd have to ask the captain of the U-boat about that."

"That's where I think you are wrong. We all, surely, have moral obligations to our fellow men and women. Do you know what atrocities I'm seeing here at the hospital from the war? Terrible things. I heard that millions of men have been killed. Using chemical weapons on human beings! For what? National pride? What about all the wives left widowed and children left fatherless?"

"Let's not argue, aroon. We have to find a way out of here together."

"I've got to go back to the operating room. I will see you later."

As she walked away through the maze of the wounded, Morgan fumed and didn't know exactly why anger surged through her. Sure she did. Men killing men was bad and wrong. And Tadgh was one of them, a killer. She thought back to their escapades in Ireland and the violence he committed. So how could she love him, then?

The next two days overwhelmed Morgan. She had worked thirty-six hours straight without sleep. Her heart went out to them, the broken boys. There had been a major Allied offensive at Loos, and the wounded German lads were piling up in the corridors, awaiting amputations or death. She crawled into her bunk and dropped into a fitful sleep.

Fritz asked for a meeting with Doctor Heinrich very early the next morning, the 29th. The good doctor showed exhaustion from the onslaught of casualties, his face haggard, bags under his eyes swelling from lack of sleep.

"I'm impressed with the nurse you brought me from your U-boat. I want her to stay with me here. She knows what she is doing, but she's late this morning."

"She's a prisoner, Doctor. Likely Irish, but we're not certain."

"But there is no evidence that she fought against us. Quite the contrary. She is fighting *for* us, helping save so many of our brave soldiers."

"My superiors have ordered me to have her partner sent to the detention camp at Limburg immediately." He paused. "She's not going to like it." He rubbed his chin. "Is the Irishman Tadgh McCarthy fit to travel?"

"He will eventually recover. His fever is down, a good sign, but there is still infection in his leg, and it would be hard for him to walk any distance."

"Will he survive if you give me enough of his medicine to get him by, and can we transport him so he doesn't have to walk?"

"Yes. I suppose so, but . . ."

"That's all I need to know. A vehicle will be here within the hour. Have him ready."

Morgan reported for duty at ten, missing Tadgh's departure by half an hour. She had overslept. With Morgan's mind clear but her body still not cooperating, she entered the ward and observed the wounded still crowding the hallways. As had become her routine, she went to check on Tadgh first and found him missing.

"*Wo ist mein Tadgh?*" she questioned one of the male orderlies, using the few German words she had picked up.

"I cannot tell you. I just came on duty. He was here yesterday," he told her, and she understood.

Morgan hunted throughout the ward and still couldn't find Tadgh. Until now she had felt safe knowing that he was near and recovering. Now panic set in. *Could he have taken a turn for the worse? My God.*

Morgan rushed to the operating area, her heart beating wildly. "Doctor Heinrich!" She had interrupted a leg amputation just as the severed limb was being discarded in the bin. The doctor ignored her while he worked to close the wound.

"This man has died," a nurse reported. "There is no pulse in his carotid artery."

Morgan imagined that Tadgh, whose leg had gone septic again, could end up like this poor soul. Like so many others who didn't survive that type of operation.

The doctor checked the patient's vital signs, shook his head, and slowly pulled a sheet up over the body. This one had too many internal complications. Turning away from the all too familiar outcome of his operations, he pulled Morgan out of the operating room and through a side door facing the beach. Before she could open her mouth, he said, "I'm sorry, dear girl. They have taken your man to Limburg. I couldn't stop them. But he will be treated fairly, and he will recover."

Morgan's heart stopped. "Why? He is not your enemy. He is an ally, if anything."

"This is war, and the military have control of these things."

"But Captain Weisbach risked his life to save him. Doesn't that mean something?"

"I just follow orders, I'm afraid."

"You, too? You damned silly men." Morgan could not hold back the tears. She was all alone now behind enemy lines. Whose enemy was she, anyway? It all seemed so grotesque and pointless.

"Come now, Morgan. It will be all right in the end. You'll see."

"How will that ever be?"

"You have friends here," he smiled. "Me, for instance. You're doing a fine job, and I need you to help me. We're saving lives. You are valuable, and as long as you are, you will live. That's the way it works."

Limburg, whatever and wherever that was, and she might never see him again.

Chapter Six
Brigade

October 31, 1915
Hotel La Plage, Ostend, Belgium

Morgan could not stop thinking about the last time she saw Tadgh. Why did they have to argue? She knew it wasn't his fault that he had military discipline. None of these men was at fault. It was the kings and politicians. Or maybe one could blame the devils who owned the companies that made the machines of war[3]. What a travesty. All she knew was that she was separated from Tadgh, and she didn't know if he was recovering from his wound.

Three days later, Fritz came by the ward. "Fräulein, I am going away to sea again tomorrow. My U-boat has been repaired."

"But Captain Weisbach is not well enough to take command yet."

"My superiors have put me in charge until he is well enough."

Morgan couldn't help herself. She angrily lashed out at Fritz. "If you are in charge, why did you allow them to send Tadgh away?"

"My superiors ordered me to detain him."

"And where exactly is Limburg? Why was he sent there?"

"Limburg is a prisoner of war camp southeast of us about 275 miles from here, halfway to Germany's southern border. That is where the Irish prisoners are kept. Your friend is Irish, no?"

"Yes, of course he is Irish. He is your *ally*, not your enemy." She threw up her hands in exasperation. "How did he get there?"

"They took him by truck."

Morgan imagined the bumpy ride and wondered what that trip would do to Tadgh's leg. "He wasn't well enough to be moved."

"Well enough to travel. The doctor gave me his medicine. They have some medical facilities at the camp."

Morgan thought of trying to escape to find Tadgh. But 275 miles? And what would she do when she got to Limburg camp. Surrender? A camp like that was intended only for men. She was stuck, and the situation seemed hopeless.

"What's to become of *me*?" Morgan frowned.

"That's what I came to tell you. I brought my wife Gerda and my two boys here to Ostend since it will be my new base. Doctor Heinrich helped me do that because of you. Apparently, you are indispensable as a nurse and he needs your skills. I had to agree to have you stay with us in a small house near the beach. Gerda says yes to this while I am gone, and she will be your guard. Will you promise to be good and not give my wife any trouble?"

"As good as I can be. I will support Doctor Heinrich, and appreciate what your wife is doing for me, if that's what you mean."

"By being good, I mean that you won't try to escape. If you do, then I can make things very difficult for your friend McCarthy."

"Don't you dare hurt him." Morgan sought his eyes.

"I won't, if you follow my orders. This is a significant risk for me and for my family. Do you understand?"

"I will not endanger your family." Morgan realized she owed him that much.

Later that day Fritz brought her to a small Tudor-style row house in Old Ostend, five blocks from the beach. Morgan was relieved to be away from the horrors of the ward and finally out in the world, even though it seemed such a foreign, dangerous, and lonely place with Tadgh gone.

"Gerda, this is Morgan," Fritz announced, as a woman in an apron opened the door. Two towheaded little boys peered out from behind their mother's legs.

"Very glad to meet you." Morgan reached out to shake Gerda's hand.

"Likewise," Gerda replied in English with a Bavarian accent. "I studied at Cambridge before I met Fritz and before the war," she added, seeing Morgan's surprise.

Morgan breathed a sigh of relief and turned her attention to the boys. "Who do we have here?"

"This is Hans, and this is Fritz," Gerda answered, grabbing each of them by the hand, and pulling them around her legs to meet their new guest. Both of them clung to her skirt.

"Come now, boys. She won't bite you." Fritz laughed, and the boys shyly stood near their mother.

"Well, young fellows," Morgan said, crouching down to meet them at their eye level. She produced two chocolates wrapped in foil paper from her worn wool coat and offered them to the boys. Chocolate was hard to come by during the war and was a real treat for them. She was given them at the ward, one of the few local delicacies still available to the medical staff for sparse distribution to the wounded men. "Look what I have here. Is it all right to give it to them?"

Gerda smiled at Morgan's generosity. The boys looked up at their mother, who nodded, and they eagerly took the candy.

"What do you boys say?" Fritz prompted them.

"*Danke,*" they cried in unison.

"*Bitte,*" Morgan answered.

"I think that we will all get along fine," Gerda laughed, offering her hand to pull Morgan to her feet. "Come in and let's have some tea. There's not much to eat, but what I have is yours to share."

Gerda gave her a warm hug.

"I've got to get back to my U-boat," Fritz announced. "We are provisioning for my mission. I leave tomorrow."

"So soon?" Gerda looked crestfallen. "I thought . . ."

"When I return, *meine Liebchen.*" He kissed the top of her head. Then turning to Morgan he said, "You remember what we discussed?" Gerda's eyebrows raised, and she looked at her husband, then back to Morgan.

"Yes, sir."

With that, Fritz was gone.

Gerda turned away, her shoulders stooped, and she shuffled into the small kitchen with its tiny icebox and old woodstove. Gerda, three inches shorter than Morgan's five-foot-seven frame, appeared to be almost thirty. Morgan's black ringleted hair and fierce green eyes contrasted with Gerda's straight blond hair and blue eyes. Under different circumstances, she would have been considered a handsome woman. But in the midst of this terrible war, worry etched her face.

For the first time since Tadgh had been snatched away from her, Morgan didn't feel so lonely. And maybe Gerda would be able to help her find out more about the place where Tadgh was being held.

While the women had tea, the boys played on the small parlor floor with blocks. Morgan could see them very neatly piling them in straight rows to make a building—typical German attention to detail and efficiency. Just as she had seen with the medical staff and with the seamen on the U-boat.

"Morgan is an unusual Irish name. In German it sounds like *tomorrow* as well as *morning.*" She smiled. "I will do what I can to protect you *today,* my dear. That's *Heute, today,* and in future, to the best of my ability, *Morgen,* and that's *tomorrow.* So in keeping us safe, that fits my name, you know, which stands for 'protected' in German," Gerda offered. "I think that both our names are apt for our situation."

"My name actually stands for 'from the sea' in Welsh, so I'm told."

"Now *that* fits you," Gerda exclaimed, leaning forward to pour more tea. "I'm sorry that we have no sugar. Are you Welsh, then, or Irish?"

"No. Not Welsh. At least I don't think so. I think, maybe Irish."

Gerda reached for Morgan's hand. "You must have been through such a fright. Tell me about your ordeal on the U-boat." Morgan could sense that the woman was pumping her for information. "What did Fritz tell you about it?"

"Just that his captain and your man were injured and that you had to take the southern route home as quickly as possible."

"I see, and what has he told you about conditions on a U-boat?" Morgan wasn't sure how much she should reveal.

"He says that it's secret, and he can't tell me. I normally do not get any information from him when he returns from a mission since our actual home is in Frankfurt, a long way from here."

"So now, why are you and your boys here in a foreign country so close to the Western Front?"

"That's what really worries me, Morgan. Something dangerous must have happened for my Fritz to have pulled strings to bring us here to be with him. He usually isn't afraid."

Morgan didn't want to upset the woman further. "U-boats are very confining to someone like me who has claustrophobia. There was a dangerous incident in which we were caught in an English net, and your husband cleared it and saved all our lives. He is a hero, you know."

"He's *my* hero, and I can't bear the thought of his dying, especially like that." She looked ashen. "Underwater, I mean."

"War is a terrible thing. I am seeing it day and night at the hospital where the young men are brought. We have to have faith in God to see them through." Morgan surprised herself with that statement. *How could God let this happen to mankind? But there is a Divine Lord. Tadgh didn't save me at sea by coincidence. There is a purpose behind my living.*

"I do pray all the time, and my boys also keep me busy." Gerda turned away, wiping at her eyes with the back of her hand.

Morgan told her new friend about the *Lusitania*, being saved by Tadgh, and about her amnesia.

"You must be a strong woman. Especially overcoming claustrophobia and the dangers in the U-boat."

"It was overwhelming. But I had the captain and my Tadgh to look after."

"Is he Irish, your Tadgh?"

"Through and through. He's not your enemy, but they've taken him to some prisoner of war camp named Limburg. Do you perhaps know anything about this detention center?"

Gerda told her that Limburg an der Lahn was a town far away but near her home in Frankfurt. She promised to help Morgan write a letter in German to authorities so she could find out more about Tadgh's condition.

"So, my dear. We both are left alone and afraid for our men." Morgan couldn't help herself as she stood up to embrace Gerda. "We've all got our crosses to bear."

When Gerda crossed herself and then hugged her new friend, Morgan realized that they weren't alone anymore. Two women, separated from their men in danger, in the middle of the war to end all wars, not twenty miles from the bloody battlefront.

Tadgh ached, exhausted and sore, and his leg throbbed. It seemed more swollen than it was at the hospital the previous week. The truck they had been on was old and creaky, and the roads when they started out must have been in the war zone, they were so bumpy. But lying inside the medical hut behind the barbed wire of a prisoner of war camp, he noticed things had calmed down. Well enough to be deloused, he was stripped and his head shaved. At least he got a clean set of prisoner clothes that weren't striped. His arms were bruised from the struggle he put up when they came for him in the hospital, before they strapped him down on the gurney. He had called out for Morgan, but they must have waited until she had gone off duty to take him. *The bastards.*

His mind raced. How could he escape and find her? What would they do with her? *Bastards.* How far apart were they? He guessed about 300 miles or so, given the roughly eight hours it had taken to get there. He had been visited by an orderly who had looked at his leg, then had given him a dose of his normal medicine to take. At least that was a good sign.

As Tadgh stewed over his predicament, a bedraggled fellow prisoner entered the tent. His threadbare clothes looked clean on the man's gaunt frame, and he did not stoop. A crisply- uniformed German soldier accompanied him, Luger in hand. Tadgh longed for his own Luger, tucked safely in his bedroom drawer at home. He vowed to join Morgan again and get them both home soon.

"They made me come in here to translate and get more information about you. My name is Sean Flaherty." The prisoner spoke with an unwavering voice. "You are in Limburg prisoner of war camp, by the way. I was captured during the Somme offensive. They are using this camp to house about 2,200 of us Irish soldiers here. I understand that you are a fellow countryman."

"Tadgh McCarthy from County Cork."

"Indeed. Where were you captured?"

"In the Celtic Sea, by a U-boat."

"Well, that's a wonder. Never heard of the tin cans taking on Irish before."

"Are you by any chance part of Redmond's Irish Volunteers, Sean?"

"Aye, Tadgh. A terrible war in the trenches, I can assure you."

"How are you being treated here?"

"Fairly, but as you can see, with meager supplies and food. We're still alive. You will be kept here until your leg is better and then transferred over to our unit. I have asked if you can join us in our hut."

Tadgh had so many questions like what plans they had for escape, but it was not the time to ask, with a German soldier hovering nearby.

"I'll see you shortly, then. Thank you for coming to see me."

It took a week for Tadgh's leg to heal well enough so that he could walk on it. During that time he had devised several fantasy escape scenarios in his mind. He had to occupy his mind with a plan, or he would go crazy. He was transferred to hut number 108, where Sean was housed. On his way across the graveled compound, Tadgh noticed that the barbed-wire boundary fences were electrified.

It turned out that Sean had been made a senior officer for the Irish contingent, given his rank of lieutenant. The huts holding fifty men were at least ventilated to limit the spread of TB and other contagious diseases among the captives. He was told that in the previous year the accommodations had been comfortable with plenty of blankets on wooden trestle beds, but their living conditions had deteriorated in the meantime. Rats that carried the germs gnawed their way through almost anything and invaded their barracks.

The men were inspected twice daily and marched around the compound for two hours in the morning and another two hours again in the afternoon. Tadgh was initially allowed to watch the exercise since his leg was still not strong enough to march very far. He would hobble after them until he could walk no more. They got two meals a day of scraps of meat with coarse bread soaked in water. It could have been cat or rat flesh for all they knew, but it kept them alive.

The second day in the hut, Tadgh finally got a chance to talk to Sean privately on a brief walk. "What are the plans for escape?"

"Nonexistent. A group of twenty tried that about six months ago by tunneling, and were caught not a quarter mile from the fence. The Germans marched them back to our parade ground and shot them all in front of the men."

"We could try again, Sean."

"Not me or the others, as far as I know. We learned our lesson."

"But, bollocks, it's our obligation to try, don't ya know."

"We're not going to get ourselves shot, lad. We don't want to go back to the Front, neither. That's suicide."

Tadgh was disgusted with Sean's attitude. A Redmond crony, afraid to fight.

"Have you ever heard of Roger Casement, Tadgh?"

Tadgh's ears pricked up. He had to proceed cautiously. "Aye. I heard he was here in Germany."

"What a traitor he is," Sean spat. "He wanted us to join what he called the Irish Brigade to turncoat away from the Allied ranks and support Germany. We drove him away, the lout."

"Did you, now." Tadgh suspected he was being tested.

"Ya, but he didn't give up. The Germans starved us to make us agree, but we resisted. A man named Kenny showed up from America to try to persuade us. Then in May, Casement's deserters Keogh and Dowling interviewed us again, along with a man named Plunkett[4]. They got about fifty of us moved to another camp nearer the Kaiser. They call it Zossen. Casement has a new underling named Robert Monteith who is here at Limburg right now trying to recruit more deserters. The nerve of the lout."

"What does he want to do with this brigade, Sean?"

"Casement is a loony fanatic. He fantasizes that this group can get back to Ireland to free the land from the English while this stupid war is still going on. What nonsense. When the Allied forces win this war, we will all be branded traitors and shot on sight if we join his ridiculous scheme."

"You don't believe in a free Ireland, Sean?"

"England will make good on its plan for Home Rule, Tadgh. After the war."

"With a divided and armed north and unarmed south by their hand?"

"Maybe that's inevitable."

"Maybe." Tadgh left it at that. He wasn't going to ostracize his countryman. He had obviously been beaten into submission. Tadgh realized he had to get to Monteith.

The next day was Sunday, November 14. Those who were Catholic turned out for open-air chapel. Father Crotty had recently been sent from Rome to minister to the inmates. Tadgh could see a soldier, smartly dressed in a green uniform with an Irish harp on the neckband, clearly different from the Germans. He was about five foot eight in height, with a small black moustache and sporting an officer's peaked cap. The soldier stood by the priest, eyeing the crowd of prisoners.

"There's the traitor, Lieutenant Monteith," Tadgh heard a prisoner nearby shout out over Father Crotty's words. The soldier stood ramrod straight and didn't react to the taunt, if he heard it.

Tadgh inched his way forward as the service droned on. He realized that it would be a mistake to try to contact Monteith in front of these men. But Father Crotty continued his sermon about Jesus' forty days in the wilderness. Tadgh could easily see the parallel, another attempt to persuade the Irish captives to make the right decision to come the aid of their country. They weren't buying it.

Monteith moved off to meet another green-uniformed soldier who approached them from the side. He wore the insignia of a sergeant major. "That's another traitor, Keogh," one of the prisoners mumbled to another of his mates. "He left us, and now he leads the defectors over at Zossen."

The service ended, and Father Crotty came down into his flock as they started to disperse. Tadgh rushed forward as fast as his gimpy leg could carry him. Drawing the priest aside, he said quietly, "My name is Tadgh McCarthy. I am new here and would like to meet with Lieutenant Monteith in private. Can you arrange that?"

"Certainly, my lad. I see you hobbling. Are you in pain?"

"Just a flesh wound, Father. It is getting better."

"You're sure, son? Which hut are you in?"

Tadgh told him where he was located in the camp.

"I will relay your message, and someone will get back to you," the priest said, as he turned to talk to an approaching prisoner.

♣ ♣ ♣ ♣

It didn't take long. The next morning during the exercise period, a German sentry approached and asked, "You McCarthy?" Tadgh nodded. "Come with me."

Tadgh was led to the Commandant's office complex at the far end of the compound while the other prisoners watched closely. Once inside, he was ushered into a side conference room. Lieutenant Monteith, I presume." Tadgh took the initiative with the officer sitting behind the desk and stepped forward to shake his hand. "And I was told that you are Sergeant Major Keogh," Tadgh added, shaking the hand of the soldier standing beside his superior.

As Monteith started his well-rehearsed speech to try to convince this potential recruit to join the brigade, Tadgh cut him off. "I heard that Joseph Plunkett was here in May, sir. What was his purpose?" He wanted to find out what these men knew.

Monteith was taken aback. "Tell me more about yourself, first," he requested, looking intently into Tadgh's eyes.

"Answer *my* question before I do that."

The man stared Tadgh down then relented. "Joseph Plunkett was here to help negotiate support from the Germans for our planned Irish insurgence against the English. Now you will answer *my* question."

Tadgh didn't want to push the man too far. He needed his support. "I am Tadgh McCarthy, and I know Plunkett and his colleagues in Dublin."

"Do you, now." Monteith seemed clearly intrigued.

"I should like to meet Roger Casement. Can you arrange that?"

"Sir Roger is under the weather at present, lad. I am his deputy. What can I do for you?"

"I'll need to talk to Mr. Casement in person, I'm afraid." Tadgh knew that Casement was a founding member of the Volunteers who had been instrumental in the successful Howth gun- running acquisition of arms a year earlier, but he had no knowledge of where these two men's allegiances lay. They could be German or English double agents, for all he knew.

"What battle were you captured at, lad?"

"I was picked up by a German U-boat in the Celtic Sea and brought to their base at Ostend in Belgium." Then Tadgh had an idea. It carried some risk. "I have a message from my superiors, but only for the ear of Roger Casement." He was lying through his teeth and hoped they wouldn't discover it.

"So you got yourself captured at sea in the hope that they would bring you to Germany and that you could escape to find Sir Roger?" Monteith raised an eyebrow.

"It worked, didn't it?"

"You've got balls, I grant you that," Monteith responded. "They could have just as easily relayed their message through Devoy in New York to the Germans in Washington."[5]

"They don't trust the Germans or their communications system. Do you know if this room is secure?"

"It is not. We have to check the premises each morning. We don't trust the Germans either, anymore," Monteith admitted. "Sir Roger is staying with friends just outside Munich. He has not been well, some recurrent illness that he first caught in the Congo. His doctor thinks it is malaria, but I honestly don't know. It has got him down, physically and emotionally."

Tadgh pressed Monteith, "You seem free to travel between here and the camp at Zossen, or so I'm told. Can you get me out of here, so I can get to Munich?"

"What have they told you about us traitors?" Monteith drummed his fingers on the desk.

"Let's just say you're not popular with the men." Tadgh leaned back in his chair and crossed his arms.

"Those prisoners? They are not patriotic for Ireland. But are you, Tadgh?" The man's eyes glittered.

"Fiercely, sir. Many in Ireland are, and you should know that. I saw the forty thousand who turned out for O'Donovan Rossa's funeral and Pearse's eulogy last August."

"You were there? Tell me what was said." Monteith and Keogh leaned forward.

Tadgh launched into a recitation of part of Pearse Padraig's speech, his arms outstretched. He remembered it since he helped his superior create it. At the end he said, "*. . . but the fools, the fools, the fools! - they have left us our Fenian dead, and while Ireland holds these graves, Ireland unfree shall never be at peace.*" Tadgh stared at the men's faces.

Monteith and Keogh seemed genuinely moved, just as Tadgh and thousands more had been during the funeral itself. Despite his earlier reservations, Tadgh's confidence in these two men grew.

"In answer to your question about arranging for your transport, I am authorized to take you to Zossen if you agree to be a member of the Irish Brigade. We are some fifty strong. But that's in the opposite direction from Bavaria where Sir Roger is lodged. I will have to check with the German General Staff in Berlin. Bernard Gronski is our main contact at German General Staff headquarters who reports to Arthur Zimmermann, the Secretary of State for Foreign Affairs." [6,7] At that moment, a German officer opened the door and stood at the threshold, pointing at his watch. "I guess I have to go." Tadgh stood up and turned toward the door, but not before shaking both men's hands and reminding them of their promise.

"We'll see what Gronski has to say about this," Monteith offered, patting Tadgh on the shoulder.

"I'd be careful what you say there. Surely you mean Casement," Tadgh whispered out of earshot of the German. He was becoming comfortable with the Irishman's loyalty, but his judgment and negotiating skills were still questionable given his last statement. No time to prod Monteith further. The waiting officer waved his Luger at them. Tadgh noticed Monteith and Keogh in hushed and animated conversation as he was ushered out at gunpoint.

Chapter Seven
Sir Roger

November 23, 1915
POW Camp, Limburg an der Lahn, Germany

Eight days later, Tadgh was called back to the prison office. His leg felt strong and the swelling was gone. This time he met with the Commandant, a squat pugnacious officer who sat behind a well-worn desk and didn't get up. He wore a scarf and gloves, which hid his stubby fingers. It was so chilly Tadgh could see his own breath in this dreary lime-green room.

"You are cold?" The commandant motioned his prisoner to the lone chair in front of him.

"No, sir." Tadgh was not going to give the man the satisfaction of knowing that his teeth were clamped to prevent chattering.

"I have been instructed to transport you to Munich under guard. You will be met there by Lieutenant Monteith. When you have finished whatever Monteith wants of you there, you will be returned to POW Camp Zossen bei Berlin. You understand?"

"Perfectly."

"You leave tomorrow morning at 0600 hours." With that, Tadgh was dismissed and the interview was over.

That afternoon, a guard marched him over to the infirmary where the camp doctor checked him over and gave him a vial with seven doses of his medicine to take with him. "You should be completely healed in a week, but get examined at your destination."

Tadgh realized that someone must have pulled some strings. The *Boche* were treating him much better than when he arrived at Limburg.

The men of hut number 108 were up and out on the parade ground the next morning when the guard came for Tadgh. They must have been surprised to see him get into the front seat of the lorry with the guard and even more astonished when the vehicle drove out through the front gate of the camp. He hadn't told them anything. As Tadgh waved goodbye from the side window, he heard the jeers, "Traitor!"

The ride to Munich was tortuous. Winding southeast through the pristine rolling hillsides, a person wouldn't have realized that this country was in the midst of war and losing thousands of men each day on both fronts. Once in awhile a convoy of army trucks would go by as a reminder of the horrors. The soldiers coming from the Western Front looked exhausted. Those heading there bore dour faces at best. Tadgh's convoy passed Frankfurt, after which the countryside turned more rural and mountainous.

After six hours of gentle climbing, Tadgh noticed a sign for the high plateau they had reached—Schwäbische Alb. The spot reminded him of home. Cattle and sheep grazed placidly in the fields. Below, a long lazy river spread out before them. It took another hour to wind their way down to the water. Tadgh saw another sign indicating the river Danube as they crossed it at a place called Ulm. As they passed quaint villages and towns, townsfolk waved. Most of the two-storied houses had high-pitched red tile roofs and ornate wooden balconies decorated with painted flower boxes. The walls appeared to be plastered stone with some exposed granite blocks and precise square-patterned exterior wood beams. The dwellings looked orderly and prepared for the oncoming winter storms, and to Tadgh, the villagers appeared happy. He wondered if they were aware that their livestock and crops were destined for a war machine that was trying to obliterate Belgium and France.

Tadgh felt that his bladder would burst as they rolled into western Munich two hours later. He tried to get his guard to stop the vehicle, but they refused to let him relieve himself. They passed through an ancient stone gate into Karlstor. The old city he glimpsed out the lorry's grimy window reminded him of Dublin with its many medieval churches and close-cropped streets. They finally came to a halt in a shopping district opposite an ornate and stately three-story stone building with a quarter-round corner façade. Above the massive door, Tadgh could see the word *Hofbräuhaus*. Since it was the supper hour, he assumed the building was a restaurant, judging by the number of people coming in and going out of the establishment.

The guard stepped out of the lorry and pointed in the direction of the building's doorway. Tadgh needed no further prompting and jumped out immediately. The German led the way in their search for a toilet, his gun hidden under his coat. Three minutes later and a pound lighter, Tadgh felt human again. Returning to the restaurant, he felt a tap on his shoulder and turned around.

"Glad you could make it, lad," Monteith said. "We've been waiting for you." When the guard put his hand up to protest, Monteith spoke to him in German. "There is no further need for your weapon. This prisoner is in my custody now. You can return to Limburg tomorrow."

Tadgh was surprised that Monteith, an obvious Irishman, had the power to command a German soldier, and in his own language. Tadgh's guard evaporated from their sight.

Come with me, Tadgh. I want you to meet someone."

"Casement?"

"No. You'll see him tomorrow." He led the way to a table occupied by a second man and introduced him as Casement's American friend, Doctor Charles Curry. After the two seated themselves, the good doctor asked, "Mr. McCarthy, how do you know my friend Sir Roger?"

"I have never met him, sir, I only know his reputation. I was there at Bachelor's Walk in July last year when the English oppressor killed unarmed Dubliners during the Howth gun-running event. Sir Roger was involved in that."

"Yes. He told me about that. Nasty business."

"We've had more than three hundred years of that *nasty business*, as you put it, sir."

"I understand, lad. You must be famished."

"Food at the camp is not the best, is it, Monteith."

"You're not there anymore. You'll find it better at Zossen."

Tadgh didn't mention that he had no intention of going to Zossen, wherever that was. The sight and smell of the Bratwurst and beer set on their table drove Tadgh mad.

"Can you tell us your message for Sir Roger?" Curry asked as they dug into their meal.

Tadgh wolfed down the first forkfuls, and his stomach rebelled. He grabbed his stein and washed down the rising bile with warm beer. Moments later, he could respond. "I'm sorry. It's a message meant only for Sir Roger." *Slow down*, he told himself.

"You need to know something before you see him. He has been visiting with my family and me at our summer home at Riederau on the Ammersee, a lake outside of Munich. Even though we have returned to the city for the winter, he has insisted on staying in the comfortable country inn out there. He is not well, you know."

"So Monteith here told me. I still need to meet with him personally, sir."

"And so you will, lad. But you and Robert will stay with me tonight, here in Munich. I noticed you have a limp."

"A slight wound. I am better, sir."

"Then I will examine the progress of that healing, son."

Monteith turned to Tadgh after downing the last of his mug of beer. "They told me, Tadgh, that if you tried to escape, they would take it out on your girl."

"Where would I escape to?" Tadgh replied, savoring the last of his own lager.

"I think that Sir Roger shares that view," Charles said, picking up the cheque for their dinner.

Tadgh enjoyed the ride out to the lake the next morning, luxurious in comparison to the last month's transportation. Charles Curry's 1909 Daimler Simplex roadster seemed designed low and wide for stability. Its 60-horsepower manual-crank engine easily cruised along at 40 miles per hour, comfortably carrying the three men. Tadgh felt much better with a full breakfast in his stomach and clean clothes from the doctor's closet on his back. The bath last night had done wonders for Tadgh's disposition, especially with Curry giving a thumbs-up after carefully inspecting the healing leg.

Ammersee Lake was a stunning sight, with the jagged, snow-covered Bavarian Alps to the south reflecting in its calm waters. The crisp November air whipping by as they traveled at high speed in the open automobile took Tadgh's breath away, and the elder tree leaves already showed orange and yellow as they heralded the shift from fall toward winter. Tadgh wished that Morgan could see this splendor of nature with him. *God, keep her safe. I am coming for you, aroon.*

On the west shore of the lake, the tiny village of Riederau sat in a combination of forest and cleared farmland, quite beautiful in late autumn. Tadgh noticed couples rowing out on the Ammersee, young ladies holding parasols to shield themselves from the bright morning sun. No wonder Sir Roger wanted to stay here as long as he possibly could. *What war?* Tadgh promised himself that he would bring Morgan here at some point. After Ireland was free.

"Sir Roger is resting in the country inn. He will be up by now, I should think," Charles said, as he stepped out of his Simplex and pointed to the lakeside guesthouse. It was a splendid three-story stone building with protruding façades to allow guests a bird's-eye view of the lake. Just the kind of Tyrolean chalet design that Tadgh had only seen in picture books in grade school. Magnificent, especially in this setting.

The men walked to Casement's second floor front suite. Curry knocked on the door, and he went in first to make sure Sir Roger was presentable.

Monteith appeared somewhat nervous. "You'll probably only get a few minutes of his time. He is busy writing his journal, for posterity you know."

"You've been here before, Monteith?"

"Several times. I am his right hand man these days. I'll stand by him whatever comes."

"Him and Gronski, you mean." Tadgh was testing his loyalty.

"Gronski is the ally. Casement is the patriot."

"Are you sure—ally, for all that?"

"Sir Roger is certainly not sure, I'll give you that much. But he isn't thinking straight and we are indebted to the Germans for our cause."

"Do you believe it?" Tadgh asked.

"What I believe doesn't matter, but the Clan na Gael believes it. In any event, we are under the thumb of the Boche, like it or not. So I comply." Monteith looked away for a brief moment.

"Not really allies, then," Tadgh pressed.

"It remains to be seen."

"You're making it sound rather grim, don't ya know." Tadgh turned to face Monteith.

"It is grim here with the Germans. But then, he'll tell you he thinks they're devious."

"It's even worse at the Front. The folk here don't appear to have a care in the world."

"Sir Roger does. More than any man should," Monteith said.

Doctor Curry returned and ushered them into the parlor room of Sir Roger's suite, then waited outside.

Casement sat in a winged armchair looking out the window onto the lake, a blazing fireplace to his right. "They're all bastards, you know," he mumbled, turning to face his visitors. "It's the curse of Prussian militarism, the embodiment of soulless efficiency."

Tadgh had seen Roger Casement from a distance in early 1914 in Dublin. He had been a dashing gentleman then, aristocratic even, with his wavy black hair, wide moustache, and full beard. In those days, his eyes would pierce right through you. They had called him the father of twentieth-century human rights investigations. He had been knighted for it, especially for his work with the British Foreign Service in the Congo.

That's when the colonial atrocities against indigenous peoples turned him against the imperialism of the British Crown. Thereafter, he took on the mantle of organizer of the Irish Volunteers wi

th Bulmer Hobson and the attendant role of arms provisioner for the Republican revolution. That was in 1913 before the war started.

Now, sitting slouched in his armchair, he looked defeated. His sunken black eyes shifted from side to side and his still-wavy hair was disheveled. He coughed from time to time.

"Sir Roger, sir, I am pleased to meet you in such an idyllic location." Tadgh offered his hand and noticed his host had a weak grip.

"They tell me you have an important message for me. From whom?"

Tadgh made his way to a chair near the fire. "It's awfully hot in here."

Casement said, "It's my malaria starting to get hold of me again, I'm afraid. Bloody Congo insects."

"I am a member of the Irish Volunteers, sir."

"Are you, now. How is my friend Eoin MacNeill?"

"Well, as far as I know."

"You know Tom Clarke, then."

"Yes sir. I'm part of his organization. Have you heard about O'Donovan's funeral and eulogy, sir? From someone who was there, I mean."

"No. Tell me."

Tadgh recounted the event and Padraig Pearse's speech. "You know the Headmaster, sir? Mister Pearse, I mean. I studied under him at Rathfornham, St. Edna's. He's the Gaelic leader, sure you know."

Casement was spellbound. "Yes, yes. I've met him. Do you think there are enough patriots, then, to muster an effective Rising, lad?"

"There was definite enthusiasm along the funeral procession." Tadgh was hedging his bets.

Casement looked at Monteith. "Where does Connolly stand?"

Tadgh didn't know the Larkinist's current intentions. Connolly, the most militant of them all, had led the Irish Citizens Army during the Irish Transport and General Workers Union Walkout of 1913. He was, as well, a socialist and syndicalist follower of James Larkin. "He's a force to be reckoned with, sir."

"Would he go it on his own?"

"He could." Tadgh was establishing his credentials to Sir Roger. Casement had clearly been in Germany since late 1914, and his information was filtered by the Clan na Gael in New York through the German Embassy in Washington.

"That's what I thought. You must know that I negotiated an important agreement with Mr. Zimmermann, the German Undersecretary for Foreign Affairs, and the Imperial Chancellor von Bethmann Hollweg last November. It allowed Germany to acknowledge the sovereign state of Ireland and to agree not to invade us for occupation."[7]

Tadgh had no such knowledge, but it sounded good to him, so he nodded. Casement was obviously proud of himself.

"Then in May, Plunkett and I negotiated a deal with the German General Staff to provide 175,000 rifles, ammunition, and officers."

It was sounding better and better to Tadgh. "That would be wonderful, sir."

"But now I think they will welch on most or all of it." Casement twisted his hands as he spoke.

"Why, sir?"

"Because they're damn devious bastards at the GGS. They want us to rise, but they don't want to anger the Americans into this confounded war."

"The Yanks didn't join when the *Lusitania* was sunk, sir."

"But they would support Britain if we started a war, lad."

"I think the fact that we have only been able to recruit 56 men for our Irish Brigade is part of the problem," Monteith offered, coming around to arrange the blanket that was slipping off his boss's legs.

"You need to tell them not to rise, McCarthy."

Damn. That's not what we want to hear. Don't bail out on us now. "We'll rise with or without the Germans, sir. But we need you to get us those munitions."

"Don't rise until we're strong enough. You've got to stop the patriots!" Sir Roger was so agitated he was shaking.

Monteith decided that the interview was over. "Come on, McCarthy. We've taken up too much of Sir Roger's time." He moved to escort Tadgh out.

"What is it you were sent to tell me, McCarthy?" Casement asked again. He hadn't forgotten.

"To inform you of the positive response to the Rossa funeral and to encourage you to bring home those weapons. We had heard that you were becoming disillusioned." Tadgh had surmised the answer from what Casement himself had said and how he had reacted.

"From whom did you hear this?"

"From Joseph Plunkett, of course." Tadgh didn't want to tell him that Plunkett was now the head of IRB's military council.

"Let's go," Monteith commanded, grabbing Tadgh's arm as he headed for the door.

Tadgh couldn't let it end this way. "Just a minute. I need your help, Sir Roger."

Monteith yanked Tadgh's arm. He obviously wanted to leave his boss alone. Tadgh dug in his heels.

"How can I help you?" Casement's voice quavered from the winged chair.

"I can't convey your message if I am incarcerated at Zossen, sir."

"Who said you were going to Zossen?"

"I did," Monteith answered, stepping back in front of his boss. "We need his skills there."

"Robert, I need that message delivered, and soon."

"We can find someone else to carry it. I will contact McGarrity in Philadelphia."

Tadgh thought of bolting. It would be easy enough, though his left leg would cause him considerable pain. Then he thought about what Monteith had said about Morgan. Was it a bluff? Surely not, but he couldn't take that chance.

"There's one more thing." Tadgh had to confess before he lost the audience. "My partner, another IRB member, is captive in Belgium."

"Is he on the Front, Tadgh?" At least Casement understood that a soldier never leaves even one man behind.

"*She* is a nurse forced into service at the German hospital in Ostend. At least that's where she was four weeks ago. I expect they would have kept her there. She's good at what she does." To offer proof, Tadgh told Casement about their submarine adventure. "I have to rescue her, sir."

"I see." Casement stared off in the direction of the fire. "What's her name, lad?"

"Morgan, sir. She means more to me than life itself."

"Is Morgan her last name?"

"It's her only name, sir, for now."

"I see. Give me some time to think about it, McCarthy." His eyes glistened. "Robert, our guest can stay with Charles for the time being. His leg is not fully mended."

"But sir . . ." Robert glanced at his boss then shot a look at Tadgh.

"Now leave me to rest. I'll call you when I've decided what to do with him. Notify Gronski that McCarthy is my aide. I will take full responsibility."

Chapter Eight
Queen Nurse

December 9, 1915
Munich, Bavaria

*T*wo weeks later Tadgh got the news from Doctor Curry to return to Riederau. The Currys had been treating him better than he had ever been looked after before. The medicine he had brought from Ostend and Limburg was all used up, but the good doctor had substituted wholesome foods still plentiful in Munich. Tadgh had never had beets before, and he didn't like them. But he ate them. His leg now felt strong. He had been doing deep knee bends and taking brisk walks the mile down to the Isar River and back. Yesterday he ran up and back, and the leg held his weight without buckling.

He was torn between the urgency to save Morgan, and Monteith's warning. That man seemed to genuinely support Casement wholeheartedly, yet Tadgh sensed the officer was on the verge of making his own decisions about the Irish Brigade with the Germans if his boss didn't snap out of his depressed physical and mental state.

"Tomorrow we will go and visit Sir Roger," Curry announced, checking Tadgh's leg once more. "It's healing nicely, judging by the scar. I think you're fit for duty. By the way, Monteith sent a message. He will be coming here to take you to Zossen."

"Isn't that up to Sir Roger?"

"Sir Roger's condition is deteriorating, I'm afraid."

Doctor Curry was right. Sir Roger was running a high fever when they arrived the next day at noon. He was more despondent than at their first meeting, but he seemed to have a purpose for this meeting that was more important than his mood. "Tadgh, I want you to return home and warn Hobson and MacNeill that the situation here is grave. I don't trust Gronski or any of the GGS for that matter."

"Meaning?"

"I'm not sure they will give us the weapons they promised nor the German officers to support us. And our Brigade is meager and not yet conditioned."

"Conditioned? They were soldiers on the Front."

"They are mostly motivated to escape and not yet committed to our cause, Tadgh."

"I noticed their reluctance at Limburg, sir. Redmond has them brainwashed."

"Damn that Redmond. They're afraid of being shot as deserters."

"A valid concern, given their circumstances, I'm afraid, Sir Roger. If I can escape, I will deliver your message. What about my partner Morgan?"

"Did you hear of *Queen Nurse* when you were in Ostend?"

"No, who is she?"

"Elisabeth Gabrielle Valerie Maria, the Queen of Belgium, married to King Albert I.[8] Did you know that Belgium tried to stay neutral like the Netherlands in this war between Germany and the rest of Western Europe in accordance with the Treaty of London in 1839? Germany tried to march through Belgium anyway, which brought England into the war. I believe King Albert's words were, 'We're not a road, we're a country.' So much of the deadly fighting has been in Belgium's lowlands. Their army is holding the line just a few miles west of Ostend from the west side of the Yser River. Only a very small northwest corner of Belgium is still intact. Alfred is leading his army into battle with a headquarters there at Furnes after his retreat from Brussels through Antwerp and finally Ostend last year. I am very impressed by the Belgians, even though we are on the other side."

"We are against our foe, England, sir, and not the Belgians."

"That's what I said."

"You started to talk about the Queen Nurse," Tadgh reminded him.

"Oh yes. The Queen has been a staunch supporter of her husband and the Belgian army. She functions as a nurse superior, organizing the hospitals and sending ambulances to the Front. She apparently fights alongside her countrymen in this way, as does the King. Quite remarkable, really. They say that the *Boche* won't fire on either of them out of respect, or maybe their Kaiser ordered it."

"Chivalry in this awful war?"

"Perhaps, lad. But I saw the atrocities at Liège and Louvain on my way to Cologne last year. On the other hand, I also saw gruesome things in the Congo that Albert's uncle, Leopold II, had inflicted there. So it's not all one-sided, you know."

"Back to Elisabeth, sir. You think she can help me save Morgan?"

"I hope so, for your sake."

Tadgh was surprised that this very sick man, with the troubles of the world on his shoulders while trapped in a hostile foreign country, would take up his personal cause. *He must really want his message delivered. But why choose me?* That's when it hit him. Casement's only contact with the outside world was through the Germans to Devoy in New York. He was cornered, forced to rely on the men whom he most suspected of deceit. He was, in fact, their prisoner.

Sir Roger's renewed coughing fit interrupted Tadgh's thoughts, and Tadgh rushed out into the anteroom seeking the doctor's aid to relieve Casement's spasm.

"It's the recurrence of malaria that he contracted while in the Congo." Doctor Curry wiped Sir Roger's brow and steadied his shoulder. Slowly the convulsive coughing subsided, leaving the poor man holding his side.

"This wretched bug. It'll do me in, I fear, if Gronski doesn't get me first."

"He'll be all right now," Curry said, as he turned to leave the room.

Tadgh could see that Casement's condition had worsened. *Those sunken eyes.*

Casement took a shallow breath and continued, "As I was saying, I have contacted the Queen through a mutual party here in Bavaria, a close childhood friend. This woman sent a letter to Her Majesty about your Morgan, and I got the reply yesterday. The Queen has an underground network of Belgian patriots who have sometimes been able to penetrate German lines. Like everything in this damned war, this is a dangerous business, Tadgh. Edith Cavell, a very brave English nurse in Belgium, found that out. The woman helped nurse soldiers from both sides and facilitated the escape of over 200 Allied soldiers from German-occupied Belgium before she was betrayed and arrested. There was an international outrage, but the Germans executed her for treason anyway, less than two months ago."

Tadgh took a few steps forward. "I've got to get to Morgan, sir."

"I know well that Queen Nurse is of the same opinion. She will try to find out where Morgan is located and get a message to her. She doesn't think it wise to try to bring her from Ostend through the enemy battlefront unless you are there by her side. You are to stay put until we get a response that she is still at the hospital there."

"I need to go now."

"No, that would not be wise. We are all being watched closely here and in Munich. You will be shot if you try to escape. You must understand one thing. Elisabeth's motivation for helping is to give Morgan, a fellow nurse, safe passage. From her perspective, you will just be along as a bodyguard. She has no direct knowledge of me or our cause here in Germany."

"Then why would she go to this trouble?"

"I don't know, but it is fortunate indeed that she is willing to help."

"What about Monteith?"

"He's back in Zossen training our Brigade, such as it is. I wish I had an officer of sufficient rank to satisfy the GGS, but he is all we have. Monteith has only recently arrived, but he seems loyal. Despite his great experience in the Boer War and the Egypt campaign, he doesn't think he is up to the job of senior Brigade officer, so he wants you to join him at Zossen. I have to dissuade him and the GGS. Let me handle this. Your job is to stay here with Charles until we hear from Queen Nurse."

A second coughing fit consumed him, and Doctor Curry rushed in to help. "We should go," Curry said, having helped his friend calm his respiratory system once more.

Sir Roger nodded, waved them out weakly, and the men made their exit.

♣ ♣ ♣ ♣

Morgan crossed off another day on the calendar Gerda had given her when she got home just before midnight on December 14. It had been seven weeks, less two days, since she last saw Tadgh. She didn't have the energy to eat anything. She had become Doctor Heinrich's right-hand nurse. He depended on her for organizing the nursing corps and for assisting him with the most difficult amputations. He even gave her an interpreter so that she could work efficiently with the nurses and orderlies who didn't speak English. Her German was improving; she knew phrases and words of the trade mostly.

Morgan watched as a family reunited, with the return of Fritz from his mission, dog-tired and filthy. Gerda didn't care. He had come home safe. The boys were overjoyed to see their Papa, but that was short-lived. Captain Raimund Weisbach had recovered and was back in command of *U-19*, getting ready for the next mission, with Fritz slated for duty to accompany him.

Fritz brought his captain home for dinner the next night. Gerda seemed upset, and Morgan could understand why. Fritz had to leave before Christmas. During the dinner that Weisbach brought from his provisioner's store, Morgan mused about the matters that she had discussed with him a fortnight earlier when he had been released from hospital. She remembered he had met with her at his request then. "I am indebted to you for saving me after I was burned," he had told her.

"It is we who are in your debt, Tadgh and I."

"I do, however, have some guilt. It is my job and I do it, but I have such remorse. You were trying to save those poor sailors on that sad ship." She thought she had detected a softening in his eyes then, but she could not be sure. Morgan deemed it better not to recount that frightful afternoon on the *Lusitania* months ago. The man was in enough pain, and she didn't want to think about all that had transpired. "What's the point of all this war, anyway?"

"I ask myself that question, Morgan, every day. But it's my job."

"And *my* job, it would seem, is to patch you all up and send you back into the battles."

"Doctor Heinrich tells me you are good at that. Perhaps we'll meet again when I return from my next mission."

Was he making advances? She had heard that he was unmarried. "I certainly hope not, for both our sakes." Morgan remembered that she had waved her arm toward the ward full of mangled humanity. To drive home her point, she had added, "Tadgh will be here shortly to rescue me."

"That's very unlikely, I'm afraid. But at least you are not also in a POW camp."

In truth, she had been consumed with worry over Tadgh. She had found the address of the camp at Limburg, and Gerda had helped her with the writing, knowing that the Germans would intercept and read the letter. Just last week she had gotten a response. At first Gerda had been afraid to read it to her, but she did. "*Tadgh McCarthy was removed from this camp on November 24 by GGS personnel. His whereabouts are unknown to us at this time.*" Morgan remembered hearing about the atrocities on both sides when prisoners were taken into the woods, shot, and thrown into shallow graves.

"Perhaps I'll see you in more peaceful circumstances then, I hope." Captain Weisbach had turned on his heel and was gone. It had seemed so long ago that they had had that conversation.

Morgan was startled out of her reverie at Fritz's home on a mid-December night when the captain said, "So I'll see you after the war, Morgan."

"Not if my Tadgh has anything to say about it, sir."

Weisbach rose, took Fritz aside to the tiny kitchen, and he not so quietly dressed him down. "You and your wife are putting us in a difficult position. The Fräulein did save my life, so I will trust your judgment, Fritz. But if she escapes, there will be retribution. I cannot let this situation stain the reputation of our ship's company. *Understand?*"

"*Jawohl, Kapitan.* She is becoming indispensable at the hospital. She will not escape for fear that we will execute her partner, McCarthy."

"Where is McCarthy now?"

"I had him sent to Limburg."

"Is he still there?"

"As far as I know, yes."

The men's conversation distressed Morgan, and when the men returned to the table, she wanted to relay her fears and disappointment.

"I must take my leave, Frau Schmidt," Weisbach said, obviously agitated. "Well then, maybe we'll meet again during the war, Fräulein Morgan, since you will be our guest here in Belgium."

Morgan let it go, remaining silent. After all, the man had saved Tadgh's life.

Fritz turned to the women after the captain abruptly left. "You both heard him, didn't you?" They both nodded. "And you're not going to get us in trouble, will you. Remember the consequences, Morgan."

The snow fell as Morgan trudged back to Gerda's home the next evening. If it hadn't been during the war that was supposed to end all wars, Christmas spirit would be filling the air. Morgan had heard the story that on December 25th the year before, there had been an unofficial truce in No Man's Land between the trenches where the soldiers had exchanged souvenirs and even played sports together. Based on the condition of the wounded soldiers who were streaming into the hospital lately, it didn't appear that would happen in 1915.

What do they say? *It's always darkest before the dawn.* She kept telling herself that as she slipped into bed. It seemed to help except in the middle of the night. Without warning, the words of the Lord's Prayer came into her head. This may have been something she had learned in childhood, as the words came to her with no effort, and she prayed. Or, maybe Tadgh had taught her the words, as it seemed like so long ago. At the end of "Forever and ever, amen," a phrase from the Bible popped into her head—again, from where, she didn't know. "My God shall provide all your needs according to his riches in glory by Jesus Christ." The words gave her comfort.

She remembered those words the next day when she encountered the priest who ministered to the gravely wounded men. During her mid-afternoon break from the operating room, Father Jan Peeters approached her and asked her to pray with him over a dying soldier. As they knelt by his mattress together, the clergyman removed a folded envelope from his robes and thrust it into her hand. Looking into her eyes, he said softly, "The Lord shall provide." Then he added, "With a little help from our Queen Nurse."

Morgan was shocked. "From where, might I ask?" She took the envelope, her hand shaking, and tucked it under her blouse, but not before she saw the official royal wax seal. She had heard about the Belgian Queen who was fighting the war just the same as any commoner. She was loved by her people, and even the Germans respected her and her husband. Morgan looked back through the ward to see if anyone might be watching her.

When she turned back to the dying soldier, the priest merely said, "De Panne, Miss," as he rose and moved off to another soul in need of prayer.

As she rushed back to the operating room, Morgan could see ambulances pulling up to the side entrance. The evening onslaught was beginning. She hurriedly scrubbed for surgery.

"Where have you been?" Doctor Heinrich wanted to know. "We have had three new cases in the last fifteen minutes."

"I needed some fresh air. The stench in here, you know."

"From now on, ask me if you need to go outside the operating room during your shift."

"Yes, sir." *The nerve of him.* That shift, as he put it, could be more than twenty-four hours long.

For the rest of the evening, Morgan agonized over what the contents of that very important letter could be. She didn't have a minute to herself to look. From a priest. That was ominous. Tadgh's death notice? Unlikely to be coming from the Belgian side unless he was killed at the Front. *God, maybe that's where GGS sent him. It's always darkest before the dawn. Maybe the Queen just heard about my good nursing work.*

All the way back to Gerda's, Morgan frequently looked over her shoulder. There had been previous times when she had been followed, and she dared not stop.

"My, my," Gerda exclaimed when Morgan flew in through the doorway. "What's the matter?"

"I'm afraid to know what's in this envelope," Morgan replied, pulling the rumpled letter from under her tunic and handing it to her. She trusted Gerda now as much as she would have trusted Tadgh. Who else could she tell?

"Is it about Tadgh? Oh Lord, it has the crown seal of Belgium." Gerda turned it over in her hands.

"Open it and read it to me." Morgan tried to subdue her shaking hands by clasping them together.

Gerda sat Morgan down and poured her some tea. Then she used her one sharp kitchen knife to open the letter with a clean slice. She scanned the contents. "It's in English." Gerda started reading it to herself first.

"Well?" Morgan drummed the table. "Gerda!"

"I'll read it aloud to you, now. *I am in communication with my childhood friend in Munich. She tells me that your friend Tadgh is alive and well.*"

Morgan snatched the letter from Gerda's hand, read it all the way through, and burst into tears. Gerda held Morgan tight, noticing how her shoulder and arm muscles were taut and rigid. She rocked her softly until she relaxed.

"Well that's a relief, isn't it, dear."

"Yes," Morgan stammered, wiping her eyes with her handkerchief.

Gerda asked, "What else does it say?"

Morgan continued, "*Your friend Tadgh is alive and well in Munich. He wants you to know that he is coming to save you. I have certain resources that may be able to aid you both in reaching our side of the Western Front.*" Gerda's eyes grew wide as she listened. "*Go to the Petrus and Paulus Church when he arrives. Since my emissary has confirmed your existence where Tadgh last saw you, as witness your receipt of my letter, I will notify your man by return correspondence through my friend that you are indeed there and as well as can be expected. Be prepared to be liberated at any time. You are in danger, so be wary. Please destroy this correspondence. Elisabeth Gabrielle Valérie Maria, Queen of Belgium.*"

Gerda lifted her chin and looked at Morgan. "We are two women with men in danger. That takes precedence over nationality. I will do anything I can to help you, Morgan."

"Thank you, Gerda. But what about the captain's threat?"

"Never you mind. We will survive, God willing."

Despite what Gerda said, Morgan worried for her friend. Yet for the first time in almost two months, Morgan had hope for her and Tadgh.

Chapter Nine
Zossen

December 23, 1915
Munich, Bavaria

Tadgh was not going to wait much longer, Gronski or no Gronski. It had been thirteen days since he had met with Sir Roger, and still there was no word. Morgan must be there because they needed her. He had a bad feeling about it.

Just as he was eating his breakfast with the Currys and looking out at the snow falling on the serene landscape, he saw Monteith stride up the walk to Doctor Curry's home in the company of a German soldier. *Damn. I've waited too long.* Just as he feared, Monteith delivered the bad news as soon as he came in.

"It's time to go to Zossen, McCarthy. I need you there."

"We need to talk to Mr. Casement before I go."

"Gronski says you must come with me, now." Monteith pointed to the armed guard beside him. "Sir Roger is incapacitated."

Curry left the room and went to his telephone. Five minutes later, he returned and slipped Tadgh a note, just as Monteith was getting him to gather up his few loaned belongings. "I've spoken to Sir Roger by telephone. There's only one device at the general store in Riederau, so they had to go and fetch him at the hotel. He says you should go with Monteith and do what you need to do."

"There. I told you so. Come along, then." Monteith tried to push Tadgh out the door, but he resisted. The guard drew his Luger.

"Charles, I am so thankful for your kindness. I will repay it someday, I assure you."

"No bother, lad. You take care of yourself." Curry winked and clapped him on the arm.

As Tadgh was thrust into the passenger seat of a waiting German Stewart truck with a staked canvas bed, he noticed a short-handled shovel strapped to the outside of the vehicle on the passenger side. While Monteith went around to jump up into the driver's seat, Tadgh looked quickly at the crumpled note in his fist. *"Morgan at Ostend Hospital. Lisa will help. Your mission crucial. Evade Monteith but don't hurt him. God speed. Casement."* Tadgh smiled. Casement thought he could get the upper hand.

The armed soldier brought up the rear on his NSU 7 PS motorcycle. Tadgh had read that they were more powerful than his Kerry 670 cc sv V twin built by Abingdon back home. Quite a machine with 60 horsepower, he remembered. It could keep up with the trucks.

Tadgh decided to play along for the time being. "Where is Zossen, Monteith?"

"It's just south of Berlin, handy enough for my visits to GGS. And convenient for Gronski to interrogate us. We are still prisoners."

"Who is this Gronski?"

"Kapitan Bernard Gronski, Chief of the *Sektion Politik*. That's the military's sabotage department of the GGS. He's responsible for the development of new chemical warfare weapons. The man is a force to be reckoned with, I can assure you. His boss assigned him to control the Ireland alliance project. He hates the duty but takes it very seriously."

"And who is this soldier?"

"One of his lackeys."

"Got you under his thumb, then. Do you think they will supply arms and men when the time comes?"

"Hard to tell. I've only been here a month or so. They are devious, though."

"Casement is gravely concerned, to use his words."

"Sir Roger has been here over a year. I trust his judgment," Monteith looked Tadgh in the eye, "although his illness concerns me."

"It puts you in a hard spot with him almost out of commission."

"It's what Devoy wants, so I'm here for better or worse. You'd better settle in. We've got a 360-mile trip ahead of us."

Ten hours, Tadgh reckoned. Plenty of time to figure out what to do. Berlin, he remembered, was in the northeastern section of Germany near the border with Poland. Not exactly close to Ostend in Belgium. By his guess it would be another 400-mile trek between the two, should he be able to escape. But how could he do that in a way that wouldn't compromise Monteith with Gronski or, more importantly, Morgan's safety, if Gronski's warning were to be real? And based on what Monteith had told him, there was every reason to believe that he would go after her. *He probably knows that Casement is starting to turn against him, and he won't let me escape since he knows I have been meeting with Sir Roger. No messages get out of Germany without his consent, I suspect.*

As they passed Nürnberg three hours later, Tadgh had a plan. He remembered something he had seen in the western countryside on their way south from Limburg. He hoped it would be the same in the east of Germany. It had to be in this time of war. If so, the timing would be everything. He closed his eyes for some rest. He would need all his strength later that evening.

Tadgh woke up. They had reached the northern edge of the Thurlinger Wold foothills at three in the afternoon. The guard pulled up even with the truck cab on the driver's side and signaled Monteith to stop. Now might be Tadgh's chance. He looked out the back of the vehicle and heard metal banging, but he could not see much from that angle. It was too early, and this wasn't the place. *Of course. The motorcycle needs petrol,* Tadgh realized, when Monteith got out and helped the guard remove a can from the truck bed. Hearing the clanking, Tadgh jumped down from the cab and sauntered around to the back where the two men stood by the motorcycle in animated conversation.

"Drive fast, you hear? This prisoner must get to Zossen tonight."

"What's the rush? They aren't expecting us until late tomorrow. I didn't know if I would have to visit Casement on this trip."

"Gronski wants him there as soon as possible."

Tadgh saw two more cans of petrol in the truck bed. Good.

The guard took out his Luger. "Hey, you there. Get back in the cab."

Tadgh could play along. He raised his arms and turned back toward the truck. The guard poured petrol while Monteith watched and stretched.

On his way around the passenger side of the Stewart, Tadgh unclipped the shovel and hopped up into the cab with it in hand. Unobserved, he stored it behind the seat, within his reach. Peering out the window at the foothills below, Tadgh could see flat, open cropland. *Good. Two more hours should do it.*

When Monteith returned to the cab, Tadgh pretended to be asleep. "Bastard, Gronski" Monteith muttered as he fired up the Stewart and headed down the hill.

One hour later, they were down on the plain, passing Leipzig. No snow on the ground on this dull cloudy day. Tadgh estimated that twilight was about an hour away. That would help. He started scouring the countryside. There, up ahead on his right, he spotted a neglected farm with no animals in the fields. This was going to work.

At a quarter after five, the light started to fade, and Monteith turned on the headlights. Tadgh guessed that they were about two hours from their destination. Two hours from unacceptable captivity, but if this worked, only a few minutes from freedom. They passed the small village of Mockrehna with a forest on the left and pastures to the right.

Lights started blinking on in the farmhouses they were passing. There was no other traffic in either direction on this straight rural road. Tadgh stretched and slid his left arm casually up and behind the driver's seat, grabbing the shovel handle midspan. A quarter of a mile ahead on the right, a dark farmhouse nestled among the trees surrounded by overgrown fields. They'd be on it in twenty seconds. *Perfect. It would be too dark to see in a few minutes. It's now or never.*

Swiftly raising his right arm high above his head and twisting to the left, Tadgh delivered a stunning downward blow to Monteith's carotid sinus causing Monteith's blood pressure to rise dangerously, and the heart to slow down. The plummeting blood pressure starved his confused brain, and he fainted. All this happened in less than three seconds.

The truck had swerved slightly and decelerated while Monteith lost consciousness. He slumped forward against the steering wheel. Tadgh yanked him upright, pressing his weight backwards against Monteith's sternum and grabbing the steering wheel with his right hand. Tadgh shifted left, shoving Monteith against the door, and positioned his own left foot onto the brake pedal. He pulled the short-handed shovel up over the seat with his left hand and placed it across his lap. Then he rolled down the driver's side window with his left hand and slowed the Stewart until it was going less than ten miles an hour.

He was counting on the guard on the motorbike to get angry at the delay and to drive up on the driver's side. Moments later, he could see him approaching in the rear view mirror. When the guard was a couple of feet behind the cab and saw that Monteith was incapacitated, the man drew his Luger, accelerating. That's when Tadgh jammed on the brake, and simultaneously, letting go momentarily of the steering wheel, he thrust the shovel out the window with both hands. Like a lance in a medieval joust, the shovel caught the guard across the throat and down he went, his motorcycle spinning out of control and coming to rest in the ditch on the side of the road.

Stopping the lorry, Tadgh shot out of the cab on the passenger side and reached the guard just as the man was starting to get up, holding his throat. Tadgh easily disabled the dazed soldier with a blow to his jaw.

Quickly, Tadgh used the guard's belt to tie his arms behind his back. Then he hoisted the man's inert form onto the bed of the truck. His size would do nicely.

Tadgh jumped into the cab on the driver's side and pushed Monteith to the middle. He was still out cold. Then he turned the Stewart around and drove up the lane to the darkened farm- house, hoping he was right that it was unoccupied. At the end of the driveway, he noticed a barn to the right of the house, at the far end of a clearing near the woods. Perfect. Minutes later, after jimmying the padlock on the door, Tadgh had the Stewart safely inside the barn. Snow had begun to fall, so at least they wouldn't freeze to death in there.

The guard moaned. Tadgh gave him another blow, this time to the neck, and he slumped, unconscious. He then stripped the man of his shirt and trousers, and dressed himself in the guard's army uniform and helmet. Not an exact fit but close enough. He slipped his own thin shirt over the guard's head and pushed his arms into the sleeves, pulling his own trousers loosely onto the man's body. That would do. He tied the guard to one of the barn's internal support posts. Tadgh felt better now, sporting the man's Luger in its holster on his right hip. He then dragged the unconscious Monteith to a separate support post twenty feet away from the guard and tied him to the post. Both captive men were well away from any implements that could help them escape. Tadgh checked Monteith's neck for a pulse. There was always the chance that a carotid blow could cause a stroke or worse. But no, there was a pulse. Tadgh guessed the man would be waking up soon.

Closing the barn door firmly, Tadgh trudged down the lane towards the road just as a military convoy came into view heading south, headlights glaring along the road through the falling snow. If they saw the motorcycle in the ditch, there would be trouble. Tadgh flattened himself behind a bush and waited. There must have been ten trucks in the line, and none of them saw the NSU. So much for German efficiency.

When the convoy had passed out of sight, Tadgh quickly ran down to the road where the motorcycle was already covered in snow. No wonder they didn't see it. Tadgh lifted it up and noticed that the front fender was pushed in against the tire. He gave it a kick, and the damn fender fell off. No problem. Tadgh tried the ignition, and the bike roared to life. It looked as if the frame and wheel spokes were still aligned. Tadgh steered the NSU up out of the ditch, then turned it around to head up the laneway into the barn. Monteith was stirring when Tadgh stopped the motorcycle beside the Stewart. He removed the two petrol cans from the truck and lashed them to the back rack of the bike. Then he checked the truck cab and found just what he needed in the driver's door pouch, a detailed road map. He pocketed it and looked for more weapons. None. Monteith was unarmed. Obvious. Gronski wouldn't permit it. Tadgh opened the bonnet of the Stewart and disabled the ignition system, taking the rotor with him.

He wasn't sure whether there were people in the house, although it looked deserted. It was time to go. There could be witnesses. Gronski be damned.

Monteith mumbled, "You won't get away with this."

Tadgh went over to him and goaded, "Just do your job and protect your boss. Sir Roger needs you." Then he gagged both Monteith and the still-unconscious guard. He locked the barn door behind him and backtracked southwest toward Leipzig.

When he reached the outskirts, Tadgh stopped under a street lamp and consulted his map that showed territory all the way to the Western Front. *Damn, 490 miles to his destination.* Fourteen hours, he estimated, if he could stay awake that long. He had to. Gronski would go after Morgan. He turned his motorcycle west towards the Netherlands border, which would lead him eventually to Belgium and his aroon. It was snowing hard. There would be no arriving at Zossen tonight.

Chapter Ten
Reunited

December 24, 1915

German General Staff Headquarters, Berlin

Bernard Gronski, **chief** of the Sektion Politik, strode up and down his office in the GGS, slapping his officer's crop against his leg. These days he had abandoned his diplomatic suit for his military uniform in deference to his superiors. "Where are they, Hans?"

Commandant Hans Pfiefer, the commander of the Camp at Zossen, had been in Gronski's office but five minutes, and he already felt like he was being grilled and served up as lunch for his superior. Gronski had a reputation for turning on his subordinates. Sometimes they just disappeared. Pfiefer had even heard the rumor that some might have become human guinea pigs for his chemical weapons experiments. "They should have arrived last night before midnight, sir. I am trying to determine whether they stayed over in Munich to see Casement. My man there went to Riederau, but Casement pleaded ignorance."

"Casement is a problem. Malaria, you say?"

"Yes, sir. Hard to deal with."

"I don't like this whole business. Damned waste of time if you ask me. But we've got to contain it. McCarthy is trouble. He's probably carrying a message from Casement. Do we have a photograph, Hans?"

"Yes, sir. Standard one taken at Limburg."

"Send a dispatch rider back along the path Monteith should have taken from Munich. They must be stopped from spreading Casement's lies at all costs. Report back here by 1600 hours."

"I will, sir." Pfiefer, who had been standing rigidly at attention throughout his interrogation, saluted smartly and made his exit.

Gronski turned to his second-in-command, Hauptman Friedric Gruber, who had heard it all. "I want you to have that hospital in Ostend watched. We won't pick up the girl yet. If he shows up, we'll detain them both. If he is not there in three days, he'll have abandoned her, I wager. Then have her shot."

Gronski hated this duty, but his orders from the Imperial Chancellor of Germany, Von Bethmann Hollweg, were to facilitate an Irish distraction. The Chancellor had negotiated with Casement. How much support would the Irish rebels get from the populace if this ineffective Irishman couldn't even convince Irish prisoners of war to fight for their country? They'd prefer to stay in the POW camps under despicable conditions. The few who agreed were an undisciplined lot, hardly military. Now their leader Casement seemed to want to call it all off. The Chancellor forbade direct communications between Casement and his superiors in Ireland. *This stupid affair could cost me my job, or worse, if McCarthy isn't stopped,* Gronski thought.

Friedric Gruber saluted and rushed out of Gronski's office. It was wise to snap to attention for the head of the Sabotage Department of the GGS.

Gerda was doing her best to get ready for Christmas with whatever meager handmade decorations she could find. Looped, colorful paper rings draped the mantel. There would be no feast to celebrate the birth of the Lord and no presents for the children. But they would make do until Papa came home from his mission. Yet Fritz had surprised her just before he left. He had given her a marvelous gift wrapped in brown paper. A beautiful, ancient-looking locket with a crown surmounting a folded hand over a heart. It was silver, and she loved it even though she couldn't get it open. She squirreled it away in her top drawer with her delicates. It was the gift of a lifetime. She'd hate to do it, but if things worsened, she could sell it for quite a few marks.

"Gerda, I'm going on-shift now," Morgan announced, as she finished the watery soup Gerda had made from the bones of a scrawny chicken they had consumed three days earlier. "I will try and get some things to bring back for the boys Christmas morning." She wasn't sure how she could do that, given that she wasn't being paid for her work.

"Don't worry about it, dear. Having you here is gift enough."

"You have been too kind, Gerda. I don't know what would have happened to me if you hadn't taken me in."

"Nonsense. You have been a great help. When young Fritz cut his finger, you stitched it up, didn't you?"

"Well, yes. It's what I do."

Gerda changed the subject. "It is a wondrous time, you know, the coming of our Lord."

"We should be thankful, no matter what our circumstances," Morgan said. "You know, last night when I was walking home, I saw a very bright star directly above us. Do you think . . . ?"

"Think what, dear?"

"That he will come tonight?" Morgan pulled her collar up to keep her neck warm.

"Who? Jesus? Yes of course. He comes every Christmas Eve."

"No, I mean Tadgh. Next to Jesus, he is my savior. He saved me once already, you know."

"It's a wonderful thought to keep with you today. Just like my positive thoughts about Fritz coming back to me. But things are not as they should be, are they?"

"We live with hope in these times, Gerda." Morgan crossed to where her friend was darning socks and hugged her tightly. "We are two peas in a pod, aren't we, now."

Gerda wiped her eyes with a corner of her apron.

"I should be home by dark tonight. We're expecting a short shift. There seems to be a lull at the Front just now."

"Jesus is coming," Gerda said. She stopped darning for a moment and stared at the ceiling. "I can feel it, a sense of calm." She picked up the thread where she left, up one row, then crosshatched in the other direction, until the hole filled in and the sock could be worn again. Even stronger than before.

Tadgh was exhausted. The snow had slowed him, the motorcycle's tires bogging down in it. Then the checkpoint near Eindhoven at the border to the Netherlands forced him to detour ten miles south through muddy fields. Now at Budel, he stopped to refill the tank with the last can of petrol. He had found three grenades and dry soldier's rations of some strange dried jerky and stale bread in the saddlebags of the motorcycle. That food had long since been consumed. The snow had stopped falling with the temperature above freezing, but his gloveless hands burned from ice on the handlebars. The guard's gloves proved to be too small, so they were useless.

Tadgh looked at his watch. One in the afternoon. *Damn, is it that late?* He checked the distance on his map. About four hours to go. He'd kill Gronski if Morgan was harmed in any way.

At the border into Belgium, he could not avoid the checkpoint. He would have to bluster his way through like the time when he, Morgan, and Wiggins smuggled arms past the English barricade outside Dublin. Tadgh pulled the Prussian helmet down tight over his ears. Maybe the soldier's goggles would help him. He unsnapped the cover on the Luger's holsteTo his surprise, the guard at the gate snapped to attention when he rolled to a stop. Tadgh returned the salute. Then the guard said something about "*das Sektion Politik*" and pulled up the barrier. Either the motorcycle or soldier's uniform he wore bore some insignia that showed he was a member of the sabotage section of the GGS. Tadgh yelled "*Danke*" in his most authoritarian baritone voice and gunned the throttle. Looking back, he saw that the border guard was still saluting. *Damn, I could have avoided that earlier detour.*

Once he had passed Antwerp, he realized that he was on the home stretch. Two more hours, give or take. He had passed several convoys of armed personnel carriers without anyone stopping him for questioning. The men and machines coming east from the Front were all pretty beaten up, and the countryside looked like pictures he had seen of burned out and bombed No Man's Land. At least the road was passable.

Finally, an hour before sunset, he stopped the bike on the outskirts of Bruges. With its intricate waterways, it looked like Venice of the North, just as he had been told in school. So picturesque, even under German occupation. They had spared the bulk of the old town. He was ten miles southeast of Ostend now. Only twenty minutes away from his aroon.

Arndt Ritter had been an orderly at the hospital in Ostend ever since the Occupation started. As a covert member of the Sektion Politik, he took his orders for sabotage—or the avoidance of it—from Hauptman Gruber. He covered Ostend and all the territory to the Western Front where the Yser River met the sea at Nieuwpoort. The Germans had driven the pugnacious Belgians back to the west side of that river last year where the defenders had made their stand, supported by the French Marine Fusiliers. They fought ferociously, battle after battle, heroically holding the line, preserving a small northwest corner of Belgian soil. Finally, in desperation on October 23, 1914, they opened the canal sluices of the Yser and flooded the eastern lowlands, including the German trenches. It forced the Prussians up and out in a final all-out attack that failed in a bloody battle. This set the western boundary of German aggression between Ypres and the North Sea coast at Nieuwpoort. There it had stayed, mired down in mud for over a year. The German generals now seemed content with holding that line in the west while they concentrated on the battles at the Eastern Front with Russia.

What had been rich pastureland intersected with ditches and canals was now a bare and sinister plain laid waste by falling bombs, shells, and shrapnel. The mucky soil lay broken by heavy traffic and plowed up by projectiles. The rows of poplars, for centuries bent by the sea winds, now stood as jagged, uprooted, and twisted stumps. In the process, hundreds of thousands of young men had died, or had been maimed on both sides. All this in the ten miles west of Ostend.

Each time he had to take an ambulance out to bring back more casualties, Arndt Ritter hated making that trip across this desolate battleground. In fact, Ritter loathed his assignment in this stagnated war zone altogether. *Why should a valuable Prussian soldier have to empty fucking bedpans? Give us the men we need, and we can break through once and for all and occupy Paris.* He'd been there once back in 1908 and longed to see the *Folies Bérgère* one more time.

While he had been handling the ablutions of maimed men in the afternoon, Ritter watched the door to the operating room closely. His boss would kill him if he mangled this assignment. The girl they called Morgan had come out several times to give instructions. He had even talked to her once. She was very efficient and a nice enough person, but Gruber's instructions were that she was the enemy . He remembered what her partner looked like from when they arrived. Septic leg wound.

The only way out of the operating room was into the ward, and he had the exit from it to the hotel lobby and street covered. The fugitive McCarthy would not elude him, if he did indeed arrive, which he doubted would happen.

Doctor Heinrich strode out of the operating room at five o'clock and gathered nurses and orderlies together in the ward. "We are not expecting a wave of casualties tonight, with it being Christmas Eve. Except for the skeleton staff who agreed to work, you are all released from duty until tomorrow. May God go with you."

He took Morgan aside and shook her hand. "You've done well here. Thank you."

"I don't know what I would have done without your support, doctor. I should be thanking you, sir." She gave the doctor a hug and turned to consult with the remaining nurses in the ward. Ten minutes later, she gathered up her coat and walked out the front door.

Ritter was conflicted. Should he follow Morgan or wait for McCarthy. He decided to wait. The fugitive would have to come to the hospital, and the girl wouldn't try to escape, he was sure of that.

An hour later, Ritter was helping an amputee try to walk when he saw a soldier wearing the Sektion Politik insignia come into the ward. The soldier looked stooped, and he was rubbing his backside, apparently saddle-sore. A messenger from Gronski? Then he looked closer as the visitor removed his helmet. *Damnation. That's McCarthy.* Ritter watched his quarry look around at all the nurses and then step through the partially open operating room door.

Ritter let his patient fall back onto the nearest mattress and rushed to the hospital military telephone in the adjacent office to call his boss. He could still see the operating room door across the ward. The telephone only rang once. "He's here," Ritter said.

"Arrest him and the girl," Gruber ordered and hung up.

A minute later McCarthy, smiling from ear to ear, emerged from the operating room with Doctor Heinrich. The doctor pointed out the door to give directions and then clapped his former patient on the shoulder. Ritter rushed from the office just in time to see Tadgh disappear out the front doorway.

From the corner of his eye, Tadgh saw the uniformed orderly's hurried actions as he exited the ward. Gronski's lackey. As Tadgh headed down Christina Straat away from the beach on foot, with a feathery-light snow starting to drift down again, he could see the orderly following at a distance. Soon the ground would be covered in a clean white mantel befitting a Christmas scene. Ten minutes later, he arrived at Number 135 Ooststraat, a nondescript village home. He had anticipated this moment for two months now. And all he had brought his lady love was danger. Then Tadgh glimpsed the orderly momentarily. He must have been lurking out of sight not even a block away. That confirmed it. He was waiting. *Should I take him now?* Tadgh was so tired and longed to be reunited with his love. The orderly could wait.

Morgan was helping Gerda skin the few potatoes that they had left for dinner when the doorknocker pounded. She remembered their talk that morning, and her heart started thumping.

"Are you expecting someone?" Morgan looked at Gerda, who shrugged her shoulders.

Through the door she heard a familiar voice, "Aroon . . . Is my love to home, do ya know?"

"My God, it's Tadgh," she cried, dropping the potato bowl on the floor as she flew to open the door. "Mavorneen. Oh Mavorneen. I'm here, waiting for you."

The door burst open, and Tadgh almost knocked her down. The two boys came running from the kitchen, and Gerda cried for joy.

Tadgh took Morgan in his arms and held her tight, tighter than ever before. He was never going to let her out of his sight, ever again. Her body responded, tingling from head to toe. Tadgh turned them away from the door and kicked it shut. "There's an orderly out there who followed me."

"But how—"

"Pay no mind right now, Morgan." Oh, her name, how he spoke it, hummed music to her ears. To him, she looked wonderful, simply wonderful.

"Won't you introduce me?" Gerda stepped forward to greet Tadgh, her hand outstretched.

"Tadgh, this is Gerda, my new good friend. She is Fritz's, the U-boat officer's, wife. They and their boys have been so good to me."

Tadgh's eyes sparkled. "Ma'am, we are forever indebted to your husband for his heroic efforts to save both of us." He shook Gerda's hand and then knelt down to give the boys a salute. They giggled and ducked behind their mother's skirts.

"What heroic acts, might I ask?" Gerda looked stern.

Morgan shook her head at Tadgh.

"He, ah . . . took over command of his U-boat when his captain was gravely injured and brought us swiftly to medical assistance here in Ostend."

Gerda looked at Morgan as if to say, *I know that you're protecting me from the worst.*

Morgan diverted the conversation. "Mavorneen, we have a path to freedom now. I have instructions from the priest at Paulus and Peterus Kirken, and I must go there. He will know what to do. You need to keep our friend the orderly here, so he will not follow me."

Morgan smiled at Tadgh and her friend and then ran to get her coat and needed papers. Gerda followed her and said, "I'm sorry to see you go, but I know it is dangerous for you, even here."

"I'm worried that there will be repercussions for you and Fritz, Gerda. Remember what Captain Weisbach said."

"Nonsense, we just put up a weary traveler and contributor at our hospital. Go with God, dear."

Morgan kissed her on her cheek. "We wish the best for you and Fritz."

"I don't think that he will survive this war, but I hold out hope."

"You have to have hope, and faith. I kept my hope that Tadgh would come for me, and he did."

"Yes, lucky for you. Now what will happen to us all?"

"We will survive. I know it, now."

Tadgh called from the living room. "Aroon, we need to go."

They returned to the living room. "You can't go alone," Tadgh stated. "Let me go with you."

"You stay here, Tadgh. Show your face to that orderly and keep him busy. I'll be right back. It's only two blocks away."

"But—"

"But nothing. I'll be all right. We can't have the church implicated."

"I have an idea." Tadgh explained his plan to Morgan.

Then she said, "Can you take him? You look so tired."

"Not to worry, love. Hurry back." To make sure that their adversary didn't notice Morgan's departure from the kitchen back door, Tadgh stepped into the front deserted street and slowly relieved himself onto the snowbank, spelling the word *English*. He could see the orderly peering out from his hiding position at the nearby intersection, watching him. He decided that he couldn't wait for the orderly to act first, as he may have already summoned help. Tadgh went back into the house and slipped out the back way. Circling around, he surprised Ritter from behind. After a scuffle in the street, Tadgh returned through the back door, dragging the inert form of the orderly behind him, and left him on the kitchen floor.

Tadgh doffed an imaginary cap and bowed low in a gallant sweeping motion. "At your service, m'lady." The boys ducked behind their mother's skirt. "Time for me to change out of these wet clothes. I feel like a chameleon."

"You *are* a chameleon, sir," Gerda said, grabbing her boys. "How else could you have eluded your captors and come to the aid of your fair damsel in distress." The boys laughed, and she steered them toward their room. "Come on, my darlings. Let's leave this knight to his task of slaying the dragon." She hated the military, and especially those who commanded her husband.

Tadgh stripped the orderly's clothes off him. Then he swapped clothing with the unconscious man. Tadgh addressed the orderly. "Now *you* are properly dressed as an agent of the Sektion Politik, and I am, for all intents and purposes, an ambulance driver."

At the same time that Tadgh was disabling Gruber's orderly, in Berlin a dissatisfied Gruber got off the telephone and called in his *Oberleutnant*. "Get permission for the *Albatros C.I* to land at Stene-Ostend Airfield tonight."

"Yes, sir. They can put out smoke pots along the runway. The light snow is expected to taper off in an hour. The runway should be cleared by your arrival."

"I haven't heard back from Ritter. I want this McCarthy stopped. Get me a car for the airport." What he didn't say was that an impatient Gronski had ordered him to the Front at Ostend.

Twenty minutes later Gruber was in the cockpit of his beloved Albatros, running through the preflight check with the ground crew. He took off from Staaken Airport and pointed his aircraft westward into the dying rays of the day. He had already calculated the need to refuel at Essen, which would take twenty minutes. The total transit time would be five hours, getting him into Ostend just after midnight.

Morgan returned twenty minutes later from meeting with the priest. "Did you take care of our friend already?" She could hear Gerda banging pots and pans in the kitchen.

"He's in your bedroom, unconscious, blindfolded, and bound."

Morgan poked her head into the bedroom and saw the man slumped in the corner. "I know him well. Arndt Ritter, I believe his name is. He must have been spying on me the whole time."

"As well he should. He surely got an eyeful."

Morgan pinched Tadgh's backside, teasing, "You look downright handsome as a German orderly, by the way."

"I try my best to impress you, aroon."

"Oh you do, you do." Morgan threw her arms around her man.

"What did you find out? There may be others coming." Tadgh asked after partially satisfying his love with a prolonged kiss.

Morgan checked her watch. "It's eight now. We're to go to the church at eleven to meet with Father Peeters. He is telegraphing the Allies on the western side of the Front through his religious communications link."

"Nurse Queen?"

"I think so."

"We need to go back to the hospital at 10:30 to get trans-portation."

"Gerda's planned a festive evening for us. It's Christmas Eve, let's celebrate it with her," Morgan urged, pulling Tadgh toward the parlor.

"It's risky to stay here."

"We stay. I owe it to her and the boys."

Tadgh stepped out the back door and and returned a few minutes later. "You weren't followed. It's likely that Ritter was working alone."

Gerda had finished preparing the meager Christmas Eve dinner of boiled potato soup with a small piece of sausage and a loaf of freshly baked rye bread, and they all sat down to eat. The children wanted a present, but their mother had none for them. Morgan went to her room and returned with a gingerbread house that she had made using pieces of dried bread, chocolates and candies that she had been storing up for this occasion. The children squealed with joy, and Gerda was moved, jumping up to embrace her friend. Even Tadgh was impressed. He marveled at the impact Morgan had on this family of the U-boat watch officer who had saved their lives. What a strange, yet wonderful quirk of fate in a time of great turmoil and cruelty.

After Christmas Eve dinner, Tadgh stood up from the table and turned toward the door. "It's time for us to leave. Thank you, Gerda."

Before Tadgh could take a step, Gerda turned to Morgan. "I have something for you, Morgan, for your love and generosity to us. Fritz gave this to me, but I'd like you to have it." From her apron she pulled out her handkerchief and unfolded it to reveal the Claddagh locket. She placed it lovingly in Morgan's hands.

"My God, Tadgh. It's your locket! I thought that I lost it on the U-boat."

"The locket?" Tadgh came over to look at it. He snapped open the clamshell. "See? My mother's picture is in it."

Morgan took her friend's hand. She knew the sacrifice that war-weary Gerda made in giving up a silver piece of jewelry. It could have meant more food on the table for her children. "Oh, Gerda, you are a saint," she said, holding her friend close. "The Lord will reward you and your children."

"And my Fritz, I hope."

"Yes, and your Fritz. We will visit you after the war."

"Can I count on it?"

"Yes, my dear friend."

"But this man Ritter knows that we're here. I hope that we have not brought you more trouble."

"Nonsense, dear. A submariner's family is above reproach."

"It worries me, madam, for all that." Tadgh interjected. "I think it wise that I tie you up for appearances. Men will come, find you bound, and you will appear innocent."

"Must you tie them up, Tadgh?" Morgan pursed her lips with worry for her friends.

"You women must trust me. It's for the best." Tadgh placed both palms on the table.

The women looked at each other and nodded in resignation. Gerda then said, "If you insist, then go ahead. I trust you."

Tadgh made sure that the knots were not too tight on the boys and their mother as they lay down on her bed.

"Why is Morgan tying us up, *Mutti*?" Hans asked.

"This is just a game, boys," Gerda explained, shifting her body closer to her children.

"I hate to leave you like this, Gerda." Morgan leaned down and gave each of them a big kiss.

"It's all right, dear. We will be fine. You go, now." Gerda smiled at her friend.

Then Tadgh had found some clean pieces of cloth in the kitchen drawer, tore them into strips, and said to Gerda, "Tell the boys this is part of the game," holding up the strips. She did so, and he gently tied their mouths closed. "I'm sorry to have to do this," he told her. Then he winked at the boys.

The couple let themselves out the front door, locking it with the key and then dropping it in the snow near the doorframe. Hopefully, Gerda would find it when the snow melted. Tadgh had checked on Ritter's condition earlier, had given him a love tap to make sure the man stayed unconscious, and had left him in the deserted alley where he had downed him. He hadn't come to.

The snow had stopped. They hurried to the hospital where they hoped to commandeer an ambulance. Luckily for them, three ambulances had come back from the Western Front earlier in the day. A motorcycle was parked alongside them. Tadgh pointed to it and said, "That old machine brought me to you."

"You came on that contraption, Tadgh?"

"Five hundred miles, my love, after four hundred more bouncing along in a truck. A fair exchange, don't ya think," Tadgh said, while he worked to get one of the ambulances started in the darkness.

"My God, Tadgh. Where were you all this time?"

"With Casement in Bavaria, my love."

As they drove south to the church, Tadgh filled her in on his adventures, staying with the Currys, and Casement's message.

"Well, weren't you living the life of ease," Morgan joked. "And me, all the while worried about whether you were dead."

"A promise is a promise."

"Don't the Currys know there is a war going on?"

"It is beautiful in Bavaria, Morgan. Someday I will take you there."

When they reached the church, Father Peeters was waiting. "We are to go to the Front opposite Furnes," he said in English, jumping in the back. Tadgh checked his map.

As they headed west out of Ostend, Morgan looked back at the city lights receding in the distance. She missed Gerda and the boys and feared for them already.

"What will happen to Gerda? I'm not sure if just tying them up will fool anybody."

"Time will tell, lass. It's the best we could do. I couldn't knock her and the boys out, like I did with Ritter."

"Certainly not. They took good care of me, didn't they," she whispered, "even though I was the enemy."

"It sounds as if you took good care of *them* as well. All of them, including the ones in the hospital."

"All the broken boys. What a waste. This damned war and you stupid men." Morgan's voice trembled with anger. She thought of Gerda, who was such a good woman and kindred spirit. If only the women could have a say in this war.

"War is not damned, my love, when it seeks righteous freedom. And we're not *all* stupid," Tadgh said.

Morgan leaned into him and nestled against his shoulder. "I wasn't talking about *you,* mavorneen."

But they both knew that she was.

Chapter Eleven
Western Front

December 25, 1915
Road to the Western Front

adgh had to be careful in the dark. The bomb and shell craters made the road barely passable, since the holes were covered with new fallen snow; he could hit any one of them and risk breaking the axle. The sky had cleared on this moonless night. Directly above them the star Polaris hovered brightly as they headed westward at midnight. It was Christmas.

"What's the plan when we get to the Front?" Tadgh asked the priest, who fiddled with his rosary the entire trip. Ahead on the horizon, flashes of light illuminated the sky, followed by booming sounds that rattled their eardrums.

"That's not lightning and thunder, is it."

"No, Morgan, artillery fire. We'll be there soon enough."

Morgan knew what that artillery could do to the human body. Shrapnel shattering the bones inside, mortar exploding interior organs. She shuddered as she strained to look out the side window at the passing devastation.

"Come back over here, aroon. It'll be all right. I'll make it right, don't ya know."

Morgan snuggled into Tadgh's right shoulder and felt better.

"We're to get to the front trench and minister to the wounded. Then wait for a signal from the Allied side," the priest, Father Peeters, spoke up from the back.

"I don't speak German," Tadgh confessed, looking back at him, momentarily.

Morgan said, "Don't worry, mavorneen. I can get by. Just follow my lead."

Tadgh admired her grit and ingenuity. His darling love. He put his right hand on her knee and kept it there, and Morgan pressed closer. She covered his hand with her own and said, "I missed you. Oh, how I missed you. I had trouble with my thoughts."

"I had faith that God would protect the righteous, aroon." Tadgh kissed her on the top of her head, taking his eyes off the road for a moment.

He didn't see the crater in the road until it was too late, and the ambulance shuddered, veered to the left, teetering at the edge of a ditch with its right wheels off the ground, threatening to flip on its side. "Tadgh, watch out!" Morgan cried as they all instinctively leaned right. Tadgh held the wheel steady, and the vehicle righted itself. Anything else and they would have crashed. *Bloody hell. Have to be more careful. Comforting Morgan would have to wait.*

Morgan moved away from Tadgh, closer to the window. Father Peeters clicked his rosary beads in the back seat and once more reminded them of God's protection.

Squinting at the war zone ahead, Tadgh said, "We can't be more than two miles away, now." Each time the guns flashed, he caught the ghostly silhouette of a torn and twisted landscape of desolation, remnants of tree trunks standing along the jagged horizon.

Gruber had heard from Gronski at six that afternoon before he took off. Monteith and the guard had untied themselves and flagged down a northbound convoy to report in as soon as they could.

"McCarthy and the girl can't be allowed to escape," Gronski ordered. "Kill them both but extract whatever message Casement may be attempting to send to his bosses first."

"Jawohl, mein Kapitan."

Six hours later, Gruber wiped his eyes as ground lights ahead flickered through the night. He'd been airborne too long in the frigid air, and the only dinner he'd eaten were the bugs in his teeth. At least coming from the east, he hadn't encountered the snow showers that had been falling at his destination. Ritter had better have the Irish couple in custody. There, on the right, he saw a line of signal lights on the snowy ground. He deftly banked and eased the throttle. The engine coughed, and he got a face full of exhaust oil. *Damn.* He'd have to have his mechanic check the fuel mixture ratio again.

Twenty minutes later, he was in the hospital's military office interrogating Doctor Heinrich. Another ten minutes and he had found Ritter, almost frozen, and still bound and gagged in the alley. "Dammit, man. You couldn't overpower a tired fugitive and a weak woman?" He sneered at Ritter. "He even stripped you of your hospital clothes—you're wearing a uniform of my motorcycle guard." Ritter turned red with humiliation.

♣   ♣   ♣   ♣

Gerda was still tied up when she heard knocking on her door at one in the morning. When she couldn't answer, she heard a single pistol shot and then heard crashing sounds in the other room. A man's voice yelled, "Check the bedrooms."

Two men burst into the room. One ordered the other to remove the gags.

Gerda felt as if her lips had been ripped off. The boys started screaming.

"Shut them up, Ritter."

"Untie my bonds, so I can quiet my boys for you," Gerda pleaded.

"I could easily stop them with a bullet." The man raised his gun.

"You wouldn't dare, whoever you are. My husband would hunt you down. He's an important man."

"Is he?" Gruber cocked his pistol and aimed it at little Hans who immediately ceased crying. "So where are they, Frau, the traitors who were living in your house?"

"I had a visitor here, is that who you mean?"

"Don't talk back to me." He stepped forward and slapped Gerda. Now she could taste blood, but she kept her resolve and stayed rigid on the bed.

"She's the wife of a U-boat officer, Gruber, sir. I found out about her past," Ritter interjected. "And look, she's tied up. They must have kept her here against her will."

Gruber stepped back and lowered his gun. Damned U-boat officers were off limits. His superiors worshipped the ground they walked on.

"Show me your visitor's room," Gruber demanded, slashing the bonds on her wrists and ankles with two swipes of the long knife he extracted from its sheath at his waist. Gerda got up slowly, her joints aching, and went to her children. "Release my boys," she demanded, starting to untie them.

"Do not touch them," he ordered. "First, the nurse's room," he growled.

She tried to stall him and desperately wanted Morgan and her man to have the best chance for freedom, even if she and Fritz couldn't be together.

He pointed the gun at her and ordered Ritter to cut the boys' bonds only if she complied. "You are holding something back. There was a man with her. Where did he go?"

"I don't know what you are talking about."

He raised his arm, gun in hand, threatening. "Woman, we know they were here, and it will go badly for you and your husband for harboring the enemy."

I have to think about my own safety and that of my boys. If my friends get away, then maybe there's a chance that Fritz and I can survive this awful war, Gerda thought. *I have stalled the men long enough. My friends should be far enough away now to be safe.* She took a deep breath, and spoke, sighing. "The couple was here, but only briefly, and they didn't say anything about where they were going. I was told they were Irish allies."

Having searched the premises in vain, Hauptman Gruber re-entered the bedroom and stood near the bed. "They didn't say anything about where they were going?" he demanded of Gerda.

"No. They just left. I expect Morgan will be returning in the morning. That's her name, Morgan." She wasn't going to compromise the priest at the Kirken or submit to these brutish officers. They were just like the ones ordering her Fritz into terrible danger. She moved to untie her boys, and this time the Hauptman didn't stop her.

"I will be back, Frau. I know you are lying, but you are, after all, an officer's wife. Do not leave your house." Hauptman Gruber turned on his heel. "Come, Ritter. They must have headed for the harbor or the Front. This woman is of no more use to us now."

"It's Christmas, you know. The day of our Savior's birth. The Lord be with you, officers," she called out and then prayed to herself. *Lord protect Morgan and her Tadgh.*

Tadgh could see the checkpoint barricade ahead. Several ambulances were lined up on the side of the road. A gruff sergeant ordered him to follow suit. Father Peeters, and then Morgan, dressed in her nurse's uniform, went off to talk to the officer coordinating triage efforts. Left on his own, Tadgh felt helpless in this environment.

When the two returned, Morgan told Tadgh, "The Allied forces are sending an artillery barrage overnight. I think they are going to attack at dawn." Helping Father Peeters up into the ambulance, she added, "We have to wait our turn. The Front is half a mile ahead."

"I heard the Germans are using the Defense in Depth tactic, so there are probably two trenches, and we are behind the last one," Tadgh said.

"What kind of tactic is that?"

"The front line is manned lightly so the attacker is initially allowed to gain some ground beyond its own artillery cover in the opening phase of an attack. Then it is counter-attacked by groups of well-placed defenders in a second position behind the front line."

"I was told there is a copse of trees still standing behind the Allied trench at the south end of Furnes. We need to be in the front German trench opposite those trees at dawn," Father Peeters said. "Can we get there in time?"

"We have to to abandon the ambulance." Tadgh checked his watch. "It's still six hours before dawn. I'm bushed—need to catch some sleep, if you'll stand guard, Morgan. Give me an hour, unless something happens."

♣ ♣ ♣ ♣

Gruber had to rouse the Ostend harbormaster at two in the morning. After checking with his men, the harbormaster reported, "No boats have left the harbor since before nine last night. It's been quiet here on Christmas Eve."

"You are certain? They would have been secretive about it—any small boat coming in from or heading out to the west."

"We patrol the harbor with three crisscross boats. They couldn't have slipped through without our knowing it, I can assure you."

He had to believe him. The only other alternative was the Western Front. But *where* on the line? Gruber had an idea. *Why didn't I think about this earlier? The only way to communicate with the Allied side quickly is by telegraph.* Transmissions would have been coded. On a long shot, they went to the closest telegraph office over by the Petreus and Paulus Kirche. *Closed.* The telegraph operator who lived above his office wasn't home either. It was Christmas. With the butt of his Luger, Gruber smashed the front window of the office. The end justified the means, in his view. The Belgian operator would keep a copy of all correspondence. An alarm went off as he and Ritter climbed through the opening.

Gruber pointed over the door. "Break that damn bell."

While he sifted through the operator's desk, the local German military police officers showed up, guns drawn. "What are you two doing in there?" one of them growled.

"Official business." Gruber turned to display his *Sektion Politik* insignia.

The police officer hated military leaders who took advantage of their position, especially on Christmas. He had just finished dealing with another hardass who had raped one of the local Belgian girls. "Put your hands up, sir. You have just destroyed public property."

93

Gruber shot him between the eyes. The other policeman ran off before Gruber could target him, too. Ritter just stood there, dumbfounded. "Nobody's going to stop me from finding McCarthy. Why do I have to do everything myself? Don't just stand there. Go turn off that alarm."

Minutes later Gruber had found copies of the five telegrams that had been sent the previous evening. "Aha." He suspected two of the five, one outbound and then another inbound a few minutes later. The Belgian operator should have notified the military of such a communication. But since it was Christmas Eve, and both contained a Christian message, he hadn't bothered. What did they mean?

Outbound 2040. *Our savior is born to Joseph and Mary. Stop. Where can they find shelter? Stop.*

Inbound 2115. *In a manger south of Bethlehem at the Inn of the trees. Stop. When dawn breaks the Magi will come. Stop.*

Ritter knew the positions well enough. "There's only one place on the Front where trees have been allowed to stand on the Allied side. It's in front of the Belgian King Albert's field headquarters. We think him an honorable adversary, and we don't shell him or his Queen."

"So, opposite Albert's field control center at dawn, then." Gruber checked his watch. Five o'clock. It would be dawn in three hours.

"Tadgh, the ambulances are moving." Morgan tugged on his sleeve.

Tadgh checked his watch. It was 0620. "Bloody hell. You were to only let me sleep for an hour."

"Tadgh, you seemed so exhausted and needed your sleep."

"Damn it, Morgan." Tadgh twisted the ignition switch, but nothing happened. He tried again. Nothing. There were four ambulances lined up behind him. "*You* talk to them," Tadgh told Morgan, pointing at the soldiers approaching their vehicle.

Morgan jumped out, grabbing a first aid kit on her way. The priest followed suit, and the two advanced to cut the soldiers off. In the meantime, Tadgh opened the bonnet of the truck and peered inside. It was too dark to see much. Then he went to the petrol tank cap and removed it. The smell of petrol was faint. Probably out of fuel. He checked the back of the vehicle. Right. No petrol cans.

Two ambulance drivers in the rear got out of their vehicles to assist. Tadgh made a decision to abandon the ambulance then, instead of later.

He hurried to interrupt Morgan and Father Peeters' talk with the soldiers. Pulling his partner aside, he said, "Tell them that the ambulance has broken down and that we will need to find help to fix it."

The priest relayed the message, but the soldiers ordered them to stay by their vehicle. Tadgh feigned compliance but then directed Morgan and Father Peeters to slip into the deep ditch paralleling the road. "Get down and move forward. Keep out of sight."

At first, the soldiers didn't see what was happening. Then one of the ambulance drivers yelled at the soldiers and pointed at the ditch. The soldiers hesitated to spring into action. It was tantamount to desertion for a soldier to leave his vehicle. Some of them jumped down into the ditch.

Tadgh and Morgan sprinted ahead full speed, but Father Peeters lagged behind.

"Keep going, Morgan," Tadgh yelled and turned around to help the priest.

"Sorry, son. I'm not cut out for this field work, I'm afraid," Father Peeters panted. Tadgh picked the willowy man up in his arms, all five feet of him, and lumbered off to catch up with Morgan. He watched the soldiers chase them half-heartedly for a few minutes before tiring of the diversion in the dark. He surmised that they weren't authorized to leave their post and saw them start to double back toward the line of ambulances still waiting for access to the battlefield.

Tadgh set Father Peeters down as soon he saw that the soldiers had given up the chase. The shelling ahead had stopped. Minutes later, they could hear voices close by, just up ahead. It must be the German trench. They were feeling their way slowly in the eerie darkness when Morgan slipped on the snow-covered ground, almost falling into the first trench. As she teetered, Tadgh lunged and pulled her back. They were soaked to the skin, and with the temperature hovering just below the freezing point on the snowy ground, they were chilled to the bone.

"Ease back there, lass," he whispered, not sure whether German soldiers were immediately in front of them.

"I've been here before to minister to the dying," Father Peeters said. "Follow me and keep down." He headed parallel to the trench for thirty feet to where they found wooden steps leading down into the dank darkness. They descended at least ten steps until their heads dipped below ground level.

If it had been dark above the trenches, inside them was pitch black. Morgan felt a cold sensation as muck oozed up through the snow and covered her boots. She heard and felt water dripping from the seams between the logs and sandbags shoring up the trench. Pacing it off, she realized this underground shelter was ten-feet wide. She wondered how many of these logs had collapsed time and again, burying the soldiers beneath the mud and slush. Plenty of them, she decided. She marveled at how quiet the night had become.

Without a word, Father Peeters grabbed her sleeve. A point of light had just appeared maybe a hundred feet away to their right, not enough to illuminate the trench. "Cigarette," he whispered.

Tadgh came loping down the trench from their left. Morgan could hear the thudding of his boots as he jogged. "There are stairs forward to our left, but no soldiers."

Morgan pointed to the right. "Over there."

"Let me go talk to them," Father Peeters offered. He disappeared into the darkness, and Tadgh soon heard a conversation in German that he couldn't make out.

Three minutes later, he was back. "They're expecting an Allied attack at dawn in about an hour. Some of the men are hurt by the shelling they took during the night. They're waiting for the orderlies and ambulances at first light. There is a whole platoon strung out to the north in this trench. Some of the more able are limping back. I'm surprised we didn't run into them."

"Did they say where we are, relative to where we are supposed to be at dawn?" Tadgh asked. He couldn't see his watch.

"We need to be a quarter mile to our left to be opposite the copse of trees."

"Let's go, then," Tadgh said.

"I think it best that I stay here, son, where I can do some good. Some of the men are in a bad way."

"Let me help you," Morgan offered, taking his hand.

"No, dear girl. You've come this far to gain your freedom. Don't jeopardize that now."

Morgan looked at Tadgh, but she could barely see him in the gloom.

"He's right, lass."

Morgan turned and hugged the priest, who marked the sign of the cross on her forehead. "Go with God," he said, and then disappeared into the darkness.

"Back up and out," Tadgh said. "I don't want to trip over German soldiers in the dark."

When they were at ground level again, they could see a sliver of light behind them at the horizon. They would be vulnerable to the Allied snipers in a few minutes. "We have to hurry, lass." Tadgh tilted his watch until he could make out the hands indicating 7:15.

They scurried to their left along the back edge of the trench, making sure that they weren't visible to anyone there. On three occasions, they heard soldiers down below them preparing for the expected onslaught.

Within ten minutes, at another set of stairs, Tadgh could see that they were at the right location. Squinting west through the gloom beyond what looked like the Allied trench, he could barely see what looked like an old farm house set in a group of scrub trees, some of which had been up-ended. They were at the Front and not at a secondary trench. A hundred yards of No Man's Land stretched before them. There were two ragged sets of barbed wire just outside each trench. *Incredible. It's been static like this for months.*

"Down we go again." Tadgh pulled Morgan after him. By now there was enough light to be able to see inside the trench. They descended into a platoon of German soldiers who were inspecting their guns and tending to their wounded. When the sergeant saw the nurse and orderly arrive, he motioned them to a man in obvious pain sprawled in the muck, his left leg twisted at an unnatural angle.

"*Kommen Sie hier*," he ordered.

"Let me do the talking," Morgan whispered, rushing forward to assist.

Morgan greeted the wounded man and then administered a needle from her first aid kit. When he had calmed, she crunched his leg to reset it. Finding wooden splints from used ammunition box slats and taking gauze from the first aid kit, she bound up the leg. "Ambulances will be here soon," she reassured him.

The sergeant was clearly impressed. "*Danke, Fräulein.*"

Tadgh wasn't sure whether he was more in awe of her nursing prowess on the front line or her ability to communicate in German after only two months.

Morgan motioned to Tadgh to help her move the soldier out of the muck. Tadgh carefully lifted him up, making sure he supported the leg from below the break, and put him on a wooden platform in a hollowed out section of the front wall of the trench. Seeing a jacket lying nearby, he used it to cover the affected leg area.

"*Danke*," the sergeant said, and moved off to ready his men for battle.

"See. Sign language works just as well, doesn't it, Tadgh." Morgan spoke in hushed tones as they stood on the fire-step leading forward, in front of the soldiers.

"Can you see the barbed wire over the top?"

"Yes, but there's a gap to the right in that overlap area."

Morgan poked her head up to look right, but Tadgh pulled her back down.

"It's too light now. We wouldn't want you to be the first casualty of the morning, my dear."

So Morgan and Tadgh stood still, awaiting the chance to break from the trench and attempt to cross No Man's Land, a hundred yards from freedom. What could be easier, and what did "Queen Nurse" have in mind? They would most likely find out in a few minutes, perhaps their last minutes on this earth.

Gruber was livid. Ritter had hit a shell hole on the road masked by the snow, and they had careened off into the torn-up countryside. The truck, with its broken front axle and smashed radiator, was finished. If only *he* had driven, he thought. They walked towards the Front. He checked his timepiece—0715. *Why aren't there any other vehicles on the road?*

"You will fry for this, Ritter. I should shoot you right now."

At that point, an ambulance approached them, heading east away from the Front. Gruber flagged it down. He would have shot the driver, had he not stopped. Lucky for him that he did.

"I need transport to the Front, immediately. Turn around."

"If I do, my patient will die, sir."

"Turn around and get out."

Once the orderly had jumped out, more because of the Luger leveled in his direction than because of the officer's rank, Gruber ordered, "Now take your patient out. Ritter, help him. When another ambulance comes from the Front, it can take you both to the hospital."

By 0725 hours they were on their way, with a sliver of light on the horizon behind them. Gruber drove. He suspected he still had some time to find the traitors, since it was still dark and silent to the west.

Fifteen minutes later, when he was stopped at the line of ambulances waiting their turn to go to the Front, Gruber spun the wheel and attempted to bypass the line. Two military officers jumped out to block the vehicle, and Gruber thought about mowing them down.

He stopped long enough to yell, "Get out of my way. There are two important fugitives trying to escape, an orderly ambulance driver and a nurse. I must get to the Front before dawn."

One officer came to the cab. "We saw them an hour ago, heading there on foot. One half mile." Seeing the *Sektion Politik* insignia, he waved them through.

Gruber jammed the accelerator down and was at the triage point ten minutes later, as far as the ambulances could go in the mud. "Where is Albert's field office?"

"Half a mile southwest, sir," Ritter told him.

Gruber took off at a run with Ritter trying to keep up behind him. The sun was now rising above the eastern wasteland.

The eight o'clock hour arrived to the sound of silence. The Germans in the trench were crouching, rifles forward with bayonets attached, expecting either an assault from the Allied forces or a barrage of artillery fire to soften them up first. Those who had them were wearing primitive gas masks that made them look like giant bug-eyed flies. *What a way for grown men to act*, Morgan thought. *What a waste of humanity and topography.*

Tadgh and Morgan positioned themselves at the bottom of the crude log stairs, holding hands quietly. Morgan pressed her body against Tadgh and felt his warmth.

Suddenly, from across No Man's Land at the Allied headquarters, a gramophone feeding loudspeakers belted out a German rendition of the Christmas carol, "*Stille Nacht.*" Morgan could see the soldiers look at each other, surprised. "Is this a trick?" one exclaimed. They were all frozen in time and place.

Before Tadgh could grab her, Morgan climbed the stairs so that she could see out. There, across No Man's Land, standing high on steps of the old farmhouse, a lone woman dressed in a Belgian Army officer's uniform waved a large white flag and sang "Silent Night." Her beautiful voice carried sweetly across the silent battlefield.

All Morgan could think of was the Madonna at the inn on Christmas heralding in the birth of her son, Jesus. The woman looked so regal. "Tadgh, come up here."

"My God, Morgan. That must be Elisabeth, *Queen Nurse.* Look at the man beside her, how he's dressed. That must be King Albert."

The Germans in the field crouched, transfixed.

"They really won't shoot the royals, Tadgh. This must be our signal. We must run for it." She wasn't sure how far she could get in her mud-caked boots.

"I don't think this is just for our benefit," Tadgh said, looking back into the trench where the confused infantrymen were discussing what to do.

"Let's go," Morgan yelled as she stepped up onto the battlefield. Tadgh chased after her, Luger drawn.

The music stopped at the end of the carol, and Queen Elisabeth called out, "*Fröhliche Weihnachten,*" in a loud, reverent voice.

The German captain below Tadgh yelled back, "Merry Christmas." The King returned the call with a reply, "*Fröhliche Weihnachten.*"

That did it. The Germans started up the stairs behind Morgan and Tadgh, crying, "*Weihnachten Waffenstillstand.*"

Morgan translated, "Christmas truce." It wasn't to be an assault at all, but a Christmas truce like last year. Tadgh quickly holstered his weapon. Unbelievable. Here were men killing each other one minute and celebrating together the next. The soldiers nearly ran Morgan over in their rush up the stairs. Seeing the Germans coming up without weapons, and the Belgians and French infantrymen following suit, Morgan thought, *What a wonderful turn of events, Gerda was right. Jesus saves all.*

They were on the German side of No Man's Land beyond the barbed wire in the crowd of mingling Allied and German soldiers when a stern voice from behind them yelled, "Halt, McCarthy."

Tadgh wheeled and dropped to the ground, taking Morgan with him. He could see a German officer with the same insignia that he had worn earlier in the day standing at the barbed wire with a Luger aimed directly at him. The infantrymen appeared oblivious in their joy to be celebrating and not fighting. The officer walked slowly forward until he was only twenty feet from the pair, his weapon now pointed directly at Morgan's chest. If Tadgh went for his own Luger, she would be dead at an instant.

"On your knees," he commanded.

Tadgh wasn't going to turn back now.

Suddenly a short Belgian soldier nearby whipped around and threw his bayonet, hitting Gruber in the chest, butt end first. That stunned him momentarily. The German recovered and turned to shoot his attacker, which gave Tadgh the moment he needed to act. He lunged forward, swooping up the bayonet and thrusting it into Gruber's heart.

The German dropped like a rag doll without firing a shot, dead before he hit the ground. Ritter poked his head up out of the trench and thought for a moment about taking action. When he saw that his boss was disabled, he disappeared back into his hole.

The Belgian soldier helped Morgan to her feet, then clasped Tadgh's hand and shook it violently. Tadgh peered into the soldier's face and realized he could be no more than fifteen years old. The boy said to them, "My job was to protect you, for my parents." He turned and pointed at the Royals. "But it is you who saved me, sir."

"You did your job well, lad."

"Prince Leopold, I presume," Morgan grinned and gave the boy a hug. She had heard that he, like his parents, was fighting for his country.

"Yes, Ma'am." The lad jumped back, apparently not wanting to look less than military.

"A fine job, to be sure, lad," Tadgh said, wiping Gruber's blood off the bayonet with his sleeve and handing it to the young man, butt first. "Smart, too. No gunshot to rattle the troops, eh."

"Yes, sir. Come now. My parents would like to meet you both."

He led them through the melee of soldiers from both sides who were happily organizing to play some form of football game. It was indeed a silent night of brief peace. Tadgh stopped briefly, looking back at the German trench, and swooped Morgan up in his arms to carry her the rest of the way to freedom. The three "wise men" bearing gifts had been the three Royals, and it was the dawn of a new life for Morgan and for him. Jesus was born.

Chapter Twelve
Premonition

Very Early Christmas Morning, 1915
Toronto, The Beaches, Canada

*L*ook out!" **Collin** O'Donnell cried out in his sleep just after midnight, his left arm flailing out, fist clenched. His new wife Kathy slept soundly facing him with her left leg curled up over his body when the blow caught her squarely on her right shoulder.

It took a second for the pain signal to reach her brain and wake her up. "Ouch."

Then Collin woke up. The girl in his dream had been in mortal danger and now his beloved beside him was in pain. "Is it the baby?"

Kathy's first pregnancy was now at the end of her second trimester. The baby had been aggressively kicking inside her womb. She continued to worry that it would be a boy, not the girl they had hoped to name after Collin's missing sister, Claire.

Being careful with the gender of their pending offspring, Kathy said, "Not unless Claire's been pounding my shoulder, my love." She rubbed where a bruise was forming. "You must have had another nightmare, like that fight in Brooklyn when one of your pugilist opponents died."

"Did I do that?" Collin sat up and kissed the injured shoulder softly, running his tongue around and around the red welt. He loved the way Kathy slept, her naked limbs wrapped around him.

"Right, you monster." Kathy lashed out and gave him a playful blow to his left temple with her right arm.

"I'm sorry, darlin'. I was asleep."

"I'll live. Good thing you didn't wallop the baby with your leg."

"It was Claire. I know it. She and her Irish lad were on a war-torn battlefield staring into the muzzle of some angry German officer's revolver. And the rest of the soldiers with different uniforms were just standing around."

Kathy sat up, turning to face her husband. She lifted his chin and stared into his hangdog black eyes.

"Come now, Collin. It's just your subconscious again. You weren't responsible for Claire's disappearance. When will you get that fact into your head? All that talk with Sam last night about the terrors of those chemicals they've been using to kill our brave soldiers must have brought in the bad dream."

"But it was so real. I could see her so clearly." Collin groaned and turned on his side facing her.

"Most nightmares seem real. Otherwise they wouldn't frighten us, would they?" Kathy wiped his brow with the corner of the bedsheet. "Come on. It's Christmas, when Jesus was born, and our little Claire is getting ready for this world. It's perfect. Let's dwell on that happy occurrence."

"Forgive me, my love. We have a lot to be thankful for, to be sure, to be sure. But I keep thinking about my sister Claire."

"You don't even know what she would look like today, do you?"

"Sometimes you just know."

"If you want to worry about something, then think about how and when we can get my mother out of our house."

"Can we talk about that tomorrow after we've had some sleep?"

"I'm not sure I'll get any more sleep at this rate with all this kicking. Feel the real Claire."

"Amazing. She's up already."

Collin's warm hand gently rubbed her stomach, soothing the flurries inside. His gentle stroking seemed to calm the baby, and Kathy imagined that the little one was curling up under her father's hand and settling into sleep. Both Collin and Kathy, however, were wide-awake in the semi-darkness, though sleep was illusive. Collin's nightmare was still fresh to him, and Kathy's belly made it impossible for her to find a comfortable position. She moved onto her side to face Collin, and he gladly wrapped himself around her. Her body was so warm and soft, and he thought she had only grown more beautiful as the pregnancy had progressed. Her eyes shone, and her skin had taken on a glow that seemed to light up his heart every time he looked her way. Although she complained that she felt ungainly and "as big as a house," he thought she had never looked so lovely. He wanted to be near her, just to touch her arm or kiss the back of her neck.

Kathy nestled closer to him so she could rest her ear against his chest. His heartbeat soothed her, as a lullaby would soon do for their baby. Her lips curled into a playful smile when Collin's body slowly responded with the unmistakable signs of arousal. She slipped her hands downward slowly, teasing Collin into anticipation.

With a stifled groan, Collin grasped her hands before she had found her target. "Oh, God, Kathy, you're making me crazy here," he whispered as he began to push urgently against her. "I'm so afraid I might hurt you and the baby. I can't, I'm too rough."

She covered his mouth with her hand to stop his protestations. "Look, this baby is strong and good, nothing can hurt her, and she's in the safest place in the whole world. Feel her," Kathy drew his hand to the bump that lay between them, in the shelter of their two bodies. "She's there, all tucked up, and our lovemaking will do her no harm. Please come to me, I need you."

How easily she made it for him to surrender to their desires. He buried his face into the sweet warmth of her neck. The position of lying on their side and facing one another to accommodate Kathy's expanding middle was awkward at first, but right away, they grew to enjoy its novelty. Although Kathy thought Collin might find more satisfaction if she turned so he could find his pleasure, he let her know that he never wanted to lose sight of her face in its exquisite rapture. He seemed to move in her with a deliberate strength to heighten her pleasure, and his unhurried movements and caresses matched her body's rhythm exactly. When he could delay no more, Collin arched his back with a series of thrusts that brought them both to heart-stopping climax. As was their custom, they remained in their close embrace, savoring their enjoyment long after their bodies had slipped from one another.

Still entwined, they fell asleep to the quiet beating of each other's hearts.

Collin awoke with the thought of how they could convince Kathy's mother Fiona to move out. Her father Ryan seemed to be trying to make amends, but he had a lot to be held accountable for. This small house on Lee Avenue was not going to be big enough for the four of them once Claire was born. He decided that he wouldn't bring it up and spoil Christmas Day.

The intensely erotic events filled Collin's mind, sweeping away the thoughts of his sister's imagined peril and his in-laws' marital problems, and he fell back asleep curled into his Kathy.

♣ ♣ ♣ ♣

The couple wasn't asleep more than half an hour before a Santa Claus of sorts landed on the walk-up porch, missing the roof entirely. He wasn't dressed in red, and he didn't have a fat round belly. He checked the front door, and finding it unlocked, quietly slipped into the darkened home.

105

Kathy's tabby cat, Silky, whom she had rescued from her parents' home when her Mother had vacated it, prowled out of the kitchen into the parlor, and enveloped the intruder's legs, purring softly. The man paid her no mind.

He went straight to his work and found the fir tree in the corner with strings of popcorn and few colored balls decorating it. One of the red balls had the word *Kathy* scrawled across it in white paint. He stopped and touched it for a moment before placing four packages at the back of the tree, hidden from view. Then he turned with a jerk, and, laying his finger aside of his nose to stifle a sudden sneeze, he quietly withdrew, patting Silky on his way out.

Fiona awoke first, with the sun streaming into her east-facing second floor bedroom that her first grandchild would soon be calling home. She would have to move out then, sometime in the beginning of March. It was a small room but cheery enough. Kathy had already painted it a pale pink because she was so hopeful that her baby would be a girl, to replace Collin's missing sister Claire. Fiona didn't have the whole story because her daughter wouldn't confide in her.

Fiona knew that Kathy partly blamed her for not setting Ryan straight years ago. When Kathy moved out of their home in Rosedale, Fiona had realized that she also needed to leave, or her daughter and family would be lost to her forever.

She pitied Ryan for his dramatic appearance at St. Aidan's Church just before Kathy walked down the aisle at her wedding, unnerving her and the others because they had not expected him to show up at all. Collin had handled the situation diplomatically, which only reinforced her belief that the lad was good for her daughter. But now that she had left Ryan, she was not fooled by his supposed turnaround, not by a long shot. She had suffered through too many years of verbal and physical abuse.

Yet a sudden ache came over Fiona this Christmas morning, the first one without her husband. She remembered the early days, when Kathy was so excited about the Christmas festivities. At least she was here with her daughter now, and soon there would be a new gift to the family, the child. *To hell with Ryan.*

Kathy heard her mother bustling around in the kitchen below making breakfast, but she did not want to get out of bed. Collin, her own dear Santa Claus, had already given her the best gift possible, the gift of love. And there he was, snoring soundly with his tousled head nuzzled into her right breast. She dared not move for fear of spoiling the moment. The chintz curtains glowed in the early sun. *Oh, my goodness!* The pendulum clock on the wall showed 9:30 already. She woke Collin up with a kiss on the cheek. "Wake up, darling. It's our last Christmas morning before Claire arrives."

Collin snorted awake and scuffed his head across her breast, almost crushing it. "What now, darlin'?" He had for once been dreaming of turkey dinner and pumpkin pie.

"Time to get up, my love. Don't you know that it's Christmas?"

"Breakfast on?"

"I suspect as much. Mother's been banging around in the kitchen for some time now. I think she's been fussing about just to get us up."

"I know it cost a pretty penny, but I hope she likes our gift."

"She needed a new coat. The one father bought her years ago is so worn." Kathy rolled out of bed and grabbed her robe, then went to the window. Opening the curtains, she exclaimed, "Look, there are skaters already out on the rink in the park. What a glorious Christmas Day. How lovely!" She laughed aloud. "There's new snow on the ground. It must have started last night after we went to bed. Mother will be so cozy in her new coat when we walk in Kew Beach Park." She smiled at her husband.

"Fiona deserves it." Collin was immediately behind her, hugging her, his hands digging under the robe. Kathy turned and kissed him fully on the lips. "Merry Christmas, my love."

"And to you the same, darlin'. I smell coffee brewing. Where's my robe? I'm famished."

"I think there's a little something under the tree for you," Collin said to Fiona after breakfast, as the women sat down on the chesterfield facing the Christmas tree. He pulled out a package wrapped in brown paper and tied with twine, containing a gray woolen scarf and matching gloves that Kathy had selected the previous week at Eaton's Department store downtown.

"Open your second gift, Mother," Kathy urged.

Fiona smiled and said, "Being here with you is my gift." She unwrapped the next festive package, held up the new woolen coat, and then hugged it.

"Oh, you children shouldn't have, and with a baby coming, it's much too expensive." Her eyes glistened.

There was a total of two gifts for each of the four of them, including baby Claire, plus one gift each for Sam, Liz, their two girls, and the new baby on the way. That's when Kathy noticed the four additional gifts behind the tree. *Strange. What is Collin up to?* They had agreed that all they could afford was two per person, especially since they were footing the bill for Fiona. Ryan was such a miser.

The expected gifts had been opened with thanks all around, with Collin getting a new model Brownie camera for his hobby and Kathy receiving a new ruffled red dress designed to hide her bulge. Then Kathy asked, "Now, what's hidden behind the tree, Collin? Looks like more packages. Didn't we have an agreement?"

"I thought you women were up to something."

They both turned to Fiona.

"Don't look at me. It's not my doing."

Silky the cat had been curled up at Fiona's feet and lazily stood and stretched, then headed for the front door, needing out. That's when Kathy saw wet boot prints in the rug near the door. "Look, Collin. Did you go out into the snow? The vestibule is all wet and dirty." They all stared. "Someone tracked in snow and dirt all the way to the tree," Kathy added.

"Did you lock the door last night, darlin'?" Collin inspected the floor.

"No, Collin, we left it unlocked as usual. Nobody ever intrudes."

"Well, someone did last night. But who?"

"Santa Claus?" Kathy asked.

"He would have come down the chimney, and not the front door, surely," Collin joked, crossing to the corner fireplace and tossing a log onto the already blazing fire.

"This is no joking matter, children. We have been *violated*." Fiona scolded them as if they were adolescents.

"I hardly think we've been harmed by these gifts, Mother. I'd venture to guess that Sam may have been responsible, that scoundrel."

"He's your best friend Liz's husband, isn't he?"

"And Collin's mentor and former boss, Mother. He's well known for his Irish shenanigans."

"I'd be careful when you open the packages up," Fiona cautioned, moving to the farthest end of the chesterfield, her eyes squinting and lips set in a line, her fingers in her ears, as if ready for a bomb to go off.

"Nonsense ladies, there is no danger here, with all these brightly-colored bows and ribbons, but it is intriguing, so it is. Let's have a look." Collin read the carefully printed nametag and handed a package to Kathy. "Someone went to a lot of trouble to wrap these gifts. This one's for the baby."

She opened the festive package carefully, slipping both the wrapping and bow under the chesterfield for safekeeping.

"Open it for heaven's sake, girl. We haven't all day. We need to get ready since we are going to the Finlays for dinner." Collin often spoke from his stomach.

"It's a bright green baby jumper," Kathy exclaimed. "How darling! Looks like it was hand-knitted. There's no name telling who it's from." She lifted the little suit and placed it over her belly. "Looks like a perfect fit. I'll bet it's from Liz. It looks like her handiwork."

Minutes later, Collin sported a new bamboo fishing rod and reel, Kathy held a silver bracelet inscribed *To Katherine with Love*, and Fiona cradled in her hand a carved wood-framed picture of Ryan and her on their wedding day.

"You did this," Fiona said, turning to her daughter and pointing at the frame. "It's a cruel gesture, seeing that it's Christmas."

"It's not my doing, Mother. Do you recognize it?"

"Of course, I recognize it, Katherine. I was there, wasn't I?"

"I mean, do you recognize the frame and all?"

"No that's new, and a fine expensive frame, I must say." Fiona gazed at the picture for a minute. "Doesn't your father look handsome? He cut quite a figure back then. Ah, but he's hardened since, the blaggard."

Kathy looked at Collin. *It must have been Father.* Collin shrugged his shoulders but came over and gave his wife a squeeze. Kathy twisted her fingers in front of her lips, as if to lock them shut with a key, and Collin nodded. But the look in his eyes revealed his thoughts to her. Her mother would really be upset if she thought her husband had been in the house. Despite her misgivings, Kathy thought it a grand and selfless show of support for the family at Christmas.

♣　♣　♣　♣

Number 10 Balsam Avenue by the beach was a cheery place when the O'Donnells arrived for Christmas dinner at noon. The Finlays had set a fine table as well as preparing a festive parlor. Norah, at four, with lovely olive skin and straight black hair, and two-year-old Dot, a curly blond, both in matching pink dresses, looked like pretty little dolls in a toy shop.

They immediately jumped up on their Unca Collie, and moments later they had him down on the parlor rug as their horsy. Collin bucked and caught the girls, one under each arm. Standing up with them as they squealed with delight, he said, "Did you make these ornaments on your tree, girls?" He set them down by the handsome seven-foot blue spruce.

Beaming from ear to ear, Dorothy cried, "I did that one." She was finally learning to speak some of her words. Collin saw that she was pointing at a green wooden tree ornament with *Dot* scrawled out in white letters.

"She's definitely Daddy's girl," Liz said, glancing over at her husband who had gotten out of his favorite chair to greet his guests.

Dot giggled and grabbed her father's trouser leg.

"What about me?" Norah bleated, holding up the end of her popcorn string draped around the spruce.

"Yes, dear. It's a fine garland, to be sure. If the dinner's a flop, we can always just eat it." Liz took Norah's hand, and together they dropped the end of the string back onto the branches. "You're more like me, Norah. More the seamstress and less the artist."

"What's a seamstress?"

"Someone who can thread a needle and string popcorn together, dear."

"Oh, I'm good at that, aren't I, Mommy?"

"I love all three of my girls." Sam, always the one to make peace, took both his daughters' hands and led them back to where Collin, now lounging near the crackling fire in the stone fireplace, was warming his hands.

"Sam and Liz, I am pleased to be invited into your cheery home," Fiona said, clasping their hands. "It has been quite a long time since I have heard the laughter of happy children." Fiona moved to the far wall near the kitchen, examining a wall-mounted painting. She pointed to it and asked, "Is this your work, Sam?"

"Yes, that's mine."

"Who are these figures in this carousel painting?"

"Those are my girls. I painted it at the Scarborough Amusement Park back in May, I think. That's right. It was the day that . . ." He stopped himself, realizing that he was about to bring up a very painful subject, one that might spoil Christmas for them all.

"Come and sit down, Fiona and Kathy." Liz waved to her husband. "Sam, you're a poor host, don't ya know. Please fetch the eggnog for our guests," she scolded, guiding Kathy's mother to the chesterfield. Liz insisted that the girls wait until after dinner to open the presents that the O'Donnells had brought them. "I'll get dinner on," Liz announced, as she disappeared into the kitchen. Kathy followed her.

While Liz was basting the turkey, Kathy shared, "Collin's having those nightmares again. This time he thinks he can see Claire in mortal danger in a battle of some kind, with soldiers milling about all around her, but there is one soldier trying to kill her."

"So is he all upset about it again, then? He looks fine today." Liz spooned some of the drippings over the top of the turkey breast.

"I managed to deflect his thinking after last night's episode."

"With a hearty breakfast?"

Kathy blushed in response.

"Really, dear. You ought to be more careful, you know, being this far along."

"You're the one to talk, with two children and another one on the way not two months behind me."

The women continued talking about their love lives with the husbands they adored while they finished the Christmas meal preparation. Once, Fiona popped her head in to ask if she could do anything to help. The women had to stop talking immediately for fear of offending her.

"You could ask Sam to pour the wine if you would be so kind, Fiona. I think that it's time to eat."

Once they were all seated at the table, Sam said, "Excuse me for a moment," and popped up, disappearing into his studio. Moments later, he reappeared with a great bouquet of Lilies of the Valley flowers in a glass vase, festooned with a big red bow, and he set it on the table in front of his wife. The girls squealed with delight, and Liz leaned forward to drink in the pungent smell of the flowers. "Well, I never. My favorites. How did you . . . ?"

"Hothouse grown, my love, 'specially for you at Christmas."

"They're beautiful, Sam. Thank you, darling," Liz gushed. She moved the vase to the center of the table, directly in front of little Norah.

"Your favorites, Mommy. They smell good," Norah exclaimed, pulling out a flower and sniffing it deeply.

"Yes, dear. I love them. Can we eat now?"

"Mommy, since you love them, and we love you, can everyone call you Lily from now on?"

"I suppose so. But everybody calls me Liz, and some even call me Mommy, you know." She smiled.

"But I like Lily," Norah said, pouting a little.

"How about Lil?" Sam broke in, always the mediator. "I like that name, too. Your mommy always smells so good, just like the flowers, doesn't she, girls?"

"Yes, Daddy." Norah was clearly pleased with herself. "Can we, Mommy, call you Lil?"

"And that way we only have to change one letter, a 'z' to an 'l'," Sam explained.

"Well, I suppose so, if you must," she beamed.

"Fine, then, it's Lil, who used to be called Liz. Let's eat now," Collin piped up.

Sam led the prayer once the bird and all the trimmings they could scrounge up during this time of war were on the dining room table. The girls started to giggle when they all held hands until Lil scolded them to be quiet. Collin eyed the brown sugar-covered sweet potato dish.

"Lord, thank you for coming to save us all, by your sacrifice on the cross. We are not wise men bearing gifts, but we love you all the same. Please look over our family, our friends, and especially all of our soldiers fighting for freedom in Europe. May they return to us victorious, safe and sound. And bless this food to our use. Amen."

The conversation during the meal of turkey, potatoes, and carrots centered on the upcoming two births. "I'd like to host a baby shower for the both of you," Fiona offered as she cut another piece of breast meat.

"We could hold it here," Sam suggested. "But when?"

"My baby is due in early March, and Lil's is due in late April, so why don't we have it on Valentine's Day?" Kathy was counting on her fingers.

"Norah, use your fork and not your fingers, girl."

"Yes, Mommy." The little girl dropped the piece of turkey back onto her plate and reached reluctantly for her fork. "I can never hold my fork right."

"Let me help you, Norah." Collin reached over and started cutting her meat for her. "There, is that better?"

"Yes. Thank you, Unca Collie."

"It would seem that our Lord's birth has stopped the war again," Sam commented, reaching over to grab the special Saturday edition of the *Toronto Telegram* from the side table.

Collin looked up from his cutting task. "How's that?"

"There was a wire telegraph message from our correspondents in Belgium overnight. Apparently King Alfred and Queen Elisabeth initiated a Christmas truce in the trenches outside their headquarters in Furnes, just like last year. The men from both sides were playing football, if you can believe that. Here, look in the late edition that I picked up at the tobacco shop this morning."

"Let me see that." Collin came around behind Sam and read the paper with him.

Kathy looked at Lil, alarmed. Collin was clenching his fists again, a sure sign of distress brought on from his fighting days back in Brooklyn as a youth.

"What is it, lad? It's just evidence that God works in mysterious ways." Sam turned to face his protégé. "He can't stop us from fighting, but He can still guide our thoughts and pause a war, if only briefly, especially on His own birthday."

"It was just a dream I had last night." Collin's voice trailed off and he looked down at his feet.

"Out with it, lad."

"It was Claire. She was on a battlefield where the soldiers on both sides were greeting each other."

Lil and Fiona stopped eating and turned to face the men at the end of the table.

"That is peculiar, I grant you. But it was just a dream, a coincidence," Kathy said, reaching for another potato and hoping for the best. But she knew this was a faint hope.

"One soldier pointed a gun at her . . . in my dream, I mean." Collin looked up at his mentor. "I had a terrible premonition."

"What happened after that, Collin?"

"I dunno. That's when I woke up."

Kathy knew that this wasn't going to end well. "Can we talk about the shower, please, and get back to eating this fine Christmas dinner?" Kathy cradled her abdomen. It seemed as if Claire would not let them forget, as she kicked violently.

"It seems too spooky to just be coincidence, Sam. I believe that she was trying to communicate with me to help her just before being shot. They say it can happen with siblings in mortal danger."

"Oh, come now, lad. You don't really believe that."

"Yes, I do." Collin looked stricken.

Kathy got up from the table and grabbed her husband's hand. "Come on. Sit right down and finish your dinner before it gets cold."

"I've got to wire Jack," Collin muttered through the rest of the meal. He didn't even seem to notice Lil's plum pudding with flaming brandy sauce, one of his favorites.

"Who's Jack?" Fiona asked Kathy privately in the washroom before coffee was served.

"Jack Jordan is the Manager of the Cunard office in Queenstown, Mother. He's the one who thinks that Claire may be alive in Ireland. Collin's been communicating with him from time to time."

"How would he think that?"

"It's a long story, but he thinks he tried to save Claire when the *Lusitania* was sinking. He was onboard. He also thinks he saw her at the Cunard office afterwards, but he is in a wheelchair and couldn't reach her in time so they could talk."

"Oh. Sounds pretty far-fetched to me, then."

"To me, too. But Collin feels so guilty about losing his sister when they were children back in Brooklyn."

Now Fiona was really confused.

"I'll tell you more about it and our trip to New York later."

"You went to New York?"

"Yes, Mother, I did, with Collin."

"Before you were married . . . alone, just you two?"

"Yes, Mother."

"Really, daughter. That's just not done." Fiona gave Kathy a look that could turn a person to stone.

"It is, nowadays, Mother. I did it, and I'm glad of it."

"When was this?" Fiona counted on her fingers.

"Last year at the beginning of July."

"Aha, I thought so. You see what can happen." Fiona pointed at her daughter's abdomen.

"Yes, and Claire will be a wonderful grandbaby, Mother."

After dinner, Collin absent-mindedly headed for the door when Norah seemed to jar him temporarily out of his mood. "C'mon, Unca Collie. Watch me open my present." Together they went to the tree and retrieved the red-wrapped dolly that Kathy had made with her pupils in the classroom as a sewing project. "Oh, I love her," Norah cried out. "See, Mommy. Her arms work." She hugged her Unca Collie. Then she remembered and moved on to kiss Kathy on the cheek. "Thank you. Thank you."

Dot looked crestfallen. Kathy went to her aid. "Here's one for you, too, Dot."

Soon both girls were playing house with their new dollies, Annabelle and Victoria. It was no coincidence that one doll had black hair and the other one blond.

"We really need to go," Collin said a few minutes later, when Kathy emerged from helping Lil wash up.

"But it's only two o'clock. Can't we stay a little longer?"

"No, I think these fine folks have probably had enough of us for one Christmas."

"Nonsense, lad. Have a cognac and put your feet up."

"The only place these feet are goin' is to the telegraph office."

"On Christmas? I doubt they're open, but you can try."

"Have to, darlin'. You and your mother can stay here 'til I get back, if you like."

"The nearest telegraph office is at Woodbine and Queen Street," Lil cautioned. She parted the curtains and looked out to the front walk. "It has started to snow again."

"It's only a mile." Collin donned his overcoat and galoshes . "I'll be back home by four."

With that he was gone, into the swirling snow. Kathy dropped down into Sam's chair by the fire, and baby Claire kicked up a fuss.

Chapter Thirteen
The Royals' Needs

December 25, 1915
De Panne, Belgium

*L*eopold ushered his prize catch into the Belgian field office. "Father, Mother, may I present Morgan and Tadgh McCarthy." Tadgh set his aroon down in front of the Royals, saluting while she curtseyed low. Freedom. "We are safe here behind the Allied lines," Leopold reassured them.

"It's just Morgan, Ma'am, not McCarthy."

"Really girl, no last name?" Queen Nurse Elisabeth, a stunning woman, regal even in army fatigues, asked, and then corrected herself. "Of course." She glanced at the couple. "The *Lusitania*. You were one of the lucky ones, weren't you. Amnesia, I understand." She reached forward, taking Morgan's hand and pulling her up.

Morgan was shocked that the Queen had that knowledge. "Saved only because of my Tadgh." She pulled a reluctant Tadgh forward and he stood next to her in front of the Queen.

"I see you brought her through again, my friend." King Albert offered Tadgh his hand. Morgan thought him a handsome ruler, with his five-foot-ten frame and a broad, handlebar moustache sculpting a sober countenance.

"Only because of your son, Your Majesty. He saved us just now." Tadgh started to bow.

"Dispense with that nonsense, Mister McCarthy. We're at war. I saw that you saved Leopold, and from where I sit, I am in your debt."

"We saved each other, Father." Leopold stood proudly.

"We must leave for De Panne," the Queen announced. "There is much to be done there, and the Front will still be here until tomorrow." She looked out onto the devastated battlefield in front of them where the combined troops were still celebrating. "At least for today, it cannot be called No Man's Land at Christmas."

"It's such a travesty, you know, the needless loss of life," Morgan said.

"That's our homeland over there, ravaged and violated." The resolute Queen pointed east beyond the trenches. "We will win it back before it's over."

"I'm sure you will, Your Grace," Morgan replied, looking into the Queen's steely gray eyes. She could understand that a cornered nation must fight, but she still thought that the war was a manufactured disaster.

The Belgian hospital in De Panne on the North Sea coast was situated just seven miles west of the Nieuwpoort Front and four miles from Furnes. It had been opened in the Grand Hôtel de l'Océan by Doctor Antoine Depage, master surgeon and chief physician to King Albert I. He had founded both the Belgian Red Cross and the International Surgical Society, the Queen explained, on their way from the Front. Albert and Elisabeth had established their residence on the top floor of this De Panne Hotel after retreating from Brussels through Antwerp and Ostend. Their small force of 65,000 men had held the line against the mighty German army at the Yser River, thereby maintaining control of a tiny northwest corner of their beloved country .

After Morgan and Tadgh washed their faces in the Royal quarters, the Queen introduced her new guests to her staff. "Morgan and Tadgh, let me introduce you to our dear friend Antoine Depage, the head of our hospital here in De Panne."

Morgan saw a rather distinguished gray-haired and bespectacled gentleman in a blood-spattered white coat. His moustache and goatee were still mostly black and full, attesting to his masculinity.

"Morgan, I have been looking forward to meeting and working with you. I understand you had an important nursing position at the Ostend hospital." Doctor Depage enthusiastically shook her hand as he spoke and then put his arm around her shoulder. "My dear, allow me to show you our facility."

Tadgh looked at Morgan, expecting her to protest. "We have to get home to Ireland as soon as possible, sir."

Elisabeth turned to Tadgh. "I'm afraid that is out of the question right now. We need you both to support our cause here in Belgium. We are hard pressed, as you know." She beckoned. "Morgan, come outside with me for a moment." The Queen guided Morgan out to the beachfront where they could be alone. The winter rollers off the North Sea crashed on the newly snow-covered beach, turning the landscape into a sandy slush.

"Doctor Depage lost his wife Marie in the *Lusitania* tragedy you know so well, my dear. She was on the ship with you, Morgan. She had been in the United States seeking funds for our cause. A very powerful woman. Marie was a compatriot. Tragically, her foot snagged in a rope on your doomed ship, and she was dragged under. Her body was one of the 289 found."

"How terrible, ma'am." The agonizing memories flooded Morgan's memory. "How did you know about me?"

"My friend in Bavaria. Your Tadgh must have mentioned it. It's good that he did because that has enabled me to convince Albert to mount your rescue. You see, Antoine has been soldiering on, but his wife's loss is taking its toll on him, I'm afraid. He is crucial to our success, Morgan. Albert relies on him. You can see that, can't you, my dear?"

"How can I help, ma'am?"

"When he heard about you and your experience on the *Lusitania*, his temperament changed for the better. You bear a remarkable resemblance to Marie, and I can see from his reaction that you remind him of her. Your skills and assistance could help him regain his spirit and make peace with his loss."

"I see, but I need to go with Tadgh."

"Tadgh is going to the Front. From what transpired today, Albert and I now want your man to be a guardian for our son Leopold."

What a mess. The Queen and King of Belgium need our help, command it in fact. We're being asked to fight for the Allies against Germany, all those boys whom I treated in Ostend. It's a good cause, but . . .

"I see that this comes as quite a shock to you, my dear. But surely you see the necessity."

"Yes, yes. Of course." What else could she say?

"Good. Come now, Morgan. Let's find you lodging at my residence."

"What about Tadgh?"

"He can come too, until Albert makes travel arrangements for him to go back to his Furnes headquarters at the Front."

Tadgh's questioning eyes told the story when they returned. Doctor Depage had left him alone at the entrance to the ward, waiting for the Queen's conversation to end.

"Come with us, Tadgh," the Queen directed, and they both followed.

Morgan and Tadgh were given two adjacent bedrooms at the far end of the Royals' top floor suite.

"I'll leave you two to freshen up. The bathroom is down that hallway to the right. We will have dinner clothes sent to your dressing rooms. Christmas dinner is at eight, and you will be our guests."

Tadgh followed Morgan into her room and closed the door. "What the hell is going on, for all that?"

"Is that how you greet me after we've been apart for over two months?" Morgan pouted.

Tadgh realized he'd made a tactical error. "Of course not, my love." He swooped her up in his tired arms, all the while never letting his hungry mouth leave hers. What a marvelous relief to be together again. Their lips and tongues explored each other shamelessly.

Tadgh's skin tasted salty, and Morgan giggled a little because she knew they had so little time before they would be summoned to dinner with the royalty. This was the only banquet she wanted, and she knew Tadgh felt the same from that look in his eye. He was far beyond words. Their feast of one another would have to begin, they were so hungry for one another's body.

They stripped their clothes from each other and kicked them away into a corner, standing once again in awe of their complete surrender to each other. Tadgh stroked and reveled in the mass of her ringletted tresses and went to his knees to kiss the dark silken hair that lightly clad her pubis. She held his head to her as he pushed his mouth in to kiss her and arched her back with a sudden gasp. They were helpless in their love, and the ability to be cool and controlled completely dissolved. He rose to meet her and buried himself deep into her body. He raised her in his arms with rough grace, and Morgan wrapped her long legs around his waist to stay with him as he lay her down on the bed. They moved together with an increasing ferocity that took their breath away, and when Tadgh spilled himself in her, they still rode each other until complete exhaustion. Tadgh refused to leave Morgan's body, so they contented one another with kisses and tastes while their breaths slowed and they fell into the sweetest rest.

When Tadgh and Morgan roused themselves at seven to prepare to meet the obligations to their hosts, she told him about her troubling conversation with the queen.

Tadgh was adamant. "I'm not going to fight for the bloody English."

"But the English aren't here in this neck of the woods."

"What woods? Even the trees have all been obliterated."

"You would be fighting for the beleaguered Belgians who have been so courageous in their outnumbered state."

"Yes, I can see that. But Casement's mission is to get German support for our cause."

"How is that going?"

"Not well. Sir Roger wants me to give that message to the Irish Volunteer leaders."

"But we should support the underdog."

"Belgium?"

"I don't think we have a choice at the moment."

"We need a plan, aroon, after some food and a long sleep. First things first."

They found robes in their rooms and quietly slipped down the hall together to the bathroom. It wouldn't do to come to dinner smelling of war and lovemaking. There in the lavatory they found kettles of water simmering on an ancient wood-burning stove. The Royals sure knew how to live, even in this temporary bivouac. Tadgh poured the bathwater, and Morgan melted into the steamy warmth, dozing off.

"Come, lass. It's 7:30. Let me wash you—then you can do me."

An aroused Morgan felt tingly under her lover's touch, and the bath cleansed body and soul. At eight on the dot, they appeared for dinner in the clothing that had been laid out for them in the dressing room adjoining their two rooms—a pressed Belgian officer's uniform for Tadgh and Belgian Red Cross nurse's uniform for Morgan. Clearly, the Queen had an eye for detail because both sets of clothes fit perfectly.

Queen Elisabeth was seated at the dining room table set up in their private chambers. It had been the bridal suite. She looked regal despite the wretched war. That evening at Christmas dinner, she was dressed in her khaki uniform, and her pendulous black pearl earrings softened her military appearance. Morgan noticed that her black, close-cropped hair framed a long face and aquiline nose, and that her penetrating gray eyes were both inquisitive and comforting. The woman's determined set of her mouth demonstrated that she was committed to the cause of her people.

Tadgh and Morgan were separated at the long mahogany dinner table, with the two men at one end and the women at the other. Leopold, seated halfway between, was attentive and quiet, absorbing his parents' demeanor and conversations. Although this was customary in European royal circles, Morgan realized that the regal family members were practicing divide-and-conquer tactics with them. She had assumed that the table settings would be frugal in a war zone, but they were using fine bone china and silver flatware. There was only one servant, and the kitchen staff was limited, the Queen told her. Morgan thought, What a difference one day could make. Just the night before, she was with Gerda and the boys, eating a frugal meal on simple crockery plates. The love flowed freely and Jesus was in the room. In contrast, here there was formality, reserved opulence, and a feast by comparison. Morgan would prefer dining with Gerda and the boys over this display any day of the week.

Queen Nurse was trying to explain. "This is a special occasion, Christmas, my dear Morgan. At the Front we eat what the other soldiers eat, no more and no less. We do have our own personal latrine facilities, however."

"Tell me, Tadgh, about how you ended up captured by the Germans in Ostend." King Albert asked, between bites of Belgian lamb, one of the delicacies he could still afford to eat.

Tadgh explained the loss of their boat, his injury, and their capture by the U-boat crew, careful not to discuss Irish politics.

"So you weren't a part of the Irish Volunteers regiment here in France, then."

"No, sir."

"Why is that, lad?"

Morgan could barely hear their conversation, but she could see that Tadgh was about to boil over and speak. She hoped to defuse the situation and said, "We're fishermen, sir. Politics does not put food on the table."

"Well, now's your chance to make amends, lad. You will come with me tomorrow and be guardian to Leopold. We depart after breakfast."

"Why not leave your son out of this, Your Majesty? It would be much safer, especially if he is your successor."

"Nonsense. He must build his character, just as I did, and like my father before me. We are fighting for our country and its people, and we all must be committed to that cause."

"But fourteen years old."

"Do you know how old Joan of Arc was when she led her country?" Leopold asked Tadgh, turning to his father for support.

"No, lad."

"Sixteen at the Siege of Orleans in 1428, sir."

King Albert beamed at his son.

"Was she, indeed?" Tadgh certainly couldn't argue with that. He could protect the boy without fighting for the English. But they had to get home to Ireland. Tadgh took a bite of lamb and a gulp of wine.

They had decided that they would sleep together, Queen Nurse be damned. They would be separated once again in the morning, exposed to the direct peril of war.

"Is our revolution going to be as bloody as this travesty?" Morgan asked when they had returned to her room for the night and crawled into bed.

"I suspect so, but on a much smaller scale, lass. The English won't give up Ireland easily."

"Is there no way to negotiate a solution, then?"

"None whatsoever. Bloody Redmond thinks we can, but it's useless. They're never going to approve Home Rule. They just threw out that carrot to get our men to fight for the Allies in the war over here. And I saw many of our men cowering in a German war camp. They'd rather be slaves to the British than escape their captivity and fight for our salvation. No. The English will not relinquish their Irish prize without a monumental fight. You can be sure of that."

"But all this suffering and death."

"Man has fought for territory and religious freedom for centuries. It is our nature and our passion."

"Do you really believe that? You saw all those broken men, on both sides. All those families torn asunder. You saw Gerda and her boys, and what is happening to their family, for God's sake."

"It can't be helped. Too much is at stake. All our valiant ancestors who fought for our freedom and a Gaelic way of life. We can't let their sacrifices die with them. We must drive the English out of Ireland."

"Even if it kills you?"

"Yes. Even if it kills all of us."

"Well, I think it's wrong. There must be another way. I'm not saying that I won't support you, Tadgh, but I can't condone all this slaughter."

"Then that's where we part ways, Morgan."

Tadgh had had enough strife for one day. "We aren't out of the woods by any stretch of the imagination. Let's not fight over this, aroon. We need some sleep."

"I agree, but this conversation is not finished by any means. I don't know who I really am, whether I'm Irish, or English, but I do know that I was trained to save lives, not to take them."

"All right. Go to sleep now."

Morgan didn't say another word and turned her back to him, pulling the linen sheets up around her head. She felt a gulf widen between them, larger than the gap she made between their bodies in the bed. One that may never reconcile.

Tadgh couldn't go to sleep even though his body was exhausted. He didn't like arguing with Morgan, but it couldn't be helped. He knew she would be loyal to him and his cause, but obviously, she didn't like what had to happen, not one little bit.

He needed a plan, and it wouldn't come to mind. His head was uncharacteristically spinning. Maddening.

He had to get help, but from whom? Clearly, the King and Queen weren't going to help them get home. Neither was Doctor Depage. They were at least in a free country, but they definitely weren't free. It would appear that he could be shot as a deserter if they tried to escape, and God knows what they would do to Morgan. Damn bad decision to head west across the Western Front. He wondered if it would have been better if they had taken the chance to cross the border into the neutral Netherlands, just as he had done a day and a half before. But that would have left them on the eastern side of the British Naval blockade, which had sealed off the northern side of the North Sea. Then they would have been boxed in east of the Dover Barrage.

Tadgh couldn't fly an aeroplane, so that method of escape was out of the question, unless he commandeered a Belgian pilot at gunpoint. Tadgh toyed with the idea and then decided it was not practical, considering Morgan's safety and the size of the dual cockpits. And besides that the aeroplanes didn't have the range to get to Ireland.

That left a boat rescue. First they'd have to travel west through France to the coast. If they could get to Le Havre, the second largest French seaport, they'd be west of the barrage. Maybe they'd have a chance, even though it would likely be teeming with English sailors and vessels—ships for the stealing?

It would be more certain if there was a friendly boat waiting for them.

What about Wiggins, their Beamish & Crawford Brewery ally, from Cork City? He had helped them get the munitions to Dublin at the time of O'Donovan Rossa's funeral. Would he be allowed to send a ship to Le Havre? The captain of his fleet, Martin Murphy, who got them out of Howth that time, would have probably done it dozens of times. Why not now, with the war on?

By three in the morning, Tadgh had a plan. It would take time, and it depended on getting the word out. He felt Morgan stir against him, her right arm draped over his abdomen. Tadgh allowed himself the luxury of a catnap against her sensuous body. At least the King and Queen didn't know that unmarried lovers were sleeping together under their roof during this terrible time of war. Or, did they?

When Morgan awoke at seven, nearly dawn, she first saw Tadgh seated at the writing desk hastily scribbling a letter on paper he must have found in the desk drawer. She got up and enfolded him with her bare arms, resting her head on his broad back as he sat there. "What are you writing, my love?" She kissed the top of his head.

"Are you still mad at me, Morgan?"

"No, why should I be?"

"But last night . . ."

"I was really tired and disheartened. So were you. Let's leave it at that, for now."

She at least realizes that we need to work together to get to freedom, Tadgh thought. "Listen to me. We don't have much time this morning."

"Not before you kiss me, silly." She leaned over his shoulder and turned his face towards hers.

Tadgh stood up and turned to face her, reaching around and pinching her backside in the process. "You vixen." He pulled her in and could feel her breasts against him as he pressed her lips to his own before she could answer. She virtually melted into him; he held her up and rocked her in his arms. "When are the Royals expecting us for breakfast?"

"They said eight o'clock." She murmured something else unintelligible into his chest.

"We can make them wait." He teased her nipple with his lips.

"Mmmm. I'd like nothing better, but they're our rescuers."

"We're still their prisoners, Morgan." Tadgh stepped back. She had broken the spell, and now so had he.

"Get your clothes on, then. We need to talk."

While Morgan dressed in her nurse's uniform, Tadgh outlined his plan. "They're not going to let me go anywhere before I have to leave for the Front. So you will need to take this note to a telegraph office later today when you can break free. It seems that they trust you, but not me."

"Can't we just escape now?"

"Without a plan in place, we wouldn't get too far. Then I'd be tried and possibly shot as a deserter."

"But you never joined their army."

"They think I should have. Therefore, I have. So listen. You will get a response, and we will be allowed to write to each other. We need a code. Do you remember the one with Padraig?"

Morgan frowned in concentration. "Yes."

"Good. I will get us land transportation when the time comes. We will meet at the telegraph office, not here at the hotel. It could take a while, maybe a couple of weeks, Morgan."

"Don't you go getting yourself killed."

"It's not my intention, aroon."

"You must make sure you are safe, for my sake."

"I'll just tell those Germans to stop shooting off their artillery then."

"Don't you joke about such things."

"Says you, popping your head up out of the trench yesterday to see what could be seen."

"Well, don't *you* do anything risky, then."

With that, they went down to breakfast and uncertain separation once again.

Chapter Fourteen
Gas Attack

December 26, 1915

German General Staff Headquarters, Berlin

On **Boxing Day,** Gronski had gotten the word about Gruber's death and McCarthy's escape from Jacobs, his direct report spy positioned in King Albert's headquarters. Gruber had been a good soldier, not an easy mark. Pity to lose him. McCarthy must certainly be a foe to be reckoned with. That damn king and queen were likely to be allies in this case. They'll consider McCarthy to be one of Redmond's Irish Volunteer POWs and will send him back to the Front. Gronski was sure of it. The Belgians needed all the help they could get. McCarthy most likely wouldn't stay there for long—only until he had an escape plan for himself and the girl. Whatever message Casement may have given the man must not reach Casement's bosses. It wouldn't be favorable to the GGS or to his own future.

Gronski got Ritter on the military telephone. "Why didn't you kill McCarthy after Gruber was knifed?"

"A gunshot would have endangered our troops who were honoring the Christmas cease-fire on the battlefield, sir. Many would have been killed on both sides."

"You could have killed him in direct combat."

"I wanted to stay alive to be able to report back to you, sir. You would have been completely in the dark about actions in the field had I been killed in the attempt."

Gronski knew that this was cowardice talking, but he needed to have this operative in Ostend, at least until he could replace Gruber. There was no other timely choice. He would have to use the new gas that his laboratory had been testing to incapacitate the Belgians. One of the benefits of being the head of the Sektion Politik was the arsenal of weapons he'd been developing. *I've been dying to try this new weapon on the enemy, anyway.*

"Do you still have that turncoat accessible to us in the Belgian trenches?"

"Yes sir—Hans Pauwels. He is a communications officer who has a brother in Limburg. We've threatened to kill the brother if our man

Hans doesn't cooperate. We can send each other coded messages if I am in our own trenches."

"How?"

"By torch at night with a code we invented."

"Good. I want him to confirm that McCarthy is still there and to make clear what his duties are. Report back."

Ritter knew that he wouldn't get a third chance to prove himself.

Morgan spent most of the day in orientation at the hospital after Tadgh, the King, and Leopold left for Furnes. Doctor Depage made sure that she was close-at-hand to witness some of his amputations. She didn't like the way the doctor eyed her. It made her uncomfortable.

Finally, at mid-afternoon, she asked for a break. The small seaside village of De Panne had a beautiful sandy beach but lacked a deepwater port or even docks. Morgan found it to be the kind of place to while away a winter's afternoon in peace, if one could forget the war. It was the dead of winter in so many ways. Fortunately, the weather had warmed a few degrees, taking the frigid chill from the air. Most of the snow had gone, leaving only sand and mud. Morgan preferred the pristine snow. It seemed to partially cleanse the horrors of the countryside.

The small country store contained a telegraph and post office, and after talking to the postmaster, she determined that letter delivery out of the immediate vicinity was sporadic at best, but the telegraph was still quick and reliable.

Morgan watched Tadgh's message go out to Cork City without question, but she was suspicious of the telegraph operator. Something about his inability to meet her eye. He just may be relaying all correspondence to the King, for all she knew. She gave the man a fictitious Belgian-sounding name to cover her tracks.

> *Your Beamish Boy is alive west of the Front. Stop. He and partner*
> *need extraction by the normal method from French LH. Stop. Can*
> *you assist and if so when. Stop. Hold response at De Panne P.O. Stop.*

When she returned to the hospital Doctor Depage was looking for her.

"Where have you been, my dear?" He grabbed her hand and jerked her toward the operating room.

Morgan didn't like how that felt. "For a walk, doctor, on my break. I wanted to see the town."

"Please don't do that again without asking first. I may need your assistance at any moment. Do you understand?"

"Perfectly."

"I would like you to join me for supper this evening at eight in the main dining room. I've had some proper clothes sent up to your room." He put his other hand on her back to guide her through the doorway.

Morgan's unease grew at the doctor's words and actions. His invitation seemed to hint at something more than a professional relationship.

Tadgh hunkered down in the same trench they had come through just a day before near sundown. He was in the process of showing the Prince how to clean a Luger when the first evening artillery shells tore a hole in the trench.[9] It made him jump even though Leopold didn't flinch in the slightest. *Who is looking after whom?*

"Lieutenant McCarthy, don't worry. They won't try to cross the field at night." Leopold took up a shovel and headed down the trench on a run. "C'mon. We've got repairs to do."

After slogging a hundred feet down the zigzagged muddy trench, the two arrived at the cave-in. Railroad ties that had previously shored up the eight-foot walls of the trench now lay askew, and the mud had slid and oozed down until it filled the trench to a depth of four feet. Two soldiers frantically dug at the sludge, using their bare hands, scooping dirt like dogs after their buried bones, but these bones happened to be attached to the flesh of soldiers. Only legs were visible from the knees down, one pair kicking wildly while another set lay still as a tomb. Tadgh thought he heard shouts from the other side of the pile.

Tadgh and Leopold immediately jumped in to help. Tadgh grabbed the kicking legs and pulled, despite the pain in his back, and Leopold used the shovel to dig on either side of the legs, to no avail. Moments later another soldier arrived and grabbed one of the legs. Together they pulled with all their might, their feet slipping and sliding in the muck. Finally, between the two of them, they managed to drag the slime-covered body from the suffocating mud. Tadgh squeezed his eyes shut from the sight of the soldier's mud-stopped mouth and eyes.

The soldier flipped his fallen comrade on his back and dug the stinking mud from his mouth. He pounded, cursing him roundly for deserting, in death, his brothers in battle. A strangled cough dislodged yet more mud from the soldier's throat, so he could take a breath. The legs kicked again and the downed soldier breathed once and spat mud. Leaning over the man, the soldier kept up the chest pumping until the man was clearly breathing on his own.

Other soldiers arrived to assist Leopold, and within minutes, they had uncovered the other body. He was dead, most likely from the ghastly wound that split his forehead. Tadgh could only imagine the panic of being buried alive. He hoped for the dead soldier's sake that the blow to his head had killed him instantly before the muck engulfed him. No one would ever know, and the family would likely be told only that he died in the line of duty.

Twenty minutes later, the soldiers had cleaned out the muck and debris and had shored up the trench. It was odd that an assault by the enemy had not followed the artillery barrage. Three soldiers had been smothered in this one shell attack, and only one had survived. They finally took the wounded soldier to the small hacked-out underground shelter in the side of the trench, just as rain started to fall. There he sat, still coated in mud, traumatized, shivering and in shock .

During the next three days, Tadgh assisted with several artillery-caused cave-ins, another one occurring within 30 feet of their position. They were all rats in a hole. If they weren't being shot at, they were being poisoned. The food at the Front was abominable with barely edible dried beef and sodden bread, which at least offset its staleness. Soldiers developed scurvy and contracted typhus, so the gas masks were often used to protect soldiers from their contagious mates. And ablution was a testy subject with latrines unfit for human use. But then life expectancy in the trenches was low anyway. Soldiers must have dreamed of home and loved ones as a way to maintain their sanity, with few thinking that they would ever see any of their loved ones again.

At least if you died in the trenches you wouldn't be trapped below the surface of the sea in a submarine. Then he thought about the cave-in. Dying, starving for breath probably wasn't much different whether it was under water or under a deluge of mud. What a waste of humanity. But following orders—now *that* was civilized.

Leopold informed him that these trenches had been at a standoff for almost a year now, with neither side being able to advance. What a disaster. Thousands of men dying without anything to show for it except holding the defensive line. Obviously, the munitions and ammunition manufacturers were making a killing as well as causing that killing.

Tadgh thought about his homeland and the need for a revolution, likely resulting in the obliteration of his beautiful green countryside. They would need to go back to the guerilla hit-and-run tactics of warfare used by the Clans. The English wouldn't be allowed to dig a trench around Dublin. Surely they wouldn't bring artillery to bear on the capital, at least not as devastating as these German Howitzers. Or would they? Tadgh decided that he had to tell Padraig Pearse about the horrors of these battle tactics in the trenches of Europe. The Irish Republican Brotherhood war council would have to evaluate the potential impact on its own people.

On the sixth day in the field, January first, Tadgh received a cryptic letter from Morgan at the same time that the Allied soldiers were getting mail from home via their communications officer Pauwels. It had come in to King Albert's field office the day before from De Panne. A message for a new year.

Mavorneen. How are you? I am fine. Wiggins overjoyed. Superiors had been worried. LH Mackarel 9 at 1 MM, B&C.

Tadgh smiled. She remembered that "mackarel" meant human cargo pickup and the time designated the number of days earlier than stated. So January eighth it would be. Tadgh fired back a letter that Pauwels took to the King's headquarters. *Excellent, aroon. Life here is bearable. Leopold is fine. 9 at 2.*

♣ ♣ ♣ ♣

Ritter heard from Pauwels on the third of January. *He's here. Guarding LIII. Letter interceptions. Girl LH Mackarel 9 at 1 MM, B&C and McC 9 at 2.*

What did the numbers mean? Could the man be less cryptic? Ritter in turn passed the message on to Gronski. Let *him* figure it out.

Gronski didn't know what the message meant except that it looked like some major event was going to happen on January 9. Not if he could help it. He'd been wanting to try out that new chemical that the laboratory had been working on. Phosgene would be more deadly than the chlorine gas they had been using, and its faint odor of moldy hay was barely detectable. The only drawback to this lethal respiratory killer was that in some cases, it might take up to 24 hours to take full effect, allowing victims the ability to fight on after dispersal. It depended on the victim. Some of the test prisoners had succumbed slowly, revealing this unfortunate characteristic.

Gronski ordered the projectiles containing phosgene to be delivered from the laboratory to the Front opposite Furnes by the fifth. There was still time.

If the wind was easterly, they would release the phosgene at dawn on the sixth so that the following German attack would come out of the sun. The new hooded gas masks with the mica eyepieces should protect his own troops against the phosgene, but that would remain to be seen. Ritter would be assigned to capture, or if necessary, kill McCarthy during the attack. If Ritter would be killed or if he deserted, then Pauwels would have to finish the job. They would lose a covert operative in the enemy camp, but that couldn't be helped.

Morgan had her hands full at the hospital. The work replaced her efforts at Ostend, which had been difficult enough. The wounded and maimed boys just had a different uniform and language—Belgian, and French with a few Canadians and no Irish. Her biggest problem remained with Doctor Depage. As Queen Nurse had remarked, Morgan was the spitting image of his dead wife. The clothes sent up for her fit her nearly perfectly, and she surmised they were Marie's. It was painful to wear them in the evenings when Morgan broke free of the operating room because it made her feel like her drowned counterpart, and that brought her back to the awful sinking and the maddening lapse of memory of anything earlier in her life. But they were beautiful custom-sewn clothes, undoubtedly acquired before the war. Unfortunately, the gorgeous shoes, one size too small, pinched her feet. As far as she knew, Morgan had never worn clothing so magnificent before. She picked an emerald dress, combined with low-heeled black leather pumps, and reluctantly put them on that first night. She surveyed herself in the full-length mirror and had to admit she looked stunning, setting her smoky green eyes on fire, but this made her feel like she was cheating on Tadgh. Then she decided that she was playing a necessary role for the moment.

That evening the Queen had passed her in the hallway of the Royal apartments. "You look very fetching, girl, just like Marie. Enjoy this respite from the war."

Morgan had bowed and then felt terribly guilty.

The good doctor had been a gentleman at their private dinners, but he gravitated toward female companionship, especially with a woman who reminded him of his dear deceased wife. Morgan could understand that. What if she lost Tadgh? She knew the feeling from her time in Ostend.

Morgan pitied Depage but admired him for his knowledge of surgery, medicine in general, and his work in establishing the Boy Scouts. Morgan was stretched in carrying on a knowledgeable conversation on most of these subjects, except where she could compare the doctor's amputation techniques to those of Doctor Heinrich's. There were certainly differences. It appeared that Depage had a higher survival rate than the Germans, and he seemed pleased with this. Morgan liked him very much. He seemed a tough man in an equally tough situation. In just a week she had become not only a responsible operating room nurse but had also become his compulsory companion. During these dinners, he kept talking about Marie, and how much he missed her. She refused to answer his persistent questions about the horrors of the sinking by saying that she had amnesia. Dwelling on the past was very destructive to his psyche. She used this defense in part to protect her own well-being as well as his. Therein lay the problem. She sensed that her leaving him would be painful, and she didn't want to hurt him further.

Morgan agonized over whether to confide in him. Would he understand and would it help him, or would he get angry and expose Tadgh and her to the King and Queen as enemies or possibly deserters? Clearly, talking directly to the Royals would be a mistake. Tadgh would be back on the seventh. She decided to stay quiet for the time being.

On January 5, the enemy had been inactive all day, and all was quiet at the Front. By evening, the wind came up from the east. The night was clear, with a full moon illuminating No Man's Land with an eerie glow. Tadgh thought the scene resembled what the moon's surface must be like—cold, empty, alien, and lonely. Each of the Belgian soldiers in his section of the trench was uncharacteristically quiet, alone with his own thoughts.

Even Leopold was silent. Finally, he said, "They're up to something over there. Usually quiet means that they'll try to attack us."

"Have they ever taken your trench on this side?"

"Not yet. Thanks Be to God. But we're worried about their weaponry development."

"Such as?"

"They're starting to manufacture armored vehicles. They call them tanks. If they bring them to the Western Front, they'll surge right over us. I've seen drawings. They roll along on giant metal belts that can breach our trenches like a steamroller and the soldiers are protected inside metal clad walls. They carry their own artillery that can swivel. Evil machines."

"Surely the Allies are also developing tanks as well."

"Of course. It will depend which army can field them in quantity first."

"I have some limited experience of the same situation in a different military service. Submarines."

"Really, Tadgh? You were on a submarine?"

"Not just any submarine. I was captured by a German U-boat. That's how Morgan and I got to Belgium."

"Tell me about that. Submarines fascinate me."

"I was injured and delirious for a time, so my knowledge is very sketchy. Submarines are very confining, and if the boat fails while submerged, it's a terrible way to go. Until this time, the Germans have had control of the sea with their U-boats, sinking merchant and military ships at will. Now the Allies have developed better detection techniques to find them under water and have started using depth charges launched from surface ships to destroy them. Morgan says we were almost sunk by one while I was unconscious. The tide will be turning against the Germans."

"Interesting. How about these gas masks?" Leopold unbuckled his mask from his belt.

"You know that in retaliation the British tried using chlorine at the Battle of Loos not thirty miles south of here back in September. The wind blew against us, and the German shelling hit some unused cylinders in the British trenches. It was a disaster. Their primitive flannel masks got hot, fogged up, and the troops who took them off were gassed. That's a terrible way to die."

Leopold looked over the newer PH helmet that they had recently been issued. "This tube helmet is made with two layers of flannel hood," he said, rubbing the material between his thumb and middle finger. "This one on the outside is treated with the chemicals sodium phenolate and something else to protect against chlorine and hydrocyanic acid. The inner layer protects my head because the chemicals attack the fabric. There's an exhaust valve fed from a metal tube that I have to hold in my mouth to avoid the fogging problem, and the two circular mica eyepieces are small, restricting my vision. What a way to fight a battle."

Tadgh took the crude mask and tried to put it on. "You know all the details, Leopold, but will it work for any new gases that the Germans invent? Besides, it doesn't look like it would fit *your* head very well."

Leopold echoed Tadgh's doubt. "It doesn't really fit because I'm still growing. I'm only fourteen, you know." He grinned.

"Yes, I know. You are brave enough to fight for your country at such a tender age, but still two years younger than Joan of Arc, don't ya know, lad."

"We do what we have to for our country and people, no matter the age."

Tadgh saw his opening. "I agree with you, Your Highness. What would you say if I told you that I am a freedom fighter for my own country?"

"Of course you are. That's why you're here."

"Not exactly. I'm here to help you save your country, that's true enough. But I really need to go home to save my own country, which continues to be in peril."

"What? Ireland? Are you at war there?"

"Not exactly, but the situation with the British is very much the same as if you Belgians were to be defeated by the Germans. They would then treat your citizens like vermin to be exterminated for centuries to come. What would you think of that?"

"Don't talk that way. We will not be defeated and that's that. And if we were, we'd rise up against the *Boche* until we defeated them."

"Precisely, lad. I can assure you that England was a terrible conqueror, and it is still our oppressor in my homeland. That's why we have to rise up, for all that."

"Is that why you were in Germany?"

He was getting too close to the truth. "No. When Morgan and I were captured by a U-boat in the Celtic Sea and brought to Belgium and Germany, we were prisoners there, and we are prisoners still."

"Prisoners? You're not in a detention camp."

"But we can't leave to go and fight our own war, can we, now."

"I see. What if I were to talk to Papa?"

"That wouldn't work, lad, but thanks for offering. Your Da and Ma have to focus on your own country, and you need all the help you can get. I understand that, believe me."

"You should just go then. I am old enough to look after myself. I was doing it before you arrived."

"Yes, and admirably, I understand. If I leave, I will be branded a deserter and shot if I'm captured, don't you see."

"But you must get back to your own battle, for your own country, I mean."

"Yes, lad, I must try, so I have talked to Corporal Janssens down the line who seems trustworthy. You know him, right? I asked him to support you, Your Highness, if something were to happen to me, and he agreed."

"But I don't need—"

"It will please your Papa."

"All right, then. For his sake. I won't tell on you."

"Thank you, lad. Now let's see if we can cinch down this infernal gas mask so that it fits you properly."

The artillery barrage started just before dawn, lighting up the sky and rearranging No Man's Land. The whir of an incoming round was menacing, and if a soldier could hear it, he had to duck. The explosion, when it hit, was deafening—if close enough, eardrum shattering. There was no time to rush to the assistance of some poor mates buried or otherwise wounded. At least it wasn't raining.

"They're coming this time," Leopold predicted, donning his helmet. "Good Brodie steel, this. They were designed by a Brit and issued to us not three months ago, you know, a great improvement on the soft peak fabric caps that were useless against the German's weaponry."

Tadgh didn't want to say what he thought. A machine gun burst would generally obliterate the entire head. He sniffed the air. "That's strange. I smell moldy hay. There's none of that around here." His nostrils started to tingle and he wanted to sneeze. "Put on your gas masks," he yelled down the line.

"Why? There's no yellow chlorine gas that I can see," Leopold replied, looking up to the edge of the trench.

"Just do it!" Tadgh ordered, his gas mask already in place. "Get up on the fire-step. Now!" He pointed to a platform some three feet off the mucky bottom of the eight-foot-deep trench that allowed soldiers to monitor the enemy's defenses.

Tadgh rushed off to warn the others, some of whom were already coughing and rubbing their eyes. "Put on your masks, for heaven's sake. Get up out of the bottom of the trench," he yelled.

When he trotted back to Leopold, the lad's gas mask was in place, and he was talking to a soldier Tadgh had not seen before. He leaned down to say, "Tadgh, meet Hans Pauwels, our communications officer."

Tadgh reached up and checked Leopold's mask, pulling the straps tighter. Then he shook the soldier's hand. He couldn't see the man's eyes, a signal of a man's character, behind the mica lenses. Jumping up on the fire-step with the other two, Tadgh took a chance and peered over the top. Incoming shells but no manned attack yet. The sun was up, and it was hard to see.

"It may be some new kind of colorless gas. I can smell it, right enough. Keep your mask on." Tadgh surveyed the trench. Some men crouched down on the fire-step, waiting. Others in the bottom of the trench appeared in distress, doubled up, heads between their knees. *This gas must be heavier than air.*

Without warning, the barrage stopped. "Get ready," Leopold said, fixing his bayonet. "Here they come," he announced, poking his head up above the edge of the trench.

The men on the fire-step stood and unleashed a volley of bullets at the Germans who were snaking through their barbed wire. Many died, caught and tangled in the wire, but many made it through and rushed across the field, shooting as they came. The Germans were gaining ground, almost breaching the barbed wire at the Belgian trench. It was time to meet the foe before they descended upon them.

"Here we go," Leopold shouted as he scrambled up out of the trench with his comrades. Tadgh stayed right beside him, covering him if necessary. During the next deadly minutes, the onslaught began, with men falling to the left and right. One Belgian beside Tadgh took a direct hit to the head, his brains splattering out of the side of his gas mask as he sank to his death. Three Germans approached the lad. Tadgh dispatched them all with his Belgian Mauser 1889 rifle, mercifully bayoneting the wounded.

Suddenly a new wave of Belgians emerged from the trench. *Where did they come from?* Tadgh realized at that moment that Belgians were using the German tactic of Defense in Depth but without the second trench. No wonder so few soldiers staffed the trench. The small German force was overwhelmed. A whistle blew and the enemy turned and ran back toward their own trench. Many Germans fell into the barbed wire and were impaled as the Belgians shot and ran after them. Those Germans who were unable to crawl back through the openings into their trenches were shot where they were sprawled. It was a slaughter, but not without Belgian casualties bloodying the field. Tadgh and Leopold reached two such unfortunate soldiers writhing in pain. Shouldering their rifles, they each grabbed hold of a fallen soldier intending to bring both of the men back to the safety of the trench.

"Not so fast." It was Pauwels who had emerged from the Belgian trench, rifle pointed at them.

"What's the meaning of this, Hans?" Prince Leopold demanded, taking a step toward Pauwels who wore the communications insignia patch on his right arm sleeve.

"I have to save my brother, Your Highness. Do not try to stop me." He stood only twenty feet away, his rifle now pointed toward Tadgh, with young Leopold between him and his target. "Step out of the way, Leopold. I don't want to shoot you."

Tadgh was at a disadvantage, hands occupied in holding his fallen comrade, his Luger holstered.

"I have to kill him, or they'll kill my brother," the communications officer went on.

"Who will, Pauwels? Who are *they*?" Tadgh stepped forward.

"The Germans at the POW camp."

"Who's pulling the strings, eh? Gronski, is it?" Tadgh asked calmly and saw Pauwels twitch his head at the mention of the would-be assassin's name. "I thought as much. I've been in Limburg POW camp. They don't shoot prisoners for no reason." Tadgh knew damn well that Gronski could order someone shot with a well-placed telephone call.

Leopold lunged for Pauwel's rifle just as the man pulled the trigger. He sliced his hand on the bayonet. The deflected shot rang out, and Tadgh felt pain at the right side of his forehead. In one fluid motion Tadgh let go of the soldier from his right hand, unholstered his Luger, and dropped into the mud. As Pauwels was swinging his rifle around for another try, Tadgh shot him cleanly between his eyes. He collapsed immediately at Leopold's feet.

Tadgh jumped up in a moment, pulled off his helmet and looked at the damage, whistling softly. A hole had punctured it on the side, so it was useless now, anyway. He felt blood trickling down his cheek, and his fingers touched it just above his right eyebrow. The moldy hay smell was gone. Then he noticed the Prince, holding his hand, with blood gushing from it. Tadgh took quick action. He pulled the dead Pauwel's scarf from around his neck and bound the Prince's hand securely. "Press down on this. Let's get you back in the trench now, safer than out here."

Leopold insisted on helping the injured soldier back through the barbed wire opening with his good arm, and down into the trench. Tadgh did likewise, dragging the other soldier with him. They left Pauwels lying grotesquely in the mud of No Man's Land, a man just trying to save his kin, but an enemy nonetheless.

By the time they reached the relative safety of the trench, the fighting had subsided. Many men in the trench were stricken by the gassing, with eye and throat irritation. Some without gas masks had succumbed, and lay still in the muck. The gas had indeed dispersed, as medics jumped down from behind the line to assist with the fallen.

The scarf wrapped around Leopold's hand, soaked red and dripping, had not stopped the bleeding. A young medic, recognizing the Prince, rushed to his assistance. He immediately applied disinfectant and bandages to the wound.

Tadgh removed Leopold's gas mask. "You look very pale, Your Highness."

"I feel quite faint." With that, the Prince's knees buckled.

Tadgh scooped him up, surprised by how feather light the young man seemed. "Where is your ambulance?"

"A quarter mile behind the line, at the end of that road."

"I'll take the Prince back to the field hospital, lad. Give me the keys."

"Yes, sir. There's a lot of work I can do here, and I can ride back in another ambulance."

As Tadgh walked out of the trench with Leopold in his arms, he looked back onto the battlefield, strewn grotesquely with deceased and dying soldiers from both sides amidst the mud, craters, and barbed wire. Except for the occasional shout of a medic or groan from the fallen, the wasteland, including the enemy trench, returned to its grave silence. Both sides honored the process of collecting their wounded and dead, dragging them back into rat holes dug into the scarred earth. A fog off the coast settled in, draping the dead in a macabre veil.

Just another day in the trenches, Tadgh thought. No side won, no ground taken. And they had all been guinea pigs while the masterminds, this time likely Gronski, the head of German chemical warfare, tried out another lethal poison. The terrifying futility of it all. What a waste of mankind.

Chapter Fifteen
Withdrawal

January 6, 1916
De Panne, Belgium

Tadgh strode into the ward a day early with young Leopold by the arm, handing the Prince over to an orderly. "Look after his hand."

"My God, Tadgh. You're alive!" Morgan rushed to embrace him. "But you're bleeding." She pulled him aside to the triage station and cleaned his grazed forehead wound with a sterile cloth. "Not another head wound, is it."

"Just a nick, don't ya know. I'm fine, aroon."

Morgan administered some salve and finished binding his head with gauze. "Just like the shoulder wound at the B&C Brewery, Tadgh? You thought you were just fine, then, too. Honestly, you men, your guns, and your bravado."

He swept her up in his arms and held her tight, her heart pumping hard against his chest. "I promised you I would be all right, and I am, can't you see, lass. What's all the fuss about?"

After a lingering kiss, she murmured in his ear, "It would appear that you didn't handle your assignment very well, mavorneen." She meant the Prince's wound, but he must have thought she meant the kiss as he covered her mouth with his lips so she couldn't speak more. Her nursing sensibilities kicked in. "I meant Leopold." Then the reverie ended.

"He'll be all right as soon as you sew up his hand and give him some nourishment. But you're right. I was supposed to keep him from harm, but it was Leopold who saved me from death by his quick action again." Tadgh told her what had happened, including the German use of a new chemical.

"I'd better go take good care of him, hadn't I then." She pulled away from his arms.

"Aye. Do that lass, then come back to me." He winked, then turned serious, his lips in a line. "I'll get us transportation in the meantime. We should leave as soon as possible."

"But you are a day early. I haven't had a chance to tell Antoine."

"*Antoine* now, is it? That's a bit close and personal, on a first-name basis. It's only been what, twelve days since you met him?"

Morgan hastened to explain, "He is really very sweet and still grieving over the loss of his wife."

"Is he now? Well, I'm not sweet, but I'm hurting to get home with you, lass."

"I can't just leave without telling him." Morgan sensed Tadgh turning from her, but she knew she had to do the right thing.

"Do what you must but recognize that we are certainly not out of the woods by any means. Gronski does not give up easily. I will be considered a deserter after we leave, even though I brought Leopold back to safety. And *your Antoine* may turn us in to the Royals before we can get out of here." She saw his hands clench into fists. "So what were you doing here with the good doctor while I was out in the muck almost getting myself killed?"

Morgan saw Tadgh's sneer and could feel her lips start to tremble. She didn't know how to turn the words so that Tadgh would understand.

Hearing no answer coming from her, he turned on his heel and disappeared through the doorway of the ward, with the door swiftly closing behind him.

♣   ♣   ♣   ♣

Back in Ostend, Ritter called up Gronski. "Your phosgene seemed to work well on their trench, but the Belgians used our Defense in Depth tactic to overwhelm our men. It was a slaughter in the end."

"McCarthy. Did you kill him?"

"I'm not sure."

"What do you mean, not sure? Did you or didn't you, man?"

Ritter had lost his nerve and stayed in the German trench to watch when the fighting started, but he wouldn't admit that to anyone, let alone Gronski. He banked on Pauwels doing the job from the Belgian side. He tried to explain, "I was approaching McCarthy, who was protecting young Leopold. I know that we are not supposed to hurt the Prince, but the lad was blocking my shot. That's when the second wave of Belgians came up out of their trench. I couldn't advance. Our fighters retreated. I saw Pauwels confronting the two of them, though."

"Did he shoot McCarthy?"

"Shots were fired." Ritter knew that it was Pauwels who had been killed, and he hoped his tone wouldn't reveal the truth.

"But did he shoot McCarthy?"

"I don't know."

Exasperated, Gronski had had enough. Judging by the vagueness of the answer, he knew Ritter had most likely disobeyed orders to save himself. He would deal with the lout later. "Get back to the Front and confirm the kill."

As a last resort, Gronski communicated directly with his own senior covert operative, Jacobs in Furnes again, using a secure coded telegram routed through his man in Paris. He cursed himself for not doing so sooner instead of working through Gruber's slimy Ostend operative. McCarthy was a worthy enemy. This action might cause him to lose this critical informant within King Albert's headquarters, but it couldn't be helped. Imperial Chancellor von Bethmann Hollweg had ordered him to squash any attempt by Casement to communicate directly with his superiors in Ireland. He was sure that McCarthy was a messenger. Failure to execute the order would likely mean incarceration or worse. "Find out if communications officer Pauwels is still alive."

Jacobs responded by coded telegram along the return path. "I was just going to contact you, sir. Unfortunately, Pauwels was killed during our attack today. And Prince Leopold was injured."

McCarthy. It had to be McCarthy. He was still alive, damn it. "Jacobs," Gronski ordered his agent. "Go immediately to De Panne, to the hospital. Look for a nurse there named Morgan. You'll find an Irishman named McCarthy with her. He is a fugitive who must not be allowed to escape to Ireland. Do you understand?"

"Yes, sir. But I can't just leave my post here at the King's headquarters."

"Do it. Now. Your life depends on it. They'll be trying to get to Le Havre for the eighth." He had guessed the code.

"Yes, sir."

"There you are, Morgan," Doctor Depage said, looking up at her with suture in hand.

"When will you be finished with this operation, doctor?"

"In about thirty minutes."

"I need to see you then."

"Meet me in my suite."

At a quarter past noon, Depage came up the service staircase. Morgan was waiting for him on the landing.

"Come up to my suite."

"I think it's better to meet here, Doctor Depage."

"*Antoine*, Morgan. I asked you to call me Antoine."

"All right. *Antoine*. Did you know that they brought Leopold into the ward this morning with a badly cut hand? He also has minor respiratory effects from a new poison gas the Germans used today near Furnes."

"A new gas, you say?"

"Tadgh says that it is almost odorless and invisible. Something about smelling a little like moldy hay. You can expect many patients shortly with respiratory problems."

"Your friend Tadgh told you this? He's back from the Front?" Doctor Depage was wringing his hands.

She nodded. "He is the one who brought Leopold in. He was responsible for him, as you know. He says that it was Leopold who saved his life fighting a Belgian soldier, one who tried to kill him during the German attack this morning."

"A Belgian soldier?"

"Someone being coerced by the Germans who happen to hold the man's brother captive."

"You said you needed to see me." The doctor pulled out a paper and carefully wadded tobacco from his pouch on it. Then he rolled it expertly in his fingers, licking along the edge to seal it.

"To tell you about Leopold and the gas, and . . ." Morgan hesitated, "that I have to leave here to return to Ireland with Tadgh, whom I love very much."

Depage pulled a match out of his white coat and struck it on the stairwell wall. "But I thought you liked it here, with me." He lit the cigarette and started puffing vigorously.

"You are doing a fine job in very difficult circumstances, Antoine. I really admire you. But I'm in love with Tadgh, and I need to help him with his mission in life, which is critical for Ireland."

Antoine flicked the cigarette down the stairs. Stepping in, he encircled Morgan's waist with his right arm. Morgan backed up a step and gently removed his arm.

"We were captured by the Germans off the coast of Ireland, and now we need to get back home. You can understand, can't you?" Morgan could see confusion in his sad eyes. He looked crestfallen as he dropped his head and kicked at the stair riser with his shoe. "You and Marie were in the same circumstances for Belgium as Tadgh and I are for Ireland, don't you see?"

"But she's gone." Antoine raised his eyes up toward the ceiling.

"If I stayed here, Tadgh would still go, and I'd be gone from him." Morgan stepped back down and took his right hand in her own.

"But you are the spitting image of her. I need you, don't you see. And my country needs you more than Ireland does. They're not even at war." He tried to pull her against him again, but Morgan pushed him away and held him firmly at arm's length with her hands pressing against his chest.

"But I thought you had feelings for me." His eyes were pleading now.

"I love Tadgh, Antoine, just like your Marie must have loved you." She was stroking his hand.

"I see your point, I suppose." Antoine closed his hand over hers.

Taking a step back and withdrawing her hand, Morgan said, "Tadgh saved me from drowning when the *Lusitania* was torpedoed. I just wish Marie had been nearby so that he could have saved her, too."

Antoine looked as if he would cry. His lips trembled and the muscles of his jaw worked. "She was a brave lady, Morgan."

"Yes, I'm sure she was." There was nothing more she could say to the poor man.

"Is there anything I can do to change your mind, my dear?"

"I'm afraid not, sir."

"I am very disappointed." Antoine took a step down the stairs. "But I understand. I will not stand in your way, nor will I tell the King and Queen about your departure until you are safely away. I owe you that."

Morgan couldn't help herself. She stepped down and flung her arms around the doctor.

"What a relief, Antoine. I wasn't sure that you would understand."

The doctor returned the hug and held on until Morgan gently pried herself away from his arms. "After the war, Tadgh and I will come and find you. Maybe we could all get together then." Morgan wiped her eyes with her sleeve.

"Perhaps, girl. I must be getting back to the operating room. We've more work to do this afternoon, don't we, nurse."

"Yes, you do, Antoine. Great work for all of Belgium."

With that, the doctor slowly descended the staircase, his shoulders stooped over. Morgan waited until he had disappeared down into the ward, salty tears slipping into the creases of her mouth. She could taste his sorrow.

♣ ♣ ♣ ♣

Later, Tadgh walked into the ward looking for Morgan. He half expected to be arrested since he had no idea what she might have said to the good doctor. Morgan was in the corner tending to an amputee.

"Nurse, can I see you for a moment?" he asked, walking up to the invalid's mattress.

Morgan went over to an orderly and pointed to the wounded man's bed, indicating that he should take over.

"What can I do for you?" she asked, pulling Tadgh towards the exit, making it appear as if he were someone off the street.

"You ready to leave yet, aroon?" Tadgh searched her face.

"Doctor Depage won't tell a soul," she whispered. "I made sure of it."

Tadgh's eyebrows raised, and he was about to speak, but she placed her index finger on her own lips, shaking her head. "He's on our side, darling."

At the door, Morgan stopped to pick up her trench coat from the rack.

"Your chariot awaits, my love." Tadgh kissed her hand as he led her out onto the street and down a deserted side alley.

Morgan leaped at Tadgh and hung on fiercely. "I was so worried about you."

Tadgh stopped in the path, returning her warmth, pressing her to him and then his lips on hers. "I missed you more."

"No, *I* missed you more."

He laughed. "I would love to do this all afternoon, but most likely Germans are tracking us as we speak." He pulled away from her, squinted into the sun, then his eyes returned to her upturned face. "I can only guess why this fierce mouser Gronski is so interested in stopping us from leaving."

"Who?"

"The German General Staff leader apparently responsible for chemical warfare development, among other diabolical war tools. The Germans must be paranoid that Casement will foul up their Irish strategy by sending a very negative report directly to the Volunteers leaders. They know I was there with Sir Roger and that they are suspicious of his motives."

"What strategy?"

"Promising munitions and other military forces for our revolution and then not likely delivering their full support."

"But why would they do that?"

"I'm guessing that a German military presence in Ireland would anger the Americans and might be the catalyst to drive them into the war. So the *Boche* strategy, coordinated with their Embassy in Washington, must be to make us think they will support us with men up until the last minute to spur on the Rising, and then not deliver anything except maybe some antiquated weapons." [10]

"It's complicated, then." Morgan grabbed Tadgh's hand. "You seem to have this all figured out. Wait. These invading Germans are your so-called ally? With more weapons surely many young Irish lads will die needlessly." Inwardly she hoped that Germany wouldn't help at all and that there would be no Rising and loss of life. *Not a good time to take a stand.*

"Not needlessly. We must restore our Gaelic authority over our homeland. All I know is that the Germans want to stop you and me at any cost. Two have tried and failed here at the Front, and they're not going to give up now." Tadgh frowned. "We'd better get going."

"You've convinced me. Where are we headed exactly ?"

"To our rendezvous at the port of LeHavre in France."

"France? We're certainly seeing Europe, aren't we now. Well traveled, we are."

"Desolate countryside over here, isn't it."

"We'll come back after we free Ireland." Morgan looked wistfully into Tadgh's brown eyes. "It'll be lush and green by then. You'll see."

"Always the optimist, aren't ya, lass. Get up in my chariot."

"This looks like the Kerry," Morgan said, jumping into the motorcycle's armor-encased sidecar, "except for this gun in front of me."

"Best I could do under the circumstances. This is an Indian. I've tested her up to sixty miles per hour. She's a beast. Got to be at least a sixty-cubic-inch engine, side mounted, as you can see."

"I like the light brown color, dear. Very fashionable. Is it full of petrol?"

"Yes, and there's an extra can on the back rack. Shall we be off?"

"Home, Jeeves." Morgan pointed in the direction of Ireland. "Did you bring the picnic?"

"Sandwiches and what fruit I could find."

"My, my. You are the resourceful one."

"You should have seen me in the trenches." He grinned.

"I did see you in the trenches. Both of them."

"So you did, my love. So you did." His life in the Belgian trench over the last few days was a story that would have to wait.

"Through good fortune we are a day earlier than I had expected. But that gives Gronski extra time to find us," Tadgh said as he started up the

Indian. "I really like this three-speed hand shift."

"Surely Gronski couldn't follow us *here*."

"It was his man in a Belgian uniform who tried to kill me in the field this morning."

Morgan didn't like the sound of that mishap. "Let's get going, then."

The road out of De Panne was better than the ones from Ostend, greatly improved beyond the conquered line. Thank God for the Belgians.

Ten minutes west out of De Panne, Morgan said, "Can't we get rid of this stupid gun? It's blocking my view." She pointed to the menacing bipod mounted machine gun in front of her, but she refused to touch it.

Tadgh brought the motorcycle to a stop at the side of the country road and stepped around to face her. "Yes, that is a wicked looking machine, Morgan. What Tadgh didn't know was that this MG8/15 could fire off 500 rounds a minute with a barrel that was water cooled to handle the heat exchange. It had a range of 2,000 yards with medium accuracy in small bursts.

Tadgh examined the bipod swivel mount closely and saw the thumbscrew dismount mechanism. He hefted the wooden stocked machine from its mount and realized that it wasn't light, maybe forty pounds.

"What's this under my feet?" Morgan asked, squirming in her seat.

"Fabric ammunition belts. Three of them." Tadgh replied, looking down between her legs.

"Will they go off?" Morgan jerked her feet up.

"Not to fret, aroon. Only when used through the machine gun." Tadgh put his hand on Morgan's knee to reassure her while he picked up one of the ammo belts out of the sidecar. "Looks like over two hundred rounds on each one." He noted with disappointment that the bullets were not the same as the 9-millimeter ones used in his Luger.

"These things could really maim a lot of men, couldn't they. I detest this."

"Yes, Morgan. This is a standard killing machine in the trenches. I saw a couple in the German trench on Christmas morning. We could sure use some of these for the Rising." The memory of the Belgian soldier's brains being splattered earlier in the day flashed through his mind.

"You men! Keep it off this sidecar."

"We might need it," Tadgh said, feeding the belt into the gun and then fastening it back down on the motorcycle.

"Don't you dare expect me to use it," Morgan cried, thrusting her arms down into the sidecar cavity.

"Don't you worry, love. If need be, I'll take charge."

"You do that, but I'd rather you throw that damn thing away."

They didn't even realize that they had crossed the border into France until they were at the outskirts of Dunkerque some twelve miles to the west. The sun was offsetting the chill from their wind-whipped exposure. Tadgh stopped to consult the German map he had folded into the Belgian officer's uniform that the Queen had given him. It mapped all the way to the Atlantic Ocean.

"We need to send a thank you note to the King and Queen when we get back to Ireland, Morgan."

"That's the least we could do. I told Antoine that we would come back and visit him after the war."

Tadgh felt his mouth turn down and fought it. "By my reckoning it is about 200 miles to Le Havre. We're going to be there a day early."

They traveled close to the coast, skirting around Calais mid-afternoon, arriving at Abbeyville, just inland from coastal Dieppe, an hour after sundown. Tadgh had turned on the gas headlamp at dusk. It had not rained, but the temperature was just above freezing.

"We need shelter for the night, my love." He could see Morgan shake, despite her coat and gloves. She wore no hat nor scarf. Tadgh himself just had his uniform, and the cold pierced through the cloth. In his hurry to get Leopold to safety, he had left his greatcoat behind in the trench.

Tadgh found a farmhouse with smoke curling out of the chimney, and he debated whether to approach the occupants. It could be risky. After another look at Morgan, he decided to chance it even though they didn't speak French.

They were greeted at the door. "*Bonsoir, Monsieur le soldat et Mademoiselle la infirmière de Belgique. Vous devez être gelé.*"

Tadgh looked at Morgan and shrugged his shoulders.

Morgan answered for both of them.

"*Oui monsieur, nous sommes froid.* Could we come out of the cold, *s'il vous plaît?*"

Tadgh glanced at Morgan, shocked by this unknown linguistic prowess. She shrugged back, as surprised as he was. How could she remember foreign words and languages, but not her own history? *Maddening.*

"*Certainement. Entrés. Je m'appel Francois Gabon. Et vous?*"

"*Je m'appel Morgan. Ici Tadgh McCarthy.*"

The man's wife rushed in from the kitchen with a warm towel and put it around Morgan's neck. "Gracious François. Let them pass. Come in, my dears, come in before you freeze to death."

Thank God she spoke English.

"Thank you, madam. We are travelers on a delicate mission and we got caught out in the cold tonight."

Good comment, Tadgh thought.

"You have held the Germans out of our part of France, so you are welcome in our home. You will stay with us for supper and the night, won't you?"

"Thank you, ma'am." Tadgh clasped her hand and the hand of her husband warmly.

After a dinner of chicken and potatoes from their own farm, with locally made beer of some sort, the farmer asked his wife, "*Demandez-leur de parler de la guerre?*"

Monique, as she was called, started to speak. "Sir . . ."

"I understand the word for war, ma'am," Tadgh responded, taking a last bite of the delicious apple pastry that Monique had served them. He turned to face François. "You want the news, I take it. Here it is. Belgians are doing a heroic job of holding the line near the Yser River, along with your French Territorial 45th and 87th divisions." He wiped his mouth with the cloth napkin. "Unless this new poisonous gas the Germans have just released is more potent than the others, our troops should be able to hold the *Boche* off."

"*C'est un méchant business, n'est pas.*"

"François says it's a nasty business."

"*Oui, madam.* Deadly."

"We are all in your debt, monsieur. Without you, we would be overrun. We may yet be. It is agonizing for us here."

Tadgh thought about his poor countrymen and the conditions back home. The English had already used chemical warfare in a sense by forcing the Irish to eat rotten black potatoes. He hoped to hell that the English bastards didn't use whatever it was the Germans used today when the Republicans rose up in Dublin. "I understand, ma'am. They are doing their best. You are safe, at least for the time being."

That seemed to quell Monique's nerves. She offered them strong coffee before bed and led them to their room for the night.

The guest bedroom was, in fact, a place in the barn with the animals. At least there was warmth from the mass of mammals in the structure, but the straw that served as a mattress stabbed through their clothing. Morgan found some kind of thick cloth material and covered the hay. The smell in the barn with the goats, sheep, and the milk cows, rivaled the trenches. Tadgh had brought the stolen Indian in out of the cold in case they were being followed and to make sure its engine didn't seize up overnight. He checked it over. At least they had plenty of petrol. That was a relief.

Morgan snuggled up to Tadgh on the wide hay hammock, clothing and all. They sank into the makeshift bed beneath them. He wrapped her in a big bear hug. This was the first time they had been alone and not exhausted in over two months. She felt safe in his arms. They were not out of the woods by any means, but tonight that didn't seem to matter. They were together and away from the war zone. It was hard to imagine what it was like for Monique, trying to keep her life going with the travesties of war on her doorstep, and not knowing when it might break her door down.

Tadgh tried to reach inside Morgan's nurse uniform, seeking warm flesh for his hands. At first, he fumbled with the buttons, and Morgan had to help him. They were on the awkward left side for the female uniform. She hesitated, wrapping her warm hands around his to lessen the shock, and then guided them under the blouse and up under her right breast. Tadgh shuddered at its softness as his hand explored the now hardening nipple.

Morgan turned inward towards him and pressed closer.

Tadgh pinched her nipple and tried with the other hand to undo the whole of Morgan's uniform. She moaned softly and the sheep in the barn bleated in response.

"Here let me help you, mavorneen." Morgan rose up on her knees and pulled off her wrap and blouse. Her breasts broke free, and Tagh's mouth was immediately on them.

Morgan leaned forward on her knees and loosened the belt of her lover's uniform trousers. He was on his knees now, facing her. With a swift move, she pulled the trousers down around his knees.

His manhood pressed through his undershorts.

"I've missed you so, aroon. Help me, please." Morgan undressed him, then quickly unfastened her skirt and dropped it into the hay. Moments later, he found her inner sanctuary, already moist. She rolled back onto the hay bed with her legs spread wide, pulling Tadgh down onto her and not letting go.

He found her then, penetrating deeply, his mouth still on her breast.

Morgan arched and squeezed, pulling him further in.

They found their rhythm, Morgan crying out as their passions rose toward their peak.

"Oh, Morgan," Tadgh cried, as they both climaxed convulsively together.

Then they collapsed back down into the hay. It didn't seem to matter that sharp blades of straw scratched Morgan's skin. They were once again reunited, one with the universe. It took only moments before Tadgh dropped off to sleep. She felt him relax on her, his breathing slowed.

Morgan was fully awake, tingling in their togetherness. She smoothed the hay bed and rolled Tadgh gently off her, onto his back. He did not stir. He must have had an exhausting day. She wondered what ordeal he had overcome at the Front. If there had been any doubt before, it had now vanished. Tadgh was her man, for sure. He had saved her from drowning, and he had come back for her twice.

Morgan mused about when her last period had been, just after Christmas when they had reached De Panne safely. She wondered if they had just made a baby. She was still tingling. What a wonderful, if sinful thought. That might change Tadgh's attitude towards revolution and potential death, wouldn't it? No, it might just anger him and drive him away. But wait. They had become as one.

Suddenly, Morgan was aware of the animals surrounding them. Three inquisitive sheep at first had gathered around, now maybe ten of them. Perhaps they could smell human lovemaking like she could. It dawned on her. Wasn't it the twelfth day of Christmas? Morgan counted on her fingers. The barn, the hay, the man and woman. And, potentially the baby, albeit nine months too early. And the sheep and other animals.

But wait, where were the wise men bearing gifts? Tadgh had brought gifts of love, protection, and freedom. Close enough.

With that happy thought, Morgan snuggled down beside her wise man, drawing their clothes up and around them both. The straw was remarkably warm. Two sheep lay down on the straw at their feet as Morgan finally drifted off to sleep with her right hand on her belly.

Later, Morgan, sound asleep, was back on the *Lusitania*, in a room with baskets of babies. There was an explosion, and a man she loved was ordering her to take her two babies and get out of the ship to save them. She couldn't quite recognize him. Was it Tadgh? They were in mortal danger. She desperately did not want to leave the man. There was smoke and a screaming mass of humanity clawing their way up the stairs. She was trapped below, then they were on deck. A woman stole one of her babies. There were boats capsizing on the deck. A boy and his mother were dead. Hundreds were dead or dying. She couldn't save them. There was fire. The ocean liner was sinking fast into foggy waters.

The nightmare changed, swirling into the battle at the Western Front, from water to cold dirty trenches. Hundreds of men dead and dying. Tadgh was caught in a trench cave-in with shells exploding all around him. Buried alive under mud and slime. She couldn't save him, or any of them, her fingernails breaking as she dug deeper. Then the swelling of the dream into near reality. Morgan dreamed she was with child.

"My God," she cried out. The startled sheep rustled away, but not before Tadgh was on his feet, Luger drawn, peering into the darkness, into nothing.

"Morgan. What is it?" Tadgh shook her gently and Morgan lurched awake.

"It was awful."

"It's all right, aroon. We're safe here." Tadgh reached down and stroked her damp brow. Then he dropped down, pulling her against him. She was shivering, so he rubbed her arms and back.

"I was on the *Lusitania*, again, and Tadgh, I remembered."

"What did you remember?" He hoped it would not be what he dreaded most of all, the memory of her identity.

Morgan relayed the gruesome details of her nightmare, ending where Tadgh was trapped in a trench cave-in.

Tadgh thought it uncanny that she had such a clear vision of the trench warfare since she had not experienced it first-hand. Perhaps her vision of the *Lusitania* disaster was an accurate remembrance. Maybe she had a husband and children. Could he have survived without her knowledge? It must be the case. There was that newspaper article he had hidden from her.

Tadgh was on the verge of telling her what he knew.

"Oh, Tadgh. I love you so. The worst part was when I thought you were being buried alive." She wrapped her arms around his neck, clinging to him. "You are my one and only, now."

"Aye lass, and you, the same." He pulled her in close and kissed the top of her head. She had saved his life three times now, and he would keep her with him, no matter what. To hell with the husband and her babies. That was another life, and she was his, now. He would never return to a life without her. He could not even imagine it.

♣ ♣ ♣ ♣

He tossed and turned in the straw, could not get comfortable, and then turned his attention to the future. Tadgh clicked into military planning mode. Traveling down into Le Havre would take about three hours. They could scout out the harbor and make sure they knew how to rendezvous the next day, but where would they stay that night? Le Havre was a major French port, the biggest on the north coast. It must be the landing and logistics depot for the English army supplying men and materiel to the Western Front. That could be dangerous. They could be questioned, given their uniforms. He decided to prevail upon the good graces of their benefactors and ask to stay at the farm for another day.

Getting safely out of Germany was clearly no simple task. You needed friends. Why, oh why, had he decided to go and help those sailors on that doomed freighter? At least Morgan survived after the *Lusitania* sinking, whereas poor Doctor Depage's wife had not. He and Morgan were better off than they had been for the last two months. He believed they were destined for greater things. God works in mysterious ways.

Chapter Sixteen
Le Havre

January 6, 1916
On the Road to Le Havre

Hugo Jacobs left De Panne just after sunset without finding Morgan. She had vanished, according to one orderly in the hospital ward. He had checked with the motor pool, and an Indian motorcycle with an armed sidecar was missing.

After receiving his orders from Gronski, he informed the King that his wounded son's bodyguard had fled, making that man a deserter. Jacobs offered to go after him. The King had already heard about the incident, and the Queen was positioned with their son at the hospital. They both wanted McCarthy and Morgan returned for questioning, so Albert agreed that Hugo should try to apprehend them. This clever idea would protect Jacobs' cover.

Before he left the Furnes headquarters, the King admonished his man, "Bring them back alive, Hugo. If you can't do that, then let them go."

Jacobs had no intention of releasing them, but he would extract Casement's message to the man's Irish leaders before he terminated them. The King be damned. He feared and obeyed his master Gronski, first and foremost.

He decided he had to go to Le Havre as soon as possible to scout around. Maybe he could figure out what MM and B&C meant ahead of the rendezvous time. And besides, Marlene, an exceptional woman who could satisfy a man's needs, lived there, and she would certainly put him up for as long as he needed.

In the morning, after Morgan and Tadgh brushed the hay out of their hair and clothing, they freshened up with a pitcher of fresh water in the farmhouse. Monique treated Tadgh and Morgan to a fine country breakfast of slices of ham, a fluffy omelet, and crusty bread. François was already out in the fields despite the light rain. "What is your mission, if I might ask?"

Monique offered warmed milk from their own cows.

"It is most secret, I'm afraid," Morgan said, gratefully accepting the milk. "Let's just say that it has something to do with the English."

"They are a good ally, aren't they, dear."

"Ally to some and foe to others," Tadgh grunted, grabbing the strawberry jam jar to coat his brown toast with the sweet red preserve.

"The Germans must think them a menace, thank God."

"I'm sure of that." Morgan cut in to change the subject. "Would it be all right for us to stay one more day, Monique? I know it must be an imposition."

"Nonsense, dear, no trouble at all. I enjoy the company. We don't get many visitors during this awful war and certainly not those who can give us information about the conditions at the Front."

"We'd like to repay you in some small way. Tadgh could help François in the fields, couldn't you, Lieutenant." Morgan met Tadgh's eyes and saw no interest. Tadgh shrugged his shoulders and then snapped to attention. He nodded assent when she gave him a dirty look. "Well, off with you then and be quick about it," she half-chided, giving him a big kiss.

"Could I have one more piece of ham first? I like the sweetness of the cure."

"Of course you can, *mon cher*. Anything for the war effort." Monique smiled.

After Tadgh departed, Morgan thought for a minute. The rain had been cold, almost like sleet, when they had come across from the barn. "Do you have anything, a scrap of material, burlap, anything that I could make a coat out of for Tadgh? He came away without his overcoat and the weather is turning frightful."

"I can do better than that, dear. François's brother Lars died in the war last year, poor lad. He left his street clothes here at the farm. I think his greatcoat might fit your lad."

"Oh, Monique, you are too kind."

The farm wife retrieved the garment and handed it to her. Morgan folded it over her arm and hastened to take it to Tadgh in the field. "This will warm you and cover up that Belgian uniform from prying eyes."

"You are truly a marvel, aroon, on many counts."

"Aren't I, though." She winked at him.

The men came in at noon for their meal, looking frozen. Their women were waiting with hot food and open arms.

Morgan realized that human beings persist despite the terrible conditions of war. Here were two men tending to a surviving farm in the dead of winter while their women took care of their needs inside the farmhouse. Where allowed, life went on. Animals were born, and then they died of natural causes. And this was as it should be. This natural order of things was the polar opposite of the bloody carnage being inflicted by the warmongers not seventy miles to the east. She decided that it was best not to rattle their hosts with details of the horrors on their doorstep. This fine French couple were completely dependent for their survival on King Albert, Queen Nurse and young Leopold, and their relatively small force of brave defenders. And these farmers, too, pressed on with resolute courage in their own way.

Hugo Jacobs arrived at the docks of Le Havre at about the same time that Morgan and Tadgh were sitting down for their meal at noon. He viewed the harbor in all its glory and took in the briny smells, the bobbing masts, and the movement of ships.

The rendezvous was presumably set for the next day, January 8, likely by boat from Ireland. Since he missed finding Morgan at the De Panne hospital, he didn't know what the woman looked like. All he had to go on was the rough description from the orderly. She was obviously a looker. Gronski had given him a fairly good description of McCarthy. And what about that Indian motorcycle with an armed sidecar? What else did he know? MM and B&C. That must mean something important about the boat that they would meet. He had already considered and ruled out an air escape. The Irish had no aeroplanes as far as he knew, and they wouldn't dare try to commandeer an allied airship. He set about scouring the waterfront for young women and for anything else he might discover in the way of troop movement.

He found many English and American ships in port, disgorging provisions, military equipment and, in the case of the British vessels, increased numbers of uniformed men. It looked as if the allies were preparing for an offensive. Hugo decided that he would need to get a coded message about this back to Gronski.

Just as he was about to give up and find supper somewhere, he spied a small ocean-going trawler rounding the north breakwater and entering the mouth of the harbor, chugging loud enough but at a near idle . The vessel couldn't have been more than fifty feet in length, black and somber, with a small, elevated wheelhouse aft. What interested Hugo most was the name on the side of the boat, *Beamish and Crawford Stout.* The boat eased into the protected harbor and made its way up toward Southampton Quay.

Jacobs fortuitously was standing on Quay de la Marine, just 300 feet across the front harbor, when an occurrence caught his attention. Two stevedores dropped what they were doing on Southampton Quay and reached for the ropes that the boat's captain threw to them, fore and aft. He appeared to be the sole occupant of the boat until another sailor emerged from the wheelhouse.

One of the stevedores apparently knew the ship's captain and called out gruffly, "Marty Murphy, you old sea dog. What brings you to this neck of the woods again in the midst of this crazy war, monsieur?"

"Émile, is it yourself, you bleedin' brawler? I'm after deliverin' stout on the B&C, what your military mongrels ordered to drown their sorrows, don't ya know." Martin swept his arm around to point to the cinched-down pallets of Beamish barrels neatly stacked on the deck. "Tie me up."

When Jacobs heard the initials B&C, he couldn't believe his good fortune. He had found his quarry. They had to be linked. MM, B&C and an Irish accent. While the stevedores berthed the B&C trawler, Gronski's spy circled around the *Bassin de la Citadelle* until he was on Southampton Quay. Keeping his distance, Jacobs waited until Murphy and his mate had battened down his trawler. Then he followed them north on Boulevard François I to a local eatery, La Sirene, where they stopped for supper. Hugo wasn't going to let Murphy out of his sight until the rendezvous took place. Marlene's sleek body would have to wait until he had dispatched McCarthy and his girl.

Seated only three booths away from his target, Jacobs ate a meal of plaice and Brussels sprouts while he waited and schemed. It would indeed be beneficial if McCarthy were to show up now rather than at the point of sailing. It would be easier to interrogate and then kill him in the backstreets of the old city tonight rather than on the open quay in broad daylight. Too many people around as witnesses. Otherwise, he might have to apprehend him at sea. All of it carried significant risk based on what he had heard about McCarthy.

That's when he got the idea. If he couldn't deal with the rogue before they sailed, he would use the French harbor police to aid him at sea. Wearing his Belgian uniform, he could enlist their help to apprehend a deserter then annihilate them all before dropping the police launch down the coast and doubling back to Furnes. He simply could not allow McCarthy to get away, or be captured by the French.

After supper, Murphy and his mate returned to their vessel and bedded down for the night. Jacobs waited in the shadows of the quay for an hour after the lights in the wheelhouse were extinguished to make sure that Murphy wasn't going to sneak off his ship. The north wind off the Channel bit deeply into his face and neck, and soon he could not feel his skin. By nine o'clock Jacobs revised his thinking. McCarthy would not likely show up in the middle of an extremely cold dark night, especially when the rendezvous was scheduled for the next day, so he decided to visit Marlene unannounced. Several months had passed since his needs had been satisfied.

When Tadgh and Morgan said goodbye to their hosts after breakfast the next morning, Morgan felt the need to promise Monique that they would return to France when the war was over. The wind had calmed slightly, but the clouds were menacing for a storm.

"Take care and win your war in Ireland," Monique called out, as Tadgh fired up the Indian. He was a little annoyed that Morgan had shared some of the information about the travesties back home.

"*Au revoir*," Morgan called back, waving, as they headed down the lane.

Two hours later at 0930, Tadgh stopped the motorcycle at the northern outskirts of Le Havre, searching for a vantage point to view the harbor. To the south, he could see ancient Fort de Sainte-Adresse perched on a hill. Fifteen minutes later, they were out on the terrace of the Fort looking down towards the estuary of the Seine River as it flowed into the English Channel. There on its north bank, the Le Havre harbor spread out before them.

Pointing and sweeping his arm across the scene below, Tadgh said, "This has been a major northern French seaport since 1517 when the town was founded by François I."

"Does this river lead to Paris?"

"Yes, aroon, to the south, and directly to the north across the channel and inland is London. The capitals of two nations, about two hundred miles apart, who were at war with each other over the ages but are now united."

"How fickle you Neanderthal men are. We're not hunter-gatherers anymore, yet you persist in killing each other anyway. If we were at peace, we could visit Paris."

"Where'd you learn that term, lass?"

"I dunno. It just came to me, even though I can't remember my real name."

"It's Morgan, so it is. Some day we will go to Paris, aroon, on our way to Bavaria, and after visiting Monique and François. Did you know that it was the Irish anatomist William King who coined the term *Neanderthal*, when fossils were found in that German area in the 1860s?"

"That figures. Germans and Irishmen, all Neanderthals."

Tadgh returned his gaze to the harbor. He saw several deepwater basins and port docks alive with military and commercial ocean-going ships of every size, from small trawlers to large destroyers. Even a huge ocean liner painted zigzag light and dark gray, a troop carrier he surmised, graced the scene. Now where, in all that maze of marine vessels, would Martin Murphy moor the B&C ship, if indeed he was there?

He decided that his friend would tie up as close to the harbor outlet as possible, between the north and south dike walls, in case they needed a fast getaway. The north end of the outer harbor entrance appeared to be the nearest quay. The inner basins each had narrow openings to the outer harbor, too tricky to navigate in a hurry. Tadgh could barely make out several smaller ships moored along that entrance sea wall. He wished that he had a pair of binoculars. There would be no time for hunting around if one of Gronski's men was still searching for them. He told Morgan, "We're going to check out the northern entrance quay first."

"I'm excited to finally find Martin and escape from the continent," Morgan said, straining to see where Tadgh was talking about. "Let's go, then."

Tadgh fired up the Indian, and they headed for the north quay.

Jacobs had been glad to see the B&C trawler still tied up at the quay when he had returned at 5:30 in the morning. He found a harbor police boat patrolling the docks a half hour later, so he hailed it and explained his mission to the two police officers on duty.

"The ship in question is tied up on Southampton Quay. I don't know when the deserters might show up to try their escape."

"Shouldn't we just seize the ship and question its crew?" one officer asked.

"I am not sure that this ship is the right one. I don't want to scare the deserters off. We will need to capture them when and if McCarthy shows up and boards her. Then we will know for certain. He is carrying spy messages for the *Boche* that we will confiscate to incriminate him. Depending on how quickly the ship makes way, we need to be ready to give chase. Can you help me?"

The two officers exchanged looks. One of them assured Jacobs, "We need to continue making our rounds of the outer harbor, but we will come to your assistance if you wave to us from the quay."

Hugo returned to Southampton Quay at seven, just as the wharf was coming alive. Murphy was busy offloading his cargo of beer with the help of two stevedores and three of their mates. There was no sign of his quarry or their motorcycle, if indeed they had stolen one. Jacobs' thoughts turned to the evening before. Marlene had been more than happy to see him. He felt that this day, January 8, was going to be a very lucky day for him. He positioned himself about a hundred yards down the quay from the B&C trawler, out of view among some crates that were not currently being moved by the many workers swarming the area.

When they reached the English Channel end of Southampton Quay, Tadgh stopped the Indian and dismounted. The quay workers paid them no mind. "You stay here, Morgan, while I scout around."

"Not on your life, my love. Where you go, I go. I wont be separated from you again."

"Fair enough." Tadgh moved the motorcycle behind a warehouse building located across the street from the quay. "Stay close," he whispered to her.

Tadgh used the buildings as cover as he progressed southward to where he could see the ships tied up along the quay. It started to drizzle, and the north wind was bitter cold.

"There. Three ships down. That black trawler. What's written on its wheelhouse?"

Morgan strained to see through the spitting rain. "Beamish & Craw—"

"That's it. Stay here. I'll be right back."

Five minutes later, huffing under the strain, Tadgh rejoined his mate hauling the machine gun over his shoulder. "C'mon, aroon. We have a ride to catch."

Murphy was chatting with Thomas, his lone crewman, by the rail when he saw a man and a woman loping southward down the quay towards his ship, the man hefting some mechanical equipment. They were a hundred yards away when he recognized the pair.

"Thomas, cast off aft. Quickly, lad. Then to the wheelhouse." Murphy himself raced to the bow, which was pointed outbound, to release the forward lines. The trawler was already running at idle.

Jacobs saw the commotion through the intensifying rain. So that's how it was, the two trying to sneak through. He darted out from behind the crates and ran down the quay brandishing his Belgian 7.65mm Colt 1903 nine-round pistol. When he realized that they were about to get away, he hailed the police launch for assistance. There would be no time to apprehend and deal with McCarthy before the boat departed. How could they be so coordinated?

Martin saw the Belgian and had the trawler slowly moving northward by the time that Tadgh and Morgan reached it. The separation between the quay and the boat was almost two feet. They turned 180 degrees and started running parallel with the trawler. Martin had the rope ladder draped over the side amidships.

"Jump, Morgan. Grab the ladder."

She hesitated, and a knot rose up in her throat. Visions of the *Lusitania* and Tadgh's hooker arose. The memories of being commanded to jump flooded her mind.

A shot rang out, ricocheting off the machine gun.

"*Jump now*, Morgan, for God's sake," Tadgh urged. He gave his love a nudge, and she leaped off the quay, landing against the side of the trawler, her body dragging through the cold harbor water. She had the wind knocked out of her but managed to secure a firm grip on the rope ladder, holding on tight.

"Martin, you old barnacle. Are we ever glad to see ya." Tadgh was lumbering parallel to the accelerating ship now, opposite the ladder.

"Take this gun." He thrust it across the three-foot span, almost breaking his arm, and the brawny Captain yanked it by the barrel into the boat.

"Halt, McCarthy. You are under arrest," Jacobs yelled out in English just as Tadgh leapt off the quay. The assailant was just thirty yards behind them. The boat was four feet away from the quay and picking up speed.

Morgan had pulled herself up out of the water and Tadgh landed just below her, his legs bent beneath him. His right hand grabbed for the second rope ladder rung above the water and slipped off. As he fell, his arm lodged behind the lowest rung. He was snagged like a fish being dragged along.

Morgan reached down with her free hand and grabbed Tadgh's collar. Another shot rang out, hitting the gunnels to the left of where Martin bent over, grabbing Morgan by her clothing, and then her limbs.

He yanked her up. Morgan thought that her arm was going to fall off. Soon, both of the escapees lay flat on the deck, gasping for air and looking back through the rain.

"Welcome aboard, mates," Captain Murphy said, hauling in the rope ladder.

The policemen on their launch pulled into the quay, having heard the shots through the rain, and Jacobs jumped aboard crying, "After them."

Two minutes later, Murphy said, "It looks like we have company." He pointed toward the police vessel barreling in their direction.

The rain pelted down harder now, sheets of it. Morgan could see into the wheelhouse where Thomas was having trouble maneuvering between the openings of the north and south dikes.

Straining to see through the rain, Tadgh regained his senses. "What company?"

"The harbor police, lad, by the looks of it. That soldier chasing you flagged them down."

On his feet now, Tadgh stared at the police launch. *Could it be Gronski himself?* Whoever it was wanted him dead in a bad way.

The trawler was now even with the harbor exit and Thomas gunned the engines. Tadgh could see that the launch was gaining and would overtake them before they got very far out into the Channel.

Tadgh found the machine gun lying where Murphy had thrown it on the deck. He quickly surveyed its condition. The ammo belt was still in place, so Tadgh released its safety and hid it behind two crates of dry goods battened down on deck.

"I have to stop for the police, Tadgh. Them's the rules, and as a commercial company we have to comply, or we'll be blackballed from using their ports."

"That soldier is a German killer sent to assassinate me and Morgan."

"I hate the bastards," Murphy replied, looking to Tadgh for guidance.

"I don't think he'll shoot us in cold blood in front of the police," Morgan offered, having regained her balance.

"Would you bet our lives on that, Morgan?"

From the launch came a shouted order. "Hello, the B&C trawler. Heave to. This is the Le Havre police."

"Tadgh, I've got to stop." Martin signaled the wheelhouse with a chopping motion across his throat.

The trawler came to a stop and was wallowing in the three-foot swells as the police launch pulled along broadside. "Prepare to be boarded," one of the two policemen from the vessel bellowed, as he nudged the launch alongside the trawler.

The German in a Belgian uniform looked determined as he jumped from the launch to the deck of the trawler, gun drawn. He hissed, "McCarthy, you are under arrest as a cowardly deserter from the Belgian army and a German spy."

Tadgh recognized Jacobs, having seen him in King Albert's headquarters. He was obviously Gronski's German spy.

One of the policemen succeeded in tying the launch to the trawler. "Who is the captain of this vessel?" the other policeman asked, as he stepped from behind the wheel of the launch, pulling his revolver from its holster.

"What message did Casement order you to deliver?" Jacobs demanded, stepping behind Morgan, grabbing her arm, and putting his Nagant M-1886 revolver to her temple. He didn't have to explain his threat.

Tadgh took a step back, his heel bumping into one of the crates. The machine gun was an arm's length away behind him. "I have no idea what you're talking about." He stalled for time.

"Five seconds and I will blow her brains out. I mean it, McCarthy. You're the one he wants."

"Gronski of the German General Staff, you mean? You're the German spy." Tadgh saw a flicker of recognition.

"Never mind. The message?"

Tadgh thought a second. *It's him or me.* "All right, let her go. I'll tell you." Tadgh took a breath, hesitated, then blurted, "Go the Rising with or without the Germans."

"You're lying."

"Which one of you is the German spy?" one of the policemen asked from his launch, brandishing his weapon.

Without losing hold of Morgan and in one motion, Jacobs turned and put a bullet in each of the two policemen's hearts. He wanted no witnesses living to tell the tale.

Morgan saw her opportunity and took it, stepping hard on their assailant's left foot and crouching down. Tadgh dove backward behind the crate.

Jacobs' shot penetrated the crate and missed McCarthy by inches. Tadgh rolled right on the deck from behind the crate, machine gun at the ready, and stitched a row of bullets through the German's abdomen. The kickback almost knocked him overboard. The man bellowed and fired once more at Tadgh, hitting the machine gun trigger and jamming it. Jacobs then fell to his knees, his eyes blazing, and attempted to raise his gun for a kill shot.

Tadgh reached under his tunic and flipped open the holster of the Luger he had taken from Gronski's guard. Before Jacobs could aim his weapon again, Tadgh pulled out his revolver, flicked the safety with his thumb, aimed, and put a bullet in Jacobs' brain.

The fight was over, leaving three men in pools of their own blood. The rain continued to fall in waves, washing Jacobs' blood to the port gunnels.

"It's a good thing they can't see us from the harbor, lad. The rain probably dampened the sounds of the gunshots," Martin remarked, looking shoreward. "I'd say that we're about half a mile out into the Channel with the drift." Then looking down into the police launch he added, "It's a shame about the coppers. They never knew what they were up against."

"Help me get this German imposter onto the police launch," Tadgh said to Martin, noticing that Morgan was already attending to the slain policemen.

"They're dead, I'm afraid, Tadgh," Morgan raised her head, a helpless look in her eyes. "I couldn't save them."

"It's war, Morgan, remember that," Tadgh said.

Martin and Tadgh dragged Jacobs' body into the launch and positioned him facing the policemen, making sure his Nagant was still attached to his stiffened fingers. Tadgh took one of the policemen's guns lying on the deck and shot Jacobs in the stomach and brain with it. Finally, he placed that gun in the policeman's hand.

"That oughtta do it," he grunted, throwing the machine gun on the deck between them.

Seconds later, they were back on board the trawler, releasing the ropes tying the two boats together. As the police launch drifted away, Tadgh commented, "Good riddance to the Western Front."

"Amen to that, mavorneen." As she stood beside him, Morgan searched for Tadgh's hand and found it.

It suddenly dawned on Tadgh that they were free from their captivity on the European continent. He looked at Morgan, and a sense of relief infected them both with that realization. Then he clapped Captain Murphy on the back as they headed for the wheelhouse. The trawler's engines sprang to life again and they headed eastward for Ireland and home.

Chapter Seventeen
Home

January 11, 1916
Entrance to Queenstown Harbor, Ireland

*T*adgh dropped to his knees on the deck of the B&C trawler when the south coast of Ireland came into view. He crossed himself and prayed to God that he would be part of the movement to free Ireland or die, despite Casement's pessimism. During the gas attack in the trenches of Belgium, he had briefly despaired of being able to fulfill this destiny. Yet his love of country and Morgan had seen him through. Clearly the Germans could not be counted on to support the revolution, but that didn't matter. The strength of young Leopold buoyed him up. *If the Belgians can preserve their country against great odds, then surely we can liberate ours. We are in the right, and the English must be vanquished.*

He saw Morgan's hair blowing like a flag on deck, her face glowing. She was a wonder—such a strong young woman who had ministered to the severely wounded, German and Allied alike, with and without his support. This was indeed the woman for him, one to support his mission and to build a life and family with afterwards. Surely her passion for saving lives would give way to the necessity for purging the British oppressor. He thought of her passion, then, and memories of their lovemaking returned, the thoughts of home in Ireland, the sharing of his bed. Her skin, soft beneath his hands. He shook his head to clear it.

Now they were coming into Queenstown Harbor, their intended destination last October when they were so dramatically sidetracked. Only four days ago, he had decided to keep silent about Morgan's past. But now, being near the Cunard operations center, he had second thoughts. Its manager, Jack Jordan, who had been third boson's mate on the *Lusitania*, held the key to Morgan's history. Her husband or lover, who wrote that impassioned plea in the *Southern Star* newspaper that only Tadgh had seen, must have been the man Morgan had dreamed about with the babies. He was alive somewhere in the world, perhaps even in Cork City. So the girl he had named Morgan was in reality named Claire. Morgan's dream, and remembrances after the freighter blew up, showed that she had had children. *She had said "my babies" after her dream, hadn't she?* Had she been on a luckless trip with them all? Likely so. Jack Jordan presumably knew everything. Morgan's stubborn amnesia still blocked the memory of her life before that fateful torpedo hit the *Lusitania.* Maybe that was for the best. For Tadgh, anyway.

God, what shall I do? He crossed himself again before standing up. How could he live with himself, knowing but not telling?

"What are you thinking, my love?" Morgan came near and held him.

"I am so thankful to be home."

"Me too, mavorneen. I did despair once or twice that we wouldn't be reunited and see our Ireland again."

Amazing, her loyalty to a country that most likely wasn't her own. "But here we are, aroon. Do you remember where we were headed when we were saved and then captured?" He knew he had to broach this crucial subject. He owed her that, whatever the outcome.

"Yes, of course. We were going to see the Cunard manager. But that isn't important to me now."

"Not important? Your history?"

"Irrelevant now. After I saw what was happening on both sides of the Western Front, and with you coming to save me, twice, that's all that matters to me, my love. Whatever happened in my life before is inconsequential. I think that is why I can't remember. Because it doesn't matter. What matters is us, now, and in the future. Don't you see?"

"Yes, aroon, I see, and I believe in us." Tadgh warmed at her outburst of love, but he still wondered about her past. He blurted out before he could stop himself, "What if you have a husband and children from before?"

"Then I would remember that now, Tadgh, wouldn't I?"

"But your dream?"

"It seemed real at the time, but now that we're home safe, I don't think so. Just another nightmare."

"I know what they're like, to be sure, Morgan." Tadgh felt guilty about what he kept from her, but he had given her the chance, and she hadn't taken it. So be it. He leaned in to give Morgan a kiss and held his tongue.

Murphy spoke up before Tadgh could dwell any further on troublesome thoughts. "Tadgh, I took the liberty to go and get your motorcycle for you, lad."

"Did you now, Martin? That was ever so kind of you. Aye, but *The Republican's* lost, don't ya know." Tadgh's face felt tight, the tears welled up inside for that other girl, the one that had carried him from mission to mission on the frothy seas.

"I knows it, lad. A mariner without his ship's like a shepherd without his sheep."

"Or an Irishman without his country."

"So it is, lad. But you've a mind to change all that, I venture."

"Aye, Martin, to be sure, to be sure."

"We'll support ya, lad, me and Wiggins, when the time comes, I mean. So it's good that you're home again safe, is it?"

"You don't know the half of it. We're happy to be here and to be alive, Martin. Thanks be to God, and you and Thomas here."

"You'd be welcome, you and the missus."

Morgan blushed. "He hasn't asked me yet, Martin."

"He will if he knows what's good for what ails him, lass, won't you, Tadgh."

Tadgh hadn't given marriage much thought. "Maybe so, you old salt, if we all survive the revolution to free Ireland. Then we'll see, won't we, aroon." Tadgh grabbed Morgan and gave her a squeeze.

Was that a proposal? If so, it took Martin Murphy to bring it to the surface. Morgan had been giving marriage to Tadgh a lot of thought while she was with brave Gerda and her family. This was what she wanted more than anything in the world, a family, her own lover. If only the revolution wasn't standing in the way. "Maybe I will join you, Tadgh, if you behave yourself."

Two hours later, they landed where they had docked several months earlier, near Murphy's cottage home on the north shores of Queenstown Harbor, and less than a half mile east of the Cunard Pier.

"We can't thank you enough for bringing us home, Martin," Tadgh said, and Morgan leapt forward to embrace their benefactor, who blushed beneath his seafaring swagger.

"'Tis nothing, lad. You know my politics. Are you sure that you won't stay with me tonight?"

"We need to get on our way. Tell Jeffrey we owe both of you, much obliged."

"No bother, lad and lassie. Call me any time."

"We undoubtedly will, Martin. The condition demands it," Tadgh said, as he held out his arms to lift Morgan gently onto the deck.

"Home, my love?"

"Soon, aroon. First, we must visit Tomas. I've got to get Casement's message to Padraig. I know it's negative, but he entrusted us with it. People tried to kill us so that we wouldn't deliver it. We owe that to Sir Roger."

When they knocked at Tomas MacCurtain's door, Tadgh's Cork Brigade boss was fortunately at home. MacCurtain ushered them into a small hallway, and the three stood in a tight circle.

"My God, Tadgh, I've just come from Dublin, and we all thought you were dead. I went to your safe house a month ago, and your boat was gone. Padraig is distressed."

"We're alive and well, Tomas. But *The Republican* is sunk."

"Where have you been off to?"

Tadgh filled him in on their adventures on the continent.

"For the love of Mary, Tadgh. The trenches?"

"We need to reconsider the value of the Irish Volunteers who support Redmond. They are patriots of a sort."

"But not to free Ireland."

"Not the ones in the prison camps in Germany. But I'm just saying, they're hard fighters. Don't count them out. And we need to discuss military tactics and equipment. If the bloody British use their trench warfare here—it's a wasteland there, don't ya know."

"They wouldn't dare, Tadgh, surely."

"You should see all the broken men and twisted landscape, sir," Morgan shook her head.

"Guerilla warfare, Tomas. Hit and run like the old days. That's what we need."

"I don't make those decisions, Tadgh. It's up to the military council, you know."

Tadgh relayed the pessimistic message from Casement intended for the head of the Irish Volunteers, Eoin MacNeill. "Can you take it to the Headmaster, Tomas? Padraig needs to hear it. The Germans clearly didn't want Casement's views known to our leadership." Tadgh explained his theory about that.

"I think you are probably right. The *Boche* want us to rise, but they don't want to propel America into the war. I'll see that Padraig gets Casement's message," MacCurtain said. "But it won't matter."

"Blood must flow," Tadgh remembered.

"Precisely. You're to continue to lie low, Tadgh."

"Is there a Rising planned?"

"You're to lie low, Tadgh, that's all you need to know."

"Let's go, Tadgh. I want to get home." Morgan tugged at his sleeve.

Tadgh was furious. Tomas knew something and he wasn't telling. Before they left, and despite his anger, Tadgh took Tomas aside into his kitchen, out of earshot of Morgan. "Since you won't tell me what is going on . . ."

"Since I can't, you mean."

"Since you won't tell me, then you owe me a favor."

"Name it."

"I need to know what happened to the babies on the *Lusitania*. Call on Jack Jordan the Cunard manager at Queenstown and ask him without saying why or who asked you. Can you do that, Tomas?"

"All the babies?"

"No, just the group that was being looked after, together down in the bowels of the ship at the time of the sinking." He tried to remember what Morgan had said. "In the nursery or something."

"How do you know this, and why does it matter?"

"You don't have a need to know." Tadgh felt somewhat better after getting that statement out.

"Oh, all right. I'll let you know what I find out."

Tadgh didn't even thank his boss as they returned to where Morgan was waiting outside by the Kerry.

"I still want to kill Boyle," Tadgh announced when they were passing through Cork City near the RIC barracks.

"Not today, mavorneen. I know he killed your parents, but you need to be at your best for that."

Tadgh slammed on the brake. "That damn Tomas knows something. We should go to Dublin and see Padraig." He turned the Kerry around and started heading northeast.

"What are you doing?" Morgan chided, grabbing hold of his right arm. "I need to go home, now, and you're exhausted."

"To hell with that. I need to find out what's goin' on." Tadgh gunned the engine and accelerated.

"Then let me off, first." Morgan stood up in the sidecar.

"Sit down, woman, before you fall out." Tadgh was yelling over the whining of the engine.

"Then stop and let me out." Morgan continued to stand.

"I hate being the last to know, after all I've done." Tadgh screamed, but then slowed the vehicle to a stop.

Morgan hopped out.

"Get back in, for heaven's sake."

She could see the fire in his eyes. The wheels were churning. This was a defiant side of Tadgh that she'd never seen before, and she didn't like it one little bit. She could be as defiant as he was. Shaking her finger at him, she stated, "Not unless you take me home right away. You're acting like a madman. Go wherever you need to, tomorrow. Today, take me home, please." *The damn revolution is more important to him than family.*

Tadgh shoulders sagged. "Get in, please. I'll take you home, girl, if you must."

Morgan jumped back into the sidecar. "Yes, I must go home."

He turned the motorcycle around and headed southwest toward Creagh. They were silent the rest of the way home, both stewing in their own thoughts. The war and all its mayhem ran counter to every fiber of her being. Morgan wondered for the first time since the Front whether she was in league with a violent warmonger, and if so, did that make her one of them, despite her beliefs?

When Tadgh and Morgan walked into the kitchen of their ancient farmhouse they had left that day almost three months earlier, they were surprised that the place had remained intact. The butter, now rancid, was still on the kitchen table. The dishes, still partly washed, were in the sink. And the walls held the cold in, up against the river air like they were. But it was a wonderful home. It seemed to bring them back together, at least for the time being.

"I'll set the fire and boil the water while you get ready for a bath," Tadgh said, as he closed and locked the front door. He remembered the intoxication and excitement of their lovemaking their first time at the An Stad Hotel and Pub just before O'Donovan Rossa's funeral last July. Now they had time, and it would be slower, stronger. Although he could not banish politics from his mind altogether, he could push those thoughts away for a bit and find comfort in his lover's embrace. He leaned forward to brush the black ringlets from her smoky green eyes and run his finger along the elegant curve of her lips. She returned him that look that never failed to arouse him. Jesus, she was shameless. *Woman, give a man some time,* his dark eyes pleaded. She knew exactly what she was doing, tangling him closer to her, her needs strong. His fingertips on her face snapped sharply with electricity, a sweet pain he hoped would never go away.

Morgan kissed his fingers and palm. In that instant, he surrendered to her and the electricity shot through his entire body. Would he always be helpless before her? Aye, he gave himself over to her, the freest thing he had ever done in his whole life. His soul that no man nor God could take from him—ever—he put into her hands for her to do with what she willed.

Morgan moved to the stairs while Tadgh stirred the fire in the stove's belly in hopes of bringing water for their bath more quickly to boil. Five minutes later bubbles erupted on the surface, and Tadgh exercised care in removing the steaming cauldrons from the stove. *Not a moment too soon for the likes of me,* Tadgh thought, as he slammed the stove door shut with his knee and turned to start up the stairs.

When he reached the top, he found Morgan standing there, examining the banister closely. Before he could voice his observation that she was still fully dressed, she turned with a question, instead of a kiss, on her lips.

"Tadgh, do you see this carving here on the banister? It's difficult to see, but you can feel it sure enough if you run your hand over it."

"My love, you have ensnared me with your wicked ways, and I will look at this mystery, yes, but no other thought but of you is in my mind. Ah, you're a right Papist, Morgan, with all this talk, hopin' to put my pleasure off. Come with me now, lass." He was loathe to be distracted from his original intent, but he could not ignore the excitement in her voice. It must be something important if Morgan was sidetracked.

Together they poured the steaming water into the bathroom tub, and Tadgh handed Morgan into it as if she was boarding a queen's barge on the ancient Nile. When he slipped in beside her, she shoved his head under the water, and he took one of her nipples into his mouth as if he were a blind babe, gently, but his lips and then his teeth became more insistent. She was turning and turning for him, heartbeat and breathing rising. Her very blood and bones sang out for him, to come and bury himself in her body. He closed his hands over her buttocks and drove into her with a power that overcame them both. He slowed his movements so he could feel her exquisite response, the signal that they were in utter union. Only then did they approach the explosion of climax and abandon, their lips, hands, and breathing quickening in pleasure. Their bodies became one in their dance, each completely inhabiting the other. Never would they be complete without their soulmate. When at last they lay exhausted in each other's arms, Tadgh wept without shame when he turned his gaze to Morgan's face and saw the sweet, sweet tears that shone on her face. They held each other with gentle reverence and kissed each other's tears away. They would have stayed floating in their embrace, but the water turned cold. Climbing from the tub, they wrapped one another in dry towels and made their way to bed.

Sinking into the eider covers, Morgan and Tadgh continued their stroking and kissing. It was as if they could not bear to be separated. As their breathing slowed and blood moved more slowly in their veins, Morgan begged Tadgh to look at the curious carving she had discovered on the banister. *Good God, this woman is insatiable, whether it be an old mystery or my body.*

Tadgh laughed with Morgan as they wound blankets about themselves and stepped out onto the landing.

"Centuries of hands have gripped here, feeling these nicks, but probably never discovering this."

"Except for you, observant one."

"There, see, just as I told you, on the back of the rail, skull and crossbones." Morgan pointed to marks carved into the old wood.

"This is interesting. I have never noticed these marks before. What's that underneath it?"

"Looks like initials of some sort. Something like the letters *JdcM* maybe. They've been here a long time, I'm sure."

Tadgh looked closely. "Let me get my glass." He padded into his secret room, behind the bedroom wall where he kept all his genealogical treasures.

After examining the marks closely under his magnifying lens, he proclaimed, "There's a faint horizontal mark in the 'c'. I think it was originally an 'e'."

"So what does 'JdeM' stand for?" Morgan asked as she peered down at the skull.

"Any student of the medieval Christian religion knows the answer," he exclaimed, running his forefinger over the ancient carving.

"I can't remember back beyond seven months ago."

"By all that's holy, the letters stand for Jacques de Molay," he whispered, almost reverently.

"Who was he, and why was he here?"

"Unless this house was here in the 1300s, he was never here," Tadgh answered mysteriously. "But let me say that Jacques de Molay was the last Grand Master of the Knights Templar." Tadgh could hardly contain himself. "Let me explain. There was a group of Christian knights who got together starting around 1120 AD to protect Christian pilgrims on their way to the Holy Land, that is, Jerusalem and areas around there." He stopped talking, took a last look at the banister then gave her a sly look under his lashes. "It's too cold here, let's get back to bed and I'll tell you everything."

When they returned to the comfort of the bed, they settled against each other, heads nestled into one shared pillow.

Morgan wanted more of the story. "Why did Christian pilgrims need protection?"

"Because Muslim nations were invading the Christian realm in that part of the world. This started a series of Holy Wars called the Crusades, which lasted for over two hundred years. These Christian knights, who came from all over Europe, fought in the eastern Mediterranean region, and eventually headquartered in Jerusalem, near what had been Solomon's Temple. So they became known as the Knights Templar." Tadgh's eyes shone as he spoke, and Morgan hadn't seen the scholarly side of Tadgh for several months.

He continued, "They were also very good businessmen, and the organization grew quite wealthy. There were some stories that they found substantial buried wealth in or under what was Solomon's Temple. But that is just hearsay." He shifted and got comfortable.

"By the end of the 1200s, they were the bank for several emerging nations. King Phillipe IV of France, for example, owed them great sums of money that he had borrowed to finance wars and other campaigns. Although they initially had the blessings of the various Popes of that time because of their good deeds for the Church, Phillipe convinced Pope Clement V, a Frenchman in the early 1300s, that the Templars were too powerful and corrupt. Phillipe had probably dreamed up this set of charges so he could gain financial control of his country."

"What happened then?" Morgan was warming to the story, but what amazed her more was Tadgh's phenomenal memory for detail. She hungered for it.

"Phillipe, with the Pope's reluctant blessing, had many of the Knights Templars arrested and thrown in jail on Friday, the thirteenth of October in 1307. This included the leaders of the organization. He had them tortured until they finally admitted to some of the charges brought against them. That was an accepted form of interrogation in those days, but human nature doesn't change. Mr. Rossa was tortured by the damn English when he was in jail many years ago, although he never succumbed to his captors."

Morgan turned her face, staring up at Tadgh. "We almost succumbed to our captors, didn't we. But go on," she urged.

"Jacques de Molay was kept in jail for seven years before the Pope finally agreed to convict him of the crimes he had admitted to under torture. In 1314, the Pope was going to sentence him to life in prison, but Jacques recanted his confession at the last minute. Phillipe quickly took matters into his own hands and had him and others slowly burned at the stake the next day."

Morgan shuddered. *War, intrigue, betrayal, again and again. History repeating itself like some sort of bad dream*, she thought. She wondered if she and Tadgh would end up as a tale in history, their story told by descendants in hushed tones, as they whispered about revolution and rebellion.

"Before he succumbed to the fire, de Molay cursed the King and the Pope and predicted they would soon die. After that the Knights Templar organization disintegrated and their immense land and monetary wealth were confiscated, much of it by Phillipe and the Pope."

"That's what the English did to the native Irish Clans in the 1500s and 1600s, wasn't it?" Morgan remembered.

"Exactly. The same barbaric travesties. Interestingly enough, both Phillipe and Pope Clement died within one year. There are many stories that have emerged through the ages about the Templars, few of which are substantiated ."

"Tell me." Morgan was intrigued. She seemed to like these Templars, their spirit, their power.

"It's a fact that many of the Knights were killed or executed at that terrible time. They were martyred for their cause. But it is purported that some survived and joined another Christian organization called the Hospitallers, which had the Pope's favor at that time. They received many of the Templars' assets from him. This group of Knights initially provided medical care for Christians in the Eastern Mediterranean region during the time of the Crusades. It is told that they were above suspicion."

Morgan's green eyes widened at the talk of medical caregivers. "Go on," she urged.

"The Pope had tried to get the Knights Templar to merge with this other order, but de Molay had refused. As it turned out, the Pope got his way in the end." He sighed, pulled the blanket up to his chin, and stared at the ceiling, growing quiet, then he looked back into lovely her eyes.

"What other stories are there, Tadgh?" Morgan asked with rapt interest. She had rested her head in the curve of his arm so her attention was focused completely on the long-ago story. As for Tadgh, he kept his eyes on her face so he would not be distracted by the creamy softness of her neck and breasts. He pulled the blanket a little more snugly around her, studiously avoiding the temptation of the nipples that winked naughtily at him, and continued the tale.

"Well, there are three that come to mind from my research. First, rumors exist that some of the Knights Templar went underground, and that the organization, much like our IRB, still operates in a clandestine way today in several countries of the world. It is said that de Molay's Naval fleet commander, Roger Bellechance, sailed with eighteen Templar ships from their main port, La Rochelle, on the west coast of France on the fateful Friday the thirteenth. They headed for safe haven in Scotland, traveling along the west coast of our Ireland to avoid England. Related rumors abound that the Templars found some artifacts of profound religious significance, or knowledge about the whereabouts of them, in or near Solomon's Temple. So the presumption is that this ongoing underground organization, if it exists, is still trying to protect these artifacts, wherever they are. Of course, there is no proof of any of this." He sat up, fluffed up the pillow beneath his head, and turned to her. With a gentle finger under her chin, he tilted her face up to look into her eyes.

She melted inside. His eyes shone, reverently almost, looking out at some distant point beyond her. "What's the third story?" Morgan could feel the back of her neck prickle and begin to go numb, as she had experienced before some time in her far distant past. This feeling had come to her before, she was sure of it.

"That brings me to why I came up with Jacques de Molay's name so quickly from the carved initials. That's why I was so startled. There is a rumor that some of the Knights retrieved the bones of Jacques de Molay after he was burned at the stake. According to this story, only his skull and femur leg bones survived, although blackened. These knights, so it is told, were furious with the King and the Pope for destroying their beloved organization in such a devious and barbaric way." He looked back into her eyes, his own spooling in dark mystery so that she could not see into them very clearly.

"They say that these knights joined the pirate organizations that ravaged the Mediterranean Sea to get revenge on their oppressors. They chose de Molay's skull and crossbones as their emblem of defiance. And some of them eventually became . . ."

Morgan flashed to the past, to a prior conversation they had had months ago before their European adventure. "Barbary pirates?" Morgan asked, remembering Tadgh's long-ago comment the first time he showed her his tiny office.

"Precisely, my dear. What a quick study you are," Tadgh said, giving her a kiss on her cheek, then caressing the nape of her neck. "Do you know what they call that black flag with the white skull and crossbones?"

"No, what?"

"The Jolly Roger."

She laughed, caught up in his intriguing story, then drifted into thought, falling silent.

Tadgh's fingers tickled her arm, and his tracing of a mysterious pattern on her skin brought her back.

"So these initials under the carved skull and crossbones could be very significant, and we do know that Jacques de Molay is revered by much of the world," he murmured, his eyelids dropping a little as his face softened and relaxed.

"I'm intrigued and puzzled at the same time," Morgan said, her mind retracing the banister letters in her memory, thinking of a mystery quite literally under their fingertips. "Of course, it could just be the meaningless scratchings by a child of some previous owner."

"Maybe. As you've said, this house is full of surprises." Tadgh stared into her green eyes, wondering where she was drifting. "What are you thinking, love?"

"The Templars, their suffering, the darkness they had seen." She felt a curtain fall over her eyes. "Could we suffer the same fate?"

"Not while I'm breathing."

She hoped that what might be about to happen in Ireland, that which her basic instinct for saving life could not avoid, would not be as ghastly as what she had seen in Belgium. She conjured images of recent memory, wondering what Antoine and Doctor Heinrich were doing at that moment, inundated at the Front with the dying. And Queen Nurse. What had *she* thought about their abrupt departure? Then she thought of Gerda and the boys, and all the poor young soldiers on both sides of that crazy war. What a bizarre and dangerous few months it had been. Yet the friendships forged in a frightening time, kinships really, had transcended national boundaries. She concluded that people were basically good, that it was the avarice of the warmongers and politicians controlling them causing horrific war and its terrible consequences. She prayed for their health and their souls, for all of them.

Tadgh broke into her reverie. "I want to explore another mystery that you have given me," and with that, he wound his arms about her waist and made ready to rediscover the heart of her body .

Chapter Eighteen
Baby Claire

March 5, 1916
Toronto General Hospital, Canada

The hospital corridors seemed to stretch endlessly to Kathy as she walked, supported between Lil and Fiona when her contractions grew steadily stronger and more painful. Drawing on their own experiences of childbirth, her best friend, and her mother agreed that the longer Kathy could stay on her feet and move, the more she could distract herself from the powerful force of the contractions. The two women also distracted the mother-to-be with comments that poked gentle fun at the menfolk who were altogether useless at this time. The best they could do was pace back and forth in the waiting room, puffing on their noxious pipes and noisily making plans for the coming child. As Kathy stopped to grip the forearms offered to support her through a new contraction bearing down on her lower back like a boxer's fist, Fiona could see Collin and Sam through the waiting room window across the hall.

She wondered where her husband Ryan was at this, the hour of the birth of his first grandchild. She thought briefly about the change she had noticed in him during the last months after she had put her foot down and refused to tolerate anymore of his shenanigans. Fortunately her daughter and Collin has allowed her to move in with them in The Beaches. The man's face showed a compassion that made her think he had grown out of his brutish behavior, but just as this occurred to her, he caught sight of her through the room's doorway and gave her a roguish wink. *Well, better not make the decision to come back to him right now. My daughter needs all my attention this minute.*

When Kathy's knees buckled under the force of the next contraction, Lil and Fiona wordlessly agreed that it was time to get her to the delivery room and make her as comfortable as possible. They helped her get onto a bed and change from her street clothes into a hospital gown. While Lil went out the door to find the midwife, Fiona helped Kathy to lie on her side to relax as much as possible. The intervals between contractions were noticeably shorter, and Fiona told Kathy to breathe when she felt the pain roll over her, so she wouldn't be too exhausted for the ordeal ahead.

When Lil returned with the midwife in tow, Kathy's brow was bathed in sweat, and she trembled with the effort to endure the next wave of pain. The midwife clucked as she rearranged Kathy onto her back and opened her legs to, as she put it, "have a quick look–see." The woman frowned with concentration as she gently probed Kathy's birth canal, then withdrew her hands and turned to Fiona and Lil standing in attendance at the bedside. "The baby is in breech position, presenting its buttocks first, so we have to call the doctor. I can feel the legs curled up and blocking the birth canal. If we don't act immediately, the baby will exhaust itself."

When Kathy heard the midwife's words, her eyes widened in fear and her hands shot out to grab onto her mother. A deep guttural moan escaped her lips, and Lil held Kathy's shoulders steady so she wouldn't fall from the bed. "Now, now, dear. Really, it will do you no good to be afraid. We will get you to an operating room, and the doctor will make everything right." The midwife's brusque response to Kathy's fear made Lil seethe with anger. *The cow has no feelings for this girl. She probably doesn't even know Kathy's name. She talks like this is a great inconvenience, she has no compassion.*

The midwife hurried from the room, and Fiona heard her summon a nurse to prepare the operating room while she contacted the doctor. She sent in another nurse to Kathy's bed who would prepare her for delivery. Fiona held tight to Kathy's hand as her daughter writhed in pain and dread. Fiona herself worried at this unexpected development and determined she would stay at Kathy's side, no matter what any doctor or midwife told her.

The nurse quickly sponged Kathy's face and neck and straightened the sheets around her before she wheeled her down the corridor. Although anyone looking at Kathy's face could tell that she was in extreme distress, the nurse wouldn't want her patient to suffer the embarrassment of exposure or add to the anxiety of any family members nearby. Kathy twisted a damp cloth in her hands and managed not to cry out when she glimpsed Collin's pale face through the waiting room window as she went by. An orderly opened the door to let the gurney pass into the operating room, and Kathy could hear the sound of running water splashing into basins, metal implements clicking against one another, and disembodied voices whispering in hushed tones. No sooner had the nurse positioned the bed directly beneath a bright electric light, then Kathy heard a door behind her whoosh open and a rosy-cheeked face came into her line of sight.

"Well, young lady, it seems you need a bit of help from me to get your little one into the world. Let's move you to your back, so we can get to work here." The doctor vigorously rubbed his hands together to warm them before he pulled off the blanket covering Kathy and gently moved her legs apart for his examination.

"Mrs. . . . uh . . . ?" His hesitation prompted Fiona to tell him Kathy's name. "Ah, yes, Mrs. O'Donnell, I will do my best to get you and your baby acquainted as soon as possible." He turned his head to the midwife who was standing nearby, "And Sister, let's get the chloroform administered to Mrs. O'Donnell here, so she's as comfortable as possible." The doctor's face disappeared, and Kathy soon felt tugging motions between her legs.

Despite the excruciating cramping she felt, Kathy concentrated as the doctor's clear voice gave her instructions to breathe the chloroform in slowly and shallowly while he massaged the baby's buttocks and legs out. The baby's stomach and chest followed soon after, but the shoulders were too wide and stopped the birthing process.

"Sister, scalpel please. Now Mrs. O'Donnell, I am making a cut to widen the passage so the baby can continue moving along here. There is pain, but you are strong and can do this."

"Just get . . . get this baby out! Now!" Kathy stammered with dry chapped lips and squeezed her eyes shut. She turned her head restlessly on the pillow, while Lil did her best to keep a cool damp cloth on Kathy's forehead. She hardly felt the pressure from the incision that allowed the shoulders to slip out, followed almost immediately by the baby's head and a rush of amniotic fluid.

As soon as the doctor had slapped the baby's backside to startle the little being into breathing, Kathy could hear a thready mewling that reminded her of a kitten's cry. The baby moved arms and legs in jerky motions as if glad to be finally free of the womb's confinement, the skin flushing a healthy pink as circulation improved. Kathy held her hands out for the baby, but the doctor quickly severed the umbilical cord, tied the stump, and handed the little one to the midwife to be weighed and measured. The doctor turned back to Kathy and pushed forcefully down on her abdomen to expel the placenta, and at long last, Kathy was at the end of her ordeal. She was exhausted but filled with a bliss unmatched by any she had experienced before. She floated in a sea of absolute calm, utterly relieved. She hardly paid attention when the doctor disappeared from the room.

Lil and Fiona, sufficiently recovered, fell into each other's arms, and wept with joy, then set about helping the nurse to change sheets, give Kathy a sponge bath, and dress her in a clean gown while the midwife swaddled the baby and placed the bundle in Kathy's waiting arms. The nurse wheeled

Kathy into the quiet recovery room where the rest of her family would soon meet the newest addition to the clan. Kathy immediately unwrapped the squirming little body to count toes and fingers. The newborn's eyes were swollen from its exertions to be born, and the little hands, so tiny, so perfect, balled up before its mouth. Just like his dad, she thought, a pugilist's son, to be sure.

Fiona turned her head sharply when she heard Kathy's startled gasp and hurried to her side, convinced that her daughter was in pain. Kathy's face was contorted with confusion, and she wailed, "Oh, Mother! What will Collin say? I have not given him a little girl. What am I to do? He will be so disappointed!"

Before Fiona could stop herself, she broke out in laughter and wreathed her face with a delighted smile. "Yes, a boy! A fine lusty little man who is the spitting image of his papa! You just watch, Daughter. When Collin claps his eyes on this baby, I'll wager that no father will be happier."

Her mother's wise words soothed Kathy, and when she saw the doctor poke his head around the door, Kathy's face lit up with joy. "Oh, Doctor, come see this baby. He's perfect—I'm in love with him already."

The doctor drew a chair to Kathy's bedside and sat down, crossing his long legs. "Mrs. O'Donnell, I am glad to make the acquaintance of your boy and pleased you have so well recovered. A breech birth can give us a scare, but there were no complications for you, and your baby cooperated fully. You are a lucky young woman." He rose from his seat and patted her hand. As he passed from the room before the father and the rest of the family made their appearance, the doctor saluted Fiona and Lil with his appreciation for their presence, supporting the new mother.

Before Kathy's father arrived, Collin had heard a muffled cry from his position in the waiting room. He would know that voice anywhere. "I've got to go to her, Sam." He stood up.

Sam grabbed his hand and held him back. "Let it be, Collin." *First Claire, and now Kathy. At least he's focused on the right woman this time.* "That's what Lil sounded like when our little Norah was born. The first is always the hardest."

"But there's something wrong. I can feel it."

"Nonsense, lad. They know what they're doing in there. It won't be long now. It is the way of nature."

Collin sat back down and looked distraught.

"Here, lad. Have a puff on my Prince Albert. It always calms me down."

Collin turned up his nose at the offer of Sam's pipe, and folded and unfolded a newspaper. When he heard Kathy cry out again, Sam put his hand on Collin's shoulder.

"How's it going at the paper?" Sam asked, cuffing his strapping protégé Collin on the chin. The young man was hanging his head again, as usual.

Collin realized that Sam started the line of questioning to get his mind off what was going on in the other room. "As well as can be expected, boss," Collin answered, focused on the pain his beloved Kathy might be going through. Was having a child like the intense heat of fire? With waves of flames? Then he remembered the flames he had experienced years before in the warehouse fire, and his past that had been headed for a life of crime, most likely, before Sam plucked him from the flames of ruin. He owed Sam, Lil, and their two daughters, the world and his life.

"I just hope it's a girl," Collin said, twisting the newspaper into a mangled mess.

"I know, my boy, it's all in God's hands. If it's a boy, I could loan you one of my girls."

"Sam, don't you be kidding me, not now. I know those young beauties are your lifeblood, but thank you, anyway."

"Aye, lad, so they are."

At that moment, Kathy's father Ryan strode into the waiting room, roses in hand.

"Well now, Collin, how's my lass doing?"

"Fine, sir, as far as I know. You are welcome to join us men in the dark, so to speak. It's been four hours since we got here. The doctor knows what he's doing. Lil and Fiona are in there helping Kathy."

"She's my only daughter, she is." Ryan's face caved in a little, the dark circles under his eyes accentuating craggy features. "Kathy's just like her mother, a fine lady. Good Lord, how I miss Fiona," Ryan said, lowering his head and scuffing the tile floor.

"Your daughter's the finest lady in Toronto in my book," Collin said, rising and clapping his father-in-law on the back. "Have my seat."

"Thanks, son. May I call you that? I owe you an apology, lad."

"How's that, sir?"

"I thought you an oaf, what with that motorcycle and all."

"I thought me an oaf if the truth be known. But your daughter, and my boss here, Samuel Stevenson Finlay, have made a man of me."

"You did it yourself, lad," Sam said, thinking about his dead brother Liam who never had a chance. *Poor Liam. He would also be proud at this moment.* It made all the difference in the world.

"I know that you agonize over the whereabouts of your sister, Collin. How's that search going?"

Collin could not believe his ears. Only a year before, he had almost come to blows because Kathy's father was so inconsiderate of his family. Now the man was all sympathy and support for others instead of himself. Ryan had had an epiphany on the wedding day, showing up at the church at the last minute, and his wife's leaving him had made the old bastard think. The prospect of a grandchild, to top that off, must have helped in some way. It seemed to have humbled the man and made him join humanity again.

"I am hoping that she is still alive in Ireland, sir. Kathy and I are going there during her summer break."

"But what about the baby?"

"Remember, Liz and I would like to look after your baby while you're gone," Sam reminded Collin.

"It's Lil, now, Sam. Norah'd be riled."

"Force of habit," Sam grinned.

"Thanks, boss. I'm sure that little Norah and Dot wouldn't mind having a baby cousin around for a few weeks. But Lil is expecting, right after Kathy. Won't it be too much for her?"

"Not at all, lad. The more the merrier. We love babies."

Collins' father-in-law chimed in, "If I could win Fiona back, then she and I could take care of the baby, too, even though we haven't had a newborn around the house for twenty-five years or so." Ryan's eyes lit up and the creases on his brow relaxed. "You are a fine example for me, Collin. Made me see the error of my ways, so to speak. I can see the love that you and my daughter share, and how you treat her. Kathy's agreed to give me a second chance, so I guess I can hope that Fiona will, too. I have done her a terrible wrong and wish to right it."

"That's the spirit."

"You have a fine wife, sir. I should know. She's been living with us nigh on these six months, as you know. If she returns to you, then I will thank you for your offer to care for your granddaughter Claire. In that case, perhaps both families can share the duties."

"That's a deal." They shook hands.

"You sure it will be a girl?"

"Absolutely, sir. It has to be." Collin raised his eyes to the ceiling as another chilling cry came through the walls.

Collin and his father-in-law rushed to the door of the waiting room just in time to see through the window, Kathy being wheeled out of the delivery room. They were rushing her down the corridor. Ryan saw the look on his wife's face and tried to give her a brave smile. It reminded him of the day when she had given birth to Kathleen—the happiest day of his life. *How did things go so terribly wrong?*

Sam came to the door. "What's all the commotion, lad?"

"They're wheelin' her somewhere else, boss. They don't look happy." Collin threw open the door and started after them down the corridor.

Sam was on him in a minute, holding him firm. "Come on back to the waiting room. You can't help her, lad. She's in good hands." He turned Collin back, though he balked.

"You convinced me not to go after Claire in Ireland or France yet, and to focus on my family, Sam. Well hell, here I am, and now you don't want me to go and help Kathy and baby Claire. She's real and just down the hall. I've got to go."

Collin tried to pull away, but Sam held him. "So you're a doctor, now? You will just get in the way, lad." Sam realized that Collin's fear for and guilt about his sister was driving his present actions. "Come on, lad, it will be all right. You'll see. We men can only do so much at these times."

Reluctantly, Collin let Sam lead him back to the waiting room.

Half an hour later, Kathy cradled her new baby, and her thoughts turned to her dear husband. What a prince he had been through all of this. The earlier altercations with her father because of Collin's questionable background were a thing of the past. He had even gotten the old boy interested in the history of his Irish O'Donnell clan. What a turnaround for them both, but he still clung to his obstinate desire to find his sister. Collin told her that the telegram inquiry he had sent to Jack Jordan at Christmas about his vision of his sister Claire on a battlefield had not borne fruit, and no more information about her was forthcoming. He said that Jack did not volunteer any information about the war in Belgium and France, either, except that he mentioned the troop ship *Aquitaine* was being sent to the port of Le Havre from time to time. He also shared with her that there had been no word back from Collin's newspaper ad in the *Southern Star*. So now Collin, *finally as it should be*, was only concerned about the birth of his baby and the health of his wife. He told her that she and the baby came first.

Fiona held her daughter's hand and touched the baby's foot. "Daughter, I would love to stay and help you with the baby, but it's time that I leave your home. You need space for the little one."

"I hope you do move back with Father," Kathy continued. "He's changed, really changed since you left him."

"Where else can I go? He certainly surprised me at the wedding, Daughter. But it's hard to make a purse out of a sow's ear." Fiona stroked the baby's fine dark hair, marveling at its softness. "We'll have to see."

Kathy reflected on her life with Collin. Who would have thought that a public schoolmarm would have met the man of her dreams, a wild Irishman so different from the man of her father's dreams. When she needed him most, Collin had saved her from bodily harm when she had been attacked, and he had protected her during their hair-raising search for his lost sister in the United States. Along the way, she had saved his life as many times as he had saved hers and her life had taken a thrilling turn for the better.

The baby stretched his legs and turned his mouth to her breast. She looked down at her son, pleased with the new little life that she and Collin had created. No matter that it wasn't a girl. Her mother was right. Her primary goal was to raise a healthy child. Kathy was proud that Collin had prioritized her and the coming baby in his life. What agony they had felt when they had learned that Claire was on board the *Lusitania* when it was torpedoed and sunk last May. She was reported lost at sea like so many others. And now new life had come into the world. She pressed the newborn close to her, relieved that they were both alive together.

It is odd what thoughts run through your head at a time like this. Like your life flashing before your eyes when you are in mortal danger. Giving birth is a mortal danger, especially the first time. She remembered the very day that they held that remembrance service for an empty casket for Claire in Toronto, and then they heard that she might have been spotted in Ireland in the company of a young Irishman, still alive. But the facts were certainly not clear, Kathy concluded. If only her husband did not feel responsible for Claire's disappearance from Brooklyn in the first place. *It wasn't his fault, poor lad. Why can't he see that? He will never give up looking,* she lamented. *His manhood and our marriage are clearly at risk until this is resolved. And now, most importantly, we have this new life to nurture.* Kathy's thoughts continued to swirl.

The midwife came into the waiting room and shook Collin's hand. "Congratulations, young man. You have a healthy baby son. Eight pounds and three ounces of a wee boy with a great mop of jet-black hair." She smiled. "That must run in the family."

"A son, you say." Collin looked dazed.

"A celebration is in order, my boy," Sam exclaimed, pulling cigars out of his waistcoat pocket.

"How's my wife doing?" Collin peered at the open door behind him.

"Your wife is tired, but she will be fine. She is a trooper, that girl. You can go on in to see her and your baby now."

The men shuffled into the recovery room and quietly stood near the bed. "Oh, Collin, it's a boy. What a surprise!" Kathy smiled. "Not what we were expecting, was it, but just look at him!" She glowed.

Collin kissed her brow. He squeezed her hand and gently stroked the curve of her cheek. "I love you more than ever, lass. Now, let me have a look at my fine son." He held out his arms.

She opened the blanket to reveal a perfect sleeping baby and handed the bundle to Collin.

"Oh, he's a handsome little thing," Collin whispered. "Looks just like me!" he beamed, cradling his son in his arms. He winked at his wife, "We can make a Claire *next* time," Collin said, smiling.

Kathy nodded, and pulled her husband with his bundle closer to her, the three of them together as one. She watched her Collin as he examined the tiny set of perfect toes and fingers. "A miracle," he said, and his eyes met hers and melted.

Then Collin noticed the others circled around the bed, Sam and Lil, Fiona and Ryan. He noticed that Kathy's mother stood next to her husband, their hands entwined, shoulders touching. "Sam, Kathy and I were convinced that the baby would be a girl, but we discussed that if we had a boy, we would name him Liam, and that we would like you and Lil to be the godparents."

"Liam," Sam whispered. "I can't imagine a better name for a young Irish lad." Sam crowded close to get a look at the child. "My brother would be proud of his namesake."

Lil smiled. Now maybe Sam's misguided guilt about the death of his younger brother would end, allowing them both to rest in peace. She squeezed her husband's hand, and he squeezed back.

The sun broke through the March storm clouds and rays of golden light streamed through the window and into the recovery room.

Map of Southwest Ireland - April 1916

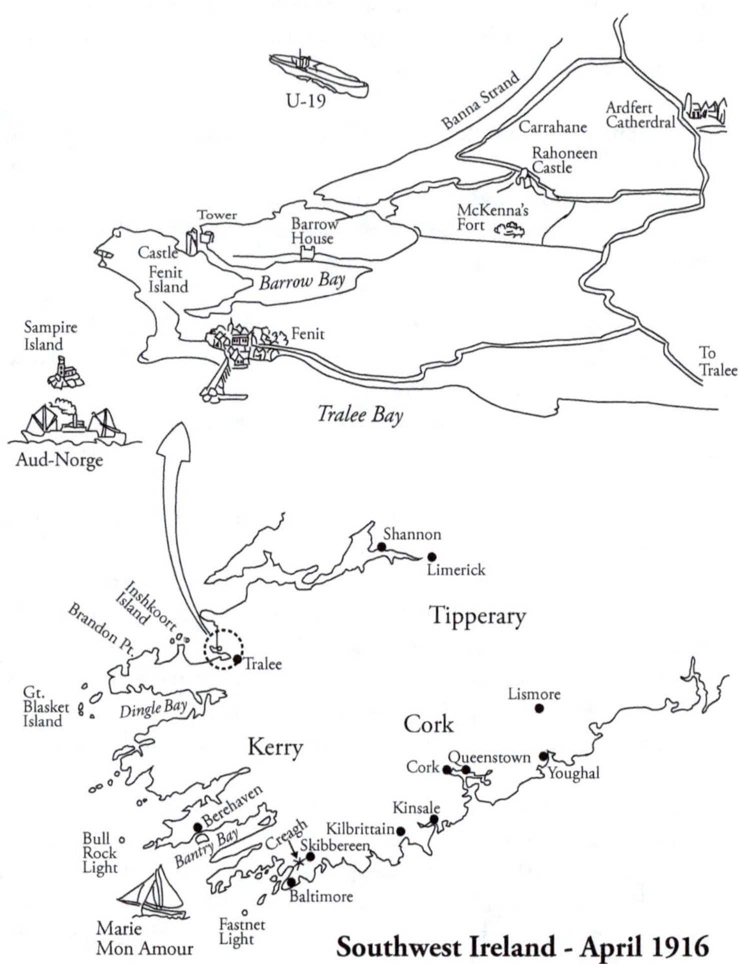

Chapter Nineteen
Sea Patrol

March 6, 1916
Creagh, County Cork, Ireland

he weather in January and February had been colder than usual with several days of snow on the ground, keeping Tadgh and Morgan mostly indoors. The latitude of Ireland closely matched that of ice-bound Labrador, yet the Gulf Stream normally kept the waters, and therefore the land, much more temperate than it did its Canadian counterpart.

Tadgh remembered that fierce storm back in 1910 when the polar maritime blasts had driven snow to a depth of two feet in the southwest portion of the country. Normally snow, if it came at all, would not last for more than a day since the air temperature was usually well above freezing. But that year the whole of southwest Ireland had been blanketed for two weeks.

This winter the Gulf Stream had more or less kept the polar winds at bay. Today, however, those winds were up, and a sleeting rain had started unexpectedly around two in the afternoon.

"I'm tired of waiting here like a caged tiger," Tadgh cursed, his muscular six-foot-one frame striding back and forth around the red-hot pot-bellied stove in the confining kitchen. "When are we going to get some orders?" He flicked his black curls out of his eyes.

"More tea, my dear?" Morgan sighed, weary of listening to his impatient rants. "It's certainly not a day fit for man nor beast, is it."

"I've been on maneuvers in worse, but I'm certainly glad to be here with you now. Don't you think you should put some clothes on? I mean, more than a robe? It can't be keeping you warm."

"But I was hoping for a repeat performance after tea, my love."

Morgan could see that her words had struck home, particularly when she purposefully bent her lithe hourglass figure over to retrieve some scones from the oven. Tadgh was contemplating his answer or attack plan when the front door knocker sounded.

Morgan dropped the pan of scones on the stovetop and rushed

upstairs for more suitable clothing.

"Who the hell would be needin' to visit us during this storm?" The Luger was in Tadgh's pocket. He flicked off the safety and then rubbed the condensed moisture off the door pane to check before opening. When he saw who it was and his condition, Tadgh threw open the door, ushered the man in, and gave him a bear hug.

"Well now, Aidan. What in heaven's name are you doing here, brother? You must be frozen through."

His younger brother made Tadgh think about the Norse god, *Jokul Frosti*, commonly called Jack Frost, with icicles dangling from his whiskers, eyebrows and his board-stiff scarf, and his face blanched from the cold. He looked almost petrified. Aidan's body shook in reaction to the warmth inside the room.

"Come over and sit down by the fire, my boy, for heaven's sake." Tadgh guided him to a chair. Aidan sagged into it and started to melt, dripping water all over the floor.

"Morgan, it's Aidan. He is chilled to the bone. Bring down the heavy blanket."

She raced down the stairs, hastily tucking in her blouse with one hand and bearing a warm blanket in the other. "Aidan, we're so glad to see you. Oh my God, you're freezing!" She worked to bundle him up in the blanket.

Aidan gave a faint smile when Morgan hugged him through the blanket and flashed her smoky green eyes his way. "So glad I made it," he chattered through clenched teeth.

Grabbing her half-filled cup from the table, she coaxed, "Here, sip some of this tea. But slowly, not too much too soon." She touched his cheek with the back of her hand. Nearly frozen, she thought. His shoulders were square, not sagging, despite his condition. Aidan was two inches shorter than his brother, but with the same burly build and curly black hair. He looked a little ruddy at the moment.

Morgan gently removed Aidan's brittle gloves. His fingers were cold as ice, but the circulation was still there. She massaged his hands and fingers. Then she noticed the good quality of his wool-lined boot tops, which may have saved his feet. Morgan removed his boots and started massaging his toes through damp socks. "Can you feel this?"

"Somewhat. There's prickles."

"Good." She pulled off his socks and examined his feet.

"Have I got frostbite?"

"Thank God, no. I think you're going to live, my boy, but just barely."

She smiled. Morgan looked up at Tadgh watching the whole procedure.

"Brother, what possessed you to leave St Edna's and come down here in this bleedin' weather, and how did you even get here?"

"I came by train to Galway. It wasn't raining like this when I started out yesterday morning. Mr. Pearse sent me with a letter for you," he answered slowly. His body stopped shaking. "And a present. I'm a courier now, don't ya know."

"Galway. Whatever for?"

"We heard that you lost *The Republican.* So I am delivering the present." Aidan broke into a grin.

Tadgh's eyes widened as he deciphered the meaning of Aidan's words. He threw on his overcoat and raced out the door down toward the dock. Sleet swirled into the kitchen through the open door, and the draft coaxed sparks to fly up out of the fireplace in the corner. Morgan pulled a thick cardigan around her and peered out the open door, watching him as he descended.

The icy steps made Tadgh stumble. He stopped short, grabbing the metal rails, and made his way down to the Ilen River where the present awaited him.

There she sat, gathering a coat of ice, cleated to the dock, sails furled. "My God. She's beautiful," Tadgh exclaimed, boarding the new hooker and then gripping the main mast. He explored the deck and new quarters. *Geotag class just like The Republican. But at least ten years newer. Unbelievable. This is Padraig's doing. And Aidan's. What a feat.* The river beyond was just starting to freeze at the shore, but the center channel was open. *How did Aidan pull it off?*

"My God, you could have died out there, Aidan," Tadgh said, when he had finally returned to the warmth of the kitchen.

"Padraig said it was important to get it to you." He shrugged.

"You're lucky you made it then, to be sure."

"It wasn't raining when I left Galway. Well, it's here I am, then," Aidan said, with a little more gusto to his voice.

"Aidan here has brought us a fine new hooker all the way from Galway, by himself, no less."

He clapped his brother on the shoulder. "You've done a good thing, lad, and made your brother very happy," he beamed. He turned to Morgan and said, "He has changed, lass. He followed through on the mission, carried out his orders—it took commitment and bravery. He's one of us, now." Then he addressed Aidan, "So glad to see you, brother. Your time at

Pearse's Military School has done you a world of good. How are they treatin' you up there?"

Aidan's face lit up. "I really like it. A bunch of us who have been through hard times are being taught how to work together towards a better future for our country."

"So then. What have you brought us? We've gotten no information directly or through Tomas MacCurtain at Cork West since January."

Aidan unbuttoned his long coat and handed his brother a sealed envelope, his fingers clumsy from the cold. "This letter from the Headmaster. It must be important. He told me to get this to you immediately. So here I am, don't ye see. He also said to destroy it if I was about to be compromised."

"We're proud of you for braving this weather to bring us this," Morgan said, taking his hand in hers and warming it.

Tadgh opened the envelope and read it to himself—

> *March 1, 1916*
> *Dear Tadgh, I am sorry to have kept you in the dark these last few months, but it couldn't be helped. We were very worried when you disappeared. I sent Tomas to find you in December. You seem to have survived quite an ordeal on the continent. We must talk about it sometime, the necessary spilling of blood. I got Casement's message you sent. We expected as much after Joseph was over there last June. But we are still counting on munitions at the very least.*
>
> *I am writing this letter and delivering it in this way because there have been some security leaks. We can't use the telephone and telegraphs anymore, except in an emergency. Aidan has proved an apt student and is becoming a trustworthy Volunteer. You can share this letter with him and with your partner, Morgan, who, as I understand it, has been with you through your travails.*

At this point Tadgh informed the others that he would read the rest of the message aloud. He continued, his voice solemn,

> *I want Aidan to stay with you for support down in Cork and Kerry. I now have great confidence in his loyalty to our cause.*

Morgan beamed a broad smile at Aidan, who acknowledged the compliment with a blush.

The IRB Military Council is planning a country-wide Rising to occur on Easter Sunday, April 23. This will be the start of our glorious Revolution. There are 12,000 Irish Volunteers who we believe are committed to supporting us in this overthrow of the English menace throughout the country. And despite Casement's views we are expecting that many more of Redmond's 100,000 National Volunteers who aren't on the continent will join us after we rise. We have not informed our Irish Volunteers or their Chief of Staff, Eoin MacNeill yet. This is because he will not rise unless the Volunteers are threatened first by the Government or by the Protestant Ulster Volunteers. The only other reasons why he might agree would be if the Home Rule Bill did not get implemented or if Conscription is forced on Ireland.

Because Asquith loaded his cabinet with wretched Ulster anti-Home Rule ministers last year, we believe that the English will not honor the Home Rule Bill when the war is over. But that isn't enough for MacNeill. On January 18, Westminster enacted the Military Service Act that requires single men between eighteen and forty-one to enlist in the war effort. Our English overlord, Chief Secretary Birrell, recognizing that Irish conscription would mean certain revolution, convinced the English parliament to exclude Irishmen at this point, but it's only a matter of time.

James Connolly, who you know as head of the Irish Citizen Army here in Dublin, has been threatening to start a revolt against the English on his own. Clarke and I met with him in January and shared some of our plans for the Rising. Connolly agreed to form an alliance with the IRB and the Irish Volunteers and he will follow our lead here in Dublin. We will seize the General Post Office as our Headquarters for the New Irish Provisional Government and we will occupy other strategic facilities in Dublin.

As you know, Tadgh, we are very short on weapons. There is a plan now in place to get help from the Germans. It is not clear at this point based on your input, whether they will provide officers or just munitions. We will use the rifles we got at Howth for Dublin, but the additional German arms that are coming will need to be distributed to the Volunteers in the rest of the Country.

The present plan is for a ship masking as a Norwegian freighter to land the arms, and perhaps men, near Fenit in Tralee Bay late on Thursday, April 20. Casement will come back from Germany by submarine after the shipment has left. He will rendezvous with the freighter at the drop point and time. I have assigned Austin Stack, who, as you know, is the Commandant of the Kerry IRB, to be responsible for this operation. I am coordinating with him.

Tadgh, I hope you like your new boat. I want you and your team to patrol the southwest coast for abnormal English naval blockade convoys from now on. Then I need you to back up Stack if it becomes necessary. I will signal you if I need your emergency support in Tralee.

There will be a Rising rehearsal here in Dublin on St. Patrick's Day. MacNeill will think it is just a parade. Birrell seems content with letting us drill. But I'm not sure about his Lord Lieutenant, Lord Wimborne. This way we will find out.

You should support the Rising under your leader Tomas MacCurtain in Cork when the time comes.

Make sure the safe house is ready and secure when we need it.

The old heart of the earth needs to be warmed by the red wine of the battlefield. God help us all.

Padraig Pearse, Headmaster, St. Edna's School.

When Tadgh finished reading the message, he threw it into the fire and watched it burn. "All right, then. We're finally goin' into action," he said, as he slapped his brother on the shoulder.

"Can the English be beaten?" Morgan asked, remembering the futility and travesty of the battle on the continent.

"Yes, if Padraig is right about getting the arms and the numbers of Volunteers who will support our cause, with their blood if necessary. We want to do this now when England is preoccupied with the war with Germany. That was Tone's plan back in '98, and it's a good one. With the support of the Germans, we can finally prevail and set Ireland free, don't ye see."

"I learned about Wolfe Tone at St. Edna's, Tadgh," Aidan said. "He was the father of our Republican movement who tried to unite all Irishmen against England in the 1798 Rebellion, wasn't he."

"Yes, but in his case the help came from the French. Just like the Spanish Armada in 1588, the landing force was thwarted by the weather," Tadgh informed them. "Now it's the Germans who may help us attack our common foe. Roger Casement believes himself to be a modern-day Florence MacCarthaigh or Wolfe Tone. He's busy in Germany soliciting help from yet another ally of Ireland against the English tyrant. I met him there."

"In Germany, Tadgh? You went there?"

"Aye, lad, not willingly. But we're home now and ready to fight."

"How'd it happen, brother? Did you go, too, Morgan?"

"We were both captured by a German U-boat out where the *Lusitania* sank. It's a long story with a happy ending, Aidan."

When Aidan said he thought his brother was fooling, Tadgh rolled his trouser leg up and showed his brother the ragged scar on his lower leg. "*The Republican* went down and the U-boat captain and his men rescued us. Then Morgan saved not only my life but also the Captain's. We were both in bad shape, and she nursed us until we could get to a German hospital in Belgium."

Aidan ran his finger over the scar on Tadgh's leg and shuddered. "That looks like a nasty wound."

"Almost killed me, brother."

Aidan turned to Morgan with his silent question. "No, Aidan, not a scratch on me." She didn't want to tell him that she almost drowned or how claustrophobic she had felt with all those sailors under the weight of the sea.

"Someday we'll tell you what it was like in the trenches of the Western Front."

"You saw them, Tadgh?"

"Fought in them, lad. Believe me. We don't want to be conscripted for that war, don't ya know."

Aidan was flabbergasted. Morgan could see that he thought he was the one with the big news.

"And don't forget Gronski," Morgan shot a look at Tadgh as she applied salve to Aidan's weathered hands.

"Who's Gronski?"

"German General Staff, brother. He tried to stop us from returning home. I wonder if he will try to thwart Casement's attempts to get the arms we need. We'll have to see how it plays out."

"It concerns me that we are siding with the Germans, who are the aggressors in Europe," Morgan interjected. "We now know it's true that millions have been killed in the trenches. Those poor boys on both sides . . ."

"But the English have killed millions of us Irishmen over the centuries," Tadgh countered. "Look at the potato famine, as an example.

That was chemical warfare with a slow death. And they're still doing it, don't ye see."

"And don't forget that they murdered our Mam and Pa" Aidan added.

"Wasn't it that rogue RIC Head Constable Boyle and his henchmen, boys?"

"Yes, aroon, and they're part of the bloody English establishment."

"I love you, Tadgh, but not the thought of wholesale bloodshed. We have been over this before." She looked away, didn't want to meet his eyes.

"And I love you, Morgan, but I agree with Padraig. I resonate with his phrase about the old heart of the earth, don't ye know."

"I'll follow you and him into hell if necessary," Aidan exclaimed, stepping out of the blanket.

Morgan noticed that, again, the differences in their fundamental philosophies of life had been enunciated, and not resolved. She believed that her commitment was to save lives just as she had done on both sides in Belgium. Yet she understood, for some equally inexplicable reason, that the British evil must be stopped somehow. Why couldn't peaceful negotiations work? Because of the stubborn, hateful nature of the human male animal.

Morgan made up a section of the second floor storage room into a bedroom for Aidan, who seemed quite content with his accommodations. Tadgh noticed that Aidan would not touch any alcohol. They really did some good up there at Padraig's school, he decided.

Tadgh wanted to change *The Republican's* name to avoid notoriety during their upcoming reconnaissance mission. "What should we call her?"

"How about *Marie Mon Amour*," Morgan offered, giving Tadgh a squeeze.

"That seems like a silly female name, but not because it's French. Who's Marie, my love?"

"Antoine's wife who died on the *Lusitania*."

"Antoine again. Oh, fair enough. *Marie Mon Amour* it is."

"Who's Antoine?" Aidan chimed in.

"Long story," they replied in unison, laughing; then they linked their little fingers with the traditional Irish incantation.

The next day, the rain had given way to sunshine, which melted the ice. They started their maneuvers, staggering the days to avoid suspicion. They headed northwest up the coast as far as the mouth of Tralee Bay on the north end of the Dingle Peninsula.

The first time that they passed Berehaven Harbor at Castletownbere on the southwest coast, at the mouth of Bantry Bay, Tadgh cautioned his mates. "There's a Royal Navy anti-submarine base here. I'll bet that's the port that the English patrol ships will sail out of. Can you see that metal loop on the point over there?"

"I see it, brother. What's it for?"

"It's a magnetometer, measuring proximity to metal. They can see a signal each time a ship passes, day or night. If they see the signal but no ship is visible, then they know a submarine is passing by at close range, likely at periscope depth."

"That's ingenious. But can they see us, mavorneen? We're mostly wood construction, I should think."

"I don't know. We've got a fair bit of metal on board."

Throughout the rest of March and early April, they patrolled. The total transit time from home to Tralee Bay was a minimum of eleven hours with favorable winds. So they would leave and arrive home in the dark. Once, when the March winds did blow, they made the round trip in sixteen hours, and twice they had to turn back because of high seas. But generally, the weather improved and what precipitation fell was rain. They only saw the occasional Royal Navy anti-submarine sloop coming in or out of Berehaven or plying the Celtic Sea south of the coast. They were not challenged or stopped. Quite often, farther offshore, they would see the smoke from convoys presumably running the gauntlet between America and England. Once they saw a flash on the southern horizon and heard the boom a second later. Another U-boat casualty, most likely. But they saw no indication of a concerted effort to intercept a shipment of arms from Germany.

On a clear sunny morning on their two-day trip in early April, Tadgh and Morgan were pretending to be fishing for mackerel. They were situated at the shoals off the island of Inishtooskert at the mouth of Tralee Bay, when Morgan noticed something unusual in the distance. "Why is that boat heading right for us?"

"Looks like a Manx Nobby trawler coming out of Fenit, so it does," Tadgh announced, squinting into the sun. "We have to be careful not to anger the local fishermen who rightly feel that these are their fishing grounds. Let me do the talking."

"Who are you and where is your port?" an old salty captain yelled from the bridge of the trawler *Slanu III.*

"We're the *Marie Mon Amour* from Galway," Tadgh hollered back, using his best Galway accent. Since this was a Gaeltacht community, the locals often spoke in the Gaelic language that only Tadgh could fully understand.

"You're trespassing on our fishing grounds. Your mates in Galway won't let us fish there. So you get out," the Captain growled as they came alongside.

"Happy to oblige," Tadgh replied as he turned the hooker into the wind. "Haul in our nets, Aidan."

"And don't come back or we'll sink your puny hooker with you on it," the captain called after them, switching to the English tongue as they headed out to sea.

"Friendly sort, love. A tad territorial, aren't they?" Morgan bristled at the animosity of the trawler captain.

"These fishing grounds are getting fished out by ships from the United Kingdom and beyond. After the Great Hunger, these good Irishmen turned to fishing for their livelihood, despite being ill-equipped. They have every right to be territorial. Each seaside community has its own local fishing area. We're just going to have to be more careful when we're in this bay, to be sure."

For the first time, on their way back to Baltimore, they spotted three Royal Navy sloops and a light cruiser patrolling west of Bantry Bay. Three days later, they passed the same patrol just coming out of Berehaven.

"They don't seem to be interested in us," Aidan observed, tracking them through binoculars.

"I guess we don't look Norwegian or German. In case they have wind of our plan, we should not go into Tralee Bay from now on."

Two days later, on Sunday April 16, they saw the patrol again, up near Great Skellig Island, about two-thirds of the way from home to Tralee Bay. "I'm guessing that they know something is up," Tadgh surmised, peering intently in their direction. "We need to tell Padraig."

"The lead ship is turning our way," Morgan alerted him, tugging on his sleeve.

"We'll stay on course for home now. Morgan, please get under the tarp, lass."

Tadgh watched carefully as the warship approached on the starboard beam. When it had closed to approximately 400 yards, it slowed until it was pacing the hooker broadside.

"That's a wicked-looking ship," Morgan exclaimed from her vantage point, peering out from under the tarp.

"She's a flower class anti-submarine sloop. *HMS Bluebell*," Tadgh read the name aloud, as he scrutinized the bridge area of the ship. "She's a fierce mouser, to be sure. Three officers are looking at us through binoculars right now. Aidan, keep folding those nets, if ya please."

"She's about 250 feet long with two stacks. She can probably make twenty knots at least. And I can see the depth charge racks clearly at her stern," Aidan said, glancing sideways from his task.

Morgan shuddered when she heard those words. Tadgh had been unconscious during that murderous attack on the U-boat. She felt compassion for Fritz and his crew and wondered if they were still alive. This destroyer looked menacing compared to the submarines, especially at close range. Yet, just like what the Biblical David did to his nemesis in ancient times, this Goliath could be brought down, but it would take more than a stone. And now, these new depth charges had changed the war. What a terrible way to die down there.

She noticed the two 4.5-inch guns and several machine guns that, thankfully, weren't pointed at the *Marie.* This cat and mouse vigil continued for at least five nerve-wracking minutes when the warship closed to 100 yards. Morgan thought for sure that they would be hailed or boarded. The sound of diesels rumbled across the waves. Suddenly, the *Bluebell* veered off to starboard and made speed for the rest of its patrol group.

"That was a close call," Tadgh exclaimed. "They've got our signature now. They must have noted our presence all three times that we saw them and finally came over to investigate. We're goin' to have to avoid them at all costs from now on. They may even suspect that we're part of the welcoming committee."

All the rest of the way home, Tadgh scanned the horizon and the shoreline for any evidence that they were being followed. He couldn't detect any.

But in Berehaven the officers on duty saw them pass by and noticed the tiny blip signature on the magnetometer. Then they notified the captain of the *Bluebell.*

Tadgh was thinking how he could get his intelligence information back to Pearse. By the time they reached home, he had decided that it was high time for him to take the risk and visit Tomas MacCurtain in Cork.

Chapter Twenty
Finally Into Action

April 17, 1916
RIC Headquarters, Cork City, Ireland

District Inspector Dean Maloney paced the floor of his Cork Royal Irish Constabulary Headquarters office downtown on South Terrace just south of the Lee River. His career was on the line and he had no clue how to deal with his orders. He hated the thought of having to rely on Darcy Boyle for advice. His Head Constable was out of control.

"What do you want?" Boyle demanded as he burst into the Inspector's office.

"Close the door," Maloney requested. "Sit down. We've been given some delicate orders that I want you to handle."

Boyle chose to stand. It gave him a height advantage over his superior.

"Captain Blinker Hall, down at the Admiralty, Room 40 in London, Whitehall, has intercepted communications between the German embassy in Washington and Berlin. He has broken their code. Apparently, the Clan na Gael leader in New York, John Devoy, is masterminding German support for the Irish Volunteers. Hall says that Republican Roger Casement is in Germany, and Hall thinks that a ship is going to bring arms for the rebels from Germany to the southwest coast of Ireland in the next few days."

"Where?" Boyle had a female hooker in Tralee that he had not dominated for almost a year. He was his father's son.

"He's not sure which day or where, but either Shannon or Tralee is a good bet. He's guessing that it will be Tralee," the Inspector said. "Casement will be there at the drop point, they understand. Admiral Bayly apparently believes Hall, and he has set up a Royal Navy blockade out of Berehaven. If they try to approach along the south coast, they'll be intercepted at sea."

"Who is Bayly?" Boyle raised his eyebrows.

"Commander-in-Chief, Coast of Ireland at the Admiralty."

"So what are your orders?" Boyle asked, leaning forward and slamming his knuckles down on Maloney's desk.

"The admiral wants us to assist the Kerry RIC in patrolling the Dingle

Peninsula and Tralee area, to stop the shipment and to arrest the traitors if they try to land there. I am putting you in charge of our part of this operation, Boyle. Take anyone you need from the detachment, and don't screw up this time," he warned. Maloney stood up and paced behind his desk.

Boyle smiled. He grabbed a cigarette out of the silver box on the desk and struck a match on the rough desk mat. "What are *you* going to be doing?" He loved seeing his boss squirm.

"I will stay here in Cork in case of an insurrection," Maloney said, importantly. "Although Chief Secretary Birrell is unconvinced, Lord Lieutenant Wimborne and Sir Neville Chamberlain are concerned about the Volunteers' St. Patrick's Day parade last month. There is something big afoot with that movement," stopping to glare at his Head Constable. "Both officials wanted to raid Liberty Hall at the beginning of the month, but Birrell stopped them. At least they have shut down the production and distribution of Republican newspapers like *The Gael.*"

Boyle smirked. "Playing safe again, are we?" Clearly a rhetorical question. Before Maloney could answer, he asked him, "Have you notified Chamberlain of Hall's findings?"

"I assume that he already knows," Maloney answered, pacing again. He certainly didn't want to be the bearer of bad news. Not good for the career.

"Is that all?" Boyle growled.

"Yes. You're dismissed." Maloney turned to face his troublesome report as Boyle headed for the door. "You have forgotten something, Head Constable."

"What?"

"You are to salute a senior officer."

Boyle spun back around, glaring. He flipped his right hand somewhere near his head and stomped to the door, not bothering to see the return salute. He despised Maloney almost as much as he did the Inspector General of the RIC, Sir Neville Chamberlain, who had run him out of Dublin last August after the stupid traffic accident while chasing after McCarthy. That bastard Chamberlain wouldn't give him the time of day now. Why should Chamberlain get the glory?

When he left the Inspector still pacing, Boyle had to admit that this might be an interesting diversion. Regardless, he was not making any headway finding the McCarthy brothers.

♣   ♣   ♣   ♣

Tadgh rode the Kerry motorcycle the next day to find MacCurtain, leaving the other two to make sure the safe house was fully provisioned.

Morgan had not been happy about his leaving. "Don't you be going after that murderous Boyle, mavorneen, I need you alive," she told him. "How about I go with you?"

"We'll see about that." Tadgh knew she worried over him, but it couldn't be helped. Later he said, "You stay here with Aidan, hold down the fort, so to speak."

Despite the protests, Tadgh left on his own that morning. MacCurtain was not at home when Tadgh arrived at the clandestine headquarters of the IRB in Blackpool, in the north end of Cork City, so he waited in the shadows. An hour later, when his boss appeared and went inside, Tadgh waited a few moments before approaching the door. At the knock, MacCurtain opened the door and invited him in to his modest parlor.

Tomas's domicile was more austere than Tadgh's Creagh home. City dwellers had to make do with less space. Here, a kitchen, tiny parlor, single bedroom, and indoor washroom appeared to be the whole abode. "Tadgh, I'm really glad you came. Saved me a drive down to your safe house." He pointed to a chair near a small table, indicating that Tadgh should sit. He then moved to a window and checked that the casement was closed. He pulled curtain panels together and turned on a low lamp. The walls and the mood were grey. Then he poured two neat thimble-full shots of Jamesons that he brought from the sideboard and set them on the table. "It's a little early in the day, but I think that the situation warrants it."

Tadgh cradled the glass. "A sizable Royal Navy patrol is placed out of Berehaven, Tomas. I think the English must know about the German arms shipment. I need you to get this information to Padraig immediately."

Tomas raised his brow. "I just came from Dublin. Padraig informed me that he brought you into our confidence. He has changed the landing date from the twentieth to the night of the twenty-third so that any knowledge of it won't pre-empt the start date of the Rising."

"I presume that the Germans know this, Tomas." Tadgh took a drink.

"Supposedly, the Clan na Gael knows, and they're connected. Casement is coming separately by U-boat and will rendezvous with the freighter at the drop point. This ship has been disguised to look like the Norwegian tramp steamer *Aud-Norge,*[11] and it will be coming south down the west coast from the area around Iceland to avoid suspicion."

"But what if the captain of the *Aud-Norge* didn't get the change in date?" Tadgh heard his voice waver. He tried to cover the worry with another drink.

"He'll either have gotten it directly or the submarine will surely communicate with him. Just in case of a misunderstanding, Michael Collins is sending three Volunteers he trusts down to the Valentia Signaling Center on the Dingle coast come Friday the twenty-first. They're to commandeer enough equipment so that they can communicate with the gunrunner when it arrives."

"Does Collins say that they will rendezvous with Casement and the weapons?" *Not good. Too many cooks,* Tadgh thought. He downed the last drop.

Tomas took his glass in hand and swirled the liquid around inside. "Austin Stack, my Tralee counterpart, has that responsibility, as well as distribution of the arms, after they and Casement are safely landed. They brought some powerful green lights down from the coal mine at Arigna to Tralee to signal the *Aud-Norge* on Sunday night."

"Where are they to come ashore, Tomas, do ya know?"

"Fenit Pier for the weapons, as I understand it. But first, Casement and two others are to be landed on Banna Strand Beach from the submarine just after midnight."

"What about German personnel support and Casement's Brigade, such as it is?" Tadgh asked, remembering the conversations from Riederau.

"Casement's pretty upset, I understand. You told me as much, lad. There may not be any Germans or Brigade members, but there will be at least twenty thousand Russian rifles and a million rounds of ammunition plus some explosive mechanisms, according to the Clan na Gael."

"Based on what I have seen down near Berehaven, they could easily be headin' into a trap, sir."

"We need those weapons, Tadgh, and this is the plan. Padraig's decided that he wants you to bring Cork's allocation of arms back to us on Monday by sea," MacCurtain explained. "You're to moor your fishing boat up at Fenit Pier after dark on Sunday night and contact Austin."

"Well, now. How am I to get them back through the blockade? Surely it would be safer to bring them by land."

"With the Rising started by then, the RIC will likely have all the roads blocked. At least that's what Padraig thinks."

Tadgh paused and took a different tack. "What did Jack Jordan find out about those children on the *Lusitania?*"

"He was suspicious of me, so he didn't spill much."

"You didn't tell him about *me,* did you?"

"Your identity is safe."

"But what about the answer? What happened?"

"They're all dead, that's what Jordan told me. All twenty-nine of them."

So Morgan's children, if she had had any with her on the ship, were dead, then. That probably meant that the man in her dream had died, as well, if he was real. He would not have left the children. Then her husband may not have been on the *Lusitania*. If she had had babies on board, they would have died. That eased Tadgh's conscience, but he realized just how sinful that thought was and crossed himself.

Tadgh definitely did not like the plan, but he didn't want to argue with Tomas. He'd been left in the dark for so long, and at least now there was some action. Tomas ushered him out. As Tadgh started back home, he couldn't help but think that the gunrunning plan was too risky. Too many late changes, and the communications chain seemed too disjointed.

Tadgh drove south through the city, heading to Barrack Street with the afternoon sun on his right. As he crossed Lee River after passing the counting house of Beamish and Crawford's Brewery, he remembered the fight to the death with Boyle's RIC goons there. Morgan had saved him that day almost a year ago—in more ways than one. He began to seethe at the thought of it, which reminded him of the agonizing memory of his parents' deaths at Boyle's hands five years earlier. *Bastard.*

He stopped when he reached Barrack Street. If he turned right, he'd be on his way home, focused on his mission for the revolution. Home to Morgan and Aidan. If he turned left along Sullivan's Quay, he could be at the RIC Barracks on South Terrace in a few minutes. That's where he would find Boyle, if he was in his office.

Tadgh fingered the Luger in his trousers pocket. It would be so easy to put a bullet in Boyle's brain. It would be worth the risk. The image of Boyle putting a Webley to his mother's head and gleefully pulling the trigger burned in his skull. He wheeled left and headed down the quay.

Five minutes later Tadgh turned south on Rutland Street just before the barracks and parked the Kerry out of sight in an alley. He adjusted his fake glasses and sailor's cap and strolled out onto South Terrace. The RIC office looked every bit like a stone jail. Even the few windows had bars on them. Undoubtedly, there would be a wanted sketch of him and Aidan pinned to their bulletin board. His chance of quickly finding Boyle inside, even if he was at work, was slim, given that Tadgh didn't know the interior layout of the building. He looked into the police van parked outside the building and found it empty. *Good.*

What am I doing here? He could hear Morgan's voice in his head, but he was so close to his adversary, at the threshold. He studied an upper window for a point of entry for his attack, but an RIC sergeant, absorbed with a piece of paper in his hand, exited the building and knocked Tadgh down, sending his hat and glasses flying.

"Excuse me, sir." The sergeant leaned down and offered a hand up, which Tadgh refused. "You all right?" the officer watched him as he got up and brushed himself off.

Tadgh reached for his hat on the ground. "Pardon me, sergeant." He kept his face turned away. "I'm jake to be sure," he mumbled, turning towards Rutland Street. *This was a bad idea. No plan.*

The sergeant reached him well after he had rounded the corner. "Your eyeglasses, sir."

"Thank you, kindly." Tadgh took them from the officer's outstretched hand.

"Can I help you, sir?" The man peered closely at him, and Tadgh looked away.

"I'm fine, I tell you. Leave me alone." For a moment, he deliberated. He could likely knock this officer out, but there were people on the street, and they were too near the RIC barracks. Not a good choice. Tadgh turned his back to the officer and strode into the alley. It was time to make tracks. What had he been thinking? It all seemed so risky now, one man against who knows how many RIC sergeants. And Padraig and Tomas would never forgive him for causing a ruckus so close to the Rising.

Sergeant Toliver called out to him, Webley in hand, "I know you. You're McCarthy! Hands up, traitor." Tadgh guessed that the constable must have recognized the motorcycle with the wicker sidecar from the wanted sketch.

Tadgh switched on the Kerry and gunned it past the startled sergeant. With one kick, he dislodged the Webley from the man's hand, and then his foot connected with his shoulder, all in one motion, bringing him down. Tadgh turned left down South Terrace and disappeared.

Toliver blew his whistle. Within seconds, three RIC constables were by his side, including Gordo James, Boyle's deputy. "McCarthy, I tell you. It was McCarthy," Sergeant Toliver shouted.

"Which way, man?"

"West. He went west."

"Get the wagon," Gordo yelled to his men.

Two minutes later, all four men sped west on South Terrace, packed in the paddy wagon that had been parked at the curb. The traffic was light until they reached Barrack Street. "Shit. Anybody see him?" Ahead on Bishop Street, the traffic was stopped for a horse-drawn milk wagon. "Not this way, sir, unless he got by them."

Gordo stared left down Barrack Street as it curved to the right ahead, with the old Elizabeth Fort high up on its right. Beyond Evergreen Street, the traffic was a snarl of carriages, horse-drawn vans, motorcars and police vehicles. Near Tower Street, he saw the Kerry, its rider trying to squeeze around the blockage. "He's heading west for Bandon Road." Gordo wheeled the wagon to the left and gunned the motor.

Tadgh squeezed past the stalled lorries, barely missing the patrons streaming out of old Lynch's Bar. He glanced over his shoulder and saw the police wagon accelerating in pursuit.

Damn. I have a critical job to do, and now I've put that task at risk. He couldn't lead them back towards his home. That's when he had an idea that was a long shot, but it could work. Timing would be everything. The turnoff was just three streets ahead.

Gordo cleared the obstruction by driving right into it. Hansoms and lorries scattered as the paddy wagon rolled through. Gordo knew that capturing McCarthy was his one chance to satisfy his demanding boss. It might even mean a promotion.

"There, he's turning left on Lough Road." Toliver pointed to his left, egging his boss on.

"I need him alive," Gordo yelled as Toliver drew his Webley and leaned out the open side window.

Tadgh glanced behind and slowed the Kerry as he approached his objective. He was hoping that his pursuers wouldn't open fire on him. He could see Cork Lough, a quarter-mile oval, coming up on his right. It was a popular park area, a shallow quarry that now held water a meter in depth. He knew that the road came within twenty feet of the lough at its southern end, down where the island overgrowth came close to the shore. He could see Cork residents out for an afternoon stroll on the footpath by the lake. This was going to be difficult.

Fortunately, the road ahead was clear. Tadgh drew his Luger and flipped off the safety just as Toliver aimed and took a shot. The bullet hit the carry bar just behind Tadgh's seat and ricocheted harmlessly away.

"Stop shooting, dammit. I want him alive, man," Gordo screamed, pounding his underling on the shoulder.

Tadgh gauged the timing. As the paddy wagon drew up close behind him, he abruptly pulled up to the left so the front of the police van came even with his back wheel on the right. The constable turned the wheel left to try to knock the Kerry over, shouting, "Pull over, McCarthy!"

In response, Tadgh calmly fired two rounds into their front right tire, which blew out immediately. The police van initially veered towards him. Tadgh hit the brake and immediately dropped behind before the paddy wagon could hit him. One more bullet through the right rear tire did the trick. Its wheels screeching, the van veered sharply to the right, jumping up and over the pedestrian walkway. It launched itself into the lough, nosing down into the edge of the island brush. Startled walkers jumped out of the way and were now pointing and laughing at the predicament of the police officers.

Tadgh waved as he accelerated south down Lough Road. Gordo and his men leaped out of the van and mucked around in the waist-deep water. Tadgh heard the man yell an expletive at the top of his lungs.

♣ ♣ ♣ ♣

When Tadgh finally returned, Morgan asked, "What did Tomas say? Are they going to stop the shipment?"

"On the contrary, my dear. It's going forward despite our information about the likely blockade, but it will be three days later," Tadgh responded. "The ship is coming from the northwest and not through the Celtic Sea. Tomas doesn't think that the English would know the landing site, or even the date, if they have wind of the possible arms landing."

Tadgh told them about their orders to bring guns to Cork.

"Sounds risky to me," Morgan drew her lovely face into an uncharacteristic frown. "Is all this necessary? A lot of people are going to get killed, aren't they?"

"We talked about this in Belgium. These are desperate times, lass," Tadgh said. "We need to gain our freedom from tyranny now, during the Great War. If we don't get these weapons, then it'll be pitchforks against machine guns, to be sure."

Aidan spoke up. "Well, then. I'm with you all the way, brother."

Tadgh looked to Morgan for the same commitment, but her nod was tentative at best. "You know I love you, desperately," she said, and moved toward him, hugging her man fiercely in a symbolic gesture, trying to hold him back.

"Aye, then. It's not clear to me that the German captains will have gotten the date-change orders. They left Germany before this decision was made. So we're going to Tralee on Thursday night in case they didn't get the message to delay."

They spent the next two days organizing, loading, and concealing equipment and provisions on the hooker for what might be a four-night voyage. They also perfected some disguises to look more like local fishermen. Morgan's outfit, with her figure, was more difficult.

Finally, at six that Thursday evening, on April 20, they emerged from the shelter of their home at Creagh and took the familiar route out to sea past Baltimore.

"Mind now. Keep an eye out for the Royal Navy," Tadgh yelled above the strong easterly wind whistling in the sails as the boat headed around Clear Island. "I don't want to give away our home port."

"Do you think they'll be out at night?" Morgan stared at the horizon.

"If they think the Germans are out there, yes, lass. Sunset is at eight-thirty. We need the cover of darkness to get by the blockade, if it's out there."

"No vessels in sight," Aidan announced at they passed north of the Fastnet lighthouse, heading west. "We've got a good ten miles per hour wind and calm seas. Couldn't be better."

Tadgh set the trim and steered into the sun. "We're going to stay close to the coast at night so that we can duck out of sight if they spot us."

By ten o'clock, it was dark and Tadgh could see the Bull Rock lighthouse winking on the horizon to the west ahead. "Everyone, pay attention. We're comin' up on the Berehaven Royal Navy Harbor. They may be listenin' with that loop magnetometer. Keep your eyes open."

Thirty minutes later, they had crossed Bantry Bay and passed Bere Island, approaching Crow Head. "We're visible now each time the Bull Rock light sweeps past us," Morgan remarked, looking west.

"It can't be helped," Tadgh answered. "We're going to pass between Dursey Head and that island called Bull Rock in about half an hour. Then we'll be past the Naval Center area. If the cruisers are out, they're far out at sea, I'm after thinkin'. So far, so good."

In the Naval Control Center at Amnikinna Point off Berehaven, the magnetometer operator called to his supervisor. "Sir, come and see this signature. I dunno, it's so faint, but it looks just like the one we saw earlier. You remember that Galway hooker the *Marie Mon Amour* we thought was suspicious."

"What would a fishing vessel be doing out at this time of night?" Ensign Johnson wondered. "I'm going to call the captain."

Captain Flood prowled the bridge of the *Bluebell* at anchor in the harbor. The Royal Navy was on high alert, ready to move into action at a moment's notice. Several naval vessels were on night patrol on the Celtic Sea.

"Captain, there's a call from Command." Ensign Cornwall handed him the new-fangled ship-to-shore. What a boon it was.

"Captain Flood, we see the signature of that fishing trawler *Marie Mon Amour* you shadowed a few days ago. It's heading west toward Dursey Head."

"What? At night?" Maybe Captain Hall was right. Flood sprang to action. "Sound general quarters." Within minutes, he had the *Bluebell* underway, set on an intercept course based on the instrument readings.

"Captain, we will lose magnetometer coverage when the hooker passes Dorsey Head, and that'll be in about ten minutes. She should be illuminated for you by the Bull Rock lighthouse then," the magnetometer signal operator announced.

Flood peered ahead from the bridge into the darkness. "We will be on scene in fifteen minutes. Contact me when you lose signal." *What a stroke of luck,* he thought as he ordered the engine room to make speed.

Tadgh saw the signal lights from the Control Center at a distance. Faintly over the water, he heard the horns sounding general quarters. "Damn it to hell, the Navy's starting after someone, and I'll bet it's us. Aidan, douse the runnin' lights, lad."

"Done, brother, but we're sitting ducks out here every time the Bull light comes round. How much of a head start do we have?"

"Five miles, but we're still two miles from the lighthouse," Tadgh calculated. "They will be comin' at twenty knots compared to our ten."

"What's the illumination distance of the lighthouse?"

"I'd guess five miles," Tadgh speculated, peering ahead towards Bull Rock.

"They'll catch us, to be sure," Aidan concluded. "Let's head into one of those coves on shore like you suggested earlier."

"No can do, brother. With the shoreline here, we'd smash on the rocks at night, and if we didn't, they'd find us under the Bull light."

"What now, Tadgh?" Morgan craned her neck in the direction of the harbor to see what was coming after them. "We can't give ourselves up."

"We won't, lass," Tadgh yelled back, while he agonized over their course of action. They could not let themselves be detained at this point. He decided that they only had one chance, and it was slim at that. He set a course directly for Bull Rock. He didn't have time to explain his plan, just what they needed to do. "Now then, Aidan and Morgan. I'm going to need your help at just the right time," he ordered. "When I tell you to lower the sails, Aidan, you lower the lug sail, and you, Morgan, lower the foresails. And have the oars ready. Got it?"

Although they didn't fully understand, they agreed, and ten minutes later, the *Marie Mon Amour* sailed directly into the illumination of the Bull Rock light, closing to a third-mile from the towering rock. Its light blinded them as they sped towards its base. When Tadgh turned his head, he could see the searchlight of the Navy vessel sweeping the sea behind them. It was gaining on them but still a mile and a half astern. Tadgh could only hope that the officers on board were not using binoculars to look at the island. Perhaps they would also be blinded by the light.

"This is crazy, brother," Aidan yelled from mid-ship. "We're either going to duck behind the island or crash into it. Either way, we're done for, to be sure. They'll find us or our debris."

Morgan was too stunned to say anything, and Aidan had said it all. She believed in Tadgh. He must have a plan, she told herself. *But what was it?* She wished he would share more of his thoughts with her. Lately, he seemed to hold things in.

Twenty seconds later, when the light came around, they were again temporarily blinded. Morgan thought they were only moments away from smashing into the near-vertical rock face. "Look out," she yelled, clinging to the mast in anticipation of the impact. *I'm going to die in this infernal sea after all.*

Chapter Twenty-One
Aud-Norge

April 20, 1916
Tralee Bay, West Coast of Ireland

At that moment, three bays to the northwest down near Fenit, on his German freighter Captain Karl Spindler consulted with his crew of twenty-two mariners. They had arrived at the rendezvous point at Inistooskert Island at four in the afternoon, as ordered. Now, seven hours later, after plying Tralee Bay for four hours searching in vain for a signal from the Irish rebels, Spindler suspected a trap. Camouflaged as the Norwegian tramp steamer *Aud-Norge*, the boat carried twenty thousand obsolete Mosin-Nagant rifles fitted with bayonets that had been captured from the Russians, along with over one million rounds of ammunition, ten machine guns, and several bombs with timing devices. But without Irishmen to receive them, these arms were useless. And without wireless on their ship, they could only use their red signal light to try establishing contact.

At one point, before nightfall, they had been close enough to the drop point at Fenit Pier to see with their binoculars the English sentries patrolling. The guards had paid the steamer no mind, or so it had seemed. As darkness settled, the Germans saw none of the expected green signal lights in the town or surrounding hills. *What could have happened?* The submarine *U-19*, carrying Roger Casement and his laughable brigade of only Monteith and Bailey, had not appeared at the rendezvous as expected, either. They had waited there for two hours for them. *Where could they be?*

"Well, crew, the men at the hilltop gun emplacement at the entrance to Tralee Bay were probably looking for us." Spindler looked each of his sailors straight in the eye. "The Sinn Féiners might be in hiding if the political situation changed after we left Germany. Since we've been at sea for two weeks to avoid suspicion, a lot could have happened. But we have our orders. We have two options. First, we can assume the worst and leave under cover of darkness tonight. Or, we can wait another day and hope that we can make contact with the rebels by then."

First Mate Dusselmann answered immediately. "We've all decided, sir. We came all this way to do a job, and we should stay another day to get it done."

Spindler expected that response and was proud of his close-knit and loyal crew. "So be it, then. Let's return to the rendezvous point and lay to in that bay against its western shore before moonrise. Perhaps our U-boat with Casement will be there waiting for us. Keep the running lights extinguished."

"Now!" Tadgh shouted as he jigged the hooker slightly to starboard. His vision was still blinded by the damn light, so he maneuvered by feel. Simultaneously, Aidan and Morgan yanked their respective halyards and the sails came billowing down. They braced themselves for impact with the rock face and waited, hugging the mast.

One second. Two seconds. Surely the boat would be mangled or worse, Morgan thought. They were now in the darkness under the beam of the light. But the collision never came. The stars disappeared, and it was as if the boat with all three of them aboard had been swallowed up by the rock. Morgan could hear the wind whistle an eerie tune, and like a bat, she sensed proximity to objects on her left and right. There was a scraping sound aloft.

"Oars out starboard, and hold on," Tadgh yelled.

Thrusting their oars outboard, Morgan and Aidan could hear and feel them bashing against rough walls on the right. Morgan almost lost her oar when it hit an outcrop. They slowed then came to an abrupt stop.

"Let's hold onto the rock on the starboard side, Aidan," Tadgh spoke quietly above the wind.

As her eyes adjusted to the darkness, Morgan, from her position in the bow could tell that they were in the middle of a tunnel that was about as wide as the hooker's length, and it appeared taller than the height of its mast. Every time the Bull light swept past, there was a glimmer of their surroundings from its reflection off the sea and back into the tunnel. She could barely make out Tadgh, at the stern, attempting to tie off to a rock protruding from the tunnel wall on their starboard side. She could see that they had come to rest roughly midway in the tunnel. The openings to the sea were about five boat lengths fore and aft, give or take.

"Drop the anchor, Morgan," Tadgh commanded, and she immediately complied. It clanked on rock only a few feet down. "We're in a hole made through Bull Rock by the sea," he explained softly. "I wasn't sure that it would be high enough to clear the mast or deep enough to clear the keel. We are almost four hundred feet below the lighthouse. Quiet now, until we know that the Navy ship is out of range."

"You could have told us, my love. I thought we were going to die."

"We may yet if you don't keep quiet, aroon." He put his index finger to his lips in case she hadn't heard him. "I thought you would have seen this natural tunnel on our previous trip past Bull Rock," he added, by way of a weak response to her question.

Five minutes passed. They could hear the throbbing of a ship's engines as it approached the island. The engine sounds grew louder and then dropped in pitch as the ship must have slowed. It must be near the rock, Morgan thought, when she heard muffled voices.

A momentary flash of light appeared at the tunnel entrance. Nobody moved a muscle. Morgan's heart was in her mouth. The illumination stopped thirty feet short of *Marie's* stern. Despite their attempts to hold her off the rock, the hooker creaked and groaned as she bumped up against the rough-hewn tunnel wall. Seconds later, the light disappeared. It seemed as if an hour had passed before the engine noise and sailors' voices faded into a watery silence, but it had only been eight minutes. *Good,* Morgan thought. *They have passed us by.*

When the sounds from the warship had died away completely, Morgan opened her mouth to speak, but Tadgh cut her off with a whisper. "You've done a fine job. But they're still hunting us, and I'd be willing to bet that they will circle back around the rock before moving on, don't ye know."

Sure enough, five minutes later, they heard the engine rumble, echoing down the tunnel ahead of them. Again the brilliant searchlight lit up the end of the tunnel, falling just short of the hooker's bow before flashing out. They waited another ten minutes until they could hear only wind and lapping noises, before anyone said a word.

"They could be scouring the coastline of Ballydonegan Bay for us at this point," Tadgh said. "We're going to have to wait here another half hour until midnight before moving on." He was guessing the time. It was too dark to see his watch.

Morgan came over to her partner and noticed his knuckles were bleeding from the beating they took on the rocks. "Let me bind your right hand, Tadgh."

"Just wipe them off, lass. I'm goin' to need the use of all my fingers for the work we have ahead of us."

Morgan didn't like that answer but returned to her post at the mast after using her sleeve to clean his hand. There she nervously played with the foresail halyard. "Tadgh, the rope's stuck."

"Don't you be puttin' the foresail up yet, lass."

"I'm not. But it's stuck."

Tadgh was at midships in a flash, tugging on the rope. "Damn. I thought I felt something when we entered the tunnel."

"What?"

"A slight drag on the *Marie*."

"I heard a scraping up there." Morgan pointed at the top of the mast, which was shrouded in darkness.

Tadgh tugged on the rope. "It looks like the top of the main mast has been damaged, make no mistake. The halyard pulley for the foresail must be damaged. The lugsail pulley may also be affected. Aidan, check your halyard."

"Aye, brother. There's a problem."

"We're not going anywhere if we can't get this fixed, don't ye know." Tadgh was, for the first time, worried. He could handle most situations if his boat was intact, but now? What if the pulleys were unusable?

"What, here in the dark?" Morgan looked incredulous.

Tadgh retrieved his torch from the cabin. Not hearing any evidence of the ship nearby, Tadgh thought it safe enough and he switched it on, being careful not to point it horizontally out of the tunnel. The beam of light, although weak, illuminated the mast near the top.

"I'm going to have to go up there. Hold this light, Morgan."

"How will you get up there?" Morgan looked worried.

"Watch me. Just like the pirates of old. Up into the riggin', mateys." Tadgh unsheathed his dagger and put it in his teeth. "Cutlasses at the ready, me hearties."

"But there's no rigging, my love. Be careful."

"Aidan, hold us fast to the rock, if you please."

This was not the first time that Tadgh had shinnied up a twenty-three-foot main mast. But it was the first time he'd attempted it in near darkness. It took a full fifteen minutes to get up, and his legs ached from constantly applying the scissors pressure against the mast. Twice he slipped a few feet and had to recover. Now he was close enough to see the damage. The top two feet of the mast was broken. The upper most edge of the tunnel had damaged but not dislodged both the lug and the foresail pulleys. He tried to spin the wheel of the main lug pulley, but it wouldn't budge. The halyard had slipped off and was wedged between the mast and the wheel frame, an easy fix.

Tadgh jerked the halyard up, out and back onto the wheel. A check of its condition showed some fraying, but he thought it would hold.

The pulley for the foresail was another matter. It looked like it had taken a direct scrape, and its axle was bent so that the wheel would not turn against its frame. Tadgh jammed his knife blade between the pulley and its case, and he tried to leverage the wheel back into position. It was still distorted. The halyard was also damaged, almost cut in two where the pulley pinched the frame.

Minutes later, he descended to the deck. "The main sail's useable, but the foresail is not. It can't be helped, and it's goin' to slow us down, so it is." He tugged on the lug halyard, and the sail started to rise.

Tadgh wasn't sure if they would make it to Tralee in time. Maybe his premonition of a delivery date foul-up would be unfounded.

"Casement, where are your Volunteers?" Captain Weisbach demanded after he had done another three-sixty with the periscope of *U-19*. "It's midnight, and we've seen no green lights since we got here four hours ago."

U-19 lurked at periscope depth, half a mile offshore from Banna Strand on the west coast of Tralee Bay, just north of Fenit Harbor. The Sampire Island light cast an eerie glow on the rolling surf at the south end of the beach. Their examination of Fenit Pier half an hour before had shown that it was well guarded.

"I don't understand it, unless they have been arrested. They knew we were coming tonight," Roger Casement responded weakly.

"Since the *Aud-Norge* was not at the rendezvous point when we arrived at eight o'clock, we should assume that they have been delayed or captured," Weisbach continued, turning to his Watch Officer Fritz, who nodded in agreement.

"So what do we do now?" Casement's adjutant Monteith asked.

"Well, I'm not taking you three back to Germany," Weisbach replied emphatically.

Roger Casement coughed before he spoke. "As agreed, you are to put us ashore tonight. I've got to get them to stop this insane Rising, especially now if the arms cannot be delivered."

Sir Roger sagged after the effort to speak, and Monteith rushed to his boss's aid, propping him up against the stairwell of the control room.

"It's your business, of course, but we've held up our end of the bargain.

Germany has brought the arms that you requested. Now we expect you to deliver a revolution. Where are your damn troops?" Weisbach was furious. Why did he have to play nursemaid to this pacifist and his "brigade" of two?

Casement was too weak and discouraged to argue. "Just let us off this infernal machine."

"We'll give it two more hours," Weisbach concluded, checking his watch. "If we haven't made contact by then, you'll have to row the dinghy through the surf to Banna Strand. I can't risk surfacing closer to shore."

"Boss, you're in no condition to be travelling on foot," Monteith observed, listening to Sir Roger's labored breathing. "The rendezvous point with Stack at the fort is about a mile and a half from the beach."

"I'm going to see this through," Casement admonished, coughing and wiping his mouth with a damp handkerchief.

"Yes, sir," Monteith muttered.

At that moment, Tadgh gave the go-ahead to cautiously paddle out of the tunnel. The wind was still up from the east. "No sign of our friend," Tadgh whispered. "Hoist the lug sail quietly."

With that accomplished, he steered north by northwest toward the Great Skellig light, skimming along at a reduced eight knots. They passed it by on their left at about two in the morning, just after the moon rose and bathed the ocean in silver.

"That warship just plain disappeared," Aidan observed.

"Lucky for us, so far. But now, we're sitting ducks again if it shows up. We lost an hour, thus far, so we won't get to Tralee Bay until well after dawn."

"What exactly are we going to do when we get there?" Morgan now sat beside her man and held his hand tight. The night chill settled under her clothes.

"Well, now. That'll depend on what we find there, won't it," Tadgh answered, as he pulled a blanket from the cabin and wrapped it around her. "In the worst case, we will sail into the fishin' harbor at Fenit and tie up like we belong there."

"Won't the locals expose us?" she asked, snuggling closer to him.

"Maybe, but we've got to take that chance. We have to get those guns."

They passed the next three and three-quarter hours heading north across the mouth of Dingle Bay without seeing another vessel. Then as dawn broke over the Slieve Mish Mountains on their right at 0545 hours, they passed Sybil Point on the Dingle Peninsula. Tadgh noticed with satisfaction that Morgan had been sleeping soundly, propped up against his shoulder.

Morgan stirred, blinking rapidly. "Is it morning?"

"Well, yes, my love. Almost. At least it's light enough to see the Three Sisters ahead on our right."

"Where's their boat?"

"They aren't women at all but three hills up ahead on the point."

"Oh, I see." But she couldn't. Morgan was rubbing the sleep from her eyes.

"Did I tell you about Smerwick, Morgan? It's the harbor town coming up on our right in a few minutes."

"No, you didn't, but is it something I need to know?" Morgan realized that a history lesson was in the making, one that would support the need for a revolution, she suspected.

"It might help you understand something. Smerwick was the place in the year 1583 where the treacherous Protestant English cornered the Irish FitzGerald and FitzMaurice clans who had received Papal forces' support for our Catholic religion. Our clans were massacred, then—men, women, and children—beheaded and thrown into the sea."

"Oh, my God, Tadgh." Morgan stopped rubbing her eyes and tears started to flow.

"Yes, and the famous Sir Walter Raleigh, so gallant in the history books, was one of the English butchers' leaders, so he was." Tadgh spat overboard.

"But does ancient butchery justify a revolution now?"

"Yes, it does. That was just one early incident, lass. They forced the dying into the sea throughout the Great Hunger. Need I continue?"

Morgan was tired of arguing. Tadgh was not going to change his beliefs or dilute his rage until blood was spilled. She just hoped that she would be there afterwards to bind his wounds when the time came.

The sea behind the hooker began to boil. Tadgh spied a familiar dark shape rising up to the surface almost directly beneath them and gripped the tiller hard. With terrifying gurgles and creaking sounds, it rose.

"Good God, Tadgh," Aidan screamed, as the black behemoth emerged from the depths with a thunderous roar. Tadgh let the lug boom swing out to kill their propulsion. It was a déjà vu for him. The submarine quickly drew alongside the hooker, looming above her and knocking whatever wind remained out of her sails.

When Morgan saw the stenciled *U-19* emblazoned on the side of the U-boat, she cried out, "It must be Captain Weisbach and Fritz. Unbelievable!"

"Hold on there, Aidan," Tadgh cautioned when his brother went for the rifle at his feet. "Leave it be."

This time only one officer appeared above the conning tower. There was no need for binoculars at this range. Tadgh and Morgan could easily recognize Captain Weisbach. "It looks like you patched our savior up just fine, aroon," Tadgh remarked, as he waved in a friendly fashion.

"Ahoy, supply ship. You got fish?" Captain Weisbach yelled in English as he waved back, laughing. "I see you replaced your old scow."

Tadgh smiled and held up a mackerel that was part of their props. Aiden could only stare at the two men with a look of confusion on his face. He was even more puzzled as neither Tadgh nor Morgan appeared to be concerned when several sailors emerged and launched a dinghy toward them.

Weisbach greeted Tadgh with a crisp salute and a handshake. "I see you decided you'd had enough of our hospitality." He nodded toward Morgan. "It is thanks to you, Fräulein, that I am even alive," he said, with an approving wink of his eye.

Morgan stepped forward and gave the captain a hug, which he happily returned. Then she peered past his collar to check the back of his neck.

Aidan looked dumbfounded but kept his mouth shut.

"Enough now, Fräulein. I am completely healed." Weisbach gently pushed her away.

"Do you have Casement on board?" Tadgh asked, cutting to the chase.

"What do you know of these matters?" Weisbach's eyebrows arched.

"I met Sir Roger near Munich."

"You're full of surprises, you are."

"We've been sent for a part of the shipment," Tadgh answered in a level tone.

"There were no green signal lights in response to our red one," Weisbach answered. "Your compatriots didn't show up last night."

"Where's Casement?"

"As agreed, we let him and his brigade of two men go ashore on Banna Strand at about 0230 hours this morning," the Captain explained. "We watched their dinghy overturn in the surf. Casement was in bad shape when he boarded my boat in Germany. I was told he had malaria. We do not know whether they survived."

"Where were they headed?"

"They mentioned that someone named Stack would pick them up at a fort a mile and a half inland. Said he had to get information to the leaders in Dublin. He's a confounding fellow. He went to all this trouble to get our help, and now he seems hell-bent on stopping your Rising. That's all I know."

"And what of the shipment, do ye know?"

"The ship was not at the rendezvous point yesterday when we arrived. We couldn't find it in Tralee Bay."

"Where was the rendezvous point?"

"One of the Magharee Islands called Inishtookskert."

"Didn't you get notified of the change in delivery date?"

"What change?"

What a fool, Tadgh thought to himself. "Delivery was supposed to be changed to Sunday."

"When did that happen?"

"More than a week ago, my superiors told me."

"Damnation. Then our supply ship could not have gotten the message, either. They sailed over two weeks ago, and they have no wireless."

"Could you have missed them in the bay?"

"Possibly, if they were trying to conceal themselves in the dark last night," Weisbach commented, stroking his chin. "But I will tell you that the area is sufficiently fortified. There are manned gun emplacements on the hilltops at the bay's entrance, a place called Bandon Point on my map. And we observed police sentries on duty at the arms drop point at midnight."

"Where might that be?"

"Fenit Pier."

"We think that the English knew we were coming and may have apprehended your Sinn Féiners."

"Sounds like it, so it does."

"We were heading out to sea to determine if there is a naval blockade when I saw you coming. We'll intercept the supply ship if it has not yet arrived and apprise the captain of the situation."

"The Royal Navy is out there," Tadgh assured him. "We were chased on our way here last night. We will continue on, into the bay. If your ship is there, or shows up, we will find an alternate landing site. Do you have any of the arms shipment on board your vessel?"

"Three cases of rifles and two of ammunition. It was all we could carry, and we couldn't put them ashore in the dinghy with Casement. They would have sunk it."

"Can we trade again?"

Weisbach nodded his assent. "They're ancient weapons, anyway. And I'm sure that you'll be generous to a fellow mariner with the fish that I can see you've got here."

Tadgh stepped forward and shook his hand. "We're even, then."

Morgan's voice cut through the silence to ask if she could see Fritz. She was anxious to see their old friend and learn any news of Gerda and their two little boys.

"Is Fritz on board? Can he join us?"

The captain shook his head. "He is my second in command. I ordered him to stay with the boat."

"Can I go and see him, then?"

Wesibach shouted orders to his men and Morgan jumped into the dinghy.

After Aidan helped the German sailors load up their dinghy with fish, two sailors rowed Morgan over to the submarine. She jumped up and soon disappeared below decks. Tadgh kept his eyes on the spot, tried to imagine her journey through the boat, with hungry German eyes following her every move.

As Morgan descended into the bowels of the U-boat, she was surprised that she wasn't afraid. It seemed as if she were coming home. The smells of oil and that obnoxious cologne greeted her nostrils and set her to sneezing. She immediately felt the warmth of the close space crowded with men, the air thick with their sweat and exhalations.

Fritz stood in the control room giving orders to his men and didn't see Morgan behind him. She tapped him on the shoulder. He whirled around and almost knocked her down, immediately breaking into a wide smile when he recognized her. He picked her up in his arms, hugging her to his chest, and tipped his head back in laughter so infectious, she couldn't help but join in.

When they both had regained their breath, Morgan lost no time in asking about Gerda and the boys.

"They are well, and we often talk about those days you were with us. A most happy time to remember." His voice faded as he turned his eyes to take in the cramped quarters and the very real feeling of anxiety and fear that hung in the air. He took a deep breath. "But how did you escape? Gerda worries for you, she will be so full of joy when I can tell her that her prayers have been answered and you got away."

"It was a trying time, yet we got across No Man's Land and eventually back to Ireland. I worried that the police had hounded you all on our account, and we had brought harm to you, Fritz."

"We submariners carry some weight. My family has been left alone."

"When we all survive our wars, we will get together in Germany, at your real home in Frankfurt, I promise."

"Well, that's something to live for, isn't it."

"As well as seeing your boys grown up and married, Fritz."

"That's my plan, Morgan, God willing. Is McCarthy with you?"

"Yes, of course. But now I have to go, and I'm supposed to take some munitions along that you brought. It's in trade for these damn fish."

Fritz queried his men and confirmed the trade. "Good riddance to these old Russian weapons. They are taking up valuable space."

After the men moved the munitions into the dinghy, Morgan turned to the men and wished them all Godspeed. She took a step up the ladder and then bounded back down to kiss Fritz right in front of his men. She was crying, as much for all the wounded men that she had seen, as for these brave souls.

"Really, Fräulein," Fritz scolded, his face turning red under his unkempt beard.

Morgan squeezed hard and held him close for a moment. Then she saw it, a tear streaking down from the corner of his eye. "There, there, now, be off with you." He gently pushed her away. *What would the men think?*

"*Auf Wiedersehen,* Fritz." She blew him a kiss as she ascended the stairwell.

"*Auf Wiedersehen,* Morgan," the entire crew called out, saluting her departure.

During the transfer of munitions to the hooker, which took two trips in the dinghy, including a hundred rounds of nine-millimeter bullets for Tadgh's Luger, Captain Weisbach asked Tadgh, "Did you get a message from Captain Schwieger with his gift of that weapon?"

"You know the saying, 'If you want peace, prepare for war'—which is why you are here," Tadgh answered, and the German smiled.

The two captains shook hands again. "We're in this fight against the English together, so we are," Tadgh stated. "How many torpedos do you have left?" he asked, stepping forward, eye to eye with his counterpart.

"A full complement—six, but that's not my mission, McCarthy," Weisbach answered, fully understanding the implication of Tadgh's question.

"Even if it means finding a way to deliver the arms?"

"As much as I'd like to, my orders are to support the clandestine delivery, not to cause an overt international incident that could bring America into the war. You understand?"

"Perfectly," Tadgh said, scowling. *I knew it.* "But what about the *Lusitania* then?" Tadgh was trying his best to get some German firepower.

"Unfortunate, truly unfortunate."

Tadgh saw that he had struck a nerve. "It's no, then?"

"That's right. Our admiral has forbidden U-boat attacks in the Celtic Sea because of the *Lusitania.*"

"To appease the Americans, then?" Tadgh crossed his arms.

"Yes, something like that." Weisbach signaled to his men in the dinghy.

"Well, at least I tried." Tadgh threw up his hands.

"After the war, then." Weisbach looked directly at Morgan and then saluted Tadgh and turned toward the submarine.

As the three Irish patriots watched the dinghy cross back to the U-boat, Tadgh said, "What is going on with the captain, Morgan?"

"What do you mean?"

"I saw the hugging, and he was staring at you just now."

"It's nothing, mavorneen. It's just my way of greeting, and he just misses contact with women, I guess." Morgan remembered the handsome captain's last words to her back at the hospital in Ostend when Tadgh's fate was uncertain. It felt good to be appreciated.

The frown on Tadgh's face said it all.

Within three minutes, *U-19* submerged, leaving no trace on the surface of the sea. In all, the encounter took less than thirty minutes, including the loading of arms. Tadgh set the sail trim, and they started off again.

"Were those the men who saved you?" Aidan needed answers. He could not make sense of the entire experience. He needed his brother to set right a world that had so suddenly turned on its head.

"Yes, the friends we met when we were on the continent," Morgan said with a twinkle in her eye. "We will tell you more details later, brother. Right now, we have problems. Big problems."

"What are we going to do? Sounds like the tyrants are in control at Fenit."

"What a bloody bollocks. We've got to find the supply ship and arrange a new drop point, brother. The Rising depends upon it." Tadgh jibed to port to catch the breeze. He realized that they had a faint hope of a positive outcome. Thank God that Weisbach had surfaced and informed them of the trap they were sailing into. Strange the quirks of fate. Or was it Divine intervention? Tadgh crossed himself and set the tiller for Tralee.

Chapter Twenty-Two
Trapped

Friday, April 21, 1916
RIC Headquarters, Tralee, Ireland

Boyle didn't like taking orders from anyone, least of all from this local Tralee Head Constable, John Kearney. At 0715 that morning, he didn't want to listen when Kearney explained the task of seeking out and apprehending three rebels who, from all reports, had landed on Banna Strand. Kearny droned, "Our intelligence from Captain Hall indicates that Roger Casement should be one of them. They're closing the net on the German gun-running ship. Those arms won't be allowed to land on Irish soil. Head Constable Boyle, are you listening to me?"

Gordo James knew that his boss was about to retaliate, so he jumped into the fray. "Head Constable Boyle is fully aware of the situation, as am I. The two of us were sent here to help. What can we do, exactly?" Boyle still looked as if he wanted to rip Kearney's throat out. Gordo knew that look all too well. His boss hated to take orders. Something about his father . . .

"I'm sending a patrol up the coast to investigate farm by farm and house by house, and I want you to go with them. We need to capture these rebels before they can get to Austin Stack, the leader of the Tralee Irish Volunteers," Kearney explained. "We have him under surveillance. And Boyle, we want them alive."

It was all he could do to keep Boyle from pummeling the man, but Gordo managed to persuade his boss to agree to the assignment and ushered him out of RIC headquarters before there was any altercation.

At 0810, the *Marie Mon Amour* passed by the first gun emplacement on Brandon Point at the entrance to Tralee Bay.

"It doesn't look like they are interested in us," Tadgh commented, as their boat passed right under their noses. "They must assume that we are just another fishing vessel coming in to begin a day's fishing in the bay."

"Unless the Naval Control Center has been in contact with those bastards," Morgan said, looking up at the cliff anxiously.

"Point well taken, my dear. *Come in to my parlor, said the spider to the fly*, eh?"

They skirted the Magharee Island chain heading into Tralee Bay. "Look, Tadgh, over there by the island." Aidan pointed southward.

Tadgh studied the two ships in the distance. One looked to be a tramp steamer flying Norwegian colors. And the other, moored alongside and dwarfed in comparison to the other vessel, was a frigate flying the Royal Navy Ensign. "Aidan, lad. Take cover behind the mast and use the binoculars to tell me the names of those vessels," Tadgh ordered. "We're probably bein' observed, so we need to keep movin' into the bay."

Aidan squinted through the binoculars. "The tramp steamer's name is *Aud-Norge* and the Navy vessel is the *Setter II*," Aidan announced, after close scrutiny from their distance of a half-mile. "The Navy ship has deck-mounted machine guns trained on the larger ship. There seems to be a boarding party on the Norwegian vessel."

"Damn," Tadgh swore. "That's our supply ship to be sure, and the bastards have got her."

"Can't we go to her rescue?"

"Just us, one Luger, and some old Russian rifles?" Tadgh countered. "Hardly a fair fight, brother. The whole Navy fleet will be here in no time."

"Is it possible that she dropped her cargo?"

"Unlikely, but it's possible." Tadgh saw that both vessels were now off the hooker's stern. "If we turn around now, it will raise suspicion. Keep an eye on them while we scout out Fenit Harbor. They would have needed a dock to unload all the crates of weapons."

"Tadgh, there's the fishing boat that stopped us a few days ago, headed toward us," Morgan yelled, tugging on his sleeve.

Tadgh wheeled around to see where Morgan pointed. He could clearly see the Manx Noby trawler coming out of Fenit Harbor. "That's just what we need right now. Another problem."

"Ahoy, *Marie Mon Amour*. Lay to and prepare to be boarded," the captain of the fishing trawler *Slanu III* bellowed at Tadgh in Gaelic as they pulled abeam of the hooker. "You were warned." Tadgh saw eight crewmen on the Noby, and they looked menacing, armed with grappling hooks. "Look on the bright side," he muttered to calm his mates. "It's probably a good thing for us that they speak Gaelic."

Before they could react further, crewmen of the *Slanu III* lassoed the hooker with their grappling hooks and pulled the boats together. Their captain jumped aboard before the boats collided, landing squarely on the aft deck of the hooker, club raised. "Come on, boys. Let's break this pipsqueak tub apart."

Morgan jumped back, but Tadgh held his ground with his Luger pointed directly at the captain's heart. This act did not go unnoticed. At the same time, he signaled Aidan with his eyes to do nothing.

"My name's Tadgh McCarthy, Captain. And your name?" he asked coolly in English, offering his right hand to shake.

Completely caught off guard, the captain stammered back in English, "Maurice Collis, Fenit Harbor." Seeing the gun leveled at him changed his demeanor. "Stand down, me lads," he ordered, and he put his hand in the air to stop his men.

Tadgh took a chance. "Are you Volunteers?"

"No, but sympathetic," Captain Collis answered cautiously. "Why?"

Tadgh eyed his face carefully as he spoke. The man stood six foot if he was an inch, and his weathered face showed the scars of a hard life at sea, pockmarked from decades of salt spray and windburn. His rough manner undoubtedly stemmed from a life of deprivation and persecution, but there was a kindliness in those green Irish eyes.

Out of necessity, Tadgh decided to trust him. "Because we are Irish Volunteers sent here on a mission."

"Not fishing?"

"Not fishing," Tadgh confirmed, as he lowered his gun.

"Hell, why didn't you say that in the first place?" the captain exclaimed and lowered his club.

Sensing the situation defused, Tadgh said, "What do you mean by *sympathetic*?"

"We'd kill the murdering English swine if we could get away with it."

"How would you like to do something significant for that cause?"

"Illegal?"

Tadgh ignored the question. "We need some intelligence about what has been happening here recently, so we do."

"The police have been swarming all over us since Tuesday," Collis explained, turning and pointing at Fenit Harbor. "They're waiting for something big to happen. We heard that two nights ago they arrested several Volunteer leaders in Tralee."

"Did the Norwegian steamer out there drop off cargo at Fenit Pier in the last day?" Tadgh pointed at the two ships now in the distance.

"Not to my knowledge."

Tadgh guessed that Collis would be knowledgeable about his homeport. So the munitions were still on the *Aud-Norge* when the Navy boarded it. It looked like a complete debacle, he decided. Even if these men could be brought to bear, they didn't have the horsepower to liberate the supply freighter. And even if they could, there was now no place to offload the munitions. Then there was the issue of starting a ruckus here two days before the surprise Rising. Pearse would be furious.

He changed his tack. "Is there a fort about a mile and a half from Banna Strand Beach, do ya know?"

"Now you're talking about my bailiwick," Collis answered enthusiastically. "I know the place. It's McKenna's Fort, to be sure. It is just the ruins of an ancient ring fort, a copse of trees, really. I live near there, just south of the Strand. Why do you ask?"

"Well, now. I've got to reach three of my compatriots who came ashore last night at the beach. They may be there yet." Tadgh also knew that they may have already been picked up or captured.

"That reminds me, so it does," Captain Collis remembered, stroking his unkempt beard. "At the Fenit docks an hour ago, I overheard some RIC guards talking about finding an overturned dinghy, a gun, and ammunition on the beach just before dawn. They were headed out to find the culprits."

"Will you help us, Captain?" Tadgh asked, offering his hand again in friendship. "Our plan was to sail into Fenit Harbor and tie up to the wharf like any other fishing trawler."

Collis clasped Tadgh's knuckles in a hard grip. "All right. I hate the English, too. But you'll have to follow my directions."

Tadgh assessed the integrity of the man and answered, "We're in your hands, Captain."

"Right. First, I will direct my crew to continue with our planned fishing trip and then accompany you on your boat here. My men can be trusted." He turned and gave his men their orders in Gaelic to continue on their day's work without him. They released the boat, and soon *Slanu III* headed toward the horizon. Captain Collis then told Tadgh, "It would be foolhardy to go to Fenit. I have a better way. Make your course for the north side of Fenit Island by the Samphire Light and just south of the Banna Strand beach."

As their boat approached the shoreline from the west, Tadgh could see the narrow channel leading east into a bay behind the island. Banna Strand beach swept away on his left to the north.

"This is my home," Collis told him. "We will be safer here. Head through the channel and mind your draft."

"Aidan, check our depth from this point on, brother," Tadgh ordered. "High tide is comin' in, which should help, so it should."

As they glided by the island into the narrow entrance to the bay, Collis narrated its history with a sweeping arm as they passed. "See that ruined castle on the right there, on Fenit Island? Not really an island. That's my ancestral home," he crowed. "It belonged to the mighty FitzMaurice Clan. They were a powerful force around here up until the Desmond Rebellion in the last few years of the sixteenth century. Do you see what's left of that round tower on the point to your left? The FitzMaurices ran a chain from there across to the castle to control access to the bay."

"Did they now, Maurice. Whatever for?" Morgan couldn't quell her curiosity.

"They charged a tariff for entry. This was a mighty harbor back then, and there was money to be made."

"It doesn't look so mighty now, does it."

"Times change, lass." Maurice looked wistfully at this home lagoon and continued his narrative. "Tragically, my FitzMaurice ancestors were squashed by the English invaders, the bastards." The captain paused for a moment, surveying the landscape. "After our Clan was almost destroyed in 1598 by the English invaders, Fenit Castle was no longer habitable. The Collis family was granted the land in this area, and there they built a home called Barrow House. We will see it ahead in the bay. The Collis family intermarried with the FitzMaurices, and I am the product of that union. I'm certainly proud of my FitzMaurice heritage, but not of my Collis ancestors from that time."

"Why is that?" Morgan asked, peering ahead to see Barrow House on the left.

"Because Captain Collis was part of the English force that destroyed the FitzMaurice Clan. Tadgh, you can tie up at the seawall where the steps are."

Tadgh swung the tiller and boom to spin the hooker so that he was pointed towards the entrance of the harbor. He nimbly brought the boat to rest against the wall. "Lower the lugsail," he ordered, and Aidan complied. After tying off, they ascended the stairs towards their new friend's home. The tide was in, so the manicured lawn was just five feet up from the sea, and supported by the rough-cut wall. Tadgh noted that the hooker would likely be beached at low tide. That could be a problem.

"You have a beautiful old home here, a mansion really," Morgan said as they approached the three-story, plastered stone façade of the imposing main house with its twelve symmetrically-arranged picture windows. "I imagine that there are stories aplenty within its walls."

"Inside and out, lass. This house has a mysterious past, much of which even I don't understand."

"We have one like that. How many bedrooms do you have?"

"The main house has seven bedrooms and a sitting room on the upper floor. We even have indoor plumbing, which of course didn't exist in the seventeenth century when it was built."

They passed a three-tiered circular fountain with opposing horseheads and headed up the outdoor marble-floored staircase to the second floor entrance. There, two crouched white lions greeted them before they crossed the threshold of the massive carved oak door. Along the way, as the captain continued to tell his story, the ancestral history took on new meaning for Tadgh and Morgan.

"Let me explain about the history of this area," Collis went on. "In the Middle Ages, the town of Ardfert, which is about two miles north of here, was a major ecclesiastical center for not only Ireland, but for all of Europe. Scholars studied there from all over the known world. This was the Irish Renaissance, and we were its leaders at the time. This bay was the harbor for ships coming from far and wide, bringing supplies, students and their masters to the great cathedral. Fenit and Tralee didn't exist in those magical days."

Tadgh thought this was quite a different man from the gruff fishing captain who had challenged them at their first meeting. *A learned man who loves the history of the Irish, a man after my own heart.*

"In 1307, when my ancestor Thomas FitzMaurice returned from the Crusades as a Knights Templar, the order was just being disbanded. Some of the knights shifted alliance, at the order of the Pope, to a sister organization, the Knights Hospitaller of Jerusalem. This group carried on the good work of providing hospitals and religious shelters to care for pilgrims seeking the Holy Land. Thomas established a Hospitaller Monastery near Ardfert, his home. In time, he became the Grand Knight for Ireland, so he did."

When Collis mentioned the role his ancestor played in the history of the Knights, Tadgh and Morgan looked at each other inquisitively and then focused on his words. This man was becoming more and more interesting, his story fascinating.

They paused at the front door while Maurice recommenced his history lesson, as he was saying, "There was another Hospitaller monastery up north in Sligo called Ballymote. Together, these two Hospitaller centers in western

Ireland provided the refuge for Knights Templar escaping persecution on their way to Scotland. So you can see that this was a very important area of the country in those days. Unfortunately, all this was destroyed by the wicked English, starting with King Henry VIII and ending with Cromwellian forces in the mid-1700s." He took a breath. "You see this door knocker?" The captain rubbed the black iron skull-shaped knob. "It came from the castle on the island."

Now Tadgh felt a strong kinship with this man. "We are of the same mind, my friend. We McCarthys suffered the same brutal fate. I am descended from the MacCarthy Reagh Clan near Cork. Our ancestors fought together at the Battle of Kinsale, I am sure." He punched him lightly on the arm. "Shall we get on our way to the fort?"

Maurice continued, unabated. "If you are descended from Florence MacCarthy Reagh, then you will know that our clan and yours fought over the territory of southwest Ireland for centuries. Florence did not fight with us in the Desmond Rebellion, but he did not fight against us. He and our Clan Chieftain Fitzthomas, rebel Sugan Earl of Desmond, did band together in 1599, after the Desmond Rebellion was lost, to continue to fight the English heretics.

"Unfortunately, both Florence and Fitzthomas were arrested and sent to the Tower of London by order of the wicked Governor of Munster, George Carew, in 1601, just months before the Battle of Kinsale. Still, their followers pressed on to support the rebels in the battle. So, yes, indeed, we are compatriots now, as our ancestors were then," Maurice agreed, clapping Tadgh on the back. "Welcome."

Morgan was amazed. Now she had two scholars who were history encyclopedias to deal with, and it fascinated her to hear them illuminate ages past. They entered the home just as a grandfather clock in the foyer chimed twice, indicating the half hour at 9:30. They knew the visit would need to be short.

"My goodness," Morgan gasped as she took in the historical opulence of the mansion's interior. "Is this circular staircase mahogany?"

"Yes, from Burma, I understand."

Morgan marveled. "And all the marble and columns in this grand foyer . . . just magnificent."

Collis ushered them into the kitchen, where he bade them to be seated. He introduced them to his wife Martha and insisted that she cook them all a proper breakfast. "Armies march on their stomachs, you know," she chortled, flipping Kerry bacon on the sizzling skillet.

"Thank you, ma'am, but we've got to be going." Tadgh looked at Maurice.

"Nonsense, lad. Sit down. It's ready and you three look famished. This won't take a minute."

Morgan led Tadgh to the table.

Unlike her lanky husband, Martha Collis was short and squat, with a kindly wrinkled face and raven hair drawn back in a bun. She brought to the table toasted slices of soda bread, a small crock of butter, and a cup of honey.

"Can I help you?" Morgan offered.

"No, lass, the eggs are almost ready and the bacon is crisp." They had only been in the house ten minutes, yet she already had their places at the table set. "The chickens were right productive this morning," she said, cracking eggs into a bowl and frothing them just enough with some water before pouring the mixture into the sizzling pan. She then turned the pan rapidly from side to side so the eggs spread over the bottom. She grinned, "The French way." She flipped the bubbling mass over and then slid it out onto a platter. Then she lifted the bacon strips out of the fry pan onto a plate. Tadgh smiled at this generous hospitality, given that they hadn't eaten anything in the last eighteen hours. Collis joined Tadgh, Morgan, and Aidan at the table to do justice to the meal. He clapped both hands on the table, palms down. "Did you know that we are also brothers with the O'Donnell Clan from that time? When they were marching south in late 1601 to engage our enemy at Kinsale, their Clan Chieftain, Red Hugh, sent his cousin to liberate my ancestor, FitzMaurice, so that he could fight on the side of the Clans."

At his words, Tadgh's and Morgan's jaws dropped open, but Collis did not seem to notice their reaction. The man was a kindred spirit. Yet not an hour ago, he threatened to destroy their hooker with them on it, thought Tadgh. The uncanny connection with the O'Donnells, and in fact, Red Hugh O'Donnell, mystified him. This history might be coincidental, yet Tadgh thought this could indeed be a pivotal day, perhaps even one of Divine intervention.

Chapter Twenty-Three
Casement

Friday, April 21, 1916
Barrow House, Near Fenit, Ireland

Tadgh kept looking at his watch and rushed them all through the meal in fifteen minutes. Even then, Martha insisted on pouring out mugs of strong tea with great lashings of sugar. Tadgh told Aidan and Morgan that they were to stay and guard the boat while he and Collis had to leave immediately.

"But we are coming with you," they responded vehemently.

Tadgh held up his hand to stop any further objections. "If we lose the hooker, we'll have a very tough time getting home. It's certain there'll be no arguments on this."

Aidan said, "I see the merit of having me ready to cast off, if need be, and I can work on the foresail lanyard problem, but I think I could be very helpful in a fight." Both he and Tadgh glanced at Morgan, whose blazing eyes let them know she was not about to play nursemaid to the hooker.

Tadgh saw the futility in further debate with Morgan. She wasn't needed to guard the boat, and he didn't really like the idea of letting her out of his sight. He was just about to agree that Morgan accompany him and the captain, with Aidan serving as boat guard, when they all heard a knock at the front door of Barrow House, followed by a voice demanding, "Maurice Collis, open the door. This is Constable Coltrain from the RIC."

Collis rushed them down into his root cellar, and on returning, pulled his forty-five-gallon pickle barrel over the floor opening. Martha banged pans about to cover the noise of shuffling people under the floor and shoved the extra breakfast plates and cutlery into the oven out of sight. The pounding on the door got louder, and she opened it without a word, ushering in Constable Frank Coltrain in the company of five men. Captain Collis recognized three of them as locals. He thought that the other two were sneering cutthroats, to be sure.

"Collis, we're looking for three chaps who overturned a dinghy in the surf off the Strand this morning. We're *concerned* about their safety,"

Constable Coltrain said, his eyes darting over the table, the kitchen, and an array of dishes stacked on the counter. "Have you seen them?"

"No, sir, I haven't," the captain said, lighting a pipe and taking a few puffs to get it going.

"Mind if we take a look around?" one of the two strangers asked.

"This here's Head Constable Boyle and his deputy, Constable Gordo James." Coltrain waved his hand at them by way of introduction. "They were sent from Cork to help us do the searches, so if you don't mind . . ."

"Fine by me. You won't find any strangers here."

While Boyle, James, and Coltrain's men searched the house and grounds, the constable stayed behind to talk to Collis. "Why are you not out with your lads fishing today?"

"Got a boat to fix. Jimmy is quite capable of running my crew for a day or so," he answered without batting an eye.

"You mean that Galway hooker you got tied up at your wall? That it?"

"That's right, Frank. Owed a friend a favor." His answer seemed to satisfy Coltrain.

Just then, they heard the sound of a crash in the back kitchen and Martha's call for her husband.

"What's going on here?" Maurice boomed, as he raced into the kitchen, Coltrain in tow.

"They've spilled our pickle barrel and want to tip it over completely," his wife cried in anger. "That's our whole year's supply until the next harvest."

Coltrain observed the damage the two men from Cork had done and shouted, "Boyle, that's enough. There's no reason to destroy these citizens' property. The perpetrators are clearly not here."

"But there's a root cellar below that we haven't checked," Gordo James protested.

Coltrain's lips set in a line. "I said that's enough. They're not here. We need to head down to Banna, closer to where they landed."

Boyle would just as soon have torn apart the place to really give the woman something to cry about, but he headed out of the house to their vehicles instead. Coltrain and the rest hurried out the door, jumped into their cars, and drove off.

The trio emerged from the cold cellar smelling of pickle brine, thankful they had not been captured. It took a few precious minutes as they washed down with lye soap to remove the odor. Tadgh had wanted to make sure that if they were captured, they could not lead the RIC back to

Barrow House with the distinct odor of pickles.

"If they go directly to Banna, there are several homes there to visit near the beach," Collis announced. "If we leave now, we should be able to get to McKenna's Fort well before they go there."

"Time's a wastin'," Tadgh urged, checking his watch. It was already eleven o'clock. "Be back soon, brother."

As the three climbed into an old Hudson, Collis told Morgan and Tadgh they would take the fastest route, a straight arrow to the fort. "And hold onto your hats," he grinned and stamped down on the accelerator. Tadgh wondered if this old clunker would hold together as they sped away.

There was no road to speak of. They headed northeast, bumping along, skirting Carrahane Strand on their left along an ancient sand track. Morgan thought that they would get stuck on two occasions, but Collis managed to get through by gunning the engine and dropping the clutch at just the right moment. The grinding of gears would have awakened the dead. As it was, the scrub brush and seashore grasses yielded a multitude of startled sea birds that flew up as they passed. "Not the stealthiest of vehicles, to be sure," Tadgh muttered, glancing back to his left toward Banna Strand.

"Not when we're caught in quicksand. But it's the best that Barrow has to offer," Collis joked, as he ground the metal teeth together once more. He reached out the driver's window to scrape caked dirt off the windshield with his bare hand. "Only another half a mile, and we'll be there."

Down the beach, the commotion of birds did not go unnoticed as they flew up out of the brush. "Follow that trail of birds," Boyle commanded.

Coltrain did not like his orders being countermanded, but he had to agree that Boyle had a point.

"Now, turn around and follow that trail," he ordered. He would deal with Boyle's insubordination later.

Morgan saw the fingerpost first. McKenna's Fort was not a building but a dense stand of scrub mulberry trees and ground vegetation that covered jumbled rocks. Whatever structure had been there was long gone, a five-foot-high dirt mound its remains. Tadgh thought the deep trench surrounding the mound looked to be an easy place to get lost in, and Collis told them it was a typical Danish Rath fort, meant for domestic rather than for military purpose.

"Pull over there behind those trees in that tall weedy area, out of sight of the road," Tadgh suggested. Strategically, he had chosen a location that was on the other side of the "fort"—hidden from view, but with access to the road downhill and around a bend from the Rath. Collis confirmed that this would lead them back south towards Fenit and Barrow Bay on the circular route.

Tadgh handed Aidan's rifle to Collis and cocked his own Luger. "You two wait here, and keep the motor running." He took off into the bushes at the edge of the Rath.

Despite Collis' objections, Morgan followed Tadgh moments later.

Tadgh found Casement in the trench, slumped against a shrub under the scant cover of some branches. His normally tailored beard was a tangled mess. The man didn't look much like the swarthy gentleman whose tintype picture appeared in the Gaelic press, and he looked much worse than when they had met in Riederau.

As Tadgh quietly approached him, he called out his name. "Roger Casement, is that yourself?" Now he could see the man's agitated state. His eyes darted from side to side like those of a caged animal. His forehead was covered with a sheen of sweat, and a rattling sound emanated from his chest area. Sir Roger's coat, trousers, and green muffler were wet and his boots were full of sea sand.

Casement did not recognize Tadgh, so he croaked out his cover name, "I'm Richard . . . Morton . . . Denham . . . Bucks, author of *Life of Saint Brendon.*"

"It's me, Tadgh McCarthy, sir, from the Ammersee."

Tadgh's voice jolted the patriot, and he looked up into his face. "The message. Did they get the message?"

"I delivered it, sir. But I don't think they will stop." Tadgh could see that this news aggravated Casement even more.

At that instant, Morgan darted out of the thicket.

"I told you to stay in the car," Tadgh growled at her.

"Where you go, I go. I just had to meet this Casement fellow that you talked about, and I so much wanted to thank him for his part in our escape from the *Boche.*" Morgan looked down at the figure. "Oh, my." She kneeled down to his level so she could check his vital signs. He recoiled from her. "I'm a nurse, sir. You need medical assistance."

Tadgh turned back to Casement. "We will get you to safety, sir."

Casement's eyes darkened, and his mouth twitched. "We've got to tell them that they're not coming. We've got to stop it and tell MacNeill," he rasped, his chest heaving with the effort.

"Who's not coming?"

"I told you before," he gasped. "The bloody Germans. They're not coming," Roger mumbled, fidgeting with his scarf. "Tell MacNeill and Hobson to stop the Rising. It's insane." His voice trailed off at the end.

"Don't exert yourself, sir," Morgan urged, trying to button his overcoat.

"Where are the others?" Tadgh asked urgently.

Casement's eyes brightened. "The brigade is coming back for me. I almost died in the surf, you know. Monteith saved me. Good lad."

Tadgh had many more questions, but they would have to wait. "Let's go now," he said gently, as he lifted him slowly to a standing position.

At just that moment, they heard a thrashing of footsteps coming from the thicket, and a rough voice ordered, "Hands up. You're surrounded!" Five men burst into the clearing, guns leveled at the three Republicans.

Tadgh knew that voice. He wheeled and trained his Luger on Boyle's forehead. How the hell did *he* get there? It would be so easy to pull the trigger and rid the world of this evil scourge. But that could get them all killed.

"Drop your gun, McCarthy," Boyle spat.

Tadgh could see that his nemesis was surprised to see him. And that gloat. *I'm going to ram it down his throat*, Tadgh vowed.

"That's the man who murdered your . . . ?" Morgan said, looking horrified. She remembered that evil face through the window of O'Donovan Rossa's hearse.

"Yes," Tadgh replied, lowering the Luger slowly. "My parents . . . in cold blood." His mouth twisted.

Coltrain spoke first. "You are all under arrest for treason against the Crown. Did you three come ashore from the German submarine?"

"No, you fool. I have been tracking this man and the woman in Ireland for a year now," Boyle sneered. "They are German spies and my prisoners. The old man is probably Casement, the only one from the U-boat."

Casement told Coltrain that his name was Richard Morton.

"Sorry, Boyle, but all three of these prisoners are coming with me to RIC headquarters in Tralee."

At this point Boyle leveled his rifle at Coltrain, and Tadgh could see that it was all Boyle could do to refrain from pulling the trigger.

"Constable Coltrain. We agree, but on one condition," Gordo James interjected, putting his hand on Boyle's weapon to push its muzzle towards the ground. Boyle tried to shrug off Gordo's hand. "We'll take these two with us in one car, and you men can take Mr. Casement here in the other. I'm sure he needs medical attention. We'll meet you in Tralee."

The Tralee Constable looked skeptical, but he saw the merit of the man's suggestion. He still believed in the integrity of the RIC force.

Collis had heard the approach of the police vehicles from the other side of the Rath. *This can't be good.* He stole his way towards the clearing on foot. With the uproar in the Rath, his approach went unnoticed. He heard and saw the whole exchange between the various policemen and realized that Tadgh and Morgan were in big trouble.

Now he had to decide if this was his fight or not. Like millions of his countrymen, he hated the English. But he had a good living, a home with a wife and three children. That was more than he could say for most of his mates. On the other hand, there was the burning desire to avenge the travesty done to his ancestors. It was one of those moments of truth that come to all men at least once in their lifetime.

After considering the situation, he figured that he had no chance against the five of them. And he knew Coltrain personally. Not a *bad* person. So he was relieved when he saw them split up. He watched the two strangers handling Tadgh and Morgan roughly as they roped their arms behind their backs. They took Tadgh's pistol from where he had dropped it and got quite agitated when they examined it.

Collis edged closer in the underbrush and watched as the two strangers loaded Tadgh and Morgan unceremoniously into the rear car. While Coltrain was busy ushering Casement into the lead vehicle, the stranger they called Boyle opened the bonnet of his police car and looked inside. Then he jumped into the driver's seat and cranked the engine. It would not turn over. Coltrain got out of his vehicle and strode over to them.

"What's the holdup, Boyle?"

"Your damn car won't start."

"Let me try," Coltrain offered, sauntering over. After several futile attempts, he got out of his vehicle.

Boyle said, "I'm sure it's just flooded. I'll get it cleared. You go on, and we'll meet you at headquarters."

Coltrain didn't like that solution. "Jamison, get over here," he yelled, and a scrappy-looking junior constable jumped out of the forward car.

"Yes, sir?"

"Go with these officers. Make sure they find their way to headquarters."

When Boyle clenched his hands into fists, a clear sign that he was about to get violent, Gordo James intervened and accepted the help.

Collis watched as Coltrain drove off to the south towards Fenit and Tralee. When they were out of sight, he heard Boyle ask Jamison, "Help me here under the bonnet, lad." When Jamison leaned over the engine, Boyle slammed the bonnet down on his head and shoulders and knocked the lad out cold.

"Gordo, put him in the boot. And reconnect those ignition wires. We need to find a different place for our interrogation."

The smaller constable dumped the body in the boot and then peered into the car's window to check that the prisoners had remained secure in the back seat. Tadgh pulled himself up and shot Gordo a look of pure defiance.

Almost directly behind the constable, Tadgh spied Collis crouched in the underbrush. Their eyes met for a second before the car started up and began to move away. Tadgh mouthed the words *Get Aidan* with the hope that Collis could read lips.

The implications of Boyle's statement were obvious to Tadgh. He realized they were in for a rough time at best. Morgan's eyes were fixed on him, and she looked terrified.

"We're going to get out of this all right, dear. Watch for my signals," Tadgh whispered lamely. In truth, he didn't have any idea yet how they were going to escape alive. He realized that bringing Jamison along was tantamount to signing the poor lad's death warrant. Nothing was going to stop Boyle from getting the information he wanted, and there would be no living witnesses afterward, unless he could find a way to stop the bastard.

The police car turned around and headed north on the dirt track in the direction of Banna Beach. Collis turned and ran, faster than he had done in a long, long time. He reached the Hudson, jumped in, and drove around the Rath and onto the road. He prayed that he wouldn't lose them. He drove a mile, turning left at the T-intersection, in pursuit at the highest speed the old Hudson could muster. He could not see the car ahead of him yet. He stopped where he had a view of the road winding down to the beach, but Boyle and his prisoners were nowhere in sight. *Damn, they*

couldn't have gotten that far ahead. He cursed himself for not taking them on before they drove away. But that action would have been suicidal.

Think, he told himself. They could have branched right. Turning, he saw the answer. Remote Rahoneen Castle, that he had just passed, stood like a sentinel on the hill situated on his right to the south, proud, even in its ruined state. It reminded him of his own ancestors, broken, but still standing. In fact, this had been the home of the Bishop of Ardfert in the glory days. When he was a boy, his father had shown him through the ruins, explaining how his ancestor Nicholas FitzMaurice had been the bishop there in the early 1400s.

He shook away the reverie and could see the police car, partially hidden by trees, parked up against the west wall above the road. He pulled off behind a clump of bushes, east of the ruins, parked the Hudson, and scurried up the hummock. Pressing himself against the broken eastern wall, from there he could see down into the open ruins.

Facing him, and about a hundred feet away, Tadgh and Morgan were tied up separately, six feet apart with their hands behind their backs, to ancient iron rings mounted in what had been an altar stone of the castle's chapel. The uphill south wall to his left, away from the road, was still standing, as was most of the westerly wall opposite him, beyond the altar. Jamison lay in a crumpled position on the ground nearby. The smaller constable called Gordo stood guard while the bigger oaf, Boyle, slapped and punched Tadgh. The man appeared to be toying with his prey and enjoying it immensely.

Collis realized that he could not possibly overpower these men by himself. He didn't fancy shooting them in cold blood from his position, even if he could be that accurate. They were, after all, the law. He had read Tadgh's lips, a trait learned at sea as a boy when his father would shout orders in the whistling gales of the Atlantic Ocean. He made a snap decision. He gambled that he could get home and back before it was too late. Running back to the car, Collis jumped in and backed quietly down the hill in neutral and headed home.

From the *Marie*, Aidan saw Collis race into the yard ten minutes later. Together, they quickly uncrated a Russian Mosin Nagant five-shot rifle, bayonet, and thirty rounds of ammunition, then sped back toward Rahoneen.

"Faster," Aidan kept yelling in Maurice's ear.

He could see fire in the boy's eyes as he set his foot down hard on the accelerator pedal. The Hudson groaned under the stress.

Chapter Twenty-Four
Peril

Friday, April 21, 1916
Rahoneen Castle Ruins, Ireland

Boyle took his time. "Come on McCarthy, I know you've got the information I need," he sneered as he pounded a fist into Tadgh's solar plexus once again.

"I don't know what you're talking about. But I know that you killed my parents." Tadgh spat out a mouthful of blood and willed his mind to stay clear.

"So you did see us then, you little bastard. Where's your pipsqueak brother, the drunk?"

"I'm going to kill you before this is over," Tadgh growled. His spit contained pieces of a broken tooth.

Boyle let out a hideous laugh. "I don't think so, McCarthy. I'll tell you what's going to happen here. First, you're going to tell me what I need to know. If you don't, then I'm going to kill your girlfriend here, but not before I've had my way with her. If you still won't talk, then I'm going to kill this fine lad here with your own Luger," he indicated Jamison's unconscious body with his gun. "And all the while I'm going to keep beating you until you bleed to death internally. I've got all afternoon."

Tadgh had no misconception about the outcome of this encounter if he didn't get his arms free. Boyle would beat up and kill them both with Jamison's Webley, then kill Jamison with Tadgh's Luger. It would be a firefight with Boyle and Gordo James claiming innocence in the matter. After taking another blow to the head, Tadgh muttered, "What is it you want from me, you bastard?"

"The same thing I wanted from your grandfather and your father." He was shouting now. "Where is the McCarthy gold? I've done my homework. You are in the bloodline."

"What makes you think that I would know anything about it?" Tadgh asked, stalling.

Boyle was whipping himself into a frenzy. "I know there's a trail in family heirlooms. And I know there's another Clan involved."

Tadgh couldn't believe his ears. It was as if Boyle had seen the Clan Pact. But he had killed Tadgh's father and mother years before he, himself, and Morgan had found it in the *Cumdac*.

"That's ridiculous mythology, Boyle. I know nothin' about any heirlooms or family gold. I'm just a simple fisherman."

"Well, maybe your woman, here, has something to say on the matter, eh?" He slapped Morgan sharply across the face.

"Is that how your mother brought you up?" Morgan said, licking blood from the corner of her mouth.

Boyle was taken aback. "You leave my mother out of this."

Tadgh detected a weakness. "Does your mother condone your murderous behavior? What kind of woman does that?" He waited for the inevitable.

Boyle delivered a vicious blow across Tadgh's mouth. "My mother was a saint."

"Was she, now? To whom? Certainly not to yourself, you bloody murderer." That incited another blow, this time to Tadgh's head.

"Your father, then." Morgan chimed in, realizing the opening.

"He'd have killed you already." Boyle turned back towards Morgan.

Morgan pressed. "Handled you roughly, did he?" Boyle twitched. Tadgh saw it. Morgan went further. "I'll bet he beat your saintly mother, didn't he?"

Before Morgan could open her mouth again, Boyle grabbed her blouse and ripped it wide open in one violent motion, exposing her breasts beneath a thin camisole.

"We'll see what you know, won't we, darlin'." When Morgan spat in his face, he laughed. "I love a spirited woman."

"Leave her alone, Boyle. She knows nothin' about it. Your fight's with me," Tadgh snarled. His wrists were raw from trying to twist out of his binding, a rope tied to the iron ring imbedded in the rock, and his struggle yielded no success. "Where did you get that ridiculous story about the heirlooms, anyway?" he asked, in part to divert the bastard's attention away from Morgan.

Boyle turned back to Tadgh and gave him an uppercut to the jaw that loosened two more teeth. Tadgh could feel blood trickling down his throat.

Being in full command, the blaggard was clearly ready to gloat. *Good.*

"My name is Boyle, from the conquering lineage of Boyles." He hissed like a snake. "Maybe you've heard of us. We owned Cork and areas east, like Youghal. We bought all the lands that Sir Walter Raleigh was given by good Queen Bess for routing your puny forefathers in the Desmond Rebellion." His voice rose. "Raleigh ordered the beheading of your kind at Smerwick in 1580, if you recall. The unfortunate ones had their limbs broken in three places each, and then they were hanged a day later. Now that I think of it, such acts would be a fitting end for you both here in that same County Kerry." Boyle could hardly contain himself.

Morgan cringed at the thought, but she held her defiant stance.

Tadgh cursed himself for not following through with trying to kill Boyle at RIC headquarters in Cork.

"We ruled from Lismore Castle until Lord Muscry attacked us during the Confederate Wars in 1643," Boyle continued, rubbing his chin with glee. "Maybe he was mad after we destroyed Kilbrittain Castle and the McCarthy Reagh Clan the year before. We laid siege to his Blarney Castle and obliterated it." Boyle seemed to relish the images conjured. "That treasure is rightfully mine as spoils of the victors, and I mean to get it, if I have to kill all the McCarthys in Ireland," he bellowed into Tadgh's face.

"Boyle, you bastard. I don't know anything about the McCarthy treasure, or if it even existed," Tadgh said, trying to catch the head constable's attention. He and Morgan were each trying to distract the murderer from harming the other

Finally, Tadgh understood Boyle's insanity. The villain was so worked up with his quest and the joy of killing slowly, he couldn't see that Tadgh had nearly worn through the rope binding his wrists, using the jagged edge of the rock as a cutting tool. He would be free at any moment.

Gordo James, sadistically enthralled with the carnage about to unfold, ached to participate. His eyes focused on the circus at the altar and then on Morgan's breasts, in particular.

Collis and Aidan had arrived and silently taken up positions behind the broken east wall just before Boyle yelled those last words about the Desmonds. All at once, this fight had become personal for Collis.

In their position overlooking the travesty below them, they discussed attack strategy in whispers. "I say we just shoot them both simultaneously from the castle wall," Aidan recommended. "You take the little one called Gordo. Boyle is mine." Aidan recognized the man who killed his parents, and he was fuming.

"I'm a fisherman, not a soldier," Collis responded honestly. "They are at least a hundred feet away from our cover. I can't guarantee that I could kill or disable one of them before they could shoot Tadgh and Morgan. That's why I didn't try earlier myself."

Aidan had to agree that this was a distinct possibility. His burly companion was an unknown quantity in the shooting department. And Aidan had had no chance to test fire the Russian weapon. It looked outdated, and its sight could be way off. He had been given some guerrilla warfare training at St. Edna's, but he had never killed a man. Yet he wanted Boyle dead in the worst way.

"Then we need a distraction," Aidan reasoned. "If you circle around the south wall and get the police car door open, you could start the vehicle rolling down the hill in plain view. That might do it." Aidan was trying to find a way for Collis to contribute without risking his life and family.

"What then?"

"Based on how you came at us this morning, Maurice, I imagine you are pretty good with your fists. You could advance on them from the west. That way we'd have them boxed in."

"I've broken up a few pub fights in my day."

Aidan figured that was an understatement. "I am sure you have. See that tree down there in the courtyard, maybe halfway the distance to them?" Aidan pointed. "It will provide me with intermediate cover because it's in a direct line between this wall and the altar. Its trunk has got to be a foot and a half in diameter." He continued. "Here's what we'll do. I will sneak down behind the tree. If I am seen, we'll have to try simultaneous shots. If I get to the tree undetected, then you start the police car rolling down the hill. In that moment when they are distracted, I'll rush Boyle and shoot him at close range before he can shoot Tadgh or Morgan. As soon as you release the car's brake, I am counting on you to attack from the west. From there you can take out the small one with your fists or your rifle. He should be preoccupied with what I'm doing at the altar. All right?" Aidan hoped that he could take out both men before Collis would be at risk.

"All right, lad. I'll follow your lead."

They could see Boyle bullying Morgan to get Tadgh to talk. He tore at her breast while fumbling with her trouser buttons, pulling at them. He grinned maniacally. They could hear Tadgh cursing as he struggled against his bonds. With the nightmare vision of how Boyle ruthlessly executed his parents burning in his memory, Aidan knew that Morgan's life was about to end. They had to act now.

"Here we go," he whispered and darted for the tree.

Just then, unexpectedly, Jamison stirred and rolled over. Aidan watched in disgust as Boyle turned from his attack and calmly used Tadgh's Luger to put a bullet in Jamison's brain. What was most revolting was the look of satisfaction on Boyle's face, the same expression of joy he had seen on that face when the man had killed his parents. Before Aidan could raise the Mosin Nagant, Morgan arched her back on the altar and kicked upwards with all her might. Her boot caught the monster squarely in his crotch. Boyle crumpled up, and with a sickening groan, fell to his knees.

Taking advantage of this commotion, Aidan stepped from behind the cover of the tree to get a clear shot. Taking a bead on Boyle's chest, he pulled the trigger. The bullet jammed in the breach of the old rifle, and it misfired.

Gordo, who was halfway between the tree and the altar, moving to the aid of his boss, had his back to Aidan. On hearing the hollow click of the hammer, he spun and fired from the hip at close range. The bullet caught Aidan in the left leg above the knee.

Before the man could get another shot off, Aidan lunged at him, pushing off from his good leg. The bayonet pierced Gordo just below the ribcage, most likely rupturing his spleen and liver. Still standing, but in the throes of death, Gordo let out a blood-curdling shriek. To be sure, the wound would be fatal. Aidan yanked the bayonet upwards to lift the sagging body from the ground and shook it like a ragdoll. Aidan landed on his bad leg and collapsed, spent, beside the body.

"Oh, Aidan!" Morgan cried, as she watched his wound gushing blood, powerless to help him.

Collis had started the police car rolling down the hill after he heard the rifle shot. He rushed to the west wall in time to see Aidan collapse and hear Morgan's cry. Then he saw Boyle, while swaying like a drunkard, raise the Luger to finish Aidan. From the wall, Collis fired at Boyle and missed, but the bullet grazed Morgan's shoulder.

Tadgh knew that what he would do next would decide it for all of them. Using all his remaining strength, he pulled on the rusty old ring, and it popped out of the stone altar with a clang. With his hands still tied behind his back, Tadgh dove the short distance into Boyle's path and swung the heavy ring, knocking the Luger from his hand.

Surprised and furious, Boyle went for his Webley. With his back turned to the murderer, Tadgh raised his arms and threw them backwards over Boyle's head. Lunging forward, Tadgh yanked on the Head Constable's thick neck, so as Boyle gagged and struggled violently for breath, the last remaining strands of the bonds on Tadgh's bleeding hands came free.

Before he could react, Boyle was upon him, Webley in hand, ready to finish him off. He grabbed Tadgh in a chokehold and put the Webley to his temple. "Tell me now what you know about the gold, McCarthy, or you're a dead man."

Tadgh couldn't breathe, and his vision blurred. He tried to shake his head to clear it, but the hold held fast. "Never will tell you," he hissed through clenched teeth. His head throbbed, pounding like a sledgehammer on granite.

They were facing Morgan, only a few feet away. In agony, she could see her man's life being squeezed out of him. She had to do something. "You bastard, let him go, and I'll tell you what you want to know."

Boyle looked up, and without letting up on his death grip on Tadgh, he pointed the gun at Morgan and shouted, "Tell me now, bitch, or he dies."

Collis could not shoot for fear of hitting his compatriots. He was about to rush Boyle who had his back to him, when he saw Aidan crawling towards the Luger.

Noticing the movement behind him, Boyle turned to fire, but Aidan reached the Luger and beat Boyle to the draw. He was deathly afraid of hitting his brother, but he had to take the shot to save their lives. The bullet nicked the flesh of Tadgh's left forearm before striking Boyle just above the heart. Both men slumped to the ground. Aidan did not have the strength to fire again.

Boyle came to first. Being woozy, and with a terrible chest pain, he no longer had the upper hand. He could hardly breathe. He stared blankly at the ground rising to meet him, and he couldn't find either gun. Then he saw Gordo lying dead in a pool of blood. Another shot rang out and caught him in the right hand. There, behind that altar, was his enemy, the shooter. McCarthy would finish him now. He had seen the police car roll by down the hill. Now alone, he did the only thing that might save his cowardly skin. Dragging himself to his feet, he lurched off after the vehicle.

Collis ignored Boyle's pathetic retreat and rushed from behind the tree to his friends' aid. He would deal with that coward later.

"Untie me first," Morgan cried, knowing that Aidan's life was in the gravest peril.

Collis pulled out his scaling knife and cut Morgan free. While he tended to Tadgh, she took care of Aidan and discovered that the bullet wound was in the lower part of his thigh, an easier wound to tourniquet. She used her blouse to tightly bind the leg, then pressed hard on the wound to stop the blood flow. Aidan's eyelids fluttered as he struggled to breathe, and she could see that he had lost a lot of blood.

"Help me here, Maurice," Morgan called him away from Tadgh, who seemed to be regaining consciousness. "I need you to press down hard on Aidan's leg so I can tend to Tadgh."

"Oh, mavorneen," she cried. Tadgh had raised himself to a sitting position, coughing and clearing his throat. She knelt down beside him and took his head gently to her bosom, as he trembled from the shock and bitter cold. Morgan moved her hands through his hair and beard, relieved that the nick on his left forearm was not serious. She covered his beautiful face with small kisses to soothe his battered skin and calm his beleaguered heart. "I love you," Morgan whispered to him again, and again. She had expected to have to patch him up in the revolution, but not so soon.

"Well, now. Is it time for tea yet, aroon?" he managed weakly and looked up at her with a twinkle in his eye. They both laughed, sharing the joy of still being alive together.

"I don't want to put a damper on your party, but we have one sick boy over here," Collis interrupted them. "Not to mention that you both have your own bullet wounds to worry about ."

Morgan's nursing training kicked her back into action. She ripped Tadgh's sleeve off to use as a temporary bandage for his forearm. "I think you'll live."

Recovering his senses, Tadgh got to his feet, and wobbly still, staggered over to check on his brother. "Morgan, Aidan looks really pale."

Morgan checked the lad's wrist. "His pulse is weak and irregular, Tadgh. We've got to get him to a hospital fast," she said through chattering teeth.

"Maurice, can Morgan use your coat? She's freezing." Collis wrapped the coat around her, and noticed the wound on her shoulder. "It's nothing," she winced.

Finally, the cobwebs cleared, and Tadgh asked, "What happened to Boyle?" Collis told him that Aidan had shot him in the chest, and even with that serious wound, the man had been able to drag himself downhill to his car. Tadgh took charge. He pried the Luger from the vise grip of

Aidan's hand and gave directions. "Maurice, let Morgan tend to Aidan's wound. Can you bring your Hudson down the hill near us?"

"Yes, I think so."

"Good. Then do it. I'll be right back."

Although Aidan's serious condition was of paramount importance, Tadgh did not want to let Boyle get away. He forced himself to function. He looked northward down at the road and saw that a tangle of bramble bushes blocked the police car's escape. He watched Boyle attempt to back it up the hill enough to get around the obstacle, but the front wheels just spun wildly in the mud, and the car was not going anywhere.

By the time Tadgh was halfway down the hill toward the car, Boyle had managed to get traction. The car backed uphill a few feet and then lurched diagonally forward onto the road.

Realizing that he couldn't reach the car in time, Tadgh fired the last four rounds in his Luger at the disappearing vehicle. The first two hit the back windshield, shattering glass. The last two hit the driver's side door. And still Boyle drove erratically down the road, accelerating until the police car sped out of sight around a bend.

When Tadgh rejoined the others, he said, "I hope I hit that bastard, but I can't be sure. If he survives, he will blame us for all the mayhem."

Collis and Morgan had positioned Aidan in the back seat of the Hudson. Morgan cradled the young man's head in her arms. Tadgh could see that she looked very worried. Collis urged him from the driver's seat to get in, so they could be on their way. As soon as Tadgh pulled the door shut, Collis slammed the car into gear and sped down the hill.

"Slow down, or Aidan's wound will split open," Morgan yelled from the back seat. It was hard to keep up the pressure on his wound in the moving car.

Collis maneuvered the car to avoid any potholes, but the old Hudson had essentially no shock absorbers. "We're going to my house," he announced, quickly checking his watch. "Aidan's going to stay with us. I am currently the leader of a small network of Hospitallers still working secretly to help our people. They took care of the sick and dying during the Famine and organized emigration to America from Fenit. Now we take care of families displaced by the English landlords. We have two doctors who have access to blood supplies and medicines. One can tend to Aidan at Barrow House without notifying the English authorities. I just hope that we aren't too late."

Tadgh looked back at Morgan, and she nodded her head in agreement.

"Did Boyle see you or your Hudson?" Tadgh asked Collis. "We don't want to put you or your family in danger, Maurice. The RIC are going to think we are the villains here if Boyle lives, and they will come after us with a vengeance."

"No, I don't think he saw me. I had good cover behind the wall and the altar. When Boyle took off, the Hudson was still to the east, safely tucked away among the trees."

"Aidan's pulse is getting weaker." Morgan didn't have to say more.

Redoubling his efforts to avoid any jarring bumps along the way to Barrow House, Collis soon drew up close to a house by the side of the country road. Bringing the car to a stop, he told Tadgh, "Doctor O'Callihan lives here. I hope he's home this afternoon." He jumped out and made for the front door. At his knock, the door opened, and Collis ushered a man carrying a medical bag out to the car to examine Aidan.

When the doctor asked Tadgh if he knew Aidan's blood type, he admitted he did not, so the doctor produced a syringe from his bag and drew a sample of Aidan's now-precious blood.

"Get him home and keep him warm," O'Callihan advised. "I'll be along presently with blood and equipment for a transfusion."

Since they were initially travelling in the same direction that Boyle had taken, Tadgh hoped to see the police car with the bastard dead at the wheel off in a ditch somewhere. But that was not to be.

On their way to Barrow House, they encountered very few cars or horse-drawn carts, and there were no RIC constables in sight. Collis drove the car around to the side of the house and stopped before the kitchen door. When he saw his wife rush out to greet them, he beckoned to her, "Quick, Martha, give us a hand here." Together, they carried Aidan into the house and carefully laid him on the bed in a basement bedroom.

"I've had occasion to care for friends who have gotten crossways with the authorities," Collis explained. "This room can be sealed from prying eyes with this outside curtain that is painted the basement wall color. We put those boxes over there up against it if we get searched. I didn't have time to get you down here earlier when the constables arrived." Tadgh could see that Collis was indeed maintaining a safe house of sorts, not unlike his own. The man was already putting it to good use. His admiration for Collis had grown immensely since their initial encounter.

A quarter of an hour later, Doctor O'Callihan drove up in his horse-drawn cart. He quickly set up a hospital room at Aidan's bedside and gave him blood and electrolytes through an intravenous injection.

Then he addressed the wound. Due to the direct pressure that Morgan had continued to apply, the bleeding had stopped. He determined that the bullet had passed clear through the leg, and although Aidan had lost a great of blood, the bullet had not damaged the femoral artery. After cleaning the area, he wrapped it with antiseptic bandages.

"Which of you did the triage here?"

When Morgan answered that she had, he asked, "Are you a nurse, ma'am?"

"Of sorts," she answered, and the doctor looked puzzled.

"Well, young lady, nurse or not, you do good work. Your attentions saved this lad's life. He should regain consciousness shortly." Then he added, "He should be ready to travel in about a week. I'll stay with him here until he wakes up."

"Thank you, Morgan." Tadgh's eyes glistened with his gratitude.

They had been so concerned with Aidan's condition that the two had forgotten all about their own injuries. Collis pointed them out to the doctor, who tended to Tadgh's arm and then Morgan's shoulder. "You're pretty banged up, my boy," he commented after examining Tadgh.

"Comes with the territory," Tadgh laughed. "You ought to see the other guy, that brawler." As a member of the clandestine Hospitaller troop, the doctor knew better than to ask what had happened.

By the time they had finished tending to the wounded, Martha had prepared a hot lunch for them all and collected some clothes for Morgan to wear that were almost her size.

"Morgan and I need to get to Cork as soon as possible," Tadgh said. "Any ideas?"

"I can't let you have the Hudson, or we would be stuck out here. Of course, you could steal a car."

"I don't think that's wise, Maurice. The roads will be heavily patrolled after what happened this afternoon. It's best if we take the hooker. I'm hoping that the Royal Navy will have stood down if they've captured the German supply ship. Be prepared for an uprising in the next few days," Tadgh cautioned.

The Collis people were full of questions that Tadgh could not, or would not, answer. In turn, Tadgh wanted to ask more about the connection between the FitzMaurices and the O'Donnells, but decided that he couldn't afford the time. Collis would just get started again into historian mode, and there were more pressing matters at hand. He had to get Casement's message and the condition of the gunrunning disaster to Pearse, personally.

Just before they left at two that afternoon, they went down to check on Aidan.

"He's got more color, and his heartbeat is stronger," Doctor O'Callihan said. "He should wake up shortly."

"I want to stay until he's awake," Morgan said, kneeling at the bedside and holding Aidan's hand.

"He'll be all right now, lass. I'll take good care of him. You go with your man."

"Thank you all," Tadgh said, helping Morgan up and preparing to go. "We are so lucky to have had your help today."

Morgan was more demonstrative. She hugged and kissed them all and then gave Aidan a tender kiss on the cheek. "He saved us, you know."

"As did Maurice, here." Tadgh clapped him on the back.

"Take good care of our brother," Morgan urged the doctor.

"Will do, Nurse."

Chapter Twenty-Five
Davy Jones' Locker

Friday, April 21, 1916
Tralee Bay, Ireland

*T*he tide had come in once again. Tadgh took the chance to sail close enough to Fenit Pier to see if the *Aud-Norge* had been escorted there by the Royal Navy. The one berth deep enough for it to anchor in stood empty.

As they passed the Magharee Islands at three o'clock, Morgan said, "Well, they're gone from here."

"Interesting, my dear," he said, as they sailed by. "The *Aud-Norge* either escaped, or the Navy diverted them to Berehaven. I can't imagine, given what we've been through, that they could have fooled the Navy with their Norwegian camouflage."

As further confirmation that the authorities felt in control again, Tadgh noticed that the gun emplacements on Brandon Point did not appear to be currently manned.

With the lug sail set and trimmed to the strong nor'westerly wind, Morgan settled beside her man at the tiller and cozied up to his warm body. "What were the chances that we would run into Maurice just when we needed him?" she asked, as they briskly plied the Celtic Sea once more.

"Well now, lass. I think that the Lord steps in when he needs to in critical situations. Do you believe in God, Morgan?" Tadgh realized that they had never talked about spiritual matters before this moment.

"Of course, I can't remember whether religion was part of my upbringing, but I believe that some force greater than Captain Weisbach brought you to me from the sea, my love. It was no coincidence that I was there, and that you saved me. After surviving the Western Trench together, I am beginning to believe that we are both part of a grander scheme than ourselves. You can call that destiny, or God, whatever you like."

"Someday we will discuss the relationship and differences between God and destiny, aroon," Tadgh suggested, and left it at that.

"I was surprised when Maurice talked about the connection between his FitzMaurice ancestors and the O'Donnell Clan," Morgan said, pulling the woolen blanket up around them both. "Do you think that they could be involved in the Clans Pact in any way?"

Tadgh adjusted the tiller. "I have no idea. They aren't mentioned in the document. The thing I find the most bizarre is that Boyle seemed to know about elements of the Pact."

"Puzzling, but how could that be?"

"Again, I have no idea, Morgan. At least we know now why he has been pursuin' and killin' my family. There is a connection between the Boyle family and mine that we need to explore in our free time, whenever we get some."

"And the Boyles apparently helped to persecute the FitzMaurices just before the Battle of Kinsale, Tadgh. It all seems connected in some mysterious way."

Tadgh added, "And in a bizarre way, even our ordeal today may have been ordained. Why was Boyle there at the Rath?"

"What do you mean?"

"We forced him to divulge why he has been attacking my family."

"I see what you mean." Morgan was left wondering once again, without answers, what *her* family history might be. What had happened to her parents? Would they be missing her? And the lover she was certain that she left behind in the choppy sea, gone down with the ship, and the babies, hers or someone else's.

The breeze tugged at the sails, and the hooker made swift progress. Despite Morgan's protests, Tadgh had found a way to hoist one of the foresails temporarily, tying the frayed halyard off near the top of the mast. Six hours later, as the twilight dimmed behind them, they approached the Bull Rock Island lighthouse. Morgan saw for the first time the hole in the vertical rock face that had sheltered them.

"My God, Tadgh. What a small opening to navigate at night with the beacon light blinding you. We could have all been killed."

"You could say that about the entire day's activities since we were here. It was our only option, to be sure."

Crossing the mouth of Bantry Bay past Berehaven posed a risk that Tadgh knew he had to take. Two hours later, they passed safely through the gauntlet without incident. Since the moon had not yet risen, they were not been able to see if the *Aud-Norge* was berthed there.

Near midnight, as they sailed up the Ilen River past Baltimore, Tadgh still kicked himself for letting Boyle get away. *Maybe he will have died from his wounds.* He promised himself to find out. With Morgan still snuggled under the blanket by his side, Tadgh guided his trustworthy little boat to its home dock. He felt secure for the first time in twenty-four hours.

"Are we home yet?" Morgan asked when the motion of the vessel stopped.

"Yes, my love," Tadgh replied. "Help me offload these three crates onto the dock, and then let's get the *Marie* inside the boathouse. We need to be on our way again. Mind that shoulder, now." He shot her a grin. She rotated her shoulder and felt the bandage. She would live.

"Can't we at least sleep in our own bed tonight and head out tomorrow?" Morgan pleaded with a look of complete exhaustion.

"Sorry, lass. We've got to get Casement's message to Padraig as soon as possible, and I don't want to risk using the telephone. You can sleep in the sidecar all the way to Cork ."

Before leaving on the Kerry, Tadgh pulled a tarpaulin over the crates with his good right arm, in case anybody came snooping around .

As they were mounting the motorcycle to leave, Morgan asked, "I see there's damage to the carrier. What happened?"

He reached back and touched the rough edge of the carrier. "A minor mishap when I went to see Tomas."

"Oh?" She shot him a look.

Tadgh came clean but left out the risky details. "I knew I should have gone with you. You endangered the mission."

"But if I'd have killed Boyle then, we wouldn't be in the fine mess we're in today."

"But they would have shot you dead, or you'd be in jail, Tadgh." She jabbed her finger at him. "You can't do that again, go after Boyle on your own."

"If he's still alive, you mean."

"That *is* what I mean, *precisely*."

Tadgh fell silent. He gunned the engine and tore off for their destination.

They arrived at MacCurtain's home at three in the morning on Saturday. "Well, Tadgh. How did it go?" he asked, as he opened the door to their knock. "Jaysus, you both look like you've been in the trenches again!" he exclaimed, when he saw their condition in the light of his parlor.

"Yes sir, we've been having a great lot of *craic* in Tralee. I've got a couple of cases of rifles and a case of ammunition, but the news is bad." Tadgh proceeded to tell his superior the events that had transpired, leaving out any mention of Boyle's true motive for interrogating them.

MacCurtain listened until Tadgh was finished and then said, "I've been worried that things weren't going well. There's a rumor in town this evening that a German supply ship has been apprehended at sea and is being escorted back to Queenstown Harbor. I was just getting ready to head down to the docks to see for myself. "

"I'd like to come with you if Morgan can stay here and get some sleep while we're gone. We've been on our feet for almost thirty hours straight."

Tomas agreed and showed her to the small bedroom near the parlor. Morgan thanked him for his kindness. "Don't open the door to anyone but us, lass," he warned her just before they left.

At 0530, the two men stood on the Cunard dock in Queenstown looking out at the harbor. A crowd in military uniform gathered at the shoreline.

"Look at that flotilla of military craft. The whole Royal Navy must be out there," MacCurtain exclaimed, indicating the silhouettes against the first hint of dawn.

Tadgh could also see RIC military vehicles and personnel two docks away. He was pleased that Boyle did not appear to be among them. How could he be, with the injury his compatriots had reported? He prayed that the murderer was dead. "I'd say that the rumors you heard are probably correct," Tadgh offered solemnly.

They waited in the shadows of a cargo warehouse until sun-up. As the sky lightened at 0630, they could see a tramp steamer emerge from the flotilla, crawling into the harbor entrance. Using his binoculars, Tadgh recognized it as the larger ship he had seen a day before near Inishtooskert Island. It still showed its Norwegian colors.

"That's the supply ship, to be sure."

"Damn," MacCurtain muttered, squinting out to sea. "That's the end of the Rising." Up until then they had been discussing potential ways of getting the arms off that ship. The German ship was tightly surrounded by escort vessels, and Tadgh recognized the *Bluebell* cruiser bringing up the rear.

"Look," Tadgh pointed out. "The supply ship is turning crossways in the channel just by the mid-channel pilot light." They watched as it ground to a halt nearly blocking the east channel. Peering through his binoculars, Tadgh narrated the action that followed. "They've run up their German colors, and the crew is assembled on deck. They're now dressed in German Navy uniforms. Holy Christ, Tomas, they're lowering their boats on the port side."

They felt as well as heard the first explosion. A cloud of dirty gray smoke belched up from the *Aud-Norge* and flames shot out of the wheelhouse, the saloon, and the ventilators.

"They're scuttling her," Tadgh said. Then they witnessed a second more violent explosion amidships, which ripped her apart. Given that the ship was rapidly sinking by the head, they could not understand why the *Bluebell* subsequently fired a shell into the inferno. It was over in a matter of minutes. The *Aud-Norge* and its critical cargo were at the bottom of Queenstown Harbor, and its crew had been captured from their boats.

"This news will travel fast to Dublin," Tadgh surmised. "Our plans have been crushed."

Just then, Tadgh noticed a man in a wheelchair at the end of the pier, swiveling around after watching the excitement out at the mouth of the harbor. Not only did he look familiar, but the man stared back at Tadgh. He waved both hands at Tadgh and then deliberately set off in his direction, rolling down the pier and shouting.

"Let's get out of here before we are recognized," Tadgh urged his superior, although it was already too late. They left the pier hurriedly and headed back to Tomas's home on the Kerry, dejected at the terrible outcome of the arms shipment.

Jack Jordan, the man in the wheelchair, was disgusted with his physical limitations, and he realized that he had missed another opportunity to find Claire. That Irishman did look familiar, he was sure of it.

Morgan had been awakened by the sounds of the explosions, her senses wracked with worry until she heard the men return. She flew to Tadgh and threw her arms about him with relief. "What happened?"

"They blew up their own ship. The weapons that we so desperately need are at the bottom of the harbor, aye, they are rusting as we speak."

"I want you to take Casement's message to Clarke, MacDermott, and Pearse," MacCurtain ordered. "The Rising was set for Sunday. I don't think that the telephones are safe anymore. Those three will have to decide what to tell MacNeill and Hobson."

"If they haven't heard already."

Before they left for Dublin, Tadgh and Morgan stopped by the B&C brewery where they hoped to find Jeffrey Wiggins. There he was in his office, hard at work at nine o'clock that fateful Easter Saturday morning.

"Tadgh, me boyo, and the fair colleen, Morgan," Wiggins exclaimed, as the pair entered and closed the door. "Do you need a ride back to France?"

When Morgan hugged him, he looked closer at her and then at Tadgh. "You've been in a scrape, that's for sure. I should not 'a been so flippant."

"We need your help again, if you please, Jeff. There are three crates under a tarpaulin on my dock. More guns for our cause. Could you pick them up and deliver them to this address?" He handed Wiggins a scrap of paper. "We have to leave for Dublin immediately."

"Certainly, me boyo. Anything for you two and the cause," Jeffrey answered. "It's pretty dull here when you're not around—just business and beer."

"We could use a dull little beer here about now," Tadgh joked. "Don't worry, there are exciting times ahead for all of us, I promise you."

Chapter Twenty-Six
Carrying the Message

Saturday, April 22, 1916
RIC Barracks, Cork City, Ireland

Maloney didn't know whether to cheer or cry. He had just received a telephone call informing him that his Head Constable Darcy Boyle had been gravely wounded in the line of duty.

"He is in hospital here in Tralee, with bullet wounds in his upper chest and in his right hand," Head Constable Kearney had said. "He and his constable, Gordon James, were part of the patrol that apprehended Sir Roger Casement and two Sinn Féiners, a man named Tadgh McCarthy and a woman, both German spies. They were bringing in the Sinn Féiners when they got the upper hand, forcing Boyle to drive to a nearby castle ruins. McCarthy's brother Aidan showed up and stabbed Constable James to death. Tadgh then killed a Tralee constable in cold blood, egged on by his mare." Kearney had related that before he collapsed from his wounds, Head Constable Boyle had told them how he tried to save the constables but got shot in the bargain. He had apparently escaped through a hail of gunfire and made it to the RIC headquarters. Boyle had said that these two rebels were the same German spies that he had chased down earlier in Dublin. Kearney had concluded, "Clearly they were part of the traitorous plot to land German weapons for the Republicans."

The story hung together—German gun-running foiled, German spies trying to help the traitor. But Maloney knew Boyle's character and wondered about the veracity of his story. He had no proof, not having been there, so the best thing to do was go along with the report. He was saddened by the death of one of his constables, especially one who had had to put up with working under Boyle.

Maloney asked Kearney, "Where are the two McCarthys and the woman now?"

The head constable had to admit, "They seem to have vanished into thin air. We have patrols controlling all the roads, but it looks as if those rebels have slipped through our net."

Maloney was glad that he was away from the action, safe in Cork. The Royal Navy had taken charge of the German prisoners from the ship that blew up without involving the local RIC. *Good. Keep your head down.*

His secretary knocked and opened the door, "District Inspector Maloney, there's another call for you."

"Good morning, Inspector. My name is Jack Jordan, manager of the Cunard Steamship Lines Queenstown office."

Maloney perked up when anyone called him Inspector. "What can I do for you today, Mr. Jordan?"

"I've been working with your Head Constable Boyle to find a missing woman from the *Lusitania* sinking, sir. They tell me that he is away on assignment. I think I've seen the Irishman who was in her company, the one with her on his motorcycle."

"Where and when did you see him?"

"This morning on our pier in Queenstown when the German ship blew up. But he disappeared again before I could get to talk with him."

Maloney remembered this man's previous questions about the woman on the motorcycle in Queenstown. Boyle had shared the information to get his boss to agree to pursue. Now he was reporting that she was at least an accomplice to murdering two constables and critically injuring his head constable. But how could he have gotten from Tralee to Queenstown on such short notice? Unlikely.

"We have a lot of people in the Cork area, son. I'm afraid you are going to have to get a local constable involved, if you see him or her again."

"I'm still in a wheelchair, not moving too fast these days. I need to find her."

"Well, then. It has just been reported to me by critically injured Head Inspector Boyle that your girl has likely murdered a police officer." Maloney had a habit of muddling the facts when it suited him.

"She's not my girl, sir, and I don't believe it."

"Boyle will be out of commission for quite some time, lad. I suggest that you contact him when he returns." With that said, the inspector terminated the conversation.

Jack slammed down the telephone. *Bastard English bureaucrat.*

At the same time, the *U-19* had been searching Tralee Bay for signal lights that Thursday evening, the Irish Volunteers Chief of Staff Eoin

MacNeill realized he had been duped. Hobson brought him news that Pearse and the IRB Military Council had been planning more than a parade for Easter Sunday. Eoin's Irish Volunteers, some twelve thousand strong, had become the muscle for a fanatical revolution led by academics. The chief of staff had believed that they all understood. The Volunteers would only rise if conscription was imposed, if the Home Rule Bill was not implemented, if they were attacked by the Authorities or by Carson's Ulster Volunteers, or if the Great War ended. None of those events had come to pass.

Eoin had heard the day before that the authorities intended to crack down on the Volunteers, but he tracked down the source and found the information to be false.

"There will be no Rising!" he and Hobson had told Pearse when they stormed into his home at Rathfarnham in southern Dublin later that Thursday evening.

"The Rising is going forward with the Volunteers," Pearse asserted as a fact, "with or without you."

On Good Friday morning, when Tadgh was busy finding Casement and facing Boyle, Pearse and other members of the IRB Military Council, not yet informed of the debacle occurring in Kerry, visited MacNeill.

"I will only speak with MacDermott, and never again with Pearse, the idealist who wants a blood sacrifice," MacNeill insisted.

"The Germans are landing arms, spearheaded by Roger Casement, that are coming ashore on Sunday in concert with our Rising in Dublin," MacDermott stated. "These arms will allow mobilization of the western half of our country. If we do not rise then, the authorities will crush us."

Having had no adverse news from Kerry, MacNeill believed him and saw the inevitability of the situation. He had been cornered. "Well, if we have to fight or be suppressed, then I suppose I'm ready to fight."

Early Saturday morning, about the time that the *Aud-Norge* was being scuttled, one of MacNeill's compatriots and a successful Dublin businessman, Michael The O'Rahilly, burst in on him.

"Eoin, they've kidnapped Bulmer Hobson."

"Who did this? Has a government crackdown started?"

"It was the IRB, sir. Also, there's been a man captured in Kerry. Don't know his name. He came off a German submarine."

"That does it!" MacNeill exploded. "I am writing countermanding the orders to all Irish Volunteer Units that cancel any instructions they may have been given to support a Rising tomorrow."

From his office in the British stronghold of Dublin Castle, Sir Matthew Nathan, Under-Secretary for Ireland, called his boss, Augustine Birrell, Chief Secretary in Asquith's Cabinet for Ireland, who was at his home in London that Saturday morning while Tadgh hurried to Rathfarnham. Nathan spoke down the telephone line, "We've stopped the arms shipment that spymaster Captain Hall predicted when he deciphered the German coded transmission between Washington and Berlin. Admiral Blythe, in Cork, heeded the warning and his fleet intercepted the Germans. What do you think of the threat now, sir? Lord Wimborne has stepped up his demands that the Sinn Féiners be rounded up this weekend."

"Well, let's review the facts, Matthew. We know that there is a revitalized militancy in the Volunteers based on their mock Rising and parade on St. Patrick's Day where MacNeill took the salute," the Chief Secretary replied. "And we've known for a year, after Asquith loaded his cabinet with Ulster anti-Home Rule members, that there would be trouble brewing. But I've been trying to avoid bloodshed by showing tolerance. As you know, that's why I stopped Major-General Friend's planned raid on Liberty Hall two weeks ago."

"Yes, sir. GOC Irish Command was upset. But what do you want us to do now?"

"Surely this defeat of the gun-running operation will stop them from rising and defuse their zeal, at least in the near-term," Birrell reasoned. "What are your thoughts on this, Matthew?"

"You are right, sir," Undersecretary Nathan dutifully agreed with his boss. "It's just that their newspaper calls for a parade on Sunday. And it *is* Easter Sunday, after all."

"Meaning?"

"Meaning, sir, that the coup would be the resurrection of the Irish people, just as Easter Sunday is the Lord's Day of Resurrection from the grave."

"So you agree with the Lord Lieutenant, do you?" Birrell pointedly asked.

"It's your decision, sir, not Wimborne's," Nathan responded, shirking his responsibility by deferring to his superior.

"I don't think that MacNeill will allow the Irish Volunteers to rise under these circumstances," the Chief Secretary stated emphatically. "We will defer a decision on rounding up the militants until after the Easter weekend. Let your men attend the Grand National Fairyhouse Races on Monday, as planned. It's only a few miles south of you if trouble brews. We will revisit this on Tuesday."

And with that our die is cast, Nathan thought as he hung up the telephone.

Tadgh almost burned out the side-valve V-twin motor of the Kerry in getting to Dublin at high speed. He was surprised that the roads were clear of roadblocks, thinking it comical that the English would have been more concerned with the funeral of Rossa than with the potential of a national insurrection at this moment. But then, he reasoned, if they had heard that the arms landing had failed, they might be assuming that there would be no Rising.

It was unbelievable to him that Morgan had been able to sleep for almost all of the six hours of their trip, despite the constant, jolting punishment handed out by the wicker sidecar.

"Morgan, we're here," Tadgh said, as they pulled into the expansive grounds of Pearse's home at St. Edna's in Rathfarnham. He hoped they were in time for tea. He knew from his time of residence there that this Hermitage had been called Odin's Rest right after its construction in the late 1700s. Tadgh thought that it looked like a giant mausoleum, with four Doric columns fronting the three-story granite-walled building. *How fitting, that its style and appearance resemble a para-military teaching facility.* The fact that the patriot Emmett had been forced to meet his lover here in a clandestine manner only added to the Gaelic appeal.

They found Pearse at home, huddled with MacDermott and MacDonagh in serious discussion. He stepped out of the parlor to meet his colleagues from Cork.

"I thought I told you to stay with the Cork Brigade. Tomas will need you."

"I had to bring you the news from Kerry, sir." He proceeded to tell Pearse everything he had told MacCurtain, as well as what they had witnessed in Queenstown Harbor.

"We had an unconfirmed report a few minutes ago about the likely fate of the German supply ship," Pearse stated, rubbing his forehead. "Thank you for the confirmation. As for Casement's message, it was probably intended for MacNeill and Hobson. Thanks for the information from Sir Roger himself, confirming that the Germans did not send officers to support us. It is as we expected."

"Our pleasure and duty, sir."

"Why the hell did they come three days early?" Pearse slammed his hand against the foyer wall in frustration.

"It would seem that they didn't get the change in date that Devoy ordered from America, sir. I didn't see any wireless aerials on the *Aud-Norge*. My guess is that the boat could not communicate with Headquarters in Berlin."

"Plunkett's aide, Michael Collins, sent some wireless experts to Valencia Island yesterday. They were supposed to commandeer wireless sets to help make contact with the supply ship and Casement's submarine on Sunday," Pearse flexed his fingers and swore. "Damn fools drove off the pier at Ballykissane, and all but one of them were drowned. That was all for nothing now that we know the ships couldn't communicate anyway."

"So much for the *Entente* with Germany then, sir."

"I never believed in Casement and the Germans anyway, Tadgh. Joseph wasn't optimistic, either. It's our fight, that's certain."

"I can assure you that Sir Roger was trying his best, Padraig."

"Well, his best wasn't good enough, Tadgh, was it now."

Tadgh did not want to point out that it was Clan na Gael and IRB communications that had broken down. That would do no good, and Pearse knew it, anyway.

"Well, then. What does all this mean for the planned Rising, sir?"

"The Rising is going ahead, Tadgh. The orders are out to all the units of the Volunteers across the country for tomorrow. They'll have to fight with pitchforks and Hurley sticks, if need be."

"Excuse me for saying so, sir, but don't you think that decision seems militarily risky?" Morgan moved so that she could hear the headmaster better.

"Blood sacrifice is necessary to cleanse the heart of the country, lass," the academic said.

"Best to keep your powder dry and wait for an advantage, sir."

"Look, Morgan. The cards are dealt, and we must play the hand while the English are diverted on the continent. Are you with us, girl?"

"I'm with Tadgh, sir, whatever the outcome. But I'm also a nurse, devoted to saving lives. You're a learned man. Surely there can be a negotiated settlement."

"They had their chance to bargain for centuries now. The bastards won't leave us alone unless we drive them out, don't ya see." Pearse looked to Tadgh to control his partner.

Tadgh was proud of Morgan for standing her ground even though he didn't agree with her, but he knew not to push the matter further. Martyrdom seemed to be the order of the day.

"C'mon, Morgan. That's enough, lass." He grabbed her hand and turned to go.

Finally, Pearse noticed that his 'soldiers' looked beaten up and exhausted. "Stay with me tonight as my guests. We will see what tomorrow brings." Morgan and Tadgh accepted his kind offer with thanks. "Margaret?" Pearse called to his mother. "Please take care of our guests. They need food and rest."

"Excuse me, I have to get back to my military council meeting," he said, turning on his heel and disappearing into the parlor behind closed doors.

At about the same time on Saturday afternoon when Tadgh was confirming to Padraig Pearse the unfortunate events in Cork and Kerry, Denis Daly was making a similar report to Michael The O'Rahilly not ten miles away.

"I was driving the lead car out of Killarney yesterday evening," he said. "Thomas McInerney was driving the communications experts in the other one. Plunkett had sent us to seize control of the wireless station on Valencia Island near Cahirciveen down the Ring of Kerry. We were to give false signals of a German naval attack on the Scottish coast in an attempt to divert the British Naval Command. Then we were to contact the *Aud-Norge* and *U-19* to help guide them to the rendezvous.

"We got separated in the dark, and north of Killorglin, McInerney inadvertently drove his car off the Ballykissane Pier into the Laune River. He was the only one of the four in that car who survived. They've got him in detention. Without the experts, I couldn't carry out the mission."

Daly then told The O'Rahilly about the fate of Casement and the *Aud-Norge*, thinking him a supporter of the Rising. The message got to MacNeill immediately.

While Tadgh and Morgan were eating supper in the Pearse dining room alone, they heard the commotion of MacNeill and Michael The

O'Rahilly's arrival and confrontation with Pearse. Their raised voices could be heard clearly through the wall.

"The arms shipment failed," MacNeill shouted. "I'm going to forbid any mobilization."

"We have used your name and influence for all they're worth, but now we don't need you anymore. It's no use you trying to stop us. Our plans are laid, and they will be carried out."

"So well laid that the police at Adfert have already upset them," MacNeill growled, and they stormed out.

Having heard this from the dining room, Morgan said to Tadgh in a low tone, "I don't know anything about military operations, but as I said to Mister Pearse, it seems foolhardy to proceed with a general Rising without the proper equipment."

"As he said, they are hell-bent on proclaiming the Irish Republic now, while England is still at war with Germany," Tadgh concluded. He put down his knife and fork, a clear sign he had no more appetite. "By doing this, I believe that they hope the nation will rally behind them with the inspiration they provide. Knowing Padraig as I do, he will lead the martyrs to sow the seeds of revolution, even if he knows this physical battle will be lost in order to achieve a moral victory."

"Now you're scaring me," Morgan groaned, then gulped her water.

"At least the cause is just, for certain."

"But do the ends justify the means, Tadgh?"

"Do we have to go over this all again? Yes, to be sure if these are the only means we are given."

"Then where is God when you need him?"

"He is our just cause and our redeemer," Tadgh stated unequivocally. "He will provide on his timetable, not ours."

"Then why not wait for his timetable?"

"Maybe this *is* his time, lass. The Germans tried, and we failed them. We are on our own. Now is the time the English overlords are most vulnerable. The Military Council must feel that it is the best time to act."

"Or maybe, with what just happened in Kerry, the Lord is telling us to slow down." Morgan glared across the table.

"It's too late for that now. Stop this nonsense talk. I won't have it." Tadgh got up from the table and stormed over to where Morgan sat clenching her serviette. She abruptly stood up and faced her partner.

"That's not how I see it, Tadgh."

"Then, let me repeat my boss's question. Are you with us?"

"I don't know. I'm confused. You're going about it all wrong."

"A good soldier follows orders. Otherwise there is anarchy, lass."

"Like lemmings over the cliff, then?"

"If that's where the lead lemming takes us, yes."

"Not this lemming, dammit." Morgan was furious. Why didn't these men listen to reason? All those maimed soldiers at the Western Front. The lucky ones. The others were dead. "I don't want to lose you, can't you see?"

"I see a country being bled to death. You're a nurse. We need to stop the bleeding." Tadgh thought that this was a fine retort.

"With much more bloodshed? No." Morgan wagged her finger in Tadgh's face.

"I'll repeat my question. Are you with us or against us?" Tadgh balled his fists, held at his side.

"I'm certainly not against you, Tadgh. I love you. I will follow you anywhere you take me. But I don't have to like it."

"Maybe you'd rather be at home dwelling on your *babies*, then." Tadgh knew immediately that this was cruel. But dammit, she deserved it.

Tears welled up in Morgan's not-so smokey green eyes. "That's not fair. You know any babies I may have had are dead and that I can't go home. I don't know where my damn home is, or who I am." She put her hands to her eyes and the tears began to flow. She was losing control, and she knew it.

"I thought you chose to be Morgan and that your home is in Creagh."

"I thought so, too . . . until now."

"C'mon lass, don't desert me now, on the eve of our revolution, and when I need you most."

"I'm not deserting you, can't you see. I'm trying to save you, all you boys with guns."

"Fine, then. Come with me. Heaven knows that we need our rest for what's ahead."

Morgan resisted when he roughly grabbed her arm. "I haven't finished my supper."

"Yes, you have, girl. It's gone cold, can't ya see?" Tadgh realized once more that there was an ocean of dissent between them. This time it was most serious.

They went to bed angry, something they vowed never to do. Once more Morgan turned to face the wall and tried to go to sleep. It was still light out. Three hours later, at eleven, having had no rest at all, she could stand it no longer. *We shouldn't go to sleep mad. The Lord knows we might be dead by sunset tomorrow.*

She turned back to face him. "Oh, Tadgh," Morgan murmured, "these matters are too heavy for me. I give up on trying to change all your minds. You are the love of my life and my true joy. I trust you to keep us safe. Promise me you won't go getting yourself killed senselessly. I need you!"

Tadgh had not slept a wink, either. "I shall keep us safe, my love, no matter what happens."

Morgan rolled into him, then, needing to show him her love. Despite their tired state, they made love before finally falling asleep in each other's arms. It was the urgent necessity to cement the bond of commitment Tadgh had just made. It gave them both great comfort at a very unsettling time.

Chapter Twenty-Seven
Easter Rising Prelude

Saturday, April 22, 1916
Dublin, Ireland

At that same moment across Dublin, when he had not heard back from Pearse that the Rising was cancelled, Eoin MacNeill finally acted with Michael The O'Rahilly. "Michael, I need you to carry this countermanding order to our Irish Volunteer Units around the country tonight. I'm counting on you." He read, "*Volunteers completely deceived. All orders for special action are hereby cancelled and on no account will action be taken.*"

"I won't stop until I've given your orders to the Volunteer leaders throughout the south," The O'Rahilly assured him. Eoin watched dejectedly as one of the few men he could still trust at this point sped off by automobile to deliver the countermand. He then summoned and dispatched a few other trusted couriers with the same message, just to be sure.

Finally, before turning in for a fitful, sleepless night, MacNeill authorized an announcement to be published in the Dublin *Sunday Independent* the next morning.

When Tadgh and Morgan awoke on Easter Sunday morning, Pearse's house was in an uproar. At breakfast, Margaret informed them, "Padraig has already left for Liberty Hall for a meeting of the Military Council."

"True to his word," Tadgh groaned, looking up from the encircled notice in the Sunday morning paper strewn all over the table.

"Who was?" Morgan stopped eating her coddled eggs that Margaret had prepared.

"MacNeill. He's published a countermanding order nationwide." He read it aloud to her.

> *Owing to the very critical position, all orders given to Irish Volunteers for tomorrow, Easter Sunday, are hereby rescinded, and no parades, marches, or other movement of Irish Volunteers will take place. Each individual Volunteer will obey this order strictly in every particular.*

He folded the paper and pocketed it. "This is really going to cripple the Rising, if it is called out at all. There is certainly no solidarity and there must be mass confusion throughout the ranks of our Volunteers by now, I should think."

"Surely they'll call it off," Morgan hoped, for all their sakes.

"One thing's for certain, Morgan. There are probably only about fifteen hundred Volunteers here in Dublin that the IRB can count on, including the two of us. The other ten thousand throughout the country will probably not rise after this since they don't have rifles. And any hope for support from a goodly fraction of John Redmond's one hundred thousand National Volunteers to join in is almost extinct by now, that's for certain." Tadgh took a great swallow of tea as if to drown his sorrow.

"What about the English forces?" Morgan asked, playing with her eggs.

"They can bring in thousands quickly. And they are military personnel with sophisticated armament, don't ya know."

"So if the Military Council votes to go forward, they are basically signing their own death warrants as well as those of many of our compatriots, aren't they, Tadgh?" She paused. "And ours."

"I'm afraid so, my love," Tadgh agreed reluctantly. "Just remember what Padraig wrote to us—*The old heart of the earth needs to be warmed by the red wine of the battlefields.* I think we know which way he'll be voting, to be sure."

Morgan's heart sank. "I'm not going to bring up our argument from last evening again, but you know where I stand, mavourneen. Don't you dare forget your commitment to me."

Tadgh was torn between his hatred of the English, his commitment to the Republican cause for freedom and his love for, and commitment to, the woman beside him. They needed their sustenance, but somehow breakfast was not that appetizing.

"We need a safe place to stay if and when things get really ugly. Not here, not at all." After giving the matter some thought during breakfast, he announced, "Morgan, I think we need to go for a drink at the pub."

"What? At this time of the morning?"

"Yes, absolutely," he responded with a twinkle in his eye. "The pubs open at eleven."

When they rose from the table and thanked Mrs. Pearse, Morgan saw that look in her eyes. Clasping the woman to her breast, she whispered, "The Lord will protect us all, including your Padraig."

"I know, dear, but even Jesus was slain to save us all," Margaret cried.

Tadgh took the serviette from the table and dabbed her eyes. "But he rose again, ma'am, didn't he, though."

"Aye, lad, but the Blessed Mother never saw him again after that."

Morgan stroked her silver locks. "They are together in heaven."

"Aye, lass, there's that."

Morgan could not think of any other words of comfort to give the dear woman.

"It's a great thing your son is doing for our country, Margaret," Tadgh offered, setting the serviette back on the table.

Morgan shot him a warning stare. Although she couldn't be certain that she was a mother, somewhere back in the deep recesses of her mind that instinct was there. She knew that she had, at some point, cared for those babies—but there was more. Oh, it was maddening, the inability to remember.

A few minutes later, as Tadgh steered the Kerry downtown, Morgan said, "Everything appears normal today. Folks decked out in their Easter finery are coming out of the churches. The sun is shining and flowers are poking through the soil in the gardens of the city. Maybe this insurrection can be averted." But really, she was thinking of the Western Front and all those mangled boys.

Tadgh chose not to respond. He knew that all this normalcy was about to change.

They arrived at the *an Stad* just after eleven. True to form, they found Tadgh's mentor, playwright Sean O'Casey, holding forth in his usual corner booth.

"Hello, Sean." Tadgh greeted him enthusiastically with a slap on the back. "Don't ya ever go home from here?"

"Tadgh, my boy. You look a sight for sore eyes. Have a drink."

Tadgh knew he could use one. "Not just yet, Sean. Can I talk to you privately, my friend?"

"If you bring the lovely Morgan with you, yes."

O'Casey excused himself from his cronies and the trio moved to sit down at a corner table, away from prying ears of the few other patrons.

"Sean, we need a favor."

"What kind of favor, son?"

"We need a place we can come to in Dublin in the next few days, Sean. It's liable to get dangerous around here. Can we stay with you tonight?"

"Yes, of course you can. But what kind of dangerous, may I ask?"

"Well, now. The kind where people get killed with bullets, Sean."

"I agree with the cause, but you know that I abhor violence, Tadgh. There have been rumors. Tell me it isn't a Rising, son."

"Ask your ICA friend Connolly," Tadgh said. "He's a big part of it."

"Not my friend anymore. Not since he's become militant. How much time have we got?"

"If it happens, maybe a day, I'd guess."

"It's mass suicide, you know," Sean groaned.

"As a literary luminary, you understand the value of martyrdom for a cause."

"But the people don't want it, Tadgh. They don't want to see their cities torn up and people killed."

"Yet they need it, don't they. We can't let the British continue to treat us like vermin."

Morgan couldn't help herself. "Sean, can I call you that?"

"Aye, lass, go on."

"Tadgh and I have already had this discussion, last night again, in fact. It seems to me prudent, given the lack of armament, to regroup and keep our powder dry until sufficient arms are available. Otherwise, we are wasting the very men needed later when there's the chance of winning. We've seen the devastation of human life at the Western Front."

"Have you now, lass? You and Tadgh?"

"Yes, Sean, that's right. But it's different here."

"In what way, Tadgh? The innocent will still get killed with the soldiers."

"As you know, Tadgh, I agree with Sean," Morgan interjected, turning to face him. "The doctors and nurses will have to patch up the fallen."

Tadgh realized that Morgan finally had an ally against his belief in the revolution. Although it was hard for him to get past his hatred for the English, he had to agree that Morgan's suggestion of waiting finally made sense, particularly since the Great War showed no signs of ending soon. But he knew Pearse's position.

"I like the way you think, Morgan," O'Casey exclaimed, obviously admiring her mental skills as well as those attributes hiding beneath her clothing. Casey was a man of rich imagination, and Morgan's figure gave him much to appreciate. "I don't actually agree with the fighting and killing part, but I agree with you that patience is a virtue."

"Well, it isn't up to us luminaries, is it," Tadgh concluded, reaching across the table and downing Sean's whiskey. "It's 35 Mountjoy Square, if I remember correctly, right?"

"That's right, son. And contrary to public belief, I do go home at night."

"I think that might be a good place to stay over the next few days, Sean."

The seven Military Council members did not struggle with *what* to do, but rather *when* to do it. At the end of the meeting, Connolly cast the deciding vote.

"Are we all agreed to go forward with the Rising but postpone its start one day until Easter Monday at noon, then?" Pearse summarized.

The three dissenters knew that they had to follow the will of the majority even though military success was very likely out of the question given the events in Kerry and MacNeill's subsequent disastrous intervention. They grumbled but nodded their assent.

Pearse noted the general depression in the room when their council ended. Tom Clarke spoke for the group, saying, "MacNeill has ruined everything. All our plans. I feel like going away to cry."

When they arrived home from church that beautiful Easter Sunday, the authorities at Dublin Castle and in London were still confident that a Rising was not in the cards, at least not immediately.

Nathan spoke to his military generals. "The Republicans would not dare rise without weapons. You and your men are authorized to go to the Grand National Fairyhouse Races tomorrow. We will potentially round up the conspirators on Tuesday."

"I object," Lord Wimborne protested.

"Overruled," the Undersecretary barked.

♣ ♣ ♣ ♣

Tadgh checked in with Pearse later in the day and found out, as he had suspected, that the Rising was on for the next day. He didn't try to dissuade his boss.

"Now that you're here, Tadgh, I want you to support Michael Mallin in capturing and holding St. Stephen's Green. It is a strategic entry point into the city. I think that the ICA may need your military expertise. Headquarters of the New Irish Republic will be in the General Post Office, the most defendable fortress in the city other than Dublin Castle."

"Why aren't you storming Dublin Castle and using it as the headquarters, sir? You can disrupt the English Army communications and operations from there."

"We discussed it, but we are not sure how many English are garrisoned there. And as you know, we will be stretched pretty thin because of MacNeill."

Tadgh saw a different motivation. "You must realize that you will be boxing in our senior staff in a building that will become the prime target of the English retaliatory forces. It's like painting a bull's-eye on our back. They will sight on the Irish flag raised above the GPO and bomb us into oblivion. It's symbolic, isn't it, gallant literary martyrdom for the cause that stirs up the population to fight for independence when Home Rule is defeated after the Great War. Am I right, sir?"

"Something like that, Tadgh. Now go along and do your duty."

On parting, Tadgh wondered if he would ever talk to his leader again.

♣ ♣ ♣ ♣

During suppertime at O'Casey's home, Tadgh got word by telephone to Peader O'Donnell, a senior student in residence at St. Patrick's College and their Clans Pact compatriot. "We need to meet with you at the *an Stad* this evening. It's critical, lad. Can you arrange it?"

"I'll be there at eight this evening. Does this have to do with our adventure?"

"Yes, and more, much more."

Later, as they sat together around a table in a private guest room, Tadgh, Morgan and Peader discussed the current political situation and their mysteries. The gaslights were turned down low, and Sean was downstairs out of earshot. It was as if they were having a séance, without a crystal ball.

"I am against futile armed insurrection, Tadgh. Civil disobedience with trade unions is a different matter."

"I understand your views, Peader, but this is the moment in history that our leadership has chosen to attack our common foe, the English tyrants."

"*Your* leadership, you mean, don't ya, Tadgh?"

"Insanity," Morgan piped up, and Tadgh shot her a wicked glance. Now she had two allies.

This was not getting them anywhere. Once again, all they could agree on was that there was a common foe. "This is my last semester," O'Donnell told them. "I graduate in June and start teaching at Arranmore this winter. I want that to happen."

After Tadgh and Morgan filled O'Donnell in on the bizarre information that they had received from Boyle and Collis, Morgan wondered aloud, "I've been thinking. What if there is another copy of the Clans Pact, and Boyle somehow got a copy of it?"

"It stands to reason that the McCarthys would have retained and hidden an original document just like Red Hugh O'Donnell did in the *Cumdach*," Tadgh conjectured. "But where?"

"I was a bit preoccupied at the time on Friday, but didn't Boyle say that his family defeated the MacCarthaigh Reagh Clan at the outset of the Confederate War in 1642?" Morgan asked.

"Yes, that's right, lass. That was my family Clan."

O'Donnell interjected. "You told us that your family owned and lived in Kilbrittain Castle, which was taken over at that time."

"Right again, lad. We now know that Florence MacCarthaigh Reagh was the McCarthy mastermind of the Clans Pact, with Red Hugh, before the Battle of Kinsale that took place not too far from his castle."

"But Florence was captured and incarcerated in the Tower of London six months before that battle," Peader got up from his seat and began to pace the room.

"Well, now. We know they formed the plan and Pact when Florence visited Donegal Castle a year or so earlier, in case the war went badly," Morgan added.

"So, it's a possibility that Florence hid his copy of the Pact somewhere in his stronghold, and that Boyle found it when they besieged the castle, mavorneen."

"And their descendants have been looking for the 'McCarthy Gold' ever since." O'Donnell stopped pacing.

"That would explain why Boyle has been torturing and killing McCarthys in the MacCarthaigh Reagh bloodline, wouldn't it, now." The reality finally hit Tadgh.

"If Florence hid it in a McCarthy relic, then it might have contained a clue as well as the Pact itself."

Tadgh leaned over from his position across the table and touched Morgan's arm. "That bears investigation when we have the time, lass. There are more pressing matters at hand."

"What about the FitzMaurice connection just before the Battle of Kinsale?" O'Donnell wondered. "What's that all about? And is it related to the Clans Pact?"

"That's truly a mystery since the FitzMaurices are not mentioned in that document, boys. It is likely a red herring, I should think." Morgan reached up from her chair and guided Peader down into his. It seemed to Morgan they had a solution to the mystery staring them right in the face, but it was shrouded in the dust of hundreds of years.

"I've been thinking, too, my love," Tadgh said, stroking his beard. "We know that St. Columba's *an Cathach* probably contains a clue that we need to decipher, right? And it is housed in the Royal Irish Academy here in Dublin." Tadgh paced the room feverishly.

"That was an exciting night at the National Museum last August, wasn't it, boys," Morgan interjected. "I guess if we can steal *an Cathach's Cumdach* in plain sight and replace it without anyone being the wiser, we can do nearly anything."

But Peader didn't like where the conversation was headed. "Not another break-in, for God's sake, and in the middle of a Rising," he cautioned, hoping Tadgh would see the foolishness of such a venture.

"No more break-ins, I assure you, lad. But we may not get another chance to be in Dublin, so we need to act now, don't ye see."

"That's a relief—if there can be relief under these circumstances, love. So what's the plan?" It helped Morgan to focus on their adventure rather than the military disaster that would likely befall them all.

"By coincidence, I happened to read in the paper at Padraig's home this morning that Reverend J. H. Lawlor, who is the Professor of Ecclesiastical Studies at Dublin University, is currently examining the relic and writing a book called the *Cathach of St. Columba*.[12] It got me to thinking about our little mystery, and that this might be a way to find out about the document in a non-invasive way."

"By pretending to be students of theology and questioning the Professor," O'Donnell finished the thought. "Tadgh, 'tis brilliant, that is."

"Thank you. He might even show us *an Cathach*, if we ask him." For the first time in many days, Tadgh's face bore that smile Morgan loved so well.

"When do you propose to try and contact him, given your other responsibilities?"

"I will have to contact you when the time comes, Peader. Will you be able to break away?"

"For this, of course," Peader responded enthusiastically.

"Let's hope we survive to follow through on this," Morgan said wistfully.

"I will fulfill my commitment to you, my love."

With that, their meeting was over. They returned to their safe houses to rest up for the ordeal ahead, whatever God and man had ordained for them.

The next morning approximately eleven hundred Irish Volunteers and their supporters turned out in Dublin. Four hundred and twenty of these, including Tadgh and Morgan, started from Liberty Hall on the north side of the Liffey River just east of O'Connell Street.

"The lucky ones are carrying the antiquated 'Howth' single shot rifles," Tadgh observed solemnly.

"The rest have pitchforks, clubs, or nothing but their own fists," Morgan said, twisting her scarf in the morning breeze. "These troops are so poorly equipped compared to their counterparts on the Western Front, and look what happened to those blokes."

"Clearly MacNeill's countermand has reduced the force considerably. Morgan, I think that we've only got about a fifth of the attendance that was expected." He pushed a gun roughly into her hands. "Here, take Boyle's Webley for defense. I've got my Luger."

She took the Webley and jammed it into her coat pocket. "Very few men and women are wearing uniforms, mavorneen. When the fighting starts, how are the English going to distinguish between rebels and the general population?"

Tadgh realized that was an excellent question.

They saw the Headquarters battalion of about three hundred peel off, heading up O'Connell Street, making for the General Post Office. This group included five of the Military Council leaders—Pearse, the President and Commander-in-Chief of the self-proclaimed "Provisional Irish Republic"; Connolly, the Commandant of Dublin; Tom Clarke, Sean MacDermott, and Joseph Plunkett. The latter, due to his ill health, was accompanied by his young *aide-de-camp,* Michael Collins, who was dressed smartly in a starched uniform.

"It's a fine day for a Rising, Mick," Tadgh shouted.

"It's a start, to be sure, Tadgh. You watch your back."

"Same to you."

Morgan overheard Connolly say to his ICA compatriot, "Bill, we're going out to be slaughtered." It didn't buoy her up with optimism.

Tadgh had met Michael The O'Rahilly on one occasion before. At the last minute, the man drove up in his dusty automobile. Seeing that the Rising was going ahead anyway, he joined the Headquarters battalion, saying, "Well, I've helped to wind up the clock, I guess I might as well hear it strike. Help me, boys. We'll load up this motorcar of mine with bombs and some of the old rifles."

True to form, MacNeill was nowhere to be found.

Morgan wished to God they were back safe in their house at Creagh. The cold wind cut through her like a lance. "It's a sorry rag tag group we've got here, Tadgh."

"But what a just cause, and that's the God's honest truth. Jesus rose for us."

"Yes, but He had to die first on the cross." That sentiment had not comforted Padraig's mother, and it did not console Morgan, now.

"But what a glorious death." Tadgh threw his arm around her, kissed her soundly, and together they marched forth.

Chapter Twenty-Eight
Abandoned

Easter Monday, April 24, 1916
The Beaches, Toronto, Canada

As far as **Collin** could tell, Fiona and Ryan were at least on speaking terms. In fact, the reunited couple would be joining the Finlay and O'Donnell Clans for the Easter Monday service at St. Aidan's Anglican Church that morning. He was glad about this, for Kathy's sake. He thought about the events that had transpired during this exciting early spring. Both Kathy and Elizabeth enjoyed new babies, Lil having given birth to an eight-pound, black-haired tyke they named Ernest on April 10. This morning they were all headed to the joyous Resurrection service that would be followed by a christening ceremony for Liam.

Kathy had dressed the baby in a white baptismal gown that Lil had sewn for the occasion, and the women all sported flowered millinery. In the sunny, though crisp, weather, the ladies secured their bonnets with pins.

Reverend McIntyre's sermon pointed out the crocuses, resplendent in the church garden and the green shoots of the coming tulips poking out of the newly tilled soil, which signaled a happy promise for the year ahead. This served as a reminder of the renewal that Christians experience at that religious point in the Church calendar. Kathy had mentioned the flowers on the way into the church. At the end of his sermon, the reverend looked out at the people gathered in the pews and added a few words, "I was just informed before this service that there is another Rising going on in this world. Perhaps the two events are not wholly unrelated. The Irish Republicans have taken to the streets in Dublin, Ireland, this morning and are rising up against the British rule. For the good of Ireland, may these warring factions come together and find peace. May God bless them all and keep them safe from harm."

Collin nudged Kathy and handed her the baby. Telegraph messages had come through to the *Toronto Telegram* newspaper, where he worked on Saturday, relaying news that on Good Friday the British had intercepted a German ship bringing guns to the rebels. He still wondered about it, but little Liam's pending baptism had taken priority. He remembered what Jack Jordan had said about the trouble Claire could be in. And now this. German spies, a German gunrunning ship stopped, insurrection. His mind and heart raced. Could Claire be mixed up in all of this?

"I've got to get out of here," he leaned close and whispered to Kathy. But he had nowhere to move. The church was packed to the rafters and they were in the center of a middle row of pews.

"Easy, Collin. I'm surprised as you are, but this is the day of our Liam's christening." Kathy looked at Sam sitting on the other side of Collin for help.

"I've got to get out and think. Sam, let me by." Collin started to get up just as the reverend began the communion chant.

Sam blocked his way. "Sit down. After the christening, we'll slip out and talk about this."

Both Sam and Kathy held the fidgeting Collin firmly by his arms to keep him still until the acolytes got to the pew.

"I've got to leave now." Collin broke free and stood up.

Kathy handed Liam to Lil beside her. "What's going on?" her best friend whispered, switching arms for her own new born baby and cradling the baby Liam.

"We'll be back. Collin's agitated about the Irish situation," Kathy leaned close to Lil and kissed baby Liam.

"Claire?"

"Of course, it's Claire. It's always Claire."

"But the christening?"

"We're going to have it, don't you worry."

As the other parishioners got up to queue for the communion rail, Sam and Kathy linked arms with Collin and headed to the back of the church. If others were curious about this, it would appear that Collin was overcome by the gravity of the occasion and needed some air. Once outside, Sam asked, "What's going on in that head of yours, my boy?" He knew quite well but wanted Collin to get it out.

"The German spy, the gun-running intercept . . ."

"What gun-running?"

"I read the wire message. The Germans tried to provide guns to the rebels on Thursday and got stopped."

"Did they, now. What has that to do with Claire? I thought you had a vision that she was in France or Belgium in the trenches."

"Remember, I told you Jack Jordan said that Claire was being branded as a German spy."

"If I recall, Mister Jordan said that the RIC told him that some woman who hasn't been identified as Claire was purported to be in the company of a suspected German spy. You're making it sound too definite, aren't you, lad?"

"Jack saw her and says it was Claire. It's all I have to go on."

"He thinks from a distance it might have been Claire, my boy."

"Well, I think that it's Claire for sure, and I think Claire's mixed up in the gun-running and now the Rising. I can feel it in my bones."

"Can you, now? Well, that's just jim-dandy." Kathy had had enough of this nonsense. "We have a happy baby boy inside who is about to be christened, if you'll remember." She could not understand how he could be so helpful when it came to her parents, yet so reckless and unsupportive when it came to his own wife and son. He was ready to fly off at the least clue about Claire's whereabouts. *He feels it in his bones?* That did not make sense to her.

"C'mon, lad. Let's go back inside. We can discuss this after Liam is baptized." Sam grabbed him by the arm to steer him back into the church.

Collin planted his feet. "I need to think ."

"Well, think about this. Come inside now, or don't come home tonight." With that, Kathy turned on her heel and disappeared into the church, stopping just short of slamming the door behind her .

"She's right, you know. We've talked about this several times before." Sam was insistent. "Wait until summer when your baby is old enough to be left with us and *then* go to Ireland, if you must."

"It'll be too late for her, Sam."

"If you are right about Claire, and I highly doubt it, what makes you think you could be more help than the lad she's purported to be with?"

"You mean the German spy? She's my sister and my responsibility."

"That's your misplaced guilt talking. I should know. We bear that cross together. Now you have a new baby to care for. Come on in and give the tyke his proper ceremony with his father." Sam opened the door and ushered a reluctant Collin inside.

Communion was over and the reverend had just asked the parents and godparents to come to the baptismal font. Kathy, now at the font with Liam in her arms, waved them in. Liam cried when the Reverend McIntyre tipped his head close to the water and poured a small amount over the infant's head. Miraculously, the baby stopped whimpering and looked angelic when the minister traced the sign of the cross on his forehead with the holy oil and welcomed Liam into the congregation's fold. Even distracted Collin was impressed with his baby's calm manner.

After the ceremony, they all went back to the Finlay home at Number 10 Balsam for a reception. Lil and the girls had done the parlor up in blue ribbons streaming from the dining room's small chandelier to the mantel of the fireplace. White balloons surrounded the candle centerpiece on the table. Sam stoked the fire to take the April chill from the room, and guests nibbled on small savories accompanied by a champagne from Kathy's family winecellar, well- stocked against the scarcity of wartime. As for Collin, he consumed quite a few O'Keefe ales as he tried to overcome his infernal demons. Kathy and Sam conversed in private and decided to let him stew in his own juices for the time being.

"I can't live with these episodes where he loses his mind over his sister," Kathy shared, twirling her hair behind her ear. She thought she had every right to be upset, especially with her newborn to care for.

"There now, lass," Sam soothed. "He's a hard nut to crack, to be sure. I'll try to knock some sense into him tomorrow when he calms down."

"Someone had better do that, Sam. I'm at my wit's end." Kathy meant what she said. Collin had erupted like this several times now, and Kathy needed him to put her and Liam first in his life.

Sam steered Kathy back into the room and sat down with the guests at a sparely-laid luncheon reminding him that shortages and rations had become a part of daily life. Thank goodness there was no shortage of champagne for toasts. He even managed to steer Kathy's father Ryan away from any mention of the Rising in Ireland with his chatter about Liam's good behavior in the face of the morning's unexpected shock of cold water and uncomfortable sensations. He noticed that Ryan held Liam on his arm and affirmed Sam's words with a tickle under Liam's chin and a soft chuckle. Kathy plucked Liam out of his grandad's hold to put him down for his nap in a quiet room. Sam relished the thought that the family had reunited.

"A fine-looking boy you have there, Collin," his mentor exclaimed , tapping some of his beloved Prince Rupert tobacco into his clay pipe. "The spitting image of you, but with his mother's eyes, don't ya know."

Sam's remarks distracted Collin from his gloomy thoughts for only a few moments, but he returned to his brooding soon enough.

♣ ♣ ♣ ♣

After lunch, they said their goodbyes and headed to their own homes. As her parents left together to go back to Rosedale, Kathy noticed that her father seemed more attentive to her mother, a stark reversal of his earlier oppressive behavior. She watched her mother lead her father by the hand down the front walk to their Model T with her mother appearing to be in full control for the first time in her life and loving every minute of it. Kathy wondered what may have happened with them when her mother had returned home after Liam's birth. Kathy hoped that her mother had found a softness in their relationship, and that the two could laugh at their own foolishness. Ryan opened the car door for his wife, and she gently kissed his cheek as she stepped up into the roadster. Maybe they had fallen in love again.

On the walk back home, along the beach boardwalk west to Lee Avenue, Kathy pushed the pram smartly with Liam tucked inside. He had been fed just before they left and slept soundly now. Collin trudged along in step, lost in his thoughts. Kathy saw that he was up to his old habit again with the fists and remembered that, contrary to his abstemious custom, he had quite a bit to drink at the reception. Kathy let him be, not knowing what would come of his mood and thoughts, but hoping his silence would not take a morose turn.

As the new family approached home at Number 24 Lee Avenue, the late afternoon sun had given way to a strong westerly wind, bringing with it the threat of rain. When they ascended to the small covered porch, Kathy saw an envelope tucked into the screen door handle, a telegram, of all things, on a holiday Easter Monday. She quickly removed it before Collin, who was lifting Liam from the pram, could see her action. She stashed it in her coat pocket, shivering when she saw the Urgent stamp on the envelope.

Once inside, and with her coat still on, Kathy scooped up Liam from his father's arms and carted him off to the nursery. Collin went straight to the icebox for another O'Keefe.

With the bedroom door closed, she ripped open the telegram addressed to Collin O'Donnell and started reading. *My God!*

Curious, Collin opened the door to see why Kathy had closed it and found her reading the document.

"What's that you're readin'?"

Kathy's first instinct was to rush past him down the stairs and burn the paper. Instead, she handed him the telegram, her hand trembling.

He narrowed his eyes when he saw that it was addressed to him. "I see you've been opening other people's mail."

"I . . . I . . . was worried."

He didn't want to hear any excuses for this invasion of his privacy and turned abruptly to the contents. "So you were going to keep this from me, were you?"

"No, no. I just wanted to find out what it said before you got upset."

"I've been upset, girl. Now I'm irate." Collin stormed around the small bedroom and woke Liam from his slumber.

"For heaven's sake, keep your voice down, Collin." Kathy was close to tears.

"I've been keeping my voice down, as you call it, for way too long. It's time now for action." Collin crumpled the paper and threw it to the floor as he stomped out of the room.

"Where are you going?" Kathy picked up Liam to soothe him and followed Collin to their own bedroom.

"To pack."

"You're not going anywhere away from me and our baby, Collin. You can't. I won't let you."

"Don't try to stop me. I've got to find Claire." He grabbed a small valise from the closet and started indiscriminately stuffing clothes from the dresser into it.

"This is crazy. I need you here. I am your wife, I am no fancy that some poor confused man—"

"I'm all talked out about this," Collin interrupted and knocked her hand away when she put it on his arm.

"But what about your job? Look, calm down. You're not used to this much alcohol. Don't ruin Liam's christening day. I think that man, Jack Jordan, must have some obsession about your sister, Collin. He's not thinking or seeing straight."

"He's the only one working to find her, isn't he, now. That's his job as manager of Cunard. And he says I should come. So I'm goin'."

"No, you're not, Collin. Hear me. Don't you dare. I'll go there with you this summer when school's out, as we planned, if you must persist in this wild goose chase. We'll take Liam with us."

"Claire'll be dead by then. I'm goin' *now*."

"She's dead already, drowned on that damned *Lusitania*, if you ask me." Kathy immediately wished she hadn't said that.

Collin clenched his fists and pounded the wall, leaving a dent. "She's not dead, I tell you. I believe Jack."

"Do you, now? Well, the two of you are loony birds. And look what you've done to the wall and to . . . Liam." In her arms, the baby, now red-faced, hiccoughed, and she could feel his tiny limbs stiffen, most likely in fear of the loud rough voices passing back and forth above his head. She rocked him, crooning.

Collin slammed the valise shut, having crammed it with as many trousers, shirts, underwear, and socks as it would hold. "The time for talk is done. I'm goin' to stay at the *Telegram* tonight, and then I'm headin' for Halifax." He started towards the stairs.

"To your newspaper office? Hear me, Collin. You leave me now, you'd better not bother coming back ."

"Come now, lass. You know I'll be back after I find Claire."

"Liam and I won't be here waiting for you."

Collin turned around at the top of the stairs. "Where would you go?"

"Never you mind."

"Don't be daft, woman."

"It's you who is daft, Collin. Now get out if you must." Kathy pointed at the stairs then buried her face in the baby's blanket.

Collin hesitated a moment and then dashed down the stairs and out into the rain. The front door slammed shut.

Kathy picked up the crumpled document that had been the cause of all this new heartache. She wanted to rush after him, but her pride stopped her. Instead, she paced the floor of her bedroom and held the baby close. At least here was someone who cared for her, needed her. She felt pressure against her blouse and knew the baby wanted to be fed. She brought him to the rocker that Collin had made for her and settled into it. She unbuttoned her blouse and held her right breast to the hungry lad's mouth, stroking his brow as she watched him search. Liam settled right in to nuzzle and suck greedily. His body relaxed and his tiny hand sought her other breast. Kathy knew he was in for a good long feed. "Your Da's a wild man, Liam. But he meant you no harm, my lad. Oh, why can't Collin see the reality of this? He's a child, too, truth be told." She gently touched Liam's cheek, and he opened his eyes wide in an expression that seemed to let his mother know she shouldn't distract him on his important mission. She read the telegram again while he suckled.

Sunday April 23. Stop. Mr. O'Donnell. Stop. No response to your newspaper advertisement. Stop. Cork police say woman and German spy accomplice responsible for double police murder Thursday during attempt to land German munitions. Stop. Considered armed

*and dangerous. Stop. Police useless and dangerous in search. Stop.
Come here to search if you want to find Claire alive. Stop. She is in
mortal danger. Stop. Space for you on Cunard troop ship Acquitania
departing Halifax harbor for Liverpool on April 26. Stop. Cargo
trawler Liverpool to Queenstown May 2. Stop. Travel to Dublin ill
advised now. Stop. Confirm via return telegram. Stop.*

Kathy could see why, in his agitated state, Collin had reacted so
vehemently to this message. On the other hand, she hoped he would
cool off overnight and come back home, stopping all this foolishness.
Immediate family comes first, or would "blood is thicker than water" be
closer to the truth?

Collin didn't come back Monday night, and Kathy was crushed. At
seven the next morning she rushed up the Finlays' front walk, rolling Liam
in his pram. The rain had stopped, but the bitter wind off the lake caused
Kathy's teeth to chatter. Or, was it something else?

Lil saw her friend through the front bedroom window and bounded
down the stairs. "This can't be good news," she called out to Sam who was
already in his studio at the back of the house. Before she could get to the
front door, she heard the barrage of knocking. Sam poked his head out of
his workshop studio as Lil reached out and opened the door. It was time
for him to be on his way to work .

"Oh, Lil, I've lost him," Kathy wailed to her friend.

"Nonsense, girl. What's happened?" Sam reached her as she entered
the parlor and gently guided Kathy to his easy chair. Lil plucked Liam
from her friend's shaking arms and pulled the blanket away from his face.
Clearly, Kathy had dressed him in haste. Her best friend looked fairly
bedraggled herself.

"As if news of the Irish Rising wasn't enough, he had a telegram
waiting at home last night. He accused me of reading his mail." Her tears
started anew. "Now he's gone."

"What do you mean *gone*, lass? What did the telegram say?"

Kathy drew the balled-up paper from her coat pocket and tossed it
onto the parlor table. Just at that moment, Sam and Lil's little girls, Norah
and Dot, came tumbling down the stairs. Norah ran up to her. "What's-a-
matter, Auntie Katie?"

"Aunt Kathy can't talk right now, Norah. You two come with me. We need to check on Ernie."

"Baby's crying, Mama," Dot said. "Need to get him."

The girls looked back down at their daddy and auntie as their mother led them back upstairs by the hand, Liam on her hip.

Sam smoothed out the telegram and read it, all the while holding Kathy's hand. "Well, now. This sheds a different light, lass."

Lil paused halfway up the stairs with the girls tugging at her skirts.

Sam realized that this was serious and got on the telephone. He wasn't going to make it to work at Riverdale Technical School on time this morning. He would have to inform the principal. They had substitutes for such family emergencies.

"Tell me what happened last night."

"He was crazy, Sam. It may have been the drink."

"Yes, he had quite a lot. Tell me."

"Collin's convinced that Jordan has seen his sister and that he is the only one who can save her. He says he has dreams, visions about it."

"What about going in the summer?"

"I tried suggesting that. He said that she'll be dead by then. When I told him that I thought she died on the *Lusitania*, it really set him off. He packed a bag and left."

"To where, I'd like to know."

"To his newspaper, he said, and then he'd take the train to Halifax. Oh, Sam. What am I going to do?"

Kathy shook like a leaf in a windstorm. Sam grabbed the throw blanket from the chesterfield and wrapped it around her.

"Well, first you're going to have some breakfast with hot tea while we figure this out."

Within thirty minutes, Kathy recovered enough in the care of her good friends to think more clearly about her situation. Lil had served up fried eggs and toast while the little girls ate their porridge. Lil's little Ernie was now sound asleep, and Kathy modestly breastfed Liam beneath a tea towel, which seemed to calm her immensely.

Sam had been quiet during the meal while his wife took over the domestic duties. He excused himself and made a telephone call to work and then another to the newspaper where he once worked and where Collin was still employed. He was told to call back after eight thirty. When he finally got through, he asked his old boss, "Is Collin O'Donnell at work this morning yet?"

The boss told him that Collin looked a mess when he himself arrived at six thirty and that he seemed overwrought about his sister in Ireland. He talked about the Rising underway and that she might be in danger.

"What else did he say?" Sam didn't want to divulge too much of Collin's guilt-driven delusions.

"He asked me to assign him as a war correspondent to Ireland immediately. It would be a great scoop for us, Sam, with the ship sailing tomorrow and all. We have a lot of Irish here in Toronto, as you well know."

"Yes, to be sure. But there's a family situation. He has a newborn son."

"He seems so anxious to find this sister of his who is in danger."

"It's my opinion, sir, that Collin should be convinced to stay home with his family."

"It's too late for that, Sam. I've already approved his new assignment and travel, given him an advance from petty cash, and he's left the office. I have to assume that my employees can handle their own affairs."

"Did he say where was he going when he left your office, sir?"

"To Union Station, I believe, to catch the eleven o'clock train to Halifax. The boat sails at eight tomorrow night."

It was incredible to Sam that Collin would ultimately decide to take off and abandon his new family. Obviously, all the coaching he had given the lad in the past, which had kept him on track until this point, had not been enough to overcome that overwhelming guilt of his. Sam wondered, given his experience with his own brother Liam, whether he would act any differently if he were in Collin's shoes. Then he thought of Lil and the kids and reflected that he himself, would not be so rash as to leave them, no matter what the circumstance.

"What did you find out?" Lil asked, when Sam returned to the kitchen.

Sam told her what he had learned from the telephone call. "You need to go to Union Station, Kathy. It's ten minutes to nine. I can drive you. There's still time."

"He's made his choice, an imaginary sister over his own wife and child. I went to New York and Rhode Island, remember. We shared all that. The officials there said she perished on the *Lusitania*. I told him last night that if he left, he need not come back. And I meant it."

Sam noticed the set to her chin, a hardness reminiscent of Kathy's father. There had to be a solution to this horrid situation. "There now, dear. You're just hurt. Anyone would be. But you love him so, or you wouldn't be so upset. We all love our dear Collin, but he's a damned fool, and we know that. But right now, you've got to try to stop him."

"I tried last night. He didn't listen to me."

"Kathy, hear me. He's just confused and there's an immediate opportunity at a time of great danger. He's not thinking straight. Go after him. I'll take you there. Think it over, now." Sam disappeared into another room then returned. Nine o'clock came and went. Kathy rocked the baby stubbornly, not even looking up. Sam called the train station to see if the train to Halifax via Montreal was on time. The trainmaster said it was, but would not confirm whether Collin O'Donnell had purchased a ticket.

The girls came down from their nap and Norah asked Kathy, "Where's Unca Collie? I miss him."

"Ya. Me, too. He's such a good horsey," Dot piped up, pulling on Kathy's trouser-clad leg.

"He's gone away, girls."

"But when can we see him?" The girls looked up at her, eyes wide.

From out of the mouths of babes. Kathy did not have an answer for them, for any of them, even herself. She suddenly realized what it would be like without Collin, without his strength or love. She pictured herself alone in the world with him away and in probable danger. Unimaginable anguish. Much worse than having to deal with his guilt-driven tantrums.

Kathy jumped up and grabbed the girls' hands. "My God, Sam, you're right. We've got to stop him!" It was ten minutes to ten when she came to her senses.

Sam had his coat on already and opened the door in a flash. He picked up his girls and gave them each a big kiss. "Well, we'd better get going." It had started raining again, harder this time.

Lil plucked Liam out of Kathy's grasp. "It's pouring buckets out there, dear. Leave the baby with me ."

"But Lil, maybe Collin will react more to Liam than to me."

"Nonsense, girl. Don't risk young Liam's life as he could catch his death in that storm." Lil ushered the two of them out the door, making sure that Sam's scarf was tightly wound around his neck and thrusting her umbrella into Kathy's hand. "Don't speed, for heaven's sake."

Sam had his Model T Ford cranked up and backed out onto Balsam Avenue before Kathy could reach the street. "Get in, girl. There's no time to waste."

The traffic moved towards downtown west on Queen Street, bogged down by the weather. Sam had to keep reaching his left arm out the window to wipe the windshield.

"Where are we now, Sam?" Kathy checked her watch. "It's 10:20," her voice quavered.

"We've just passed Woodbine Avenue." Sam didn't want to remind her that she had refused to budge for over an hour.

They had just crossed over the Don River at 10:35, and Sam thought they might make it in time until he saw the traffic at a dead standstill up ahead. He could see St. Paul's Basilica up on the left, near Parliament Street. They were trapped behind an accident with cars hemming them in all around. "This damned rain."

"Sam, hurry!"

"I'm trying, lass. It doesn't look good." They waited a full five minutes without moving, the rain smearing the windshield.

Then when the auto ahead inched forward, Sam seized the opportunity to turn out left. He stuck his head out the window to get a better view. Automobiles moved smartly eastbound, but there were some gaps if he could time it right. He could barely see a laneway up ahead through the driving rain, just before Sumach Street, leading south.

Sam immediately took the chance, steering Lizzie out into the opposing traffic lane, and missed clipping a Buick's rear fender as it raced by and swerved. Before he could reach the laneway, another Model T emerged from the rain, bearing down on them. Sam veered left, which knocked Kathy's head against the side window. He heard her cry out but couldn't help her. That maneuver saved them from a head-on collision, but the eastbound car scraped his car side in passing.

A few seconds later, he made a sharp left into the alley. Another oncoming automobile whizzed by. "Damn," Sam exclaimed, peering ahead. He knew there had to be damage to his automobile, probably to his running board, but thankfully he and Kathy were just a bit shaken up. At least his tires were holding up.

Sam wove around garbage cans and empty produce boxes as he snaked his way down to King Street, turning west, and saw yet more traffic ahead. He veered left onto Sumach Street, and minutes later, headed west onto Eastern Avenue. Good, they were closing in on Front Street, where the Union Station was located.

He glanced at his watch.10:45. It would be close. "Kathy, get ready to jump out when we get to the station. There won't be time to park. The train for Montreal leaves from Track Twelve at eleven sharp. You got that, lass?"

"Yes, Sam. I got it. I just don't know what I'm going to say to him."

"Tell him you and Liam love him, girl."

"Oh, I will. And I do."

Up ahead, Sam could see a commotion on the left—in the vicinity of the train station—probably spouses and other loved ones seeing their soldiers off to the war. Sam checked his watch—10:52. "You're going to have to run for it, Kathy. Up there on the left. Hurry, lass."

Kathy jumped out of Lizzie, nearly knocking over a woman near the curb. She didn't even try to open the umbrella in the driving rain. She came across the mob of people streaming in and out of the cavernous Union Station and had to muscle her way through.

"Where is Track Twelve?" she cried out to anyone who would notice her. A matron on her way out of the building pointed across the huge rotunda. "It's over there, but we've already said the goodbyes, girl. You'd best hurry as the trains are on time today." With that, the woman disappeared, swept up in the mass of humanity.

Kathy checked her watch—10:57. She pushed ahead through the maze. Bustling along the tunnel, Kathy spied the number 12 on the wall to the right. As she scrambled up the first steps on the flight of stairs, she heard a train whistle sound. It was the most hollow, mournful sound she had ever heard. Above her, someone yelled, "All aboard."

She fought against the tide of women with children coming down from the platform. "Let me by." Every time she took a step up, she would get knocked back. "Let me up, I beg you."

She could see the train on the track up above through the mass of women. Soldiers leaned out of the windows, hoping to catch a glimpse of their loved ones, or to say one last word of comfort. Women were crying on the platform, some searching for their mate in the windows. Finally, elbows out, Kathy pushed up, free of the crowd.

Once on the platform, she scanned the windows for any sign of Collin. Not seeing him, she pushed forward so she could look into the passenger cars ahead. The train started to roll.

Sitting amongst all these young soldiers, Collin thought they looked so splendid in their smart uniforms with their kit bags by their sides. His hearing loss had kept him from the fight, making him feel inferior. He noticed that they each had a holstered sidearm on their right hip. He wondered what these men would look like a fortnight hence in the trenches he had read accounts about and how many would be lucky enough to be alive still. All this wasted humanity, standing up and straining out the windows to catch a last glimpse of the ones they were leaving behind, in most cases for good. He thought of the ones he was leaving behind—Kathy and wee Liam. He loved them so. He was the lucky one. He wasn't a young man going to the Front and likely not coming home. But Kathy told him not to return if he made the choice to leave. *I thought she understood that I need to find Claire, or I'm not a man, for all that. It has to be now. No more time for talk and delay.* He looked at the men around him and then out the window. *There's no one out there to see me off.*

The train picked up speed. The locomotive cleared the platform. Kathy stopped and frantically scanned the cars rolling by. Some of the soldiers whistled at her through the windows.

In desperation, Kathy called out repeatedly, "Collin!"

"Hey, look at that dame out there, the one calling out to some bloke named Collin. What a dish," one of the soldiers at the window near Collin yelled to his mate.

Collin startled out of his melancholy. "Where? Let me see." He pushed the soldier aside and thrust his head out the window. He didn't hear the soldier's complaint as he followed the sound, a lilting voice he knew so well. There she was on the platform behind them now, scanning the windows of the car immediately behind and calling out his name. Collin looked up at the emergency cord and thought of pulling it. Then he thought of Claire, poor Claire. He was sure that she was in mortal danger in war-torn Ireland, and that both Kathy and Liam were at least safe at home in Canada.

"I'm here, Kathy. I love you and Liam," Collin screamed at the top of his lungs as he leaned out the window.

But the last of the train cars had rumbled out of the station, steel wheels screeching and drowning out their searching voices.

Abandoned

THE END of Book Two

Book Three titled *Rising* is coming soon!

CAST OF CHARACTERS

North America – Historical

John Devoy—Leader of Clan na Gael in New York, U.S.

Dorothy Finlay—Sam and Lil's Younger Daughter

Elizabeth Finlay (Lil)—Sam's Wife

Ernest Finlay—Sam and Lil's Newborn Son

Norah Finlay—Sam and Lil's Elder Daughter

Samuel Stevenson Finlay—Artist & Director of Art at Riverdale High School, Toronto, Canada

Joseph McGarrity—Leader of Clan na Gael in Philadephia, U.S.

Reverend Edward McIntyre—Minister, St. Aidans Church, Toronto, Canada

North America – Fictional

Collin O'Donnell—Young Irishman in Toronto

Fiona O'Sullivan—Kathleen's Mother

Kathy O'Donnell (Kathleen)—Young Irish Woman in Toronto, Collin's Wife. Nee O'Sullivan

Liam O'Donnell—Kathy and Collin's Son

Ryan O'Sullivan—Kathleen's Father

Europe – Historical

Albert I—King Albert I of Belgium during WWI

Herbert Henry Asquith—British Prime Minister during WWI

Daniel Bailey—Sergeant, Second Member of Casement's Brigade, Landed Banna Strand, Ireland

Augustine Birrell—British Secretary for Ireland

Lewis Bayly—Vice Admiral, Commander-in-Chief, Coast of Ireland

George Carew—British Lord Totnes, President of Munster, Ireland, 1600

Sir Roger Casement—Irish Volunteers, Ambassador to Germany, Recruiter of Irish Brigade

Sir Neville Chamberlain—Chief Inspector, Royal Irish Constabulary (RIC) Ireland

Thomas Clarke—Lead Member of Irish Republican Brotherhood (IRB)

Pope Clement V—Supported French King Philippe IV in Terminating Knights Templar

Michael Collins—Member, Irish Volunteers, Joseph Plunkett's Aide in Easter Rising

James Connolly—Head of the Irish Citizens Army (ICA)

Dr. Charles Curry—Supporter of Roger Casement in Bavaria

Dr. Antoine DePage—King Albert I physician, Head of Belgium Field Hospital, De Panne, Founded Belgium's Red Cross

Marie DePage—Dr, DePage's Wife, Nurse Advocate in America, *Lusitania* Victim

Queen Elisabeth—Queen Elisabeth Gabrielle Valérie Maria, Wife of Albert I of Belgium, called Queen Nurse

Thomas FitzMaurice—Knight Templar, 1307, Kerry, Ireland, Grand Knight Hospitaller, Ancestor of Maurice Collis

James FitzThomas—James FitzThomas FitzGerald, Sugan Earl of Desmond, Maurice's Ancestor, Captured & Jailed mid-1601 before the Battle of Kinsale

Captain Flood—Captain of HMS *Bluebell*

Lovick Friend—British Major General, Commander-in-Chief, for Ireland in WWI

William Hall (Blinker)—British Captain, Director of British Intelligence, Broke German Code

John Bulmer Hobson—Member of IRB, Helped form Irish Volunteers, Supported MacNeill

Von Bethmann Hollweg—Imperial Chancellor of Germany, WWI

John Kearney—Tralee Head Constable, RIC

Michael Keogh—Sergeant Major, Recruiter, Casement's Brigade at Zossen, Germany

Reverend J.H. Lawlor—Professor of Ecclesiastical Studies, Dublin University Researcher and Author for the Cathach of St. Columba

Leopold III—Prince Leopold, son of King Albert I and Queen Elisabeth

Tomas MacCurtain—Head of IRB for Cork

Sean MacDermott—IRB Leader, Member of Military Committee

Thomas MacDonagh—IRB Leader, Assistant Principal St. Edna's School

Eoin MacNeill—Chief of Staff, Irish Volunteers

Florence MacCarthaigh—Clan Chieftain in 1601, Arrested by George Carew before Battle Reagh of Kinsale in January 1602

Thomas McInerney—Irish Volunteer, Drove Car off Bridge, Captured by British

Michael Mallin—IRB Commandant of St. Stephen's Green, ICA Soldier

Jacques de Molay—Last Head of the Knights Templar. Burned at the Stake in 1314

Captain Robert Monteith—Casement's Commander of the Irish Brigade, Camp Zossen, First Member of Casement's Brigade. Landed at Banna Strand

Sir Matthew Nathan—British Undersecretary for Ireland

Sean O'Casey—Irish Playwright, Tadgh's Literary Mentor

Peader O'Donnell—College Student, Later to be a Revolutionary Leader

Red Hugh O'Donnell—Last Free Chieftain, O'Donnell Clan in 1601, Battle of Kinsale

Michael The O'Rahilly—Director of Arms, Irish Volunteers, Allegiance to Eoin MacNeill

Padraig Pearse—Lead Member of the IRB and School Master St. Edna's

King Philippe IV—King of France. Terminated Knight's Templar in 1307

Joseph Plunkett—Member IRB, Visited Casement and GGS in Germany, mid-1915

John Redmond—Irish Nationalist Politician, Organized National, Volunteers to Fight for the Allied Cause in WWI, Believing Britain Would Pass Irish Home Rul

Kapitan Karl Spindler—Captain of German *Aud-Norge* Gun-running Ship

Austin Stack—Head of IRB for Tralee

Wolfe Tone—Father of Irish Republicanism and Leader of 1798 Rebellion

Kapitan Raimund Weisbach—Watch Officer on *U-20* then Kapitanleutnant of *U-19*

Lord Wimborne—Ivor Churchill Guest, British Lord Lieutenant for Ireland

Arthur Zimmermann—Secretary of State, Foreign Affairs, Germany in WWI

Europe – Fictional

Darcy Boyle—Head Constable, Royal Irish Constabulatory (RIC), Cork City

Captain Maurice Collis—Fishing Captain, Fenit, Ireland, Descendant of the FitzMaurice Clan, Supporter of Tadgh

Martha Collis—Wife of Maurice Collis

Frank Coltrain—RIC Constable, Tralee. Captured Sir Roger Casement Hauptmann Friederic Gruber Bernard Gronski's Second in Command at GGS, WWI

François Gabion—Farmer in France Who Sheltered Tadgh and Morgan

Monique Gabion—François's Wife Who Sheltered Tadgh and Morgan

Bernard Gronski—Head of Sektion Technik of the German General Staff, WWI

Dr. Heinrich—Head Doctor, German Field Hospital, Ostend, Belgium in WWI

Hugo Jacobs—Albert I's Advisor, Furnes Headquarters, Gronski's Direct Spy in Belgium

Gordon (Gordo) James—Constable RIC Cork, and Boyle's Henchman

Jack Jordan—Third Boson's Mate, HMS *Lusitania*, Manager Cunard Operations, Queenstown, Ireland

Dean Maloney—District Inspector, RIC Cork

Aidan McCarthy—Tadgh's Younger Brother, Irish Volunteer

Tadgh McCarthy—Young Irish Revolutionary. Member of Cork IRB, Communications and Transportation Specialist

Morgan—Woman Rescued by Tadgh McCarthy, His Partner

Martin Murphy—Captain of Supply Ships for Beamish & Crawford (B&C) Brewery

Doctor O'Callihan—Hospitaller Doctor at Fenit, Ireland

Hans Pauwels—Communications Officer at Albert I's Headquarters at Furnes, Gruber's Spy in Belgium

Father Jan Peeters—Priest, St. Petrus and Paulus Church, Ostend, Belgium

Hans Pfiefer—Kommandant of Zossen Prisoner of War Camp. WWI

Arndt Ritter—Sektion Technik spy in Ostend Posing as an Orderly/ Ambulance Driver. Works for Gruber

Fritz Schmidt—Watch Officer, Second in Command to Weisbach on *U-19*

Gerda Schmidt—Fritz's Wife, Mother of Young Sons Hans and Fritz

Jeffrey Wiggins—Transportation Leader, Beamish & Crawford (B&C) Brewery, Cork City, Ireland, and Tadgh's Colleague

HISTORICAL BACKGROUND

Reference	Subject	Novel	Background
1	Casement	p. 39	318
2	German Invasion of Belgium	p. 39	303
3	Machines of WWI	p. 43	305
4	Irish Prisoners at Limburg and Zossen	p. 49	319
5	US/German Communications	p.52	320
6	Gronski	p.53	320
7	Zimmermann	p. 53	317
8	King Albert I	p. 64	304
9	Horrors of War in the Trenches–de Wiart Speech and PPCLI	p. 129	304, 310
10	German Support to the Irish USA War Entry	p. 147	316
11	Aud-Norge, German Gun-running Ship	p. 203	322
12	The *Cathach* of Saint Columba	p. 276	325

World War I and the Belgian Campaign Triumph that Saved France

Historians still debate today, more than a hundred years after the start of the war to end all wars of 1914—1918, about what caused the horrific conflict that killed more than seventeen million people worldwide. Of course, they all agree that the straw that broke the camel's back was the assassination of Archduke Franz Ferdinand or Austria and his wife, Sophie, Duchess of Hohenberg, on June 28, 1914 by a Serbian nationalist. But what was the camel?

It's complicated. Many alliances and treaties had been established in the nineteenth and early twentieth centuries as nationalism was on the rise within European countries, Russia, and the Ottoman Empire, and with the colonies and allies of these countries. This caused an inevitable chain reaction after the archduke and his wife were killed. You can see from the accompanying Venn diagram that Serbia sat right in the middle between the Triple Entente Allied Powers of Russia, Britain and France and the Quadruple Alliance Central Powers of Germany, Austria-Hungary and the Ottoman Empire. Italy switched allegiance in 1915 to join the Allied Powers.

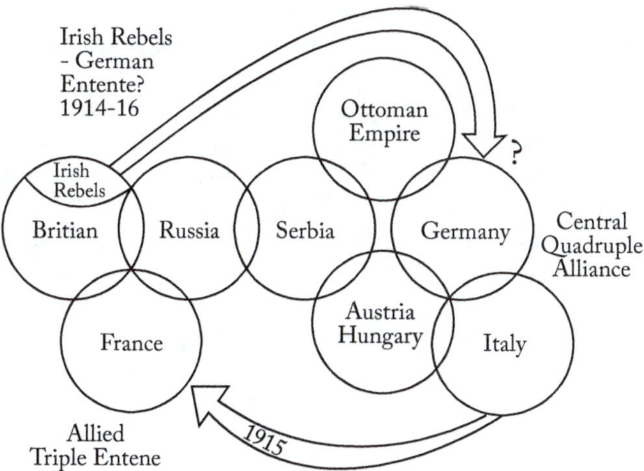

Of course, the causes included lust for territory and power. King Wilhelm II of Prussia was the last Emperor (Kaiser) of the German Empire. When he dismissed Chancellor Otto von Bismark in 1890 who had been crafting alliances with Britain and Russia, the die was cast. The Kaiser was carelessly outspoken, sometimes making ill-advised comments un-vetted by his advisors including the military. It is interesting to note that he was the grandson of Queen Victoria of Britain.

His Chancellor, Theobald von Bethmann Hollweg, continued to try to mend fences with Britain prior to 1914, but Germany was already aligning with Austria/Hungary. Paul von Hindenburg and Erich Lundenorff, Germany's highest-ranking generals at the start of the war, were said to have directed policy almost exclusively without civilian government or citizenry consideration.

Russia had started to mobilize towards western conquest in 1913, which in turn forced Germany to do likewise in defense. Meanwhile France had fortified its borders with Germany, also in a defense posture. When the Austrian/Serbian situation exploded with the assassination of the archduke, senior British diplomat Sir Edward Grey suggested mediation. His letter to the Austrians was facilitated by von Bethmann, who removed the last sentence before passing it on to Vienna, reading "*Also, the whole world here is convinced, and I hear from my colleagues that the key to the situation lies in Berlin, and that if Berlin seriously wants peace, it will prevent Vienna from following a foolhardy policy*"(Fritz Fischer, 1967).

Kaiser Wilhelm II heard about this after the fact when war was inevitable on July 26, 1914 and refused to accept his Chancellor's resignation saying, "*You've made this stew, now you're going to eat it!*" (Butler, David Allen, The Burden of Guilt: How Germany Shattered the Last Days of Peace, Summer 1914, Casement Publishers, p 103).

Punch Cartoon by F. H. Townsend
Published in August 1914

The German generals felt that they must conquer France rapidly before Russia would be fully mobilized to attack Germany. They realized that they would have to march through Belgium to avoid the French defenses. This counterclockwise attack near the North Sea was called the Schlieffen plan. I will concentrate this WWI narrative in this theater of operations because of my storyline, recognizing that the First World War was indeed that—a massive and horrific worldwide conflict.

[2] Britain and Prussia had signed the London Treaty in 1839, which called for the neutrality of Belgium among other nations like the Netherlands in any future European Wars. When the German military tried to pass through Belgium to conquer France in 1914, it violated that treaty. Theobold von Bethmann Hellwig was dismayed when Britain declared war on Germany, questioning, *Are you going to war over "ein Fetzen Papier?"* (a scrap of paper). (Zuckerman, Larry, 2004, *The Rape of Belgium*, The Untold Story of World War I, New York University Press, p 43). Apparently Germany had thought that their war would be only limited to France on the Western Front and that it would be over quickly, *"by Christmas."* They didn't count on Belgium, a country of seven

million people, stopping Germany, a country of 65 million people, from advancing through its territories.

[8] King Albert I of Belgium declared, *"Belgium is a nation, not a road."* His queen, Duchess Elisabeth Gabrielle Valérie Marie of Bavaria, a Wittelsbach princess whose ancestry was in the Prussian Empire, was devoted to her husband and their country of Belgium. In 1914, together she, with Albert and their first son Leopold III, then thirteen, led their country's resistance against the Germans, fighting alongside their countrymen and women. Elisabeth, who spearheaded the nursing efforts at the battlefield, became known as Queen Nurse. The Belgian royal couple was respected by the Germans.

The Belgians were forced to first evacuate their capital Brussels, then Antwerp on October 10, 1914, and then Ostend, under the onslaught of the Germans. The Germans were merciless with both military and civilian personnel. This offensive, the Race to the Sea, was named The Rape of Belgium with good cause. Starvation, execution for resistance, occupation, and moral decimation were viciously imposed on the citizenry, many of whom fled to neutral Netherlands.

But once the Belgian army under Albert I retreated west across the Yser River in Flanders, they took their final stand in the very southwest corner of their country, backed right up to the North Sea and France. There they bravely held the line, including winning the first Battle of Ypres in late October and November 1914. During the same period, in a last ditch effort to stop the Germans near the North Sea, the Belgians flooded West Flanders at Nieuwpoort, including the German trenches.

Thus, they won the day, establishing the trenches that would remain intact throughout the war. This heroic fight by the meager but ferocious Belgian army and their supporters diverted the might of Germany long enough for the Allied Forces to build up a line of trenches from Switzerland to meet up with the Belgians at the North Sea at Nieuwpoort at the mouth of the Yser River, a total of 475 miles in all. Belgium was still free in the small sliver west of the Yser River and Germany was denied their northern path into France. See the map of Europe titled 'World War 1, December 1915' to be found at the outset of this novel.

This herculean effort was described by the Belgian Minister of Justice Carton DeWiart in his inspiring address in London June 1915 seeking support, which can be read in its entirety at http://www.firstworldwar. com/source/yser_dewiart.htm [9]

Poorly supplied and with only the aid of a few divisions of French Marine Fusiliers, 60,000 exhausted Belgian soldiers killed or wounded more than their total army numbers, from a massive, well equipped and supplied German army, while only losing a quarter of their own strength. Only by flooding the Yser valley did they eventually bring Germany to a halt.

But this was just the start of the western conflict which would last for another four brutal years. The second battle of Ypres in May 1915 was another ferocious fight. The Belgians held their ground until French Marine Fusiliers and the Princess Patricia's Canadian Light Infantry, among others, could come to their aid.

It is into this deadly struggle that I immerse our characters Tadgh and Morgan six months later. Germany has entrenched with its forward command and naval center in Ostend, ten miles east of the Western Front. To all intents and purposes, that front was still where it had been when the Yser was flooded a year earlier. The German General Staff (GGS) had decided to hold the line on the Western Front while they diverted manpower to the very real threat of the Russians on the Eastern Front.

The stagnation of the war was not indicative of the ongoing loss of life. Casualties continued to grow at a staggering pace. Without the advent of armored vehicles like tanks, neither army could advance unchecked. Artillery and machine gun fire did most of the damage, and trench duty was usually a death sentence, in the most pitiful conditions imaginable, on both sides. What might have been a war of several months, stretched on for four years until the United States finally entered the war on the side of the Allied Powers, and with the help of new war machines including tanks, the U.S. tipped the scales in favor of the Allied Powers.

The War Machines of WWI [3]

The Great War, as they also called it, may have been spurred on by arms manufacturers like Krupp, Fokker and Mauser in Germany, and Vickers, Webley and Lee-Enfield in Britain, among many others. They certainly did profit from the war financially. The new technologies of dreadnought battleships, submarines, aircraft and dirigibles, tanks, machine guns, flamethrowers, and chemical weapons like phosgene all advanced the arms industries product lines that mercilessly killed human beings in large numbers.

Was the German naval build-up the principal cause of deteriorating Anglo-German relations in the 1900 to 1914 timeframe? Possibly. Germany never came close to catching up with Britain as can be seen below with the dreadnought class comparison (Ferguson Niall, *The Pity of War* ISBN 978-0-465-05712-2).

Wilhem II pushed for a competitive German navy. Grand Admiral Alfred von Tirpitz led the naval armament efforts with four funding initiatives from 1898 to 1912, while the British Royal Navy expanded its fleet to keep ahead of the Germans. The revolutionary new ships based on the Dreadnought, which was launched in 1906, gave Britain a battleship that far outclassed any other in Europe (Blyth, Robert J. and Andrew Lambert, 2011, *The Dreadnought in the Edwardian Age*, Ashgate). At the start of the war, Britain had 29 dreadnought class ships of 2.2 million tonnes with 209,000 naval personnel compared to Germany with 17 dreadnought class ships of 1 million tonnes and 79,000 naval personnel (Ferguson, Niall, 1999, *The Pity of War* p.85, Basic Books).

As a result of this imbalance, Britain was able to employ naval blockades, in the North Sea for example, in an attempt to cut off critical supplies to their enemies.

Germany, in turn, focused on the use of U-boat submarines to attack and sink Allied naval and civilian shipping supplying critical supplies to Britain and other Triple Entente Allies.

The story of the technologies which were rapidly developed and extensively deployed during this terrible war have been chronicled by A. Torry McLean and are here presented with permission from Tar Heel Junior Historian 32, no. 2 (Spring 1993): 25-30, copyright NC Museum of History, as follows:

> *"One of the saddest facts about World War I is that millions died needlessly because military and civilian leaders were slow to adapt their old-fashioned strategies and tactics to the new weapons of 1914. New technology made war more horrible and more complex than ever before. The United States and other countries felt the effects of the war for years afterwards. The popular image of World War I is soldiers in muddy trenches and dugouts, living miserably until the next attack. This is basically correct. Technological developments in engineering, metallurgy, chemistry, and optics had produced weapons deadlier than anything known before. The power of defensive weapons made winning the war on the western front all but impossible for either*

side.

When attacks were ordered, Allied soldiers went "over the top," climbing out of their trenches and crossing no-man's-land to reach enemy trenches. They had to cut through belts of barbed wire before they could use rifles, bayonets, pistols, and hand grenades to capture enemy positions. A victory usually meant they had seized only a few hundred yards of shell-torn earth at a terrible cost in lives. Wounded men often lay helpless in the open until they died. Those lucky enough to be rescued still faced horrible sanitary conditions before they could be taken to proper medical facilities. Between attacks, the snipers, artillery, and poison gas caused misery and death.

Airplanes, products of the new technology, were primarily made of canvas, wood, and wire. At first they were used only to observe enemy troops. As their effectiveness became apparent, both sides shot planes down with artillery from the ground and with rifles, pistols, and machine guns from other planes. In 1916, the Germans armed planes with machine guns that could fire forward without shooting off the fighters' propellers. The Allies soon armed their airplanes the same way, and war in the air became a deadly business. These light, highly maneuverable fighter planes attacked each other in wild air battles called dogfights. Pilots who were shot down often remained trapped in their falling, burning planes, for they had no parachutes. Airmen at the front did not often live long. Germany also used its fleet of huge dirigibles, or zeppelins, and large bomber planes to drop bombs on British and French cities. Britain retaliated by bombing German cities.

Back on the ground, the tank proved to be the answer to stalemate in the trenches. This British invention used American-designed caterpillar tracks to move the armored vehicle equipped with machine guns and sometimes, light cannon. Tanks worked effectively on firm, dry ground, in spite of their slow speed, mechanical problems, and vulnerability to artillery. Able to crush barbed wire and cross trenches, tanks moved forward through machine gun fire and often terrified German soldiers with their unstoppable approach.

Chemical warfare first appeared when the Germans used poison gas during a surprise attack in Flanders, Belgium, in 1915. At first, gas was just released from large cylinders and carried by the wind into nearby enemy lines. Later, phosgene and other gases were loaded into artillery shells and shot into enemy trenches. The Germans used this weapon the most, realizing that enemy soldiers wearing gas masks did not fight as well. All sides used gas frequently by 1918. Its use was a frightening development that caused its victims a great deal of suffering, if not death.

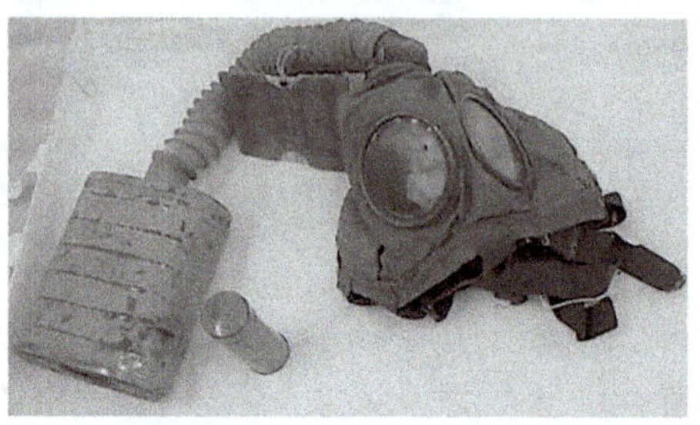

Gas Mask. WWI. Used in France.
NC Museum of History Collections.
Accession no. H.1999.1.406.

Both sides used a variety of big guns on the western front, ranging from huge naval guns mounted on railroad cars to short-range trench mortars. The result was a war in which soldiers near the front were seldom safe from artillery bombardment. The Germans used super– long-range artillery to shell Paris from almost eighty miles away. Artillery shell cratered, moonlike landscapes where beautiful fields and woods had once stood.

Perhaps the most significant technological advance during World War I was the improvement of the machine gun, a weapon originally developed by an American, Hiran Maxim. The Germans recognized its military potential and had large numbers ready to use in 1914. They also developed air-cooled machine guns for airplanes and improved those used on the ground, making them lighter and easier to move. The weapon's full potential was demonstrated on the Somme battlefield in July 1916 when German machine guns killed or wounded almost 60,000 British soldiers in only one day.

"Browning Machine Gun. Model 1917."
1918. NC Museum of History.
Accession No. H.1918.31.9.

At sea, submarines attacked ships far from port. In order to locate and sink German U-boats, British scientists developed underwater listening devices and underwater explosives called depth charges. Warships became faster and more powerful than ever before and used newly invented radios to communicate effectively. The British naval blockade of Germany, which was made possible by developments in naval technology, brought a total war to civilians. The blockade caused a famine that finally brought about the collapse of Germany and its allies in late 1918. Starvation and malnutrition continued to take the lives of German adults and children for years after the war.

The firing stopped on November 11, 1918, but modern war technology had changed the course of civilization. Millions had been killed, gassed, maimed, or starved. Famine and disease continued to rage through central Europe, taking countless lives. Because of rapid technological advances in every area, the nature of warfare had changed forever, affecting soldiers, airmen, sailors, and civilians alike."

I have attempted to use this knowledge regarding the unfortunate timing of the development and deployment of these deadly war machines in my novel to show the inhumanity and futility of this horrific war in the trenches of Europe. There is a terrible similarity between this war of merciless bombardment on forces that are pinned down in a hole in the ground, and the subsequent Irish Easter Rising where the rebels are subjected to merciless bombardment while they are holed up in the General Post Office and elsewhere in Dublin. The numbers of casualties are greatly different, but the demoralizing terror of those involved must have been similar.

The Princess Patricia Canadian Light Infantry (P.P.C.L.I.) - Valor in the Trenches [9]

Canadians at Ypres, painting by William Barnes Wollen,
1916 provided by P.P.C.L.I Museum, Calgary, Canada

The front cover art on this novel, so splendidly painted by the renowned military artist William Barnes Wollen, graphically depicts the brave fight of the Princess Patricia Canadian Light Infantry during the Battle of Frezenberg on May 8, 1915, as part of the second Battle of Ypres in the southwestern Flanders plain. I chose this image because I feel it epitomizes the patriotic and valiant struggle by the soldiers in the western trenches of Belgium and France at that time. It also shows the desperate conditions that the soldiers had to endure for years, if they lived so long. I am indebted to The P.P.C.L.I Museum, Calgary, Canada, which owns and proudly displays the original of this painting, for permission to use this illustrative image on the cover of my novel and the account of the battle herein. I think their story is an inspiration for all of us who cherish the moral value of history. I would like to share it with you here.

At the outbreak of WWI, Canada was lacking military forces. The bond of the British colonists was still strong at a time when the United States was still in an isolationist posture. Captain Hamilton Gault offered $100,000 to create a battalion of Canadian soldiers. This was accepted by the Government on August 10, 1914, and the P.P.C.L.I. was formed in

Ottawa Canada and approved by the Governor General of Canada HRH, The Duke of Connaught and Strathearn. The regiment was named after his daughter, Princess Patricia of Connaught.

Under the leadership of Captain Gault and Lieutenant-Colonel Francis Farquhar, both of whom had fought in the Boer War, the 1,092-man regiment mobilized quickly in Ottawa. They had to wait for a convoy to protect the troop ship from enemy U-boat attack during the Atlantic crossing, so they finally reached the Western Front on December 20, the first Canadian combat unit to participate in the war.

The Patricias first took their place in the trenches on January 6, 1915, at a location known to the British Army's soldiers as "Dickiebush." When Francis Farquhar, the first commanding officer, was killed in action at St. Eloi on March 20, 1915, he was replaced by Lt. Col H. Buller, another British regular who had served with him on the staff of the Governor General before the war.

On May 8, the stout defense of Bellewaerde Ridge during the Battle of Frezenberg established the reputation of the Patricias, but at a tremendous cost. When they came out of the line, they had lost 500 men in three days. The tattered remains were commanded by a lieutenant, all other officers having been killed or wounded.

I appreciate the opportunity to share some of the documentation of the action on that fateful day on Bellewaerde Ridge, titled *Princess Patricia's Canadian Light Infantry, 1914-1919* by Ralph Hodder-Williams formerly Lieutenant, P. P. C.L.I. It is fact and not fiction, which makes it all the more horrific.

". . . The early hours of May 8 were unnaturally quiet, but an hour or two after dawn the German artillery opened fire and the shelling rapidly became intense. At about 7 a.m. the heavier guns joined in, and so violent a bombardment began as could only announce a general action. Bellewaerde Ridge became an inferno, and to those in the trenches "the whole world seemed alive and rocking with the flashing and crashing of bursting shells." The guns gradually concentrated their fire upon the British lines between the Menin road and Frezenberg, and the 80th Brigade received its full force. Major Gault reported 'very very heavy shelling,' and the 4th K.R.R. warned the Brigade that 'this heavy bombardment leads to supposition that attack may be coming.' The Patricias were unprotected from the enfilading fire of machine guns on the high ground at the right flank and from the

artillery in Bodmin Copse, and the effect of the bombardment on the bad and exposed trenches was most disastrous. Bursts of shrapnel mowed down the men, high explosive 'more or less obliterated the front line,' destroyed one of the Patricias' four machine guns and put another out of action, blew away the wire and cut the Regiment off from all communication with its supports. Casualties came so fast that Major Gault soon ordered every 'employed'—man—signallers, pioneers, orderlies, officers' servants—into the support line to make good the losses. Shortly after 8 a.m. he succeeded in communicating the state of affairs to the Brigade by runner in the following account:

Have been heavily shelled since 7 a.m. Sections of front trenches made untenable by enemy's artillery, but have still about 160 rifles in front line. German infantry has not yet appeared. Should they rush our front trenches will at once counter-attack if possible, but do not propose to risk weakening my support lines. Will advise O.C. Rifle Brigade should I require support. In lulls of gun fire there is heavy fire from rifles and machine guns. Please send me two m.g.'s if possible. I have only two left in front line. None in support.

A second message read:

Should this continue all day, would like support this evening in case of heavy night attack. Most of my wire gone.

About the time that these messages were sent, and during something of a lull in the gun fire, particularly heavy machine-gun fire swept the Patricias to keep down the heads of the garrison, and the enemy were seen by No. 2 Company swarming out of their lines and massing for the attack. Thin as it was, the front line was still strong enough to bring a deadly fire to bear. Every man who could 1 handle a rifle used it with good effect and the attack was broken. Not more than 80 or 100 Germans reached cover behind hedges and in some ruined buildings a short distance in front of the British line. Most of these were soon driven out by concentrated rifle fire, and were seen crawling back over the ridge into safety. But two, or possibly three, machine-gun crews established themselves in the ruined buildings. These added point-blank fire to the enfilading guns of the artillery, which opened up again as soon as the infantry attack was seen to have failed; and during the second hour the support position was almost as badly punished as the front line had been during the first. But the front line still received its share and was now completely blown to pieces in several places, notably on the extreme right, and gradually became untenable. Most of No. 1 Company, and later the right of No. 2, had to fall back in small parties upon the support trench. The main assault was delivered at, or very soon after, 9 a.m. 'There seemed,' wrote an eyewitness, 'to be an astounding silence with just an occasional rifle shot, and then we realized that the German infantry were upon us.' On the left, the remnant of No. 2 Company again brought a heavy aimed fire upon the open ground in front which brought the enemy to a standstill, and this though their machine guns had been buried. The Germans lost very heavily and were forced to retire. On the right, however, the front line trench in some places was obliterated and abandoned, and the enemy—" there seemed to be dozens of them" climbed over and through the broken wire into the trench, bayoneting the wounded as they came. It was touch-and-go for the next few minutes . . . . the Patricias rallied instantly, and the Germans were pinned down to the few bays of the battered right trench which they had entered in the first rush. Even so the situation was sufficiently desperate. The Germans in the captured trench could now fire point-blank into No. 2 Company, whose position they completely enfiladed. As soon as the enemy had installed themselves they set up a row of small white flags. For a moment the Patricias thought this might be a sign of surrender; but they soon realized that the object was to mark the extent of the advance for the German gunners, who now concentrated their fire on the support line. Toward the end of the bombardment four officers had fallen in quick succession. Major Gault, wounded early in the day, was again hit, and so severely wounded that he was unable to move about the line. He sent word by Captain H. S. Hill instructing Captain Agar Adamson to take over the command. It was clear that the support line must be held at all costs. The right of No. 1 Company's position had long since gone and the left had by now become untenable. Captain H. S. Dennison had sent back the remnant of the garrison under Lieutenant D. A. Clarke, and himself stayed behind with Lieutenant P. E. Lane and a handful of men to cover the withdrawal. Neither Dennison nor Lane was ever seen again and few of their men survived; nor can the tale ever be told of this rear-guard's devotion to duty. On the left, No. 2 Company clung to what remained of their trench for some time longer, and, almost without cover, they kept up a hot and effective fire upon the enemy lying massed behind the hedge and round the farm buildings in the centre of the position. At last, when they ran out of ammunition and found both their flanks being turned, they too began to fall back along the shallow communication trench. This they held until it was completely blown in, and many of them were killed as they exposed themselves during the withdrawal in places where the trench had ceased to exist or was choked with the bodies of their dead comrades. Single-handed N.C.O.'s and men covered the whole retirement from the front line with extraordinary daring. Some remained behind in trenches, others lay out in the open, others again waited at the head of the communication trench,—all sniping at every German who showed himself. Sergeant W. Jordan and Lance-Corporal J. M. Christie accounted for large numbers with their rifles; while other N.C.O.'s, conspicuously Sergeant L. Scott and Lance-Corporal A. G. Pearson, handled the withdrawal brilliantly where the officers had fallen. 1 Private J. Bushby 'assisted wounded from a trench that was already in the hands of the Germans. He attempted to rescue a comrade who was half-buried in the trench although while doing so he had to keep at bay two Germans who were trying to bayonet him.' By 10 a.m., save for a few isolated posts, the front line had been abandoned. The 4th K.R.R. on the right, who had suffered from the bombardment almost as severely as the Patricias, escaped the worst of the German attack. In the lull of the artillery fire they brought a company of the Rifle Brigade into their support trenches. Another company from the Rifle Brigade pushed forward with magnificent courage a little later through the barrage to strengthen the Patricias, and reached the line most opportunely while the German attack was still in progress. The garrison of Bellewaerde Ridge cheered the reinforcements and took new heart. Well it might, for even those men of the Rifle Brigade who were laden with ammunition boxes carried half a dozen bandoliers of cartridges as well. Above all they brought machine guns. "On the 8th of May," said a wounded P.P. C.L.I, sergeant in a speech at Shorncliffe on the first birthday of the Regiment, 'we saw the Angels, and they wore the letters 'R.B.' on their shoulders; and the biggest of the Angels were those who bore the machine guns on their shoulders too.' Captain Agar Adamson, by this time wounded, arranged for the distribution of ammunition, decided that the machine-gun sections should remain with the Patricias unless they were urgently needed elsewhere, and then personally led the men from the Rifle Brigade in rear of the support line to his extreme left, whence they counterattacked and not only lessened the pressure but gave some cover to the exposed left flank. This relief, however, could only be temporary. Major John Harington, commanding the 4th Rifle Brigade, came up to the ridge, crawled along the front to form an opinion of the state of affairs and reported:

P.P. have suffered 75 per cent casualties and the position is critical. Reinforcements badly wanted at once. All my battalion is up.

. . . All but five officers, 80 per cent of the men were gone; there was a great gap on the flank; the crumbling ditch that did duty for a trench was open to fire from three sides. But the iron grip on the ridge was never loosed, and the officer commanding the Shropshires reported in the heat of the fight that not one man from the Patricias was coming back except an occasional stretcher-bearer on duty. Little by little the tension slackened. The 4th K.R.R. on the right stood their ground as gallantly as the Patricias. The Shropshires, Argyll and Sutherland Highlanders and 3rd K.R.R. were all instructed to support the Patricias and to watch their left; and before 3 p.m. a platoon of the Shropshires who brought up ammunition were scattered by Captain Agar Adamson's direction along the line. A short time later the Germans made a final sally, which weakened, wavered, collapsed under the answering rifle fire. Then they fell back leaving their dead and wounded behind them. The 4th K.R.R. and the Patricias had saved the day . . ."

Original Ric-A-Dam-Doo Flag
P.P.C.L.I. Museum, Calgary, Canada

This was indeed a desperate and valiantly decisive day on the Western Front, yet just one day out of the 1,550 total days of the war to end all wars on one of the fronts.

One final word about the P.P.C.L.I., which relates to the Gaelic heritage. The original camp flag for the P.P.C.L.I. was hand-sewn by Princess Patricia herself. It became known by the regiment as *Ric-A-Dam-Doo,* around which they rallied. Various sources claim that "Ric-A-Dam-Doo" is a presumably phonetic version of the Gaelic for "cloth of thy mother," but this claim has been denounced by several Gaelic scholars. Another plausible account is that the phrase was a derivation of *Am Freiceadan Dubh*, which translates to "The Black Watch." Hamilton Gault was in fact a member of a Highland Regiment prior to WWI. Indeed, there were Irish and Scottish Canadians willing to lay down their lives for liberty and justice.

This leads to the next section of historical background. How did the Irish Republicans attempt to utilize this inevitable and terrible world war to assist them in their own fight for liberty and justice at home on the Emerald Isle?

Potential Entente between Irish Republicans and Germany [10]

The Clan na Gael Irish Republican leaders, John Devoy in New York, and Joseph McGarrity in Philadelphia, realized, like Wolfe Tone and Red Hugh O'Donnell before them, that the best time to strike for freedom is when the enemy, Britain, was preoccupied with other wars. In 1600 the remaining Clans, O'Donnell, Florence MacCaltaigh Reagh and Hugh O'Neill allied with Spain. In 1798, Tone allied with France. In 1914, the Clan na Gael sought an entente with Germany and the Central Powers. The Clan na Gael president at the time was John Kenny, a businessman who regularly traveled abroad from the United States. Leading members John Devoy and Jeremiah O' Donovan Rossa were two of the Cuba 5 group of expatriates who had been released from a British prison by Queen Victoria in 1871 and exiled to America. Together they had been successful in generating assets and connections to be able to fund the Irish Republicans (Irish Republican Brotherhood or IRB). Further, they were in a country that was neutral to the world war for its first two and a half years.

The Clan na Gael created a plan to approach Germany for munitions and military personnel support for a revolution against Britain in Ireland. They first took their plan to Johan Heinrich von Bernstorff, the German

Ambassador to the United States, who was sympathetic. Collectively they decided that Kenny should travel to Germany to discuss this proposal with the Kaiser. He met with von Flutow, the German Ambassador in Rome who was cautiously supportive in early September. He then travelled on to Germany but could not meet with Kaiser Wilhelm II, instead proposing the plan to former chancellor, Prince von Beulow. The Germans seemed interested in the prospects of an entente, yet they were concerned about international repercussions and the mounting support of a large percentage of Irish Volunteers fighting for Britain in WWI, based on Irish politician John Redmond's assurances of home rule after the war.

[7] Arthur Zimmermann was a career diplomat who had been in service to his native Germany since 1896. Although Zimmermann was the Undersecretary of State for Foreign Affairs when war broke out, he was the real strategist and negotiator with foreign powers, since the secretary was ineffective. At that time, Arthur was crafting potential alliances with revolutionary forces of the Allied adversaries, namely the Bolsheviks in Russia, the Ghadar Party in the United States inciting independence for India, and, after Kenny's visit, the Clan na Gael in the United States and the Republicans in Ireland. Unfortunately for Germany, Zimmermann attempted to make an alliance with Mexico in 1917, and his supposedly secure telegram was intercepted by the Allies. He offered Mexico the return of Arizona, Texas, and New Mexico if they would support Germany in a war with America ("Arthur Zimmermann Profile," *Britannica.com*). This exposed initiative may have been the straw that broke that camel's back, resulting in the United States entering the war with the Allies.

Back in the fall of 1914 after Kenny's visit, John Devoy communicated with Arthur Zimmermann through secure encrypted communications via von Bernstorff who was instrumental in developing the possibility of entente. Zimmermann was cautiously interested—anything to thwart his enemy, Britain. On the other hand, Germany wanted to keep the United States out of the war in Europe until they had beaten France, Belgium, and Britain. With a relatively large Irish population in America, there was a significant risk if Germany were to pro-actively support an Irish revolution.

Sir Roger Casement
Painting by Norman Teeling

[1] Sir Roger Casement (1 September 1864–3 August 1916) was an Irish-born civil servant, a career employee for the British Foreign Office as a diplomat at the turn of the twentieth century. Casement first worked for commercial interests in Africa before joining the British Colonial Service.

In 1891 he was appointed as a British consul, a post in which he faithfully served for approximately twenty years. During the Boer War when he was investigating colonial atrocities against indigenous peoples, Casement decided that imperialism, as it was being exploited, was flawed. He was honored in 1905 for his Casement Report on the Congo, which exposed social injustices. Then he was knighted in 1911 for his important investigations of human rights abuses in Peru. As a result, he became known as the "father of twentieth-century human rights investigations." (https://en.wikipedia.org/wiki/Roger_Casement)

Casement came home temporarily from Africa in 1904, and joined the Gaelic League of 1893, which was attempting to revive the Gaelic language. He felt strongly that the British House of Lords, offers notwithstanding, would never grant Ireland Home Rule. Therefore, in 1905, he supported Arthur Griffith and his fledgling Sinn Féin party, that advocated for Irish independence, achieved through non-violent strikes and boycotts.

By 1913, he was friends with Eoin MacNeill, who was forming the Irish Volunteers to counteract the Ulster Volunteers in the Protestant north. Together they wrote its manifesto, but Sir Roger realized that armed insurrection would be the only Republican voice that would be heard by the British. He took it as his calling to organize that armament. He went to the United States to solicit funds for the organization.

In July 1914, with war about to break out on the continent, Casement helped to organize the Howth Gun Running operation that secured 900 Mauser rifles for the Irish Volunteers. This gave him credibility with John Devoy and Joseph McGarrity. Shortly thereafter, he assisted John Devoy in preparing the proposal for German support. It was Casement's idea to get the Germans to free Irish prisoners of war to join an Irish Brigade that would return home and fight for independence from Britain.

The clandestine Irish Republican Brotherhood (IRB) was the revolutionary arm in Ireland, linked closely to the Clan na Gael in America. Casement was not allowed into this IRB circle, which had members in the Volunteers as well. His interface was with MacNeill and his compatriot Bulmer Hobson.

In October 1914, Casement was chosen to be the ambassador to Germany for the Republicans. The British were aware of his movements and attempted to intercept him as he passed through Norway, to no avail. In November that same year, Casement negotiated a declaration from Zimmermann in Berlin, as follows:

> *The Imperial Government formally declares that under no circumstances would Germany invade Ireland with a view to its conquest or the overthrow of any native institutions in that country. Should the fortune of this Great War, that was not of Germany's seeking, ever bring in its course German troops to the shores of Ireland, they would land there not as an army of invaders to pillage and destroy but as the forces of a Government that is inspired by goodwill towards a country and people for whom Germany desires only national prosperity and national freedom (Dudgeon, Jeff "Casement's War" Drb. ie. retrieved January 2016).*

[4] Then, on December 27, he gained agreement to implement his Irish Brigade plan, again from Zimmermann of the German General Staff in Berlin. The Irish recruits would come from the 2,200 prisoners being held at the Limburg an der Lahn POW camp near Frankfurt. By this agreement, they were to be trained on the use of the new machine guns. The brigade would be transferred to the Zossen POW camp, just south of Berlin, where they would be trained, and would have much better living conditions.

[5] [6] Zimmermann assigned Rudolph Nadolny, who was heading up the Sektion Politik Berlin des Generalstabs of the GGS, to make the Irish "entente" a reality. Nadolny was cautioned to strictly control the communications from Casement outward to America, allowing no direct contact from him to Ireland. The German ambassador in the United States, von Bernsdorff, was the conduit between the Clan na Gael and Berlin (GGS). Nadolny considered this assignment to be a nuisance since his main job at that time was sabotage and biological warfare development. He must have understood, however, that his career depended upon his successful management of the potential Irish alliance for Zimmermann. Since I needed a German antagonist who was responsible for the development of chemical and not biological warfare, I chose to change his name from Rudolph Nadolny to the fictitious Bernard Gronski.

It would appear that Casement, in turn, offered to help the Germans start a similar POW recruitment program with the captive Indian soldiers in what was called the Hindu-German Conspiracy, to rid India of the British Raj rule. At this point, Casement felt that Germany would honor the overarching agreement to provide arms and trained German military personnel when the time came for Irish Republicans to rise.

Count von Lüttichau of the German General Staff (GGS) was ordered to show Casement the travesties of war in late 1914. He was taken to Andenne in Belgium where the German army in August had executed 350 Belgian civilians, partly prompted by panic over *francs tireurs*, French for irregular military or resistance saboteurs.

Since Sir Roger had witnessed a similar travesty levied by the Belgians under King Albert's father, Leopold II, in the Congo years earlier, he rationalized this brutality as justified retribution.

In 1915, Casement's pleas to win over the prisoners at Limburg fell largely on deaf ears. The Irish prisoners who had fought in the Allied trenches branded him a traitor. They rightly believed that they would be considered British traitors if they chose to side with the Irish Republicans in a battle that Britain would undoubtedly win. Joseph Plunkett, a key member of the IRB in Ireland and responsible for militarization, was sent to Germany mid-1915 to bolster support without Casement's knowledge of his role back in Ireland. Both he and Casement decided that the German efforts were tepid at best. By that time in July, Casement had recruited less than sixty brigade members, and their allegiance to the Irish cause was questionable.

Later in 1915, Sir Roger travelled to Bavaria to deal with a bout of malaria originally contracted in the Congo years earlier. While in the care of an American, Dr. Charles Curry, in Munich, at Curry's vacation property at nearby Riederau on Lake Ammersee, he wrote his diaries while he directed brigade preparations from a distance and waited for action in Ireland. He was quite sick when he returned to Ireland the following April.

Sensing Sir Roger's problems, Tom Clarke, a senior IRB leader, sent Corporal Robert Monteith from Ireland to handle the recruitment and training of the Irish Brigade.

> Monteith was *36 years old, about 5-feet-9 inches tall, formerly a sergeant major in the royal riding artillery (the RHA) in the English army. Robert had participated in the Boer War and the Indian border wars, served in Egypt, and was wounded twice. At the outbreak of WWI he had a position in the armory in Dublin and at the same time was a drill captain in the Irish Volunteers. He was offered the rank of captain in the English army but declined and was expelled from Dublin to Limerick (http://www.irishbrigade.eu/recruits/monteith. html*—A German Military Attaché in New York, writing to Berlin on 21 Sep 1915).

When Monteith arrived in Berlin on October 22, 1915, he was put in an awkward spot between Nadolny and his ill boss, Roger Casement. Further, he did not consider himself experienced enough to lead the brigade training and implementation, and the Germans, in turn, did not consider him of sufficient rank for the assignment.

Isolated in Bavaria, Sir Roger became more and more discouraged about the prospects for the Germans implementing his plan, to the point that he attempted to send word back to MacNeill and Bulmer in March 1916 that the German support would be weak at best, urging them not to rise yet. That effort was unsuccessful. The courier went missing somewhere in Scandinavia.

In April 1916, Germany provided the Irish with 20,000 outdated Mosin-Nagant 1891 rifles confiscated from the Russians, ten machine guns and accompanying ammunition, but no German officers—a fraction of the 200,000 rifles Casement had requested, and with no military expertise to offer. Clan na Gael had sent $100,000 to Ireland to fund the rising, and at that time, with just three weeks to go, they sent another $25,000, exhausting the Clan's funds. The news that the arms were to be delivered at Fenit on Thursday night, April 20, 1916, came through German channels from John Devoy in America. This conduit through encrypted German communications was compromised. Captain 'Blinker' Hall of the Admiralty in London Room 40 had broken the code in late 1915. Britain now knew that guns would be provided along the southwest coast just before Easter, but not exactly where and when.

It was Casement who pushed the Germans not to send the Irish Brigade, such as it was, to Ireland. Instead, he would bring Robert Monteith and one other man, Beverley (Bailey) with him. They would travel by U-boat and would meet the gun-running ship at the drop point in Tralee Bay. They began their voyage in *U-20*, the submarine that sank the *Lusitania*, but quickly turned back due to rudder trouble and switched to *U-19*, captained by Raimund Weisbach, a former watch officer who had fired the fatal torpedo on *U-20* almost a year earlier. Before returning to Ireland, Casement, still a very sick man, entrusted his friend Dr. Curry in Bavaria with his memoirs for posterity.

[11] The German cargo vessel *Libau*, disguised as a Norwegian ship *Aud-Norge*, left Luebeck, Germany approximately two weeks before the rendezvous. Flying the Norwegian flag, the ship sailed around the north of Scotland, and although seen by Royal Navy warships, it passed unchallenged through the blockade between the Faeroe Islands and Iceland. After a stormy voyage, which saw them having to sheltering off Rockall, they finally arrived and anchored off the agreed rendezvous point on Thursday afternoon, April 20, 1916.

Unknown to either German vessel, because of a lack of the newfangled radio equipment onboard, Thomas Clarke had decided to delay the delivery by three days until Easter Sunday, April 23, to avoid compromising the rising then planned to start on that day. Neither ship got the message.

As a result, the rendezvous to be signaled by a set of green lights ashore, never took place. In any event, the Royal Navy and RIC constables in Tralee were waiting for the shipment. The activities that occurred are described in the novel, including:

   a) The failed mission by Plunkett's men to commandeer a communications facility in Kerry to give false signals to the British and then communicate with the *Aud-Norge*

   b) Casement's rocky boat ride ashore onto Banna Strand

   c) His subsequent capture at McKenna's Fort

   d) The scuttling of the *Aud-Norge* by its Captain Karl Spindler and his crew early Saturday morning at the mouth of Queenstown Harbor The gun-running plot was foiled, and the impact on the prospect of success for the rising was disastrous.

Sir Roger Casement was arrested for treason, and after a lengthy trial, was hanged on August 3, 1916, the last of the Easter Rising conspirators to be executed.

The rest of the events in Dublin leading up to the Rising, which was postponed one day until Monday, April 24, are well documented in the novel.

Some time ago, an unknown poet wrote "Lonely Banna Strand." The Wolfe Tones band picked it up as a song. In 1965, when Roger Casement's body was finally brought to Dublin to be laid to rest in the Republican Glasnevin Cemetery, Derek Warfield from the band wrote the final verse:

Ballad of Roger Casement
by the Wolfe Tones Band

'Twas on Good Friday morning, all in the month of May,

A German ship was lying there, beyond there in the Bay,

With twenty thousand rifles all ready for to land,

But no answering signal came from the lonely Banna Strand.

A motorcar was dashing through the early morning gloom

A sudden crash, and in the sea they went to meet their doom

Two Irish lads lay dying there just like their hopes so grand

They could not give the signal now on lonely Banna Strand.

"No signal answers from the shore," Sir Roger sadly said,

"No comrades here to welcome me: alas, they must be dead,

But I must do my duty and so I mean to land."

So in a boat he pulled ashore on lonely Banna Strand.

The R.I.C. were hunting for Sir Roger high and low.

They found him at McKenna's ford: Said they, "You are our foe."

Said he, "I'm Roger Casement, I came to Ireland,

To try and free my countrymen on lonely Banna Strand."

They took Sir Roger prisoner, and they sailed for London town,
And in the Tower they named him a traitor to the Crown.
Said he, "I am no traitor", but his trial he had to stand,
For bringing German rifles to lonely Banna Strand.
'Twas in an English prison that they led him to his death,
"I'm dying for my country," he said with his last breath,
He's buried in a prison yard, far from his native land,
And the wild waves sing his requiem on the lonely Banna Strand.
They took Sir Roger home again in the year of '65,
And with his comrades of '16 in peace and tranquil lies.
His last wishes have been fulfilled: he's home in Ireland,
And the waves will roll in peace again on lonely Banna Strand.

These lyrics are included with the gracious consent from the Wolfe Tones Band.

There is an interesting side-note regarding Kapitanleutnant Raimund Weisbach. When doing my research, I found it to be coincidental that this decorated naval officer (he received two iron crosses, among other medals) was not only the second-in-command watch officer on the *U-20* who fired the fatal torpedo that sank the grand ocean liner *Lusitania*, but he was also the captain of *U-19* that delivered Roger Casement and his two brigade soldiers back to Ireland in April 1916.

Both events are historical facts and critical elements of my story. This is where the real fun comes for me as an author. This is the point in each episode of the television series, *The A-Team*, where George Peppard would say, "I love it when a plan comes together!"

It was therefore serendipitous that I could utilize this officer to link my characters from Ireland in late 1915 to the battlefields of Belgium and the POW camps of Germany. Of course, this part of the story is fictitious. In fact, Raimund only became a *Kapitanleutnant* of U-boat 19 in March 1916, and his first mission in that capacity was to return Casement to Ireland in April. Also, as a result of the worldwide condemnation of Germany for sinking the *Lusitania*, and then in August the *S.S. Arabic*, both off the south coast of Ireland, Chancellor von Bethmann ordered the cessation of unrestricted submarine warfare in the Irish Sea/English Channel corridor temporarily during the latter half of 1915. They only restarted this wartime attack process there in February 1917.

So here is a good example of what I meant when I wrote on the masthead page of my novels, *the depiction of the historical persons in these novels is not coincidental, and to the best of my knowledge, is accurate to events and their character in life. Some historical aspects may be augmented or adjusted for dramatic purposes.*

Finally, despite the terrible risks in the U-boats of WWI, Raimund Weisbach, whose submarine was sunk in 1917 with the loss of all but five crew members, himself sank 36 ships in his U-boat captain's career and lived to the ripe old age of 84 years.

Nadolny did attempt to get Casement to take his whole Irish Brigade of 56 men back to Ireland in April 1916. Casement balked, given his pessimistic view of the chances for success for the Rising, the lackluster participation of the brigade members, and with very limited German support. He went around Nadolny, convincing German-American Jacob Noeggerath to intercede with the German Admiralty. They agreed to deliver Casemant and only two brigade members back to Ireland via submarine, leaving the rest of the brigade in Germany. Devoy, in America, had requested that Casement stay in Germany, likely to avoid having him interfere with the planned Rising (*Prelude to the Easter Rising, Roger Casement in Imperial Germany,* by Doerries, Reinhard R. 2000).

The *Cathach* of Saint Columba [12]

It is purported in the mists of Gaelic time, that Saint Columba wrote this famous Roman vulgate psalter, see the historical background section of The Irish Clans, Searchers, Book One of the Series, page 439. This sacred relic was housed in the Royal Irish Academy in 1916 at the time of the Easter Rising. Reverend Hugh Jackson Lawlor, who became Dean of St. Patrick's Cathedral, was actually examining this relic in 1916 and attempting to separate damaged folios and restore faded wording. His report is contained in the Proceedings of the Royal Irish Academy, Volume 33, section C, No. 11, on pages 243-443 as published by Hedges, Figgis and Co. on September 4, 1916. At this time he was Professor of Ecclesiastical Studies at Dublin University.

So it was appropriate for Tadgh to find a reference to this effect in the newspaper on that famous Easter Sunday morning at Padraig Pearse's home in Rathfarnham, Ireland.

AUTHOR'S NOTE

It has been quite a year since I published the first book in *The Irish Clans* series of novels. Researching and writing are exciting, editing is drudgery, and self-marketing is very challenging to say the least.

In March 2016, we launched *Searchers* at the Temple Bar Pub in Dublin, Ireland, a key pub in my novel, with the assistance of its owner, Mr. Tom Cleary. I was encouraged by the enthusiasm of the pub crowd with my talk on the moral fiber of history. Ireland is a land of literary enthusiasts, to be sure.

In April, we launched the novel at St. Aidan's Church in The Beaches of Toronto with attendance of many friends and family descendants of my grandfather, Sam Finlay, an important character in the novel. It was a grand reunion. This experience alone made all the effort to write this novel worthwhile.

Since I left the main characters at sea, literally as well as figuratively, in *Searchers, Book One* in the Series, I chose to take them into the fray of WWI on the continent in *Entente, Book Two,* consistent with the historical efforts by the Irish revolutionaries to forge an alliance with Germany at that time.

Sir Roger Casement, knighted by the British crown for humanitarian actions in the Congo prior to WWI, subsequently became a staunch supporter of humanitarian rights of the Irish people. As a member of the Irish Volunteers under Eoin MacNeill and in conjunction with the controlling Clan na Gael in America, principally John Devoy and Joseph McGarrity, he was a main spokesman for the rebels while he resided in Germany from late 1914 to April 1916. He gained agreement that Germany would not invade Ireland for settlement. Unfortunately, however, his attempts to sway 2,200 Irish Volunteer prisoners of war in Germany to form an Irish Brigade to fight for freedom back in Ireland were essentially unsuccessful, despite support from Joseph Plunkett of the Irish Republican Brotherhood, and he became very disillusioned about the prospects of a viable entente/alliance with Germany.

Germany, on the other hand, was walking a tightrope, wanting Ireland to become a thorn in England's side during the war, yet not wanting to anger the United States into the war in early 1916. This gave rise to foreign intrigue for all parties concerned. Bernard Gronski, head of Sektion Politik of the German General Staff, was given the task of handling this fragile *entente.* He was clearly more comfortable developing new chemical warfare weapons to be used at the front, but he knew that his career depended upon controlling Sir Roger and his communications back to his masters in the United States and Ireland.

History is a harsh teacher. Had we learned from the horrors of WWI (over 17 million died), then fascism and WWII might have been avoided (over 60 million died). A generation of patriots fought for the moral high ground in the horrible trenches of WWI. Let's not let their deaths be in vain, as McCrae urged in his famous WWI poem, "In Flanders Fields." He, too, died in those ghastly trenches upholding moral standards of freedom, integrity, equality, humanity, and valor.

I have attempted to preserve historical truth in my writing. Now there's an oxymoron. History is written by the victors. After the first book in my series, **Searchers**, was published, a discovery of a family detail at my Toronto book launching was unearthed. My cousin Mary informed me that our grandmother actually went by the nickname "Lil" and not "Liz." How do you get "Lil" out of "Elizabeth"?

Be that as it may, I was confronted with a quandary. For the remaining novels in the series, should I retain "Liz" for continuity or switch to "Lil" for historical truth? I asked my readership who voted two to one in favor of historical truth. Henceforth, motherly Liz will become matronly Lil. "A rose by any other name," as the Bard once said. I trust you approve of the segue.

I hope you love reading *Entente* as much as I did writing it, as we pursue the historical road to freedom for the Irish Republicans and the romantic adventures of Clans warriors and their feisty women.

ACKNOWLEDGMENTS

The author is indebted to Manzanita Writers Press of Angels Camp, California, for their tireless support in editing, production, and marketing of these novels. Of particular note are its founding director and creative editor Monika Rose, and editor Suzanne Murphy, as well as book designer Connie Strawbridge and eBook designer Jennifer Hoffman, who took me under their wings to rope my manuscripts into shape. Thank you, ladies!

There are a number of readers who have given me constructive feedback of *Entente,* including Bob Kolakowski, Kathy Archer, Victoria Bors, and Joy Roberts. Thank you all.

Most of all, I wish to express my undying love and appreciation to the woman who has for thirty years been the wind beneath my wings, my darling wife Kathy. She has wholeheartedly supported this new journey in our lives, even though it wasn't in our plans when we retired from the aerospace business more than a decade ago.

I have chosen to dedicate this second book of the Irish Clans saga to all the men and women who fought to defend their countries and allies during World War I. They soldiered on and died under the most perilous and pitiful conditions imaginable. We honor them still. This dedication was a tough decision since my beloved Kathy is my muse, and to her I owe everything. I hope that you will continue to allow me to be the wind beneath your wings, my love. Grandly and forever.

The front cover art depicts the terrible trench warfare in Belgium in 1915. This painting by William Barnes Wollen, renowned military artist, is titled "Canadians at Ypres" depicting the second battle of Ypres. I am appreciative of the Princess Patricia's Canadian Light Infantry Museum of Calgary, Canada, for allowing me to utilize this graphic image, which, if anything, presents a more favorable picture of the green battlefield than actually existed. It is their valiant efforts that are depicted in this illustrative painting (see also the historical notes at the back of this novel).

I would also like to acknowledge the inspirational speech by the Belgian Minister of Justice, Carton de Wiart, given in London in June 1915, describing the heroic defense of Belgium.

The article by A. Torry McLean, presented in the Spring 1993 Tar Heel Junior Historian, is provided in part in the historical notes, thanks to the Tar Heel Junior Historian Association, North Carolina Museum of History. It gives an excellent summary of the machinery of warfare in WWI.

The image of the soldier and angel nurse on the dedication page and back cover is intended to depict Tadgh and Morgan fresh from the trenches of the Western Front in WWI. This image is taken from a British War Poster titled *Belgian Red Cross*, which was used to solicit funds for that humanitarian group. This poster resides at The United States Library of Congress as Image LC-USZC4-11243, and the painting was skillfully done by Charles Buchel in 1915. I thank the Library of Congress for the use of this image.

Finally, but certainly not least, the back cover portrait of Sir Roger Casement is one of a set of Easter Rising commemorative paintings by the very talented artist Mr. Norman Teeling. You will note the brilliant emotional content in Norman's works of art. I thank him for allowing me to share his painting with you in this way, and for his friendship along this literary journey of mine.

ABOUT THE AUTHOR

Stephen Finlay Archer

The author writes Irish historical fiction. His latest eight-novel series, *The Irish Clans*, covers the Irish revolutionary period from 1915 to 1923. This Irish family saga, full of swashbuckling characters and page-turning action, tells the true story of Ireland's conflict with England. It is also a personal portrayal since the fictitious story involves his own ancestral family as they are drawn into the conflict of their Irish homeland, while residing in his birthplace of Toronto, Canada.

Archer lives in Northern California with his wife Kathy. He is a member of Writers Unlimited in California Goldrush Country and the North American Historical Novel Society. Before his retirement, he was an Aerospace Manager directing large-scale, delivery-in orbit, satellite systems for the U.S. Navy and NASA/NOAA.

Stephen Finlay Archer's books are available on Amazon.com and directly from the author, publisher, and Ingram distribution.

Stephen can be reached at:

Email: stephenfinlayarcher@gmail.com
Website: www.stephenfinlayarcher.com
LinkedIn: (Stephen Finlay Archer)
Twitter: @StephenFinlayArcher
Facebook: StephenFinlayArcher
Blog: www.stephenfinlayarcher.com/blog